PENGUIN BOOK

WORK SUSPENDED AND
OTHER STORIES

Evelyn Waugh was born in Hampstead in 1903, second son of the late Arthur Waugh, publisher and literary critic, and brother of Alec Waugh, the popular novelist. He was educated at Lancing and Hertford College, Oxford, where he read Modern History. In 1927 he published his first work, a life of Dante Gabriel Rossetti, and in 1928 his first novel, *Decline and Fall*, which was soon followed by *Vile Bodies* (1930), *Black Mischief* (1932), *A Handful of Dust* (1934), and *Scoop* (1938). During these years he travelled extensively in most parts of Europe, the Near East, Africa, and tropical America. In 1939 he was commissioned in the Royal Marines and later transferred to the Royal Horse Guards, serving in the Middle East and in Yugoslavia. In 1942 he published *Put Out More Flags* and then, in 1945, *Brideshead Revisited. When the Going Was Good* and *The Loved One* were followed by *Helena* (1950), his historical novel. *Men at Arms*, which came out in 1952, is the first volume in a trilogy of war memoirs, and won the James Tait Black Prize; the other volumes, *Officers and Gentlemen* and *Unconditional Surrender*, were published in 1955 and 1961. Evelyn Waugh was received into the Roman Catholic Church in 1930 and his earlier biography of the Elizabethan Jesuit martyr, *Edmund Campion*, was awarded the Hawthornden Prize in 1936. In 1959 he published the official *Life of Ronald Knox*. For many years he lived with his wife and six children in the West Country. He died in 1966.

EVELYN WAUGH

WORK SUSPENDED

and Other Stories

INCLUDING
CHARLES RYDER'S SCHOOLDAYS

PENGUIN BOOKS

Penguin Books Ltd, Harmondsworth, Middlesex, England
Penguin Books, 40 West 23rd Street, New York, New York 10010, U.S.A.
Penguin Books Australia Ltd, Ringwood, Victoria, Australia
Penguin Books Canada Ltd, 2801 John Street, Markham, Ontario, Canada L3R 1B4
Penguin Books (N.Z.) Ltd, 182–190 Wairau Road, Auckland 10, New Zealand

—

Work Suspended and Other Stories first published by Chapman & Hall 1943
Scott-King's Modern Europe first published by Chapman & Hall 1946
Published together in Penguin Books 1951
Basil Seal Rides Again first published by Chapman & Hall 1963
This volume published in Penguin Books 1967
Reprinted 1976, 1977, 1978, 1981
Charles Ryder's Schooldays first published in *The Times Literary Supplement* 1982
This volume, including *Charles Ryder's Schooldays*, published in Penguin Books 1982
Reprinted 1983

—

—

Filmset, printed and bound in Great Britain by
Hazell Watson & Viney Ltd, Aylesbury, Bucks
Set in VIP Palatino

CONTENTS

MR LOVEDAY'S LITTLE OUTING

1

'You will not find your father greatly changed,' remarked Lady Moping, as the car turned into the gates of the County Asylum.

'Will he be wearing a uniform?' asked Angela.

'No, dear, of course not. He is receiving the very best attention.'

It was Angela's first visit and it was being made at her own suggestion.

Ten years had passed since the showery day in late summer when Lord Moping had been taken away; a day of confused but bitter memories for her; the day of Lady Moping's annual garden party, always bitter, confused that day by the caprice of the weather which, remaining clear and brilliant with promise until the arrival of the first guests, had suddenly blackened into a squall. There had been a scuttle for cover; the marquee had capsized; a frantic carrying of cushions and chairs, a table-cloth lofted to the boughs of the monkey-puzzler, fluttering in the rain; a bright period and the cautious emergence of guests on to the soggy lawns; another squall; another twenty minutes of sunshine. It had been an abominable afternoon, culminating at about six o'clock in her father's attempted suicide.

Lord Moping habitually threatened suicide on the occasion of the garden party; that year he had been found black in the face, hanging by his braces in the orangery; some neighbours, who were sheltering there from the rain, set him on his feet again, and before dinner a van had called for him. Since then Lady Moping had paid seasonal calls at the asylum and returned in time for tea, rather reticent of her experience.

Many of her neighbours were inclined to be critical of Lord Moping's accommodation. He was not, of course, an ordinary inmate. He lived in a separate wing of the asylum, specially devoted to the segregation of wealthier lunatics. They were given every consideration which their foibles permitted. They might choose their own clothes (many indulged in the liveliest fancies), smoke the most expensive brands of cigars, and, on the anniversaries of their certification, entertain any other inmates for whom they had an attachment to private dinner parties.

The fact remained, however, that it was far from being the most expensive kind of institution; the uncompromising address, 'County Home for Mental Defectives', stamped across the notepaper, worked on the uniforms of their attendants, painted, even, upon a prominent hoarding at the main entrance, suggested the lowest associations. From time to time, with less or more tact, her friends attempted to bring to Lady Moping's notice particulars of seaside nursing homes, of 'qualified practitioners with large private grounds suitable for the charge of nervous or difficult cases', but she accepted them lightly; when her son came of age he might make any changes that he thought fit; meanwhile she felt no inclination to relax her economical régime; her husband had betrayed her basely on the one day in the year when she looked for loyal support, and was far better off than he deserved.

A few lonely figures in great-coats were shuffling and loping about the park.

'Those are the lower class lunatics,' observed Lady Moping. 'There is a very nice little flower garden for people like your father. I sent them some cuttings last year.'

They drove past the blank, yellow brick façade to the doctor's private entrance and were received by him in the 'visitors' room', set aside for interviews of this kind. The window was protected on the inside by bars and wire netting; there was no fireplace; when Angela nervously attempted to move her chair further from the radiator, she found that it was screwed to the floor.

'Lord Moping is quite ready to see you,' said the doctor.

'How is he?'

'Oh, very well, very well indeed, I'm glad to say. He had rather a nasty cold some time ago, but apart from that his condition is excellent. He spends a lot of his time in writing.'

They heard a shuffling, skipping sound approaching along the flagged passage. Outside the door a high peevish voice, which Angela recognized as her father's, said: 'I haven't the time, I tell you. Let them come back later.'

A gentler tone, with a slight rural burr, replied, 'Now come along. It is a purely formal audience. You need stay no longer than you like.'

Then the door was pushed open (it had no lock or fastening) and Lord Moping came into the room. He was attended by an elderly little man with full white hair and an expression of great kindness.

'That is Mr Loveday who acts as Lord Moping's attendant.'

'Secretary,' said Lord Moping. He moved with a jogging gait and shook hands with his wife.

'This is Angela. You remember Angela, don't you?'

'No, I can't say that I do. What does she want?'

'We just came to see you.'

'Well, you have come at an exceedingly inconvenient time. I am very busy. Have you typed out that letter to the Pope yet, Loveday?'

'No, my lord. If you remember, you asked me to look up the figures about the Newfoundland fisheries first?'

'So I did. Well, it is fortunate, as I think the whole letter will have to be redrafted. A great deal of new information has come to light since luncheon. A great deal . . . You see, my dear, I am fully occupied.' He turned his restless, quizzical eyes upon Angela. 'I suppose you have come about the Danube. Well, you must come again later. Tell them it will be all right, quite all right, but I have not had time to give my full attention to it. Tell them that.'

'Very well, Papa.'

'Anyway,' said Lord Moping rather petulantly, 'it is a matter of secondary importance. There is the Elbe and the Amazon and the Tigris to be dealt with first, eh, Loveday? . . .

Danube indeed. Nasty little river. I'd only call it a stream myself. Well, can't stop, nice of you to come. I would do more for you if I could, but you see how I'm fixed. Write to me about it. That's it. *Put it in black and white.*'

And with that he left the room.

'You see,' said the doctor, 'he is in excellent condition. He is putting on weight, eating and sleeping excellently. In fact, the whole tone of his system is above reproach.'

The door opened again and Loveday returned.

'Forgive my coming back, sir, but I was afraid that the young lady might be upset at his Lordship's not knowing her. You mustn't mind him, miss. Next time he'll be very pleased to see you. It's only today he's put out on account of being behindhand with his work. You see, sir, all this week I've been helping in the library and I haven't been able to get all his Lordship's reports typed out. And he's got muddled with his card index. That's all it is. He doesn't mean any harm.'

'What a nice man,' said Angela, when Loveday had gone back to his charge.

'Yes, I don't know what we should do without old Loveday. Everybody loves him, staff and patients alike.'

'I remember him well. It's a great comfort to know that you are able to get such good warders,' said Lady Moping; 'people who don't know, say such foolish things about asylums.'

'Oh, but Loveday isn't a warder,' said the doctor.

'You don't mean he's cuckoo, too?' said Angela.

The doctor corrected her.

'He is an *inmate*. It is rather an interesting case. He has been here for thirty-five years.'

'But I've never seen anyone saner,' said Angela.

'He certainly has that air,' said the doctor, 'and in the last twenty years we have treated him as such. He is the life and soul of the place. Of course he is not one of the private patients, but we allow him to mix freely with them. He plays billiards excellently, does conjuring tricks at the concert, mends their gramophones, valets them, helps them in their crossword puzzles and various – er – hobbies. We allow them

10

to give him small tips for services rendered, and he must by now have amassed quite a little fortune. He has a way with even the most troublesome of them. An invaluable man about the place.'

'Yes, but why is he here?'

'Well, it is rather sad. When he was a very young man he killed somebody – a young woman quite unknown to him, whom he knocked off her bicycle and then throttled. He gave himself up immediately afterwards and has been here ever since.'

'But surely he is perfectly safe now. Why is he not let out?'

'Well, I suppose if it was to anyone's interest, he would be. He has no relatives except a step-sister who lives in Plymouth. She used to visit him at one time, but she hasn't been for years now. He's perfectly happy here and I can assure you *we* aren't going to take the first steps in turning him out. He's far too useful to us.'

'But it doesn't seem fair,' said Angela.

'Look at your father,' said the doctor. 'He'd be quite lost without Loveday to act as his secretary.'

'It doesn't seem fair.'

2

Angela left the asylum, oppressed by a sense of injustice. Her mother was unsympathetic.

'Think of being locked up in a looney bin all one's life.'

'He attempted to hang himself in the orangery,' replied Lady Moping, *'in front of the Chester-Martins.'*

'I don't mean Papa. I mean Mr Loveday.'

'I don't think I know him.'

'Yes, the looney they have put to look after papa.'

'Your father's secretary. A very decent sort of man, I thought, and eminently suited to his work.'

*

Angela left the question for the time, but returned to it again at luncheon on the following day.

'Mums, what does one have to do to get people out of the bin?'

'The bin? Good gracious, child, I hope that you do not anticipate your father's return *here*.'

'No, no. Mr Loveday.'

'Angela, you seem to me to be totally bemused. I see it was a mistake to take you with me on our little visit yesterday.'

After luncheon Angela disappeared to the library and was soon immersed in the lunacy laws as represented in the encyclopedia.

She did not re-open the subject with her mother, but a fortnight later, when there was a question of taking some pheasants over to her father for his eleventh Certification Party she showed an unusual willingness to run over with them. Her mother was occupied with other interests and noticed nothing suspicious.

Angela drove her small car to the asylum, and, after delivering the game, asked for Mr Loveday. He was busy at the time making a crown for one of his companions who expected hourly to be anointed Emperor of Brazil, but he left his work and enjoyed several minutes' conversation with her. They spoke about her father's health and spirits. After a time Angela remarked, 'Don't you ever want to get away?'

Mr Loveday looked at her with his gentle, blue-grey eyes. 'I've got very well used to the life, miss. I'm fond of the poor people here, and I think that several of them are quite fond of me. At least, I think they would miss me if I were to go.'

'But don't you ever think of being free again?'

'Oh yes, miss, I think of it – almost all the time I think of it.'

'What would you do if you got out? There must be *something* you would sooner do than stay here.'

The old man fidgeted uneasily. 'Well, miss, it sounds ungrateful, but I can't deny I should welcome a little outing once, before I get too old to enjoy it. I expect we all have our secret ambitions, and there *is* one thing I often wish I could do. You mustn't ask me what . . . It wouldn't take long. But I do feel that if I had done it just for a day, an afternoon even, then I would die quiet. I could settle down again easier, and devote myself to the poor crazed people here with a better heart. Yes, I do feel that.'

There were tears in Angela's eyes that afternoon as she drove away. 'He *shall* have his little outing, bless him,' she said.

3

From that day onwards for many weeks Angela had a new purpose in life. She moved about the ordinary routine of her home with an abstracted air and an unfamiliar, reserved courtesy which greatly disconcerted Lady Moping.

'I believe the child's in love. I only pray that it isn't that uncouth Egbertson boy.'

She read a great deal in the library, she cross-examined any guests who had pretensions to legal or medical knowledge, she showed extreme goodwill to old Sir Roderick Lane-Foscote, their Member. The names 'alienist', 'barrister' or 'government official' now had for her the glamour that formerly surrounded film actors and professional wrestlers. She was a woman with a cause, and before the end of the hunting season she had triumphed. Mr Loveday achieved his liberty.

The doctor at the asylum showed reluctance but no real opposition. Sir Roderick wrote to the Home Office. The necessary papers were signed, and at last the day came when Mr Loveday took leave of the home where he had spent such long and useful years.

His departure was marked by some ceremony. Angela and Sir Roderick Lane-Foscote sat with the doctors on the stage of the gymnasium. Below them was assembled everyone in the institution who was thought to be stable enough to endure the excitement.

Lord Moping, with a few suitable expressions of regret, presented Mr Loveday on behalf of the wealthier lunatics with a gold cigarette case; those who supposed themselves to be emperors showered him with decorations and titles of honour. The warders gave him a silver watch and many of the non-paying inmates were in tears on the day of the presentation.

The doctor made the main speech of the afternoon. 'Remember,' he remarked, 'that you leave behind you nothing but our warmest good wishes. You are bound to us by ties that none will forget. Time will only deepen our sense of debt to you. If at any time in the future you should grow tired of your life in the world, there will always be a welcome for you here. Your post will be open.'

A dozen or so variously afflicted lunatics hopped and skipped after him down the drive until the iron gates opened and Mr Loveday stepped into his freedom. His small trunk had already gone to the station; he elected to walk. He had been reticent about his plans, but he was well provided with money, and the general impression was that he would go to London and enjoy himself a little before visiting his stepsister in Plymouth.

It was to the surprise of all that he returned within two hours of his liberation. He was smiling whimsically, a gentle self-regarding smile of reminiscence.

'I have come back,' he informed the doctor. 'I think that now I shall be here for good.'

'But, Loveday, what a short holiday. I'm afraid that you have hardly enjoyed yourself at all.'

'Oh yes, sir, thank you, I've enjoyed myself *very much*. I'd been promising myself one little treat, all these years. It was short, sir, but *most* enjoyable. Now I shall be able to settle down again to my work here without any regrets.'

Half a mile up the road from the asylum gates, they later discovered an abandoned bicycle. It was a lady's machine of some antiquity. Quite near it in the ditch lay the strangled body of a young woman, who, riding home to her tea, had chanced to overtake Mr Loveday, as he strode along, musing on his opportunities.

CRUISE

(LETTERS FROM A YOUNG LADY OF LEISURE)

S.S. Glory of Greece

DARLING,

Well I said I would write and so I would have only goodness
it was rough so didnt. Now everything is a bit more alright
so I will tell you. Well as you know the cruise started at Monte
Carlo and when papa and all of us went to Victoria we found
that the tickets didnt include the journey there so Goodness
how furious he was and said he wouldnt go but Mum said
of course we must go and we said that too only papa had
changed all his money into Liri or Franks on account of
foreigners being so dishonest but he kept a shilling for the
porter at Dover being methodical so then he had to change it
back again and that set him wrong all the way to Monte Carlo
and he wouldnt get me and Bertie a sleeper and wouldnt
sleep himself in his through being so angry Goodness how
Sad.

Then everything was much more alright the purser called
him Colonel and he likes his cabin so he took Bertie to the
casino and he lost and Bertie won and I think Bertie got a bit
plastered at least he made a noise going to bed he's in the
next cabin as if he were being sick and that was before we
sailed. Bertie has got some books on Baroque art on account
of his being at Oxford.

Well the first day it was rough and I got up and felt odd in
the bath and the soap wouldnt work on account of salt water
you see and came into breakfast and there was a list of so
many things including steak and onions and there was a
corking young man who said we are the only ones down may
I sit here and it was going beautifully and he had steak and
onions but it was no good I had to go back to bed just when
he was saying there was nothing he admired so much about
a girl as her being a good sailor goodness how sad.

16

The thing is not to have a bath and to be very slow in all movements. So next day it was Naples and we saw some Bertie churches and then that bit that got blown up in an earthquake and a poor dog killed they have a plaster cast of him goodness how sad. Papa and Bertie saw some pictures we weren't allowed to see and Bill drew them for me afterwards and Miss P. tried to look too. I havent told you about Bill and Miss P. have I? Well Bill is rather old but clean looking and I don't suppose hes very old not really I mean and he's had a very disillusionary life on account of his wife who he says I wont say a word against but she gave him the raspberry with a foreigner and that makes him hate foreigners. Miss P. is called Miss Phillips and is lousy she wears a yachting cap and is a bitch. And the way she makes up to the second officer is no ones business and its clear to the meanest intelligence he hates her but its part of the rules that all the sailors have to pretend to fancy the passengers. Who else is there? Well a lot of old ones. Papa is having a walk out with one called Lady Muriel something or other who knew uncle Ned. And there is a honeymoon couple very embarrassing. And a clergyman and a lovely pansy with a camera and white suit and lots of families from the industrial north.
So Bertie sends his love too. XXXXXXetc.

Mum bought a shawl and an animal made of lava.

POST-CARD

This is a picture of Taormina. Mum bought a shawl here. V. funny because Miss P. got left as shed made chums only with second officer and he wasnt allowed ashore so when it came to getting into cars Miss P. had to pack in with a family from the industrial north.

S.S. Glory of Greece

Darling,

Hope you got P.C. from Sicily. The moral of that was not to make chums with sailors though who I've made a chum

17

of is the purser who's different on account he leads a very cynical life with a gramophone in his cabin and as many cocktails as he likes and welsh rabbits sometimes and I said but do you pay for all these drinks but he said no that's all right.

So we have three days at sea which the clergyman said is a good thing as it makes us all friendly but it hasn't made me friendly with Miss P. who won't leave poor Bill alone not taking any more chances of being left alone when she goes ashore. The purser says theres always someone like her on board in fact he says that about everyone except me who he says quite rightly is different goodness how decent.

So there are deck games they are hell. And the day before we reach Haifa there is to be a fancy dress dance. Papa is very good at the deck games especially one called shuffle board and eats more than he does in London but I daresay its alright. You have to hire dresses for the ball from the barber I mean we do not you. Miss P. has brought her own. So I've thought of a v. clever thing at least the purser suggested it and that is to wear the clothes of one of the sailors I tried his on and looked a treat. Poor Miss P.

Bertie is madly unpop. he wont play any of the games and being plastered the other night too and tried to climb down a ventilator and the second officer pulled him out and the old ones at the captains table look *askance* at him. New word that. Literary yes? No?

So I think the pansy is writing a book he has a green fountain pen and green ink but I couldn't see what it was. XXXX Pretty good about writing you will say and so I am.

POST-CARD

This is a photograph of the Holyland and the famous sea of Gallillee. It is all v. Eastern with camels. I have a lot to tell you about the ball. *Such* goings on and will write very soon. Papa went off for the day with Lady M. and came back saying enchanting woman Knows the world.

18

S.S. Glory of Greece

Darling,

Well the Ball we had to come in to dinner in our clothes and everyone clapped as we came downstairs. So I was pretty late on account of not being able to make up my mind whether to wear the hat and in the end did and looked a corker. Well it was rather a faint clap for me considering so when I looked about there were about twenty girls and some woman all dressed like me so how cynical the purser turns out to be. Bertie looked horribly dull as an apache. Mum and Papa were sweet. Miss P. had a ballet dress from the Russian ballet which couldnt have been more unsuitable so we had champagne for dinner and were jolly and they threw paper streamers and I threw mine before it was unrolled and hit Miss P. on the nose. Ha ha. So feeling matey I said to the steward isnt this fun and he said yes for them who hasnt got to clear it up goodness how Sad.

Well of course Bertie was plastered and went a bit far particularly in what he said to Lady M. then he sat in the cynical pursers cabin in the dark and cried so Bill and I found him and Bill gave him some drinks and what do you think he went off with Miss P. and we didn't see either of them again it only shows into what degradation the Demon Drink can drag you him I mean.

Then who should I meet but the young man who had steak and onions on the first morning and is called Robert and said I have been trying to meet you again all the voyage. Then I bitched him a bit goodness how Decent.

Poor Mum got taken up by Bill and he told her all about his wife and how she had disillusioned him with the foreigner so tomorrow we reach Port Said d.v. which is latin in case you didn't know meaning God Willing and all to go up the nile and to Cairo for a week.

Will send P.C. of Sphinx.

XXXXXX

POST-CARD

This is the Sphinx. Goodness how Sad.

POST-CARD

This is temple of someone. Darling I cant wait to tell you I'm engaged to Arthur. Arthur is the one I thought was a pansy. Bertie thinks egyptian art is v. inartistic.

POST-CARD

This is Tutankhamens v. famous Tomb. Bertie says it is vulgar and is engaged to Miss P. so hes not one to speak and I call her Mabel now. G how S. Bill wont speak to Bertie Robert wont speak to me Papa and Lady M. seem to have had a row there was a man with a snake in a bag also a little boy who told my fortune which was v. prosperous Mum bought a shawl.

POST-CARD

Saw this Mosque today. Robert is engaged to a new girl called something or other who is lousy.

S.S. Glory of Greece

Darling,
Well so we all came back from Egypt pretty excited and the cynical purser said what news and I said *news* well Im engaged to Arthur and Bertie is engaged to Miss P. and she is called Mabel now which is hardest of all to bear I said and Robert to a lousy girl and Papa has had a row with Lady M. and Bill has had a row with Bertie and Roberts lousy girl was

awful to me and Arthur was sweet but the cynical purser wasnt a bit surprised on account he said people always get engaged and have quarrels on the Egyptian trip every cruise so I said I wasnt in the habit of getting engaged lightly thank you and he said I wasnt apparently in the habit of going to Egypt so I wont speak to him again nor will Arthur.

All love.

S.S. Glory of Greece

Sweet,

This is Algiers *not* very eastern in fact full of frogs. So it is all off with Arthur I was right about him at the first but who I am engaged to is Robert which is *much* better for all concerned really particularly Arthur on account of what I said originally first impressions always right. Yes? No? Robert and I drove about all day in the Botanic gardens and Goodness he was Decent. Bertie got plastered and had a row with Mabel – Miss P. again – so thats all right too and Robert's lousy girl spent all day on board with second officer. Mum bought shawl. Bill told Lady M. about his disillusionment and she told Robert who said yes we all know so Lady M. said it was very unreticent of Bill and she had very little respect for him and didn't blame his wife or the foreigner.

Love.

POST-CARD

I forget what I said in my last letter but if I mentioned a lousy man called Robert you can take it as unsaid. This is still Algiers and Papa ate *dubious oysters* but is all right. Bertie went to a house full of tarts when he was plastered and is pretty unreticent about it as Lady M. would say.

21

POST-CARD

So now we are back and sang old lang syne is that how you spell it and I kissed Arthur but wont speak to Robert and he cried not Robert I mean Arthur so then Bertie apologised to most of the people hed insulted but Miss P. walked away pretending not to hear. Goodness what a bitch.

PERIOD PIECE

LADY AMELIA had been educated in the belief that it was the height of impropriety to read a novel in the morning. Now, in the twilight of her days, when she had singularly little to occupy the two hours between her appearance downstairs at a quarter past eleven, hatted and fragrant with lavender water, and the announcement of luncheon, she adhered rigidly to this principle. As soon as luncheon was over, however, and coffee had been served in the drawing-room; before the hot milk in his saucer had sufficiently cooled for Manchu to drink it; while the sunlight, in summer, streamed through the Venetian blinds of the round-fronted Regency windows; while, in winter, the carefully stacked coal-fire glowed in its round-fronted grate; while Manchu sniffed and sipped at his saucer, and Lady Amelia spread out on her knees the various shades of coarse wool with which her failing eyesight now compelled her to work; while the elegant Regency clock ticked off the two and a half hours to tea time – it was Miss Myers' duty to read a novel aloud to her employer.

With the passing years Lady Amelia had grown increasingly fond of novels and of novels of a particular type. They were what the assistant in the circulating library termed 'strong meat' and kept in a hidden place under her desk. It was Miss Myers' duty to fetch and return them. 'Have you anything of the kind Lady Amelia likes?' she would ask sombrely.

'Well, there's this just come in,' the assistant would answer, fishing up a volume from somewhere near her feet.

At one time Lady Amelia had enjoyed love stories about the irresponsible rich; then she had had a psychological phase; at the moment her interests were American, in the school of brutal realism and gross slang. 'Something else like *Sanctuary* or *Bessie Cotter*,' Miss Myers was reluctantly obliged to demand. And as the still afternoon was disturbed by her delicately modulated tones enunciating page by page, in scarcely comprehensible idiom, the narratives of rape and betrayal, Lady Amelia would occasionally chuckle a little over her woolwork.

'Women of my age always devote themselves either to religion or to novels,' she said. 'I have remarked among my few surviving friends that those who read novels enjoy far better health.'

The story they were reading came to an end at half-past four.

'Thank you,' said Lady Amelia. 'That was *most* entertaining. Make a note of the author's name, please, Miss Myers. You will be able to go to the library after tea and see whether they have another. I hope you enjoyed it.'

'Well, it was very sad, wasn't it?'

'Sad?'

'I mean the poor young man who wrote it must come from a terrible home.'

'Why do you say that, Miss Myers?'

'Well, it was so far fetched.'

'It is odd you should think so. I invariably find modern novels painfully reticent. Of course until lately I never read novels at all. I cannot say what they were like formerly. I was far too busy in the old days living my own life and sharing the lives of my friends – all people who came from anything but terrible homes,' she added with a glance at her companion; a glance sharp and smart as a rap on the knuckles with an ivory ruler.

There was half-an-hour before tea; Manchu was asleep on the hearth rug, before the fireless grate; the sun streamed in through the blinds, casting long strips of light on the Aubusson carpet. Lady Amelia fixed her eyes on the embroidered, heraldic firescreen; and proceeded dreamily. 'I suppose it would not do. You couldn't write about the things which actually happen. People are so used to novels that they would not believe them. The poor writers are constantly at pains to make the truth seem probable. Dear me, I often think, as you sit, *so kindly*, reading to me, "If one was just to write down quite simply the events of a few years in *any* household one knows . . . No one would believe it." I can hear you yourself, dear Miss Myers, saying, "Perhaps these things *do* happen, very occasionally, once in a century, in terrible homes"; instead of which they are constantly happening, every day, all round us – or at least, they were in my young days.

'Take for example the extremely ironic circumstances of the succession of the present Lord Cornphillip.

'I used to know the Cornphillips very well in the old days,' said Lady Amelia – 'Etty was a cousin of my mother's – and when we were first married my husband and I used to stay there every autumn for the pheasant shooting. Billy Cornphillip was a *very* dull man – very dull indeed. He was in my husband's regiment. I used to know a great many dull people at the time when I was first married, but Billy Cornphillip was notorious for dullness even among my husband's friends. Their place is in Wiltshire. I see the boy is trying to sell it now. I am not surprised. It was very ugly and very unhealthy. I used to dread our visits there.

'Etty was entirely different, a lively little thing with very nice eyes. People thought her fast. Of course it was a *very* good match for her; she was one of seven sisters and her father was a younger son, poor dear. Billy was twelve years older. She had been after him for years. I remember crying with pleasure when I received her letter telling me of the engagement . . . It was at the breakfast table . . . she used a very artistic kind of writing paper with pale blue edges and bows of blue ribbon at the corner . . .

'Poor Etty was always being artistic; she tried to do something with the house – put up peacocks' feathers and painted tambourines and some very modern stencil work – but the result was always depressing. She made a little garden for herself at some distance from the house, with a high wall and a padlocked door, where she used to retire to think – or so she said – for hours at a time. She called it the Garden of

Her Thoughts. I went in with her once, as a great privilege, after one of her quarrels with Billy. Nothing grew very well there – because of the high walls, I suppose, and her doing it all herself. There was a mossy seat in the middle. I suppose she used to sit on it while she thought. The whole place had a nasty dank smell . . .

'Well we were all delighted at Etty's luck and I think she quite liked Billy at first and was prepared to behave well to him, in spite of his dullness. You see it came just when we had all despaired. Billy had been the friend of Lady Instow for a long time and we were all afraid she would never let him marry but they had a quarrel at Cowes that year and Billy went up to Scotland in a bad temper and little Etty was staying in the house; so everything was arranged and I was one of her bridesmaids.

'The only person who was not pleased was Ralph Bland. You see he was Billy's nearest relative and would inherit if Billy died without children and he had got very hopeful as time went on.

'He came to a very sad end – in fact I don't know *what* became of him – but at the time of which I am speaking he was extremely popular, especially with women . . . Poor Viola Chasm was terribly in love with him. Wanted to run away. She and Lady Anchorage were very jealous of each other about him. It became quite disagreeable, particularly when Viola found that Lady Anchorage was paying her maid five pounds a week to send on all Ralph's letters to her – *before* Viola had read them, that was what she minded. He really had a most agreeable manner and said such ridiculous things . . . The marriage was a great disappointment to Ralph; he was married himself and had two children. She had a little money at one time, but Ralph ran through it. Billy did not get on with Ralph – they had very little in common, of course – but he treated him quite well and was always getting him out of difficulties. In fact he made him a regular allowance at one time, and what with that and what he got from Viola and Lady Anchorage he was really quite comfortable. But, as he said, he had his children's future to consider, so that Billy's marriage *was* a *great* disappointment to him. He even talked of emigrating and Billy advanced him a large sum of money to purchase a sheep farm in New Zealand, but nothing came of that because Ralph had a Jewish friend in the city who made away with the entire amount. It all happened in a very unfortunate manner because Billy had given him this lump sum on the understanding that he should not expect an allowance. And then Viola and Lady Anchorage were greatly upset at his talk of leaving and made other arrangements so that in one way and another Ralph found himself in very low water, poor thing.

'However he began to recover his spirits when, after two years, there was no sign of an heir. People had babies very much more regularly when I was young. Everybody expected that Etty would have a baby – she was a nice healthy little thing – and when she did not, there was a great deal of ill-natured gossip. Ralph himself behaved very wrongly in the matter. He used to make jokes about it, my husband told me, quite openly at his club in the worst possible taste.

'I well remember the last time that Ralph stayed with the Cornphillips; it was a Christmas party, and he came with his wife and his two children. The eldest boy was about six at the time and there was a very painful scene. I was not there myself, but we were staying nearby with the Lockejaws and of course we heard all about it. Billy seems to have been in his most pompous mood and was showing off the house when Ralph's little boy said solemnly and very loudly, "Daddy says that when I step into your shoes I can pull the whole place down. The only thing worth worrying about is the money."

'It was towards the end of a large and rather old-fashioned Christmas party, so no one was feeling in a forgiving mood. There was a final breach between the two cousins. Until then, in spite of the New Zealand venture, Billy had been reluctantly supporting Ralph. Now the allowance ceased once for all and Ralph took it in very bad part.

'You know what it is – or perhaps, dear Miss Myers, you are so fortunate as not to know what it is – when near relatives begin to quarrel. There is no limit to the savagery to which they will resort. I should be ashamed to indicate the behaviour of these two men towards each other during the next two or three years. No one had any sympathy with either.

'For example, Billy, of course, was a Conservative. Ralph came down and stood as a Radical in the General Election in his own country and got in.

'This, you must understand, was in the days before the lower classes began going into politics. It was customary for the candidates on both sides to be men of means and, in the circumstances, there was considerable expenditure involved. Much more in fact than Ralph could well afford, but in those days Members of Parliament had many opportunities for improving their position, so we all thought it a very wise course of Ralph's – the first really sensible thing we had known him do. What followed was *very* shocking.

'Billy, of course, had refused to lend his interest – that was only to be expected – but when the election was over, and everybody perfectly satisfied with the result, he did what I always consider a *Very Wrong Thing*. He made an accusation against Ralph of corrupt practices. It was a matter of three pounds which Ralph had given to a gardener whom Billy had discharged for drunkenness. I daresay that all that kind of thing has ceased nowadays, but at the time to which I refer it was universally customary. No one had any sympathy with Billy, but he pressed the charge and poor Ralph was unseated.

'Well, after this time, I really think that poor Ralph became a little unsettled in his mind. It is a very sad thing, Miss Myers, when a middle-aged man becomes obsessed by a grievance. You remember how difficult it was when the Vicar thought that Major Etheridge was persecuting him. He actually informed me that Major Etheridge put water in the petrol tank of his motor-cycle and gave sixpences to the choir boys to sing out of tune – well, it was like that with poor Ralph. He made up his mind that Billy had deliberately ruined him. He took a cottage in the village and used to

28

embarrass Billy terribly by coming to all the village fêtes and staring at Billy fixedly. Poor Billy was always embarrassed when he had to make a speech. Ralph used to laugh ironically at the wrong places, but never so loudly that Billy could have him turned out. And he used to go to public houses and drink far too much. They found him asleep on the terrace twice. And, of course, no one on the place liked to offend him, because at any moment he might become Lord Cornphillip.

'It must have been a very trying time for Billy. He and Etty were not getting on at all well together, poor things, and she spent more and more time in the Garden of Her Thoughts and brought out a very silly little book of sonnets, mostly about Venice and Florence, though she could never induce Billy to take her abroad. He used to think that foreign cooking upset him.

'Billy forbade her to speak to Ralph, which was very awkward, as they were always meeting one another in the village and had been great friends in the old days. In fact Ralph used often to speak very contemptuously of his cousin's manliness and say it was time someone took Etty off his hands. But that was only one of Ralph's jokes, because Etty had been getting terribly thin and dressing in the *most* artistic way, and Ralph *always* liked people who were chic and plump – like poor Viola Chasm. Whatever her faults –' said Lady Amelia, 'Viola was always chic and plump.'

'It was at the time of the Diamond Jubilee that the crisis took place. There was a bonfire and a great deal of merry making of a rather foolish kind and Ralph got terribly drunk. He began threatening Billy in a very silly way and Billy had him up before the magistrates and they made an order against him to keep the peace and not to reside within ten miles of Cornphillip. "All right," Ralph said, in front of the whole Court, "I'll go away, but I won't go alone." And will you believe it, Miss Myers, he and Etty went off to Venice together that very afternoon.

'Poor Etty, she had always wanted to go to Venice and had written so many poems about it, but it was a great surprise to us all. Apparently she had been meeting Ralph for some time in the Garden of Her Thoughts.

'I don't think Ralph ever cared about her, because, as I say, she was not at all his type, but it seemed to him a very good revenge on Billy.

'Well, the elopement was far from successful. They took rooms in a very insanitary palace, and had a gondola and ran up a great many bills. Then Etty got a septic throat as a result of the sanitation and while she was laid up Ralph met an American woman who was *much* more his type. So in less than six weeks poor Etty was back in England. Of course she did not go back to Billy at once. She wanted to stay with us, but, naturally, that wasn't possible. It was very awkward for everyone. There was never, I think, any talk of a divorce. It was long before that became fashionable. But we all felt it would be very inconsiderate to Billy if we had her to stay. And then, this is what will surprise you, Miss Myers, the next thing we heard was that Etty was back at Cornphillip and about to have a baby. It was a son. Billy was very pleased about it and I don't believe that the boy ever knew, until quite lately, at luncheon with Lady Metroland, when my nephew Simon told him, in a rather ill-natured way.

'As for poor Ralph's boy, I am afraid he has come to very little good. He must be middle-aged by now. No one ever seems to hear anything of him. Perhaps he was killed in the war. I cannot remember.

'And here comes Ross with the tray; and I see that Mrs Samson has made more of those little scones which you always seem to enjoy so much. I am sure, dear Miss Myers, you would suffer much less from your *migraine* if you avoided them. But you take so little care of yourself, dear Miss Myers . . . Give one to Manchu.'

ON GUARD

1

MILLICENT BLADE had a notable head of naturally fair hair; she had a docile and affectionate disposition, and an expression of face which changed with lightning rapidity from amiability to laughter and from laughter to respectful interest. But the feature which, more than any other, endeared her to sentimental Anglo-Saxon manhood was her nose.

It was not everybody's nose; many prefer one with greater body; it was not a nose to appeal to painters, for it was far too small and quite without shape, a mere dab of putty without apparent bone structure; a nose which made it impossible for its wearer to be haughty or imposing or astute. It would not have done for a governess or a 'cellist or even for a post office clerk, but it suited Miss Blade's book perfectly, for it was a nose that pierced the thin surface crest of the English heart to its warm and pulpy core; a nose to take the thoughts of English manhood back to its schooldays, to the doughy-faced urchins on whom it had squandered its first affection, to memories of changing room and chapel and battered straw boaters. Three Englishmen in five, it is true, grow snobbish about these things in later life and prefer a nose that makes more show in public — but two in five is an average with which any girl of modest fortune may be reasonably content.

Hector kissed her reverently on the tip of this nose. As he did so, his senses reeled and in momentary delirium he saw the fading light of the November afternoon, the raw mist spreading over the playing-fields; overheated youth in the scrum; frigid youth at the touchline, shuffling on the duckboards, chafing their fingers and, when their mouths were emptied of biscuit crumbs, cheering their house team to further exertion.

'You will wait for me, won't you?' he said.

'Yes, darling.'

'And you will write?'

'Yes, darling,' she replied more doubtfully, 'sometimes . . . at least I'll try. Writing is not my best thing, you know.'

'I shall think of you all the time Out There,' said Hector. 'It's going to be terrible – miles of impassable waggon track between me and the nearest white man, blinding sun, lions, mosquitoes, hostile natives, work from dawn until sunset single handed against the forces of nature, fever, cholera . . . But soon I shall be able to send for you to join me.'

'Yes, darling.'

'It's bound to be a success. I've discussed it all with Beckthorpe – that's the chap who's selling me the farm. You see, the crop has failed every year so far – first coffee, then sisal, then tobacco, that's all you can grow there, and the year Beckthorpe grew sisal everyone else was making a packet in tobacco, but sisal was no good; then he grew tobacco, but by then it was coffee he ought to have grown, and so on. He stuck it nine years. Well if you work it out mathematically, Beckthorpe says, in three years one's bound to strike the right crop. I can't quite explain why, but it is like roulette and all that sort of thing, you see.'

'Yes, darling.'

Hector gazed at her little, shapeless, mobile button of a nose and was lost again . . . 'Play up, play up,' and after the match the smell of crumpets being toasted over a gas-ring in his study . . .

2

Later that evening he dined with Beckthorpe, and, as he dined, he grew more despondent.

'Tomorrow this time I shall be at sea,' he said, twiddling his empty port glass.

'Cheer up, old boy,' said Beckthorpe.

Hector filled his glass and gazed with growing distaste round the reeking dining-room of Beckthorpe's club. The last awful member had left the room and they were alone with the cold buffet.

'I say, you know, I've been trying to work it out. It *was* in three years you said the crop was bound to be right, wasn't it?'

'That's right, old boy.'

'Well, I've been through the sum and it seems to me that it might be eighty-one years before it comes right.'

'No, no, old boy, three or nine, or at the most twenty-seven.'

'Are you sure?'

'Quite.'

'Good . . . you know it's awful leaving Milly behind. Suppose it *is* eighty-one years before the crop succeeds. It's the devil of a time to expect a girl to wait. Some other blighter might turn up, if you see what I mean.'

'In the Middle Ages they used to use girdles of chastity.'

'Yes, I know. I've been thinking of them. But they sound damned uncomfortable. I doubt if Milly would wear one even if I knew where to find it.'

'Tell you what, old boy. You ought to give her something.'

'Hell, I'm always giving her things. She either breaks them or loses them or forgets where she got them.'

'You must give her something she will always have by her, something that will last.'

'Eighty-one years?'

'Well, say twenty-seven. Something to remind her of you.'

'I could give her a photograph – but I might change a bit in twenty-seven years.'

'No, no, that would be most unsuitable. A photograph wouldn't do at all. I know what I'd give her. I'd give her a dog.'

'Dog?'

'A healthy puppy that was over distemper and looked like living a long time. She might even call it Hector.'

'Would that be a good thing, Beckthorpe?'

'Best possible, old boy.'

So next morning, before catching the boat train, Hector hurried to one of the mammoth stores of London and was shown the livestock department. 'I want a puppy.'

'Yes, sir. Any particular sort?'

'One that will live a long time. Eighty-one years, or twenty-seven at the least.'

The man looked doubtful. 'We have some fine healthy puppies, of course,' he admitted, 'but none of them carry a guarantee. Now if it was longevity you wanted, might I recommend a tortoise? They live to an extraordinary age and are very safe in traffic.'

'No, it must be a pup.'

'Or a parrot?'

'No, no, a pup. I would prefer one named Hector.'

They walked together past monkeys and kittens and cockatoos to the dog department, which, even at this early hour, had attracted a small congregation of rapt worshippers. There were puppies of all varieties in wire-fronted kennels, ears cocked, tails wagging, noisily soliciting attention. Rather wildly, Hector selected a poodle and, as the salesman disappeared to fetch him his change, he leant down for a moment's intense communion with the beast of his choice. He gazed deep into the sharp little face, avoided a sudden snap and said with profound solemnity:

'You are to look after Milly, Hector. See that she doesn't marry anyone until I get back.'

And the pup Hector waved his plume of tail.

3

Millicent came to see him off, but, negligently, went to the wrong station; it could not have mattered, however, for she was twenty minutes late. Hector and the poodle hung about the barrier looking for her, and not until the train was already moving did he bundle the animal into Beckthorpe's arms with instructions to deliver him at Millicent's address. Luggage labelled for Mombasa 'Wanted on the voyage' lay in the rack above him. He felt very much neglected.

That evening as the ship pitched and rolled past the Channel lighthouses, he received a radiogram: MISERABLE TO MISS YOU WENT PADDINGTON LIKE IDIOT, THANK YOU THANK YOU FOR SWEET DOG I LOVE HIM FATHER MINDS DREADFULLY LONGING TO HEAR ABOUT FARM DONT FALL FOR SHIP SIREN ALL LOVE MILLY.

In the Red Sea he received another: BEWARE SIRENS PUPPY BIT MAN CALLED MIKE.

After that Hector heard nothing of Millicent except for a Christmas card which arrived in the last days of February.

4

Generally speaking, Millicent's fancy for any particular young man was likely to last four months. It depended on how far he had got in that time whether the process of extinction was sudden or protracted. In the case of Hector, her affection had been due to diminish at about the time that she became engaged to him; it had been artificially prolonged during the succeeding three weeks, during which he made strenuous, infectiously earnest efforts to find employment in England; it came to an abrupt end with his departure for Kenya. Accordingly the duties of the puppy Hector began with his first days at home. He was young for the job and wholly inexperienced; it is impossible to blame him for his mistake in the matter of Mike Boswell.

This was a young man who had enjoyed a wholly unromantic friendship with Millicent since she first came out. He had seen her fair hair in all kinds of light, in and out of doors, crowned in hats in succeeding fashions, bound with ribbon, decorated with combs, jauntily stuck with flowers; he had seen her nose uplifted in all kinds of weather, had even, on occasions, playfully tweaked it with his finger and thumb, and had never for one moment felt remotely attracted by her.

But the puppy Hector could hardly be expected to know this. All he knew was that two days after receiving his commission, he observed a tall and personable man of marriageable age who treated his hostess with the sort of familiarity which, among the kennel maids with whom he had been brought up, meant only one thing.

The two young people were having tea together. Hector watched for some time from his place on the sofa, barely stifling his growls. A climax was reached when, in the course of some barely intelligible back-chat, Mike leant forward and patted Millicent on the knee.

It was not a serious bite, a mere snap, in fact; but Hector had small teeth as sharp as pins. It was the sudden, nervous speed with which Mike withdrew his hand which caused the damage; he swore, wrapped his hand in a handkerchief, and at Millicent's entreaty revealed three or four minute wounds. Millicent spoke harshly to Hector and tenderly to Mike, and hurried to her mother's medicine cupboard for a bottle of iodine.

Now no Englishman, however phlegmatic, can have his hand dabbed with iodine without, momentarily at any rate, falling in love.

Mike had seen the nose countless times before, but that afternoon, as it was bowed over his scratched thumb, and as Millicent said, 'Am I hurting terribly?', as it was raised towards him, and as Millicent said, 'There. Now it will be all right,' Mike suddenly saw it transfigured as its devotees saw it and from that moment, until long after the three months of attention which she accorded him, he was Millicent's besotted suitor.

The pup Hector saw all this and realized his mistake. Never again, he decided, would he give Millicent the excuse to run for the iodine bottle.

5

He had on the whole an easy task, for Millicent's naturally capricious nature could, as a rule, he relied upon, unaided, to drive her lovers into extremes of irritation. Moreover, she had come to love the dog. She received very regular letters from Hector, written weekly and arriving in batches of three or four according to the mails. She always opened them; often she read them to the end, but their contents made little impression upon her mind and gradually their writer drifted into oblivion so that when people said to her 'How is darling Hector?' it came naturally to her to reply, 'He doesn't like the hot weather much, I'm afraid, and his coat is in a very poor state. I'm thinking of having him plucked,' instead of, 'He had a go of malaria and there is black worm in his tobacco crop.'

Playing upon this affection which had grown up for him, Hector achieved a technique for dealing with Millicent's young men. He no longer growled at them or soiled their trousers; that merely resulted in his being turned from the room; instead, he found it increasingly easy to usurp the conversation.

Tea was the most dangerous time of day, for then Millicent was permitted to entertain friends in her sitting-room; accordingly, though he had a constitutional preference for pungent, meaty dishes, Hector heroically simulated a love of lump sugar. Having made this apparent, at whatever cost to his digestion, it was easy to lead Millicent on to an interest in tricks; he would beg and 'trust', lie down as though dead, stand in the corner and raise a fore paw to his ear.

'What does SUGAR spell?' Millicent would ask, and Hector would walk round the tea table to the sugar-bowl and lay his nose against it, gazing earnestly and clouding the silver with his moist breath.

'He understands everything,' Millicent would say in triumph.

When tricks failed Hector would demand to be let out of

the door. The young man would be obliged to interrupt himself to open it. Once on the other side Hector would scratch and whine for re-admission.

In moments of extreme anxiety Hector would affect to be sick – no difficult feat after the unwelcome diet of lump sugar; he would stretch out his neck, retching noisily, till Millicent snatched him up and carried him to the hall, where the floor, paved in marble, was less vulnerable – but by that time a tender atmosphere had been shattered and one wholly preju-dicial to romance created to take its place.

This series of devices, spaced out through the afternoon and tactfully obtruded whenever the guest showed signs of leading the conversation to a more intimate phase, distracted young man after young man and sent them finally away, baffled and despairing.

Every morning Hector lay on Millicent's bed while she took her breakfast and read the daily paper. This hour from ten to eleven was sacred to the telephone and it was then that the young men with whom she had danced overnight attempted to renew their friendship and make plans for the day. At first Hector sought, not unsuccessfully, to prevent these assigna-tions by entangling himself in the wire, but soon a subtler and more insulting technique suggested itself. He pretended to telephone too. Thus, as soon as the bell rang, he would wag his tail and cock his head on one side in a way that he had learned was engaging. Millicent would begin her con-versation and Hector would wriggle up under her arm and nuzzle against the receiver.

'Listen,' she would say, '*someone* wants to talk to you. Isn't he an angel?' Then she would hold the receiver down to him and the young man at the other end would be dazed by a shattering series of yelps. This accomplishment appealed so much to Millicent that often she would not even bother to find out the name of the caller but, instead, would take off the receiver and hold it directly to the black snout, so that some wretched young man half a mile away, feeling, perhaps, none too well in the early morning, found himself barked to silence before he had spoken a word.

At other times young men badly taken with the nose would attempt to waylay Millicent in Hyde Park when she was taking Hector for exercise. Here, at first, Hector would get lost, fight other dogs and bite small children to keep himself constantly in her attention, but soon he adopted a gentler course. He insisted upon carrying Millicent's bag for her. He would trot in front of the couple and whenever he thought an interruption desirable he would drop the bag; the young man was obliged to pick it up and restore it first to Millicent and then, at her request, to the dog. Few young men were sufficiently servile to submit to more than one walk in these degrading conditions.

In this way two years passed. Letters arrived constantly from Kenya, full of devotion, full of minor disasters – blight in the sisal, locusts in the coffee, labour troubles, drought, flood, the local government, the world market. Occasionally Millicent read the letters aloud to the dog, usually she left them unread on her breakfast tray. She and Hector moved together through the leisurely routine of English social life. Wherever she carried her nose, two in five marriageable men fell temporarily in love; wherever Hector followed their ardour changed to irritation, shame and disgust. Mothers began to remark complacently that it was curious how that fascinating Blade girl never got married.

6

At last in the third year of this régime a new problem presented itself in the person of Major Sir Alexander Dreadnought, Bart, M.P., and Hector immediately realized that he was up against something altogether more formidable than he had hitherto tackled.

Sir Alexander was not a young man; he was forty-five and a widower. He was wealthy, popular and preternaturally patient; he was also mildly distinguished, being joint-master of a Midland pack of hounds and a junior Minister; he bore a war record of conspicuous gallantry. Millie's father and mother were delighted when they saw that her nose was having its effect on him. Hector took against him from the first, exerted every art which his two and a half years' practice had perfected, and achieved nothing. Devices that had driven a dozen young men to frenzies of chagrin seemed only to accentuate Sir Alexander's tender solicitude. When he came to the house to fetch Millicent for the evening he was found to have filled the pockets of his evening clothes with lump sugar for Hector; when Hector was sick Sir Alexander was there first, on his knees with a page of *The Times*; Hector resorted to his early, violent manner and bit him frequently and hard, but Sir Alexander merely remarked, 'I believe I am making the little fellow jealous. A delightful trait.'

For the truth was that Sir Alexander had been persecuted long and bitterly from his earliest days – his parents, his sisters, his schoolfellows, his company-sergeant and his colonel, his colleagues in politics, his wife, his joint-master, huntsman and hunt secretary, his election agent, his constituents and even his parliamentary private secretary had one and all pitched into Sir Alexander, and he accepted this treatment as a matter of course. For him it was the most natural thing in the world to have his ear-drums outraged by barks when he rang up the young woman of his affections; it was a high privilege to retrieve her handbag when Hector dropped it in the Park; the small wounds that Hector was able to inflict on his ankles and wrists were to him knightly scars. In his more ambitious moments he referred to Hector in Millicent's hearing as 'my little rival'. There could be no doubt whatever of his intentions, and when he asked Millicent and her mamma to visit him in the country, he added at the foot of the letter, 'Of course the invitation includes Hector.'

The Saturday to Monday visit to Sir Alexander was a nightmare to the poodle. He worked as he had never worked before; every artifice by which he could render his presence odious was attempted and attempted in vain. As far as his host was concerned, that is to say. The rest of the household responded well enough, and he received a vicious kick when, through his own bad management, he found himself alone with the second footman, whom he had succeeded in upsetting with a tray of cups at tea-time.

Conduct that had driven Millicent in shame from half the stately homes of England was meekly accepted here. There were other dogs in the house – elderly, sober, well-behaved animals at whom Hector flew; they turned their heads sadly away from his yaps of defiance, he snapped at their ears. They lolloped sombrely out of reach and Sir Alexander had them shut away for the rest of the visit.

There was an exciting Aubusson carpet in the dining-room to which Hector was able to do irreparable damage; Sir Alexander seemed not to notice.

Hector found a carrion in the park and conscientiously rolled in it – although such a thing was obnoxious to his nature – and, returning, fouled every chair in the drawing-room; Sir Alexander himself helped Millicent wash him and brought some bath salts from his own bathroom for the operation.

Hector howled all night; he hid and had half the household searching for him with lanterns; he killed some young pheasants and made a sporting attempt on a peacock. All to no purpose. He staved off an actual proposal, it is true – once in the Dutch garden, once on the way to the stables, and once while he was being bathed – but when Monday morning arrived and he heard Sir Alexander say, 'I hope Hector enjoyed his visit a little. I hope I shall see him here *very, very* often,' he knew that he was defeated.

It was now only a matter of waiting. The evenings in London were a time when it was impossible for him to keep Millicent under observation. One of these days he would wake up to hear Millicent telephoning to her girl friends, breaking the good news of her engagement.

Thus it was that after a long conflict of loyalties he came to a desperate resolve. He had grown fond of his young mistress;

often and often when her face had been pressed down to his he had felt sympathy with that long line of young men whom it was his duty to persecute. But Hector was no kitchen-haunting mongrel. By the code of all well-born dogs it is money that counts. It is the purchaser, not the mere feeder and fondler, to whom ultimate loyalty is due. The hand which had once fumbled with the fivers in the livestock department of the mammoth store, now tilled the unfertile soil of equatorial Africa, but the sacred words of commission still rang in Hector's memory. All through the Sunday night and the journey of Monday morning, Hector wrestled with his problem; then he came to the decision. *The nose must go.*

7

It was an easy business; one firm snap as she bent over his basket and the work was accomplished. She went to a plastic surgeon and emerged some weeks later without scar or stitch. But it was a different nose; the surgeon in his way was an artist and, as I have said above, Millicent's nose had no sculptural qualities. Now she has a fine aristocratic beak – worthy of the spinster she is about to become. Like all spinsters she watches eagerly for the foreign mails and keeps carefully under lock and key a casket full of depressing agricultural intelligence; like all spinsters she is accompanied everywhere by an ageing lap-dog.

AN ENGLISHMAN'S HOME

1

MR BEVERLEY METCALFE tapped the barometer in the back hall and noted with satisfaction that it had fallen several points during the night. He was by nature a sun-loving man, but he believed it was one of the marks of a true countryman to be eternally in need of rain. He had made a study and noted the points of true countrymen. Had he been of literary habit and of an earlier generation, his observations might have formed a little book of aphorisms. The true countryman wore a dark suit on Sundays unlike the flannelled tripper from the cities; he loved a bargain and would go to any expense to do his marketing by private treaty instead of through the normal channels of retail trade; while ostensibly sceptical and conservative he was readily fascinated by mechanical gadgets; he was genial but inhospitable, willing to gossip for hours across a fence with any passing stranger, but reluctant to allow his closest friends into his house . . . These and a hundred other characteristics Mr Metcalfe noted for emulation.

'That's what we need – rain,' he said to himself, and opening the garden door stepped into the balmy morning air. There was no threat in the cloudless heavens. His gardener passed, pushing the water-barrow.

'Good morning, Boggett. The glass has dropped, I'm glad to say.'

'Ur.'

'Means rain.'

'Noa.'

'Down quite low.'

'Ah.'

'Pity to spend a lot of time watering.'

'Them'll burn up else.'

'Not if it rains.'

'Am't agoin to rain. Don't never rain around heres except you can see clear down-over.'

'See clear down-over?'

'Ur. Can always see Pilbury Steeple when rain's a-coming.'

Mr Metcalfe accepted this statement gravely. 'These old fellows know a thing or two that the scientists don't,' he would often remark, simulating an air of patronage which was far from sincere. Boggett, the gardener, was not particularly old and he knew very little; the seeds he planted seldom grew; he wrought stark havoc whenever he was allowed to use the pruning-knife; his ambition in horticulture went no further than the fattening of the largest possible pumpkin; but Mr Metcalfe regarded him with the simple reverence of peasant for priest. For Mr Metcalfe was but lately initiated into the cult of the countryside, and any features of it still claimed his devotion – its agricultural processes, its social structure, its vocabulary, its recreations; the aspect of it, glittering now under the cool May sunshine, fruit trees in flower, chestnut in full leaf, the ash budding; the sound and smell of it – Mr Westmacott calling his cows at dawn, the scent of wet earth and Boggett splashing clumsily among the wallflowers; the heart of it – or what Mr Metcalfe took to be its heart – pulsing all round him; his own heart beating time, for was he not part of it, a true countryman, a landowner?

He was, it is true, a landowner in rather a small way, but, as he stood on his terrace and surveyed the untroubled valley below him, he congratulated himself that he had not been led away by the house agents into the multitudinous cares of a wider territory. He owned seven acres, more or less, and it seemed to him exactly the right amount; they comprised the policies of the house and a paddock; sixty further acres of farmland had also been available, and for a day or two he had toyed with the rather inebriating idea of acquiring them. He could well have afforded it, of course, but to his habit of mind there was something perverse and downright wrong in an investment which showed a bare two per cent yield on his capital. He wanted a home, not a 'seat', and he reflected on the irony of that word; he thought of Lord Brakehurst, with whose property he sometimes liked to say that his own 'marched' – there was indeed a hundred yards of ha-ha between his paddock and one of Lord Brakehurst's pastures. What could be less sedentary than Lord Brakehurst's life, every day of which was agitated by the cares of his great possessions? No, seven acres, judiciously chosen, was the ideal property, and Mr Metcalfe *had* chosen judiciously. The house-agent had spoken no more than the truth when he described Much Malcock as one of the most unspoilt Cotswold villages. It was exactly such a place as Mr Metcalfe had dreamed of in the long years in the cotton trade in Alexandria. Mr Metcalfe's own residence, known for generations by the singular name of Grumps, had been rechristened by a previous owner as Much Malcock Hall. It bore the new name pretty well. It was 'a dignified Georgian house of mellowed Cotswold stone; four recep., six principal bed and dressing rooms, replete with period features'. The villagers, Mr Metcalfe observed with regret, could not be induced to speak of it as 'the Hall'. Boggett always said that he worked 'up to Grumps', but the name was not of Mr Metcalfe's choosing and it looked well on his notepaper. It suggested a primacy in the village that was not undisputed.

Lord Brakehurst, of course, was in a class apart; he was Lord Lieutenant of the County with property in fifty parishes. Lady Brakehurst had not in fact called on Mrs Metcalfe, living as she did in a world where card-leaving had lost its importance, but, of the calling, there were two other households in Much Malcock, and a border-line case – besides the vicar, who had a plebeian accent and an inclination to preach against bankers.

The rival gentry were Lady Peabury and Colonel Hodge, both, to the villagers, newcomers, but residents of some twenty years' priority to Mr Metcalfe.

Lady Peabury lived at Much Malcock House, whose chimneys, soon to be hidden in the full foliage of summer, could still be seen among its budding limes on the opposite slope of the valley. Four acres of meadowland lay between her property and Mr Metcalfe's, where Westmacott's plump herd enriched the landscape and counterbalanced the slightly suburban splendour of her flower gardens. She was a widow and, like Mr Metcalfe, had come to Much Malcock from abroad. She was rich and kind and rather greedy, a diligent reader of fiction, mistress of many Cairn terriers and of five steady old maidservants who never broke the Crown Derby.

Colonel Hodge lived at the Manor, a fine gabled house in the village street, whose gardens, too, backed on to Westmacott's meadow. He was impecunious but active in the affairs of the British Legion and the Boy Scouts; he accepted Mr Metcalfe's invitation to dinner, but spoke of him, in his family circle, as 'the cotton wallah'.

These neighbours were of unequivocal position; the Hornbeams at the Old Mill were a childless, middle-aged couple who devoted themselves to craftsmanship. Mr Hornbeam senior was a genuine, commercial potter in Staffordshire; he supported them reluctantly and rather exiguously, but this backing of unearned quarterly cheques placed them definitely in the upper strata of local society. Mrs Hornbeam attended church and Mr Hornbeam was quite knowledgeable about vegetables. In fact, had they preferred a tennis court to their herb garden, and had Mr Hornbeam possessed an evening-suit, they might easily have mixed with their neighbours on terms of ostensible equality. At the time of the Peace Ballot, Mrs Hornbeam had canvassed every cottage in bicycling distance, but she eschewed the Women's Institute, and in Lady Peabury's opinion failed to pull her weight in the village. Mr Metcalfe thought Mr Hornbeam Bohemian, and Mr Hornbeam thought Mr Metcalfe Philistine. Colonel Hodge had fallen out with them some time back, on a question relating to his Airedale, and cut them year in, year out, three or four times a day.

Under their stone-tiled roofs the villagers derived substantial comfort from all these aliens. Foreign visitors impressed by the charges of London restaurants and the splendour of the more accessible ducal palaces often express wonder at the wealth of England. A half has not been told them. It is in remote hamlets like Much Malcock that the great reservoirs of national wealth seep back to the soil. The villagers had their Memorial Hall and their club. In the rafters of their church the death-watch beetle had been expensively exterminated for them: their scouts had a bell tent and silver bugles; the district nurse drove her own car; at Christmas their children were surfeited with trees and parties and the cottagers loaded with hampers; if one of them was indisposed port and soup and grapes and tickets for the seaside arrived in profusion; at evening their menfolk returned from work laden with perquisites, and all the year round they feasted on forced vegetables. The vicar found it impossible to interest them in the Left Book Club.

'God gave all men all earth to love,' Mr Metcalfe quoted, dimly remembering the lines from a calendar which had hung in his office in Alexandria, 'but since our hearts are small, Ordained for each one spot should prove, Beloved over all.'

He pottered round to the engine-house where his chauffeur was brooding over batteries. He popped his head into another outbuilding and saw that no harm had befallen the lawnmower during the night. He paused in the kitchen garden to nip the blossom off some newly-planted blackcurrant which must not be allowed to fruit that summer. Then, his round finished, he pottered in to breakfast.

His wife was already there.

'I've done my round,' he said.

'Yes, dear.'

'Everything coming along very nicely.'

'Yes, dear.'

'You can't see Pilbury Steeple, though.'

'Good gracious, Beverley, why should you want to do that?'

'It's a sign of rain when you can.'

'What a lot of nonsense. You've been listening to Boggett again.'

She rose and left him with his papers. She had to see the cook. Servants seem to take up so much time in England; she thought wistfully of the white-gowned Berber boys who had pattered about the cool, tiled floors of her house in Alexandria.

Mr Metcalfe finished his breakfast and retired to his study with pipe and papers. The *Gazette* came out that morning. A true countryman always reads his 'local rag' first, so Mr Metcalfe patiently toiled through the columns of Women's Institute doings and the reports of a Council meeting on the subject of sewage, before he allowed himself to open *The Times*.

Serene opening of a day of wrath!

2

Towards eleven o'clock Mr Metcalfe put aside the cross-word. In the lobby by the garden-door he kept a variety of garden implements specially designed for the use of the elderly. Selecting from among them one which had newly arrived, he sauntered out into the sunshine and addressed himself to the plantains on the lawn. The tool had a handsomely bound leather grip, a spliced cane handle and a head of stainless steel; it worked admirably, and with a minimum of effort Mr Metcalfe had soon scarred a large area with neat little pits.

He paused and called towards the house, 'Sophie, Sophie, come and see what I've done.'

His wife's head emerged from an upper window. 'Very pretty, dear,' she said.

Encouraged, he set to work again. Boggett passed.

'Useful little tool this, Boggett.'

'Ur.'

'Think we ought to sow seed in the bare patches?'

'Noa.'

'You think the grass will grow over them?'

'Noa. Plantains'll come up again.'

'You don't think I've killed the roots?'

'Noa. Makes the roots powerful strong topping 'em off same as you've done.'

'Well, what ought I to do?'

'Bain't nothing you can do with plaintains. They do always come up again.'

Boggett passed. Mr Metcalfe looked at his gadget with sudden distaste, propped it petulantly against the sundial, and with his hands in his pockets stared out across the valley. Even at this distance Lady Peabury's aubretias struck a discordant note. His eyes dropped and he noticed, casually at first, then with growing curiosity, two unfamiliar figures among Westmacott's cows. They were young men in dark, urban clothes, and they were very busy about something. They had papers in their hands which they constantly consulted; they paced up and down the field as though measuring it; they squatted on their haunches as though roughly taking level; they pointed into the air, to the ground, and to the horizon.

'Boggett,' said Mr Metcalfe sharply, 'come here a minute.'

'Urr.'

'Do you see two men in Mr Westmacott's field?'

'Noa.'

'You don't?'

' 'Er bain't Mr Westmacott's field. 'E've a sold of 'er.'

'Sold it! Good heavens! Who to?'

'Couldn't rightly say who 'e've a sold 'er to. Gentleman from London staying at the Brakehurst. Paid a tidy price for 'er too I've a heard said.'

'What on earth for?'

'Couldn't rightly say, but I reckon it be to build hissel a house.'

Build. It was a word so hideous that no one in Much Malcock dared use it above a whisper. 'Housing scheme', 'Development', 'Clearance', 'Council houses', 'Planning' – these obscene words had been expunged from the polite vocabulary of the district, only to be used now and then, with the licence allowed to anthropologists, of the fierce tribes

49

beyond the parish boundary. And now the horror was in their midst, the mark of Plague in the court of the Decameron.

After the first moment of shock, Mr Metcalfe rallied for action, hesitated for a moment whether or no to plunge down the hill and challenge the enemy on his own ground, and decided against it; this was the moment to act with circumspection. He must consult Lady Peabury.

It was three-quarters of a mile to the house; the lane ran past the gate which gave access to Westmacott's field; a crazily-hung elm gate and deep cow-trodden mud, soon in Mr Metcalfe's imagination to give place to golden privet and red gravel. Mr Metcalfe could see the heads of the intruders bobbing beyond the hedge; they bore urban, purposeful black hats. He drove on, miserably.

Lady Peabury was in the morning-room reading a novel; early training gave a guilty spice to this recreation, for she had been brought up to believe that to read a novel before luncheon was one of the gravest sins it was possible for a gentlewoman to commit. She slipped the book under a cushion and rose to greet Mr Metcalfe.

'I was just getting ready to go out,' she explained.

Mr Metcalfe had no time for politenesses.

'Lady Peabury,' he began at once, 'I have very terrible news.'

'Oh dear! Is poor Mr Cruttwell having trouble with the Wolf Cub account again?'

'No; at least, he is; there's another fourpence gone astray; on the credit side this time, which makes it more worrying. But that isn't what I came about. It is something that threatens our whole lives. They are going to build in Westmacott's field.' Briefly, but with emotion, he told Lady Peabury what he had seen.

She listened gravely. When he had finished there was silence in the morning-room; six little clocks ticked among the chintzes and the potted azaleas. At last Lady Peabury spoke:

'Westmacott has behaved very badly,' she said.

'I suppose you can't blame him.'

'I do blame him, Mr Metcalfe, very severely. I can't understand it at all. He always seemed a very decent man . . . I was
thinking of making Mrs Westmacott secretary of the Women's
Institute. He had no right to do a thing like that without
consulting us. Why, I look right on to that field from my
bedroom windows. I could never understand why you didn't
buy the field yourself.'

It was let for £3 18s.; they had asked £170 for it; there was
tithe and property tax on top of that. Lady Peabury knew
this.

'Any of us could have bought it at the time of sale,' said Mr
Metcalfe rather sharply.

'It always went with your house.'

In another minute, Mr Metcalfe felt, she would be telling
him that *he* had behaved very badly; that *he* had always
seemed a very decent man.

She was, in fact, thinking on just those lines at the moment.
'I daresay it's not too late even now for you to make an offer,'
she said.

'We are all equally threatened,' said Mr Metcalfe. 'I think
we ought to act together. Hodge won't be any too pleased
when he hears the news.'

Colonel Hodge had heard, and he was none too pleased.
He was waiting at the Hall when Mr Metcalfe got back.

'Do you know what that scoundrel Westmacott has done?'

'Yes,' said Mr Metcalfe rather wearily, 'I know.' The
interview with Lady Peabury had not gone off quite as he
had hoped. She had shown no enthusiasm for common
action.

'Sold his field to a lot of jerry builders.'

'Yes, I know.'

'Funny, I always thought it was *your* field.'

'No' said Mr Metcalfe, 'never.'

'It always used to go with this house.'

'Yes, I know, but I didn't happen to want it.'

'Well, it's put us all in a pretty nasty fix, I must say. D'you
suppose they'd sell it back to you now?'

'I don't know that I want to buy it. Why, they'll probably want a building-land price – seventy or eighty pounds an acre.'

'More, I daresay. But, good heavens man, you wouldn't let that stop you. Think how it would depreciate your property having a whole town of bungalows right under your windows.'

'Come, come, Hodge. We've no reason to suppose that it will be bungalows.'

'Well, villas then. You surely aren't sticking up for the fellows?'

'Certainly not. We shall all suffer very much from any development there. My belief is that it can be stopped by law; there's the Society for the Protection of Rural England. We could interest them in it. The County Council could be approached. We could write letters to the papers and petition the Office of Works. The great thing is that we must all stand together over this.'

'Fat lot of change we shall get out of that. Think of the building that's gone on over at Metbury.'

Mr Metcalfe thought, and shuddered.

'I should say that this was one of the times when money talked loudest. Have you tried Lady Peabury?'

For the first time in their acquaintance Mr Metcalfe detected a distinctly coarse strain in Colonel Hodge. 'I have discussed it with her. She is naturally very much concerned.'

'That field has always been known as Lower Grumps,' said the Colonel, reverting to his former and doubly offensive line of thought. 'It's not really her chicken.'

'It is all our chickens,' said Mr Metcalfe, getting confused with the metaphor.

'Well, I don't know what you expect me to do about it,' said Colonel Hodge. 'You know how I'm placed. It all comes of that parson preaching Bolshevism Sunday after Sunday.'

'We ought to get together and discuss it.'

'Oh, we'll discuss it all right. I don't suppose we shall discuss anything else for the next three months.'

*

No one in Much Malcock took the crisis harder than the Hornbeams. News of it reached them at midday by means of the village charwoman who dropped in twice a week to despoil their larder. She told them with some pride, innocently assuming that all city gentlemen – as she continued to regard Mr Hornbeam, in spite of his homespuns and his beard – would welcome an addition to their numbers.

Nervous gloom descended on the Old Mill. There was no explosion of wrath as there had been at the Manor; no moral condemnation as at the House; no call to action as had come from the Hall. Hopeless sorrow reigned unrelieved. Mrs Hornbeam's pottery went to pieces. Mr Hornbeam sat listless at the loom. It was their working hour; they sat at opposite ends of the raftered granary. Often, on other afternoons, they sang to one another catches and refrains of folk music as their busy fingers muddled with the clay and the shuttles. Today they sat in silence each, according to a Japanese mystical practice, attempting to drive the new peril into the World of Unbeing. It had worked well enough with Colonel Hodge and the Airedale, with the Abyssinian War, and with Mr Hornbeam senior's yearly visit, but by sunset the new peril remained obstinately concrete.

Mrs Hornbeam set their simple meal of milk, raisins, and raw turnip; Mr Hornbeam turned away from his elm platter. 'There is no place for the Artist in the Modern World,' he said. 'We ask nothing of their brutish civilization except to be left alone, to be given one little corner of land, an inch or two of sky where we can live at peace and occupy ourselves with making seemly and beautiful things. You wouldn't think it was too much to ask. We give them the entire globe for their machines. But it is not enough. They have to hunt us out and harry us. They know that as long as there is one spot of loveliness and decency left it is a standing reproach to them.'

It was growing dark; Mrs Hornbeam struck a flint and lit the rush lights. She wandered to the harp and plucked a few poignant notes. 'Perhaps Mr Metcalfe will stop it,' she said.

'That we should be dependent for the essentials of life upon a vulgarian like that . . .'

It was in this mood that he received an invitation from Mr Metcalfe to confer with his neighbours at Much Malcock House on the following afternoon.

The choice of meeting place had been a delicate one, for Lady Peabury was loth to abdicate her position of general leadership or to appear as leader in this particular matter; on the other hand, it touched her too closely for her to be able to ignore it. Accordingly the invitations were issued by Mr Metcalfe, who thereby accepted responsibility for the agenda, while the presence of the meeting in her morning-room gave something of the atmosphere of a Cabinet meeting at the Palace.

Opinion had hardened during the day and there was general agreement with Colonel Hodge's judgement: 'Metcalfe has got us into this hole by not buying the field in the first place; it's up to him to get us out of it.' Though nothing as uncompromising as this was said in front of Mr Metcalfe, he could feel it in the air. He was the last to arrive. Lady Peabury's welcome to her guests had been lukewarm. 'It is very kind of you to come. I really cannot think that it is necessary, but Mr Metcalfe particularly wished it. I suppose he intends telling us what he is going to do.' To Mr Metcalfe she said, 'We are full of curiosity.'

'Sorry to be late. I've had a day of it, I can tell you. Been to all the local offices, got on to all the Societies, and I may as well tell you at once, there's nothing doing from that end. We are not even scheduled as a rural area.'

'No,' said Colonel Hodge, 'I saw to that. Halves the potential value of one's property.'

'*Schedules*,' moaned Mr Hornbeam, 'that is what we have become. We must be *scheduled* to lead a free life.'

'. . . And so,' persisted Mr Metcalfe, in his board-room manner, 'we are left to find the solution ourselves. Now this young man has no particular reason, I imagine, for preferring this district above any other in the country. The building has not yet begun; he has no commitments. I cannot help feeling that if he were tactfully approached and offered a reasonable profit on the transaction, he might be induced to re-sell.'

'I am sure,' said Lady Peabury, 'we shall all owe a deep debt of gratitude to Mr Metcalfe.'

'Very public spirited of you,' said Colonel Hodge.

'Profits, the cancer of the age . . .'

'I am perfectly willing,' said Mr Metcalfe, 'to bear my share of the burden . . .' At the word 'share' his hearers stiffened perceptibly. 'My suggestion is that we make a common fund proportionate to our present land holdings. By a rough calculation I work that out as being in the ratio of one to Mr Hornbeam, two to Colonel Hodge, two to myself, and five to our hostess here. The figures could be adjusted,' he added as he noted that his suggestion was falling a little flat.

'You can count me out,' said Colonel Hodge. 'Couldn't possibly run to it.'

'And me,' said Mr Hornbeam.

Lady Peabury was left in, with a difficult hand to stake. Delicacy forbade recognition of the vital fact that Mr Metcalfe was very much the richer – delicacy tempered with pride. The field must be saved, but there seemed no system of joint purchase by which she could honourably fail to bear the largest part. Duty called, clearly and unmistakably, to Mr Metcalfe alone. She held her cards and passed the bidding. 'Surely,' she said, 'as a business man you must see a great many objections to joint ownership. Do you propose to partition the field, or are we all to share the rent, the tithe and the tax? It would be highly inconvenient. I doubt if it is even legal.'

'Certainly, certainly. I merely wished to assure you of my readiness to cooperate. The field, as such, is of no interest to me, I can assure you. I would willingly stand down.'

There was a threat, almost a lack of politeness in his tone. Colonel Hodge scented danger.

'Wouldn't it be best,' he said, 'to find out first if this fellow is willing to re-sell. Then you can decide which of you keep it.'

'I am sure we shall be very interested to hear the results of Mr Metcalfe's negotiations,' said Lady Peabury.

She should not have said that. She would gladly have recalled the words the moment after they were uttered. She had vaguely wanted to say something disagreeable, to punish Mr Metcalfe for the discomfort in which she found herself. She had not meant to antagonize him, and this she had unmistakably done.

Mr Metcalfe left the House abruptly, almost precipitately, and all that evening he chafed. For fifteen years Mr Metcalfe had been president of the British Chamber of Commerce. He had been greatly respected by the whole business community. No one could put anything across him, and he would not touch anything that was not above-board. Egyptian and Levantine merchants who tried to interest Metcalfe in shady business went away with a flea in the ear. It was no good trying to squeeze Metcalfe. That was his reputation in the Union Club, and here, at home, in his own village, an old woman had tried to catch him napping. There was a sudden change. He was no longer the public spirited countryman; he was cards - on - the - table - brass - tacks - and - twenty - shillings - in - the - pound - treat - him - or - mind - your - step Metcalfe, Metcalfe with his back up, fighting Metcalfe once again, Metcalfe who would cut off his nose any day to spite his face, sink any ship for a ha'p'orth of tar that was not legally due, Metcalfe the lion of the Rotarians.

'She should not have said that,' said Colonel Hodge, reporting the incident to his wife over their horrible dinner. 'Metcalfe won't do anything now.'

'Why don't *you* go and talk to the man who's bought the field?' said Mrs Hodge.

'I might . . . I think I will . . . Tell you what, I'll go now.' He went.

He found the man without difficulty, since there was no other visitor staying at the Brakehurst Arms. An inquiry from the landlord elicited his name – Mr Hargood-Hood. He was sitting alone in the parlour, sipping whisky and soda and working at *The Times* crossword.

The Colonel said, 'Evening. My name is Hodge.'

'Yes?'

'I daresay you know who I am.'

'I'm very sorry, I'm afraid . . .'

'I own the Manor. My garden backs on to Westmacott's field – the one you've bought.'

'Oh,' said Mr Hargood-Hood, 'was he called Westmacott? I didn't know. I leave all these things to my lawyer. I simply told him to find me a suitable, secluded site for my work. He told me last week he had found one here. It seems very suitable. But he didn't tell me anyone's name.'

'You didn't pick this village for any particular reason?'

'No, no. But I think it perfectly charming,' he added politely.

There was a pause.

'I wanted to talk to you,' said Colonel Hodge superfluously. 'Have a drink.'

'Thank you.'

Another pause.

'I'm afraid you won't find it a very healthy site,' said the Colonel. 'Down in the hollow there.'

'I never mind things like that. All I need is seclusion.'

'Ah, a writer, no doubt.'

'No.'

'A painter?'

'No, no. I suppose you would call me a scientist.'

'I see. And you would be using your house for week-ends?'

'No, no, quite the reverse. I and my staff will be working here all the week. And it's not exactly a house I'm building, although, of course, there will be living quarters attached. Perhaps, since we are going to be such close neighbours, you would like to see the plans . . .'

'. . . You never saw such a thing,' said Colonel Hodge next morning to Mr Metcalfe. 'An experimental industrial laboratory he called it. Two great chimneys – have to have those, he said, by law, because of poison fumes, a water tower to get high pressures, six bungalows for his staff . . . ghastly. The odd thing was he seemed quite a decent sort of fellow. Said it hadn't occurred to him anyone would find it objectionable. Thought we should all be interested. When I brought up the subject of re-selling – tactful, you know – he just said he left all that to his lawyer . . .'

3

Much Malcock Hall.

Dear Lady Peabury,

In pursuance of our conversation of three days ago, I beg to inform you that I have been in communication with Mr Hargood-Hood, the purchaser of the field which separates our two properties, and his legal representative. As Col. Hodge has already informed you, Mr Hargood-Hood proposes to erect an experimental industrial laboratory fatal to the amenities of the village. As you are doubtless aware, work has not yet been commenced, and Mr Hargood-Hood is willing to re-sell the property if duly compensated. The price proposed is to include re-purchase of the field, legal fees and compensation for the architect's work. The young blackguard has us in a cleft stick. He wants £500. It is excessive, but I am prepared to pay half of this if you will pay the other half. Should you not accede to this generous offer I shall take steps to safeguard my own interests *at whatever cost to the neighbourhood*.

Yours sincerely,

Beverley Metcalfe

P.S. – I mean I shall sell the Hall and develop the property as *building lots*.

Much Malcock House.

Lady Peabury begs to inform Mr Metcalfe that she has received his note of this morning, the tone of which I am unable to account for. She further begs to inform you that she has no wish to increase my already extensive responsibilities in the district. She cannot accept the principle of equal obligation with Mr Metcalfe as he has far less land to look after, and the field in question should rightly form part of your property. She does not think that the scheme for developing his garden as a housing estate is likely to be a success if Mr Hargood-Hood's laboratory is as unsightly as is represented, which I rather doubt.

'All right,' said Mr Metcalfe. 'That's that and be damned to her.'

4

It was ten days later. The lovely valley, so soon to be defiled, lay resplendent in the sunset. Another year, thought Mr Metcalfe, and this fresh green foliage would be choked with soot, withered with fumes; these mellow roofs and chimneys which for two hundred years or more had enriched the landscape below the terrace, would be hidden by functional monstrosities in steel and glass and concrete. In the doomed field Mr Westmacott, almost for the last time, was calling his cattle; next week building was to begin and they must seek other pastures. So, in a manner of speaking, must Mr Metcalfe. Already his desk was littered with house agents' notices. All for £500, he told himself. There would be redecorations; the cost and loss of moving. The speculative builders to whom he had viciously appealed showed no interest in the site. He was going to lose much more than £500 on the move. But so, he grimly assured himself, was Lady Peabury. She would learn that no one could put a fast one over on Beverley Metcalfe.

And she, on the opposing slope, surveyed the scene with corresponding melancholy. The great shadows of the cedars lay across the lawn; they had scarcely altered during her long tenancy, but the box hedge had been of her planting; it was she who had planned the lily pond and glorified it with lead flamingoes; she had reared the irregular heap of stones under the west wall and stocked it with Alpines; the flowering shrubs were hers; she could not take them with her where she was going. Where? She was too old now to begin another garden, to make other friends. She would move, like so many of her contemporaries, from hotel to hotel, at home and abroad, cruise a little, settle for prolonged rather unwelcome visits on her relatives. All this for £250, for £12 10s. a year, for less than she gave to charity. It was not the money; it was Principle. She would not compromise with Wrong; with that ill-bred fellow on the hill opposite.

Despite the splendour of the evening, an unhappy spirit obsessed Much Malcock. The Hornbeams moped and drooped; Colonel Hodge fretted. He paced the threadbare carpet of his smoking-room. 'It's enough to make a fellow turn Bolshie, like that parson,' he said. 'What does Metcalfe care? He's rich. He can move anywhere. What does Lady Peabury care? It's the small man, trying to make ends meet, who suffers.'

Even Mr Hargood-Hood seemed affected by the general gloom. His lawyer was visiting him at the Brakehurst. All day they had been in intermittent, rather anxious, consultation. 'I think I might go and talk to that Colonel again,' he said, and set off up the village street, under the deepening shadows, for the Manor House. And from this dramatic last minute move for conciliation sprang the great Hodge Plan for appeasement and peace-in-our-time.

5

'. . . the Scouts are badly in need of a new hut,' said Colonel Hodge.

'No use coming to me,' said Mr Metcalfe. 'I'm leaving the neighbourhood.'

'I was thinking,' said Colonel Hodge, 'that Westmacott's field would be just the place for it . . .'

And so it was arranged. Mr Hornbeam gave a pound, Colonel Hodge a guinea, Lady Peabury £250. A jumble sale, a white-elephant tea, a raffle, a pageant, and a house-to-house collection, produced a further 30s. Mr Metcalfe found the rest. It cost him, all told, a little over £500. He gave with a good heart. There was no question now of jockeying him into a raw deal. In the rôle of public benefactor he gave with positive relish, and when Lady Peabury suggested that the field should be reserved for a camping site and the building of the hut postponed, it was Mr Metcalfe who pressed on with the building and secured the old stone tiles from the roof of a dismantled barn. In the circumstances, Lady Peabury could not protest when the building was named the Metcalfe-Peabury Hall. Mr Metcalfe found the title invigorating and was soon in negotiation with the brewery for a change of name at the Brakehurst Arms. It is true that Boggett still speaks of it as 'the Brakehurst,' but the new name is plainly lettered for all to read: The Metcalfe Arms.

And so Mr Hargood-Hood passed out of the history of Much Malcock. He and his lawyer drove away to their home beyond the hills. The lawyer was Mr Hargood-Hood's brother.

'We cut that pretty fine, Jock. I thought, for once, we were going to be left with the baby.'

They drove to Mr Hargood-Hood's home, a double quadrangle of mellow brick that was famous far beyond the county. On the days when the gardens were open to the public, record crowds came to admire the topiary work, yews and boxes of prodigious size and fantastic shape which gave perpetual employment to three gardeners. Mr Hargood-Hood's ancestors had built the house and planted the gardens in a happier time, before the days of property tax and imported grain. A sterner age demanded more strenuous efforts for their preservation.

'Well, that has settled Schedule A for another year and left something over for cleaning the fish-ponds. But it was an anxious month. I shouldn't care to go through it again. We must be more careful next time, Jock. How about moving east?'

Together the two brothers unfolded the inch ordnance map of Norfolk, spread it on the table of the Great Hall and began their preliminary, expert search for a likely, unspoilt, well-loved village.

EXCURSION IN REALITY

1

THE commissionaire at Espinoza's restaurant seems to maintain under his particular authority all the most decrepit taxicabs in London. He is a commanding man; across his great chest the student of military medals may construe a tale of heroism and experience; Boer farms sink to ashes, fanatical Fuzzi-wuzzies hurl themselves to paradise, supercilious mandarins survey the smashing of their porcelain and rending of fine silk, in that triple row of decorations. He has only to run from the steps of Espinoza's to call to your service a vehicle as crazy as all the enemies of the King-Emperor.

Half a crown into the white cotton glove, because Simon Lent was too tired to ask for change. He and Sylvia huddled into the darkness on broken springs, between draughty windows. It had been an unsatisfactory evening. They had sat over their table until two because it was an extension night. Sylvia would not drink anything because Simon had said he was broke. So they sat for five or six hours, sometimes silent, sometimes bickering, sometimes exchanging listless greetings with the passing couples. Simon dropped Sylvia at her door; a kiss, clumsily offered, coldly accepted; then back to the attic flat, over a sleepless garage, for which Simon paid six guineas a week.

Outside his door they were sluicing a limousine. He squeezed round it and climbed the narrow stairs that had once echoed to the whistling of ostlers, stamping down to the stables before dawn. (Woe to young men in Mewses! Oh woe to bachelors half in love, living on £800 a year!) There was a small heap of letters on his dressing-table, which had arrived that evening while he was dressing. He lit his gas fire and began to open them. Tailor's bill £56, hosier £43; a reminder that his club subscription for that year had not yet been paid;

his account from Espinoza's with a note informing him that the terms were strict, net cash monthly, and that no further credit would be extended to him; 'it appeared from the books' of his bank that his last cheque overdrew his account £10 16s. beyond the limit of his guaranteed overdraft; a demand from the income-tax collector for particulars of his employees and their wages (Mrs Shaw, who came in to make his bed and orange juice for 4s. 6d. a day); small bills for books, spectacles, cigars, hair lotion and Sylvia's last four birthday presents. (Woe to shops that serve young men in Mewses!)

The other part of his mail was in marked contrast to this. There was a box of preserved figs from an admirer in Fresno, California; two letters from young ladies who said they were composing papers about his work for their college literary societies, and would he send a photograph; press cuttings describing him as a 'popular', 'brilliant', 'meteorically successful', and 'enviable' young novelist; a request for the loan of two hundred pounds from a paralysed journalist; an invitation to luncheon from Lady Metroland; six pages of closely reasoned abuse from a lunatic asylum in the North of England. For the truth, which no one who saw into Simon Lent's heart could possibly have suspected, was that he was in his way and within his limits quite a famous young man.

There was a last letter with a typewritten address which Simon opened with little expectation of pleasure. The paper was headed with the name of a Film Studio in one of the suburbs of London. The letter was brief and businesslike.

Dear Simon Lent [a form of address, he had noted before, largely favoured by the theatrical profession],

I wonder whether you have ever considered writing for the Films. We should value your angle on a picture we are now making. Perhaps you would meet me for luncheon tomorrow at the Garrick Club and let me know your reactions to this. Will you leave a message with my night secretary some time before 8 a.m. tomorrow morning or with my day secretary after that hour?

Cordially yours,

Below this were two words written in pen and ink which

seemed to be *Jewee Mecceee* with below them the explanatory typescript (*Sir James Macrae*).

Simon read this through twice. Then he rang up Sir James Macrae and informed his night secretary that he would keep the luncheon appointment next day. He had barely put down the telephone before the bell rang.

'This is Sir James Macrae's night secretary speaking. Sir James would be very pleased if Mr Lent would come round and see him this evening at his house in Hampstead.'

Simon looked at his watch. It was nearly three. 'Well . . . it's rather late to go so far tonight . . .'

'Sir James is sending a car for you.'

Simon was no longer tired. As he waited for the car the telephone rang again. 'Simon,' said Sylvia's voice, 'are you asleep?' . . .

'No; in fact I'm just going out.'

'Simon . . . I say, was I beastly tonight?'

'Lousy.'

'Well, I thought you were lousy, too.'

'Never mind. See you some time.'

'Aren't you going to go on talking?'

'Can't, I'm afraid. I've got to do some work.'

'*Simon*, what *can* you mean?'

'Can't explain now. There's a car waiting.'

'When am I seeing you – tomorrow?'

'Well, I don't really know. Ring me up in the morning. Good night.'

A quarter of a mile away, Sylvia put down the telephone, rose from the hearthrug, where she had settled herself in the expectation of twenty minutes' intimate explanation and crept disconsolately into bed.

Simon bowled off to Hampstead through deserted streets. He sat back in the car in a state of pleasant excitement. Presently they began to climb the steep little hill and emerged into an open space with a pond and the tops of trees, black and deep as a jungle in the darkness. The night butler admitted him to the low Georgian house and led him to the library, where Sir James Macrae was standing before the fire, dressed in ginger-coloured plus-fours. A table was laid with supper.

'Evening, Lent. Nice of you to come. Have to fit in business when I can. Cocoa or whisky? Have some rabbit pie; it's rather good. First chance of a meal I've had since breakfast. Ring for some more cocoa, there's a good chap. Now what was it you wanted to see me about?'

'Well, I thought *you* wanted to see *me*.'

'Did I? Very likely. Miss Bentham'll know. She arranged the appointment. You might ring the bell on the desk, will you?'

Simon rang and there instantly appeared the neat night secretary.

'Miss Bentham, what did I want to see Mr Lent about?'

'I'm afraid I couldn't say, Sir James. Miss Harper is responsible for Mr Lent. When I came on duty this evening I merely found a note from her asking me to fix an appointment as soon as possible.'

'Pity,' said Sir James. 'We'll have to wait until Miss Harper comes on tomorrow.'

'I think it was something about writing for films.'

'Very likely,' said Sir James. 'Sure to be something of the kind. I'll let you know without delay. Thanks for dropping in.' He put down his cup of cocoa and held out his hand with unaffected cordiality. 'Good night, my dear boy.' He rang the bell for the night butler. 'Sanders, I want Benson to run Mr Lent back.'

'I'm sorry, sir. Benson has just gone down to the studio to fetch Miss Grits.'

'Pity,' said Sir James. 'Still, I expect you'll be able to pick up a taxi or something.'

66

2

Simon got to bed at half-past four. At ten minutes past eight the telephone by his bed was ringing.

'Mr Lent? This is Sir James Macrae's secretary speaking. Sir James's car will call for you at half-past eight to take you to the studio.'

'I shan't be ready as soon as that, I'm afraid.'

There was a shocked pause; then the day secretary said: 'Very well, Mr Lent. I will see if some alternative arrangement is possible and ring you in a few minutes.'

In the intervening time Simon fell asleep again. Then the bell woke him once more and the same impersonal voice addressed him.

'Mr Lent? I have spoken to Sir James. His car will call for you at eight forty-five.'

Simon dressed hastily. Mrs Shaw had not yet arrived, so there was no breakfast for him. He found some stale cake in the kitchen cupboard and was eating it when Sir James's car arrived. He took a slice down with him, still munching.

'You needn't have brought that,' said a severe voice from inside the car. 'Sir James has sent you some breakfast. Get in quickly; we're late.'

In the corner, huddled in rugs, sat a young woman in a jaunty red hat; she had bright eyes and a very firm mouth.

'I expect that you are Miss Harper.'

'No. I'm Elfreda Grits. We're working together on this film, I believe. I've been up all night with Sir James. If you don't mind I'll go to sleep for twenty minutes. You'll find a thermos of cocoa and some rabbit pie in the basket on the floor.'

'Does Sir James live on cocoa and rabbit pie?'

'No; those are the remains of his supper. Please don't talk. I want to sleep.'

Simon disregarded the pie, but poured some steaming cocoa into the metal cap of the thermos flask. In the corner Miss Grits composed herself for sleep. She took off the jaunty red hat and laid it between them on the seat, veiled her eyes with two blue-pigmented lids and allowed the firm lips to relax and gape a little. Her platinum-blonde wind-swept head bobbed and swayed with the motion of the car as they swept out of London through converging and diverging tram lines. Stucco gave place to brick and the façades of the tube stations changed from tile to concrete; unoccupied building plots appeared and newly-planted trees along unnamed avenues. Five minutes exactly before their arrival at the studio Miss Grits opened her eyes, powdered her nose, touched her lips with red, and pulling her hat on to the side of her scalp, sat bolt upright, ready for another day.

Sir James was at work on the lot when they arrived. In a white-hot incandescent hell two young people were carrying on an infinitely tedious conversation at what was presumably the table of a restaurant. A dozen emaciated couples in evening dress danced listlessly behind them. At the other end of the huge shed some carpenters were at work building the façade of a Tudor manor house. Men in eyeshades scuttled in and out. Notices stood everywhere. 'Do not Smoke.' 'Do not Speak.' 'Keep away from the high-power cable.'

Miss Grits, in defiance of these regulations, lit a cigarette, kicked some electric apparatus out of her path, said, 'He's busy. I expect he'll see us when he's through with this scene,' and disappeared through a door marked 'No admittance.'

Shortly after eleven o'clock Sir James caught sight of Simon. 'Nice of you to come. Shan't be long now,' he called out to him. 'Mr Briggs, get a chair for Mr Lent.'

At two o'clock he noticed him again. 'Had any lunch?'

'No,' said Simon.

'No more have I. Just coming.'

At half-past three Miss Grits joined him and said: 'Well, it's been an easy day so far. You mustn't think we're always as slack as this. There's a canteen across the yard. Come and have something to eat.'

An enormous buffet was full of people in a variety of costume and make-up. Disappointed actresses in languorous

attitudes served cups of tea and hard-boiled eggs. Simon and
Miss Grits ordered sandwiches and were about to eat them
when a loud-speaker above their heads suddenly announced
with alarming distinctness, 'Sir James Macrae calling Mr Lent
and Miss Grits in the Conference Room.'

'Come on, quick,' said Miss Grits. She bustled him through
the swing doors, across the yard, into the office buildings
and up a flight of stairs to a solid oak door marked 'Conference. Keep out.'

Too late.

'Sir James has been called away,' said the secretary. 'Will
you meet him at the West End office at five-thirty.'

Back to London, this time by tube. At five-thirty they were
at the Piccadilly office ready for the next clue in their treasure
hunt. This took them to Hampstead. Finally at eight they
were back at the studio. Miss Grits showed no sign of
exhaustion.

'Decent of the old boy to give us a day off,' she remarked.
'He's easy to work with in that way – after Hollywood. Let's
get some supper.'

But as they opened the canteen doors and felt the warm
breath of light refreshments, the loud-speaker again announced: 'Sir James Macrae calling Mr Lent and Miss Grits in
the Conference Room.'

This time they were not too late. Sir James was there at the
head of an oval table; round him were grouped the chiefs of
his staff. He sat in a greatcoat with his head hung forward,
elbows on the table and his hands clasped behind his neck.
The staff sat in respectful sympathy. Presently he looked up,
shook himself and smiled pleasantly.

'Nice of you to come,' he said. 'Sorry I couldn't see you
before. Lots of small things to see to on a job like this. Had
dinner?'

'Not yet.'

'Pity. Have to eat, you know. Can't work at full pressure
unless you eat plenty.'

Then Simon and Miss Grits sat down and Sir James
explained his plan. 'I want, ladies and gentlemen, to introduce

69

Mr Lent to you. I'm sure you all know his name already and I daresay some of you know his work. Well, I've called him in to help us and I hope that when he's heard the plan he'll consent to join us. I want to produce a film of *Hamlet*. I daresay you don't think that's a very original idea – but it's Angle that counts in the film world. I'm going to do it from an entirely new angle. That's why I've called in Mr Lent. I want him to write dialogue for us.'

'But surely,' said Simon, 'there's quite a lot of dialogue there already?'

'Ah, you don't see my angle. There have been plenty of productions of Shakespeare in modern dress. We are going to produce him in modern speech. How can you expect the public to enjoy Shakespeare when they can't make head or tail of the dialogue. D'you know I began reading a copy the other day and blessed if *I* could understand it. At once I said, "What the public wants is Shakespeare with all his beauty of thought and character translated into the language of every day life." Now Mr Lent here was the man whose name naturally suggested itself. Many of the most high-class critics have commended Mr Lent's dialogue. Now my idea is that Miss Grits here shall act in an advisory capacity, helping with the continuity and the technical side, and that Mr Lent shall be given a free hand with the scenario . . .'

The discourse lasted for a quarter of an hour; then the chiefs of staff nodded sagely; Simon was taken into another room and given a contract to sign by which he received £50 a week retaining fee and £250 advance.

'You had better fix up with Miss Grits the times of work most suitable to you. I shall expect your first treatment by the end of the week. I should go and get some dinner if I were you. Must eat.'

Slightly dizzy, Simon hurried to the canteen where two languorous blondes were packing up for the night.

'We've been on since four o'clock this morning,' they said, 'and the supers have eaten everything except the nougat. Sorry.'

Sucking a bar of nougat Simon emerged into the now

deserted studio. On three sides of him, to the height of twelve feet, rose in appalling completeness the marble walls of the scene-restaurant; at his elbow a bottle of imitation champagne still stood in its pail of melted ice; above and beyond extended the vast gloom of rafters and ceiling.

'*Fact*,' said Simon to himself, 'the world of action . . . the pulse of life . . . Money, hunger . . . *Reality*.'

Next morning he was called with the words, 'Two young ladies waiting to see you.'

'Two?'

Simon put on his dressing-gown and, orange juice in hand, entered his sitting-room. Miss Grits nodded pleasantly.

'We arranged to start at ten,' she said. 'But it doesn't really matter. I shall not require you very much in the early stages. This is Miss Dawkins. She is one of the staff stenographers. Sir James thought you would need one. Miss Dawkins will be attached to you until further notice. He also sent two copies of *Hamlet*. When you've had your bath, I'll read you my notes for our first treatment.'

But this was not to be; before Simon was dressed Miss Grits had been recalled to the studio on urgent business.

'I'll ring up and tell you when I am free,' she said.

Simon spent the morning dictating letters to everyone he could think of; they began – *Please forgive me for dictating this, but I am so busy just now that I have little time for personal correspondence . . .*' Miss Dawkins sat deferentially over her pad. He gave her Sylvia's number.

'Will you get on to this number and present my compliments to Miss Lennox and ask her to luncheon at Espinoza's . . . And book a table for two there at one forty-five.'

'Darling,' said Sylvia, when they met, 'why were you out all yesterday, and *who* was that voice this morning?'

'Oh, that was Miss Dawkins, my stenographer.'

'Simon, what *can* you mean?'

'You see, I've joined the film industry.'

'*Darling*. Do give me a job.'

71

'Well, I'm not paying much attention to casting at the moment – but I'll bear you in mind.'

'Goodness. How you've changed in two days!'

'Yes!' said Simon, with great complacency. 'Yes, I think I have. You see, for the first time in my life I have come into contact with Real Life. I'm going to give up writing novels. It was a mug's game anyway. The written word is dead – first the papyrus, then the printed book, now the film. The artist must no longer work alone. He is part of the age in which he lives; he must share (only of course, my dear Sylvia, in very different proportions) the weekly wage envelope of the proletarian. Vital art implies a corresponding set of social relationships. Co-operation . . . co-ordination . . . the hive endeavour of the community directed to a single end . . .'

Simon continued in this strain at some length, eating meantime a luncheon of Dickensian dimensions, until, in a small miserable voice, Sylvia said: 'It seems to me that you've fallen for some ghastly film star.'

'Oh God,' said Simon, 'only a virgin could be as vulgar as that.'

They were about to start one of their old, interminable quarrels when the telephone boy brought a message that Miss Grits wished to resume work instantly.

'So that's her name,' said Sylvia.

'If you only knew how funny that was,' said Simon scribbling his initials on the bill and leaving the table while Sylvia was still groping with gloves and bag.

As things turned out, however, he became Miss Grits' lover before the week was out. The idea was hers. She suggested it to him one evening at his flat as they corrected the typescript of the final version of their first treatment.

'No, really,' Simon said aghast. 'No, really. It would be quite impossible. I'm sorry, but . . .'

'Why? Don't you like women?'

'Yes, but . . .'

'Oh, come along,' Miss Grits said briskly. 'We don't get much time for amusement . . .' And later, as she packed their

72

manuscripts into her attaché case she said, 'We must do it again if we have time. Besides I find it's so much easier to work with a man if you're having an *affaire* with him.'

3

For three weeks Simon and Miss Grits (he always thought of her by this name in spite of all subsequent intimacies) worked together in complete harmony. His life was redirected and transfigured. No longer did he lie in bed, glumly preparing himself for the coming day; no longer did he say every morning 'I *must* get down to the country and finish that book,' and every evening find himself slinking back to the same urban flat; no longer did he sit over supper tables with Sylvia, idly bickering; no more listless explanations over the telephone. Instead he pursued a routine of incalculable variety, summoned by telephone at all hours to conferences which rarely assembled; sometimes to Hampstead, sometimes to the studios, once to Brighton. He spent long periods of work pacing up and down his sitting-room, with Miss Grits pacing backwards and forwards along the other wall and Miss Dawkins obediently perched between them, as the two dictated, corrected and redrafted their scenario. There were meals at improbable times and vivid, unsentimental passages of love with Miss Grits. He ate irregular and improbable meals, bowling through the suburbs in Sir James's car, pacing the carpet dictating to Miss Dawkins, perched in deserted lots upon scenery which seemed made to survive the collapse of civilization. He lapsed, like Miss Grits, into brief spells of death-like unconsciousness, often awakening, startled, to find that a street or desert or factory had come into being about him while he slept.

The film meanwhile grew rapidly, daily putting out new shoots and changing under their eyes in a hundred unexpected ways. Each conference produced some radical change in the story. Miss Grits in her precise, invariable voice would read out the fruits of their work. Sir James would sit with his head in his hand, rocking slightly from side to side and giving vent to occasional low moans and whimpers: round him sat the experts – production, direction, casting, continuity, cutting and costing managers, bright eyes, eager to attract the great man's attention with some apt intrusion.

'Well,' Sir James would say, 'I think we can O.K. that. Any suggestions, gentlemen?'

There would be a pause, until one by one the experts began to deliver their contributions . . . 'I've been thinking, sir, that it won't do to have the scene laid in Denmark. The public won't stand for travel stuff. How about setting it in Scotland – then we could have some kilts and clan gathering scenes?'

'Yes, that's a very sensible suggestion. Make a note of that, Lent . . .'

'I was thinking we'd better drop this character of the Queen. She'd much better be dead before the action starts. She hangs up the action. The public won't stand for him abusing his mother.'

'Yes, make a note of that, Lent.'

'How would it be, sir, to make the ghost the Queen instead of the King . . .'

'Yes, make a note of that, Lent . . .'

'Don't you think, sir, it would be better if Ophelia were Horatio's sister. More poignant, if you see what I mean.'

'Yes, make a note of that . . .'

'I think we are losing sight of the essence of the story in the last sequence. After all, it is first and foremost a Ghost Story, isn't it . . .'

And so from simple beginnings the story spread majestically. It was in the second week that Sir James, after, it must be admitted, considerable debate, adopted the idea of incorporating with it the story of *Macbeth*. Simon was opposed to the proposition at first, but the appeal of the three witches proved too strong. The title was then changed to *The White Lady of Dunsinane*, and he and Miss Grits settled down to a prodigious week's work in rewriting their entire scenarios.

4

The end came as suddenly as everything else in this remarkable episode. The third conference was being held at an hotel in the New Forest where Sir James happened to be staying; the experts had assembled by train, car and motor-bicycle at a moment's notice and were tired and unresponsive. Miss Grits read the latest scenario; it took some time, for it had now reached the stage when it could be taken as 'white script' ready for shooting. Sir James sat sunk in reflection longer than usual. When he raised his head, it was to utter the single word:

'No.'

'No?'

'No, it won't do. We must scrap the whole thing. We've got much too far from the original story. I can't think why you need introduce Julius Caesar and King Arthur at all.'

'But, sir, they were your own suggestions at the last conference.'

'Were they? Well, I can't help it. I must have been tired and not paying full attention . . . Besides, I don't like the dialogue. It misses all the poetry of the original. What the public wants is Shakespeare, the whole of Shakespeare and nothing but Shakespeare. Now this scenario you've written is all very well in its way – but it's not Shakespeare. I'll tell you what we'll do. We'll use the play exactly as he wrote it and record from that. Make a note of it, Miss Grits.'

'Then you'll hardly require my services any more?' said Simon.

'No, I don't think I shall. Still, nice of you to have come.'

Next morning Simon woke bright and cheerful as usual and was about to leap from his bed when he suddenly remembered the events of last night. There was nothing for him to do. An empty day lay before him. No Miss Grits, no Miss Dawkins, no scampering off to conferences or dictating of dialogue. He rang up Miss Grits and asked her to lunch with him.

'No, quite impossible, I'm afraid. I have to do the continuity for a scenario of St John's Gospel before the end of the week. Pretty tough job. We're setting it in Algeria so as to get the atmosphere. Off to Hollywood next month. Don't suppose I shall see you again. Good-bye.'

Simon lay in bed with all his energy slowly slipping away. Nothing to do. Well, he supposed, now was the time to go away to the country and get on with his novel. Or should he go abroad? Some quiet café-restaurant in the sun where he could work out those intractable last chapters. That was what he would do . . . sometime . . . the end of the week perhaps.

Meanwhile he leaned over on his elbow, lifted the telephone and, asking for Sylvia's number, prepared himself for twenty-five minutes' acrimonious reconciliation.

BELLA FLEACE GAVE A PARTY

BALLINGAR is four and a half hours from Dublin if you catch the early train from Broadstone Station and five and a quarter if you wait until the afternoon. It is the market town of a large and comparatively well-populated district. There is a pretty Protestant church in 1820 Gothic on one side of the square and a vast, unfinished Catholic cathedral opposite it, conceived in that irresponsible medley of architectural orders that is so dear to the hearts of transmontane pietists. Celtic lettering of a sort is beginning to take the place of the Latin alphabet on the shop fronts that complete the square. These all deal in identical goods in varying degrees of dilapidation; Mulligan's Store, Flannigan's Store, Riley's Store, each sells thick black boots, hanging in bundles, soapy colonial cheese, hardware and haberdashery, oil and saddlery, and each is licensed to sell ale and porter for consumption on or off the premises. The shell of the barracks stands with empty window frames and blackened interior as a monument to emancipation. Someone has written *The Pope is a Traitor* in tar on the green pillar box. A typical Irish town.

Fleacetown is fifteen miles from Ballingar, on a direct uneven road through typical Irish country; vague purple hills in the far distance and towards them, on one side of the road, fitfully visible among drifting patches of white mist, unbroken miles of bog, dotted with occasional stacks of cut peat. On the other side the ground slopes up to the north, divided irregularly into spare fields by banks and stone walls over which the Ballingar hounds have some of their most eventful hunting. Moss lies on everything; in a rough green rug on the walls and banks, soft green velvet on the timber – blurring the transitions so that there is no knowing where the ground ends and trunk and masonry begin. All the way from Ballingar there is a succession of whitewashed cabins and a dozen or so fair-size farmhouses; but there is no gentleman's house, for all this was Fleace property in the days before the Land Commission. The demesne land is all that belongs to Fleace-town now, and this is let for pasture to neighbouring farmers. Only a few beds are cultivated in the walled kitchen garden; the rest has run to rot, thorned bushes barren of edible fruit spreading everywhere among weedy flowers reverting rankly to type. The hot-houses have been draughty skeletons for ten years. The great gates set in their Georgian arch are perma-nently padlocked, the lodges are derelict, and the line of the main drive is only just discernible through the meadows. Access to the house is half a mile farther up through a farm gate, along a track be-fouled by cattle.

But the house itself, at the date with which we are dealing, was in a condition of comparatively good repair; compared, that is to say, with Ballingar House or Castle Boycott or Knode Hall. It did not, of course, set up to rival Gordontown, where the American Lady Gordon had installed electric light, central heating and a lift, or Mock House or Newhill, which were leased to sporting Englishmen, or Castle Mockstock, since Lord Mockstock married beneath him. These four houses with their neatly raked gravel, bathrooms and dyna-mos, were the wonder and ridicule of the country. But Fleacetown, in fair competition with the essentially Irish houses of the Free State, was unusually habitable.

Its roof was intact; and it is the roof which makes the difference between the second and third grade of Irish country houses. Once that goes you have moss in the bedrooms, ferns on the stairs and cows in the library, and in a very few years you have to move into the dairy or one of the lodges. But so long as he has, literally, a roof over his head, an Irishman's house is still his castle. There were weak bits in Fleacetown, but general opinion held that the leads were good for another twenty years and would certainly survive the present owner.

Miss Annabel Rochfort-Doyle-Fleace, to give her the full name under which she appeared in books of reference, though she was known to the entire countryside as Bella Fleace, was the last of her family. There had been Fleaces and Fleysers living about Ballingar since the days of Strongbow, and farm buildings marked the spot where they had inhabited a stockaded fort two centuries before the immigration of the Boycotts or Gordons or Mockstocks. A family tree emblazed by a nineteenth-century genealogist, showing how the original stock had merged with the equally ancient Rochforts and the respectable though more recent Doyles, hung in the billiard-room. The present home had been built on extravagant lines in the middle of the eighteenth century, when the family, though enervated, was still wealthy and influential. It would be tedious to trace its gradual decline from fortune; enough to say that it was due to no heroic debauchery. The Fleaces just got unobtrusively poorer in the way that families do who make no effort to help themselves. In the last generation, too, there had been marked traces of eccentricity. Bella Fleace's mother – an O'Hara of Newhill – had from the day of her marriage until her death suffered from the delusion that she was a Negress. Her brother, from whom she had inherited, devoted himself to oil painting; his mind ran on the simple subject of assassination, and before his death he had executed pictures of practically every such incident in history from Julius Caesar to General Wilson. He was at work on a painting of his own murder at the time of the troubles, when he was, in fact, ambushed and done to death with a shot-gun on his own drive.

It was under one of her brother's paintings – Abraham Lincoln in his box at the theatre – that Miss Fleace was sitting one colourless morning in November when the idea came to her to give a Christmas party. It would be unnecessary to describe her appearance closely, and somewhat confusing, because it seemed in contradiction to much of her character. She was over eighty, very untidy and very red; streaky grey hair was twisted behind her head into a horsey bun, wisps hung round her cheeks; her nose was prominent and blue-veined; her eyes pale blue, blank and mad; she had a lively smile and spoke with a marked Irish intonation. She walked with the aid of a stick, having been lamed many years back when her horse rolled her among loose stones late in a long day with the Ballingar Hounds; a tipsy sporting doctor had completed the mischief, and she had not been able to ride again. She would appear on foot when hounds drew the Fleacetown coverts and loudly criticize the conduct of the huntsman, but every year fewer of her old friends turned out; strange faces appeared.

They knew Bella, though she did not know them. She had become a by-word in the neighbourhood, a much-valued joke.

'A rotten day,' they would report. 'We found our fox, but lost it again almost at once. But we saw Bella. Wonder how long the old girl will last. She must be nearly ninety. My father remembers when she used to hunt – went like smoke, too.'

Indeed, Bella herself was becoming increasingly occupied with the prospect of death. In the winter before the one we are talking of, she had been extremely ill. She emerged in April, rosy cheeked as ever, but slower in her movements and mind. She gave instructions that better attention must be paid to her father's and brother's graves, and in June took the unprecedented step of inviting her heir to visit her. She had always refused to see this young man up till now. He was an Englishman, a very distant cousin, named Banks. He lived in South Kensington and occupied himself in the Museum. He arrived in August and wrote long and very amusing letters to all his friends describing his visit, and later translated his experiences into a short story for the *Spectator*. Bella disliked him from the moment he arrived. He had horn-rimmed spectacles and a B.B.C. voice. He spent most of his time photographing the Fleacetown chimney-pieces and the moulding of the doors. One day he came to Bella bearing a pile of calf-bound volumes from the library.

'I say, did you know you had these?' he asked.

'I did,' Bella lied.

'All first editions. They must be extremely valuable.'

'You put them back where you found them.'

80

Later, when he wrote to thank her for his visit – enclosing prints of some of his photographs – he mentioned the books again. This set Bella thinking. Why should that young puppy go poking round the house putting a price on everything? She wasn't dead yet, Bella thought. And the more she thought of it, the more repugnant it became to think of Archie Banks carrying off her books to South Kensington and removing the chimney-pieces and, as he threatened, writing an essay about the house for the *Architectural Review*. She had often heard that the books were valuable. Well, there were plenty of books in the library and she did not see why Archie Banks should profit by them. So she wrote a letter to a Dublin bookseller. He came to look through the library, and after a while he offered her twelve hundred for the lot, or a thousand for the six books which had attracted Archie Banks' attention. Bella was not sure that she had the right to sell things out of the house; a wholesale clearance would be noticed. So she kept the sermons and military history which made up most of the collection, the Dublin bookseller went off with the first editions, which eventually fetched rather less than he had given, and Bella was left with winter coming on and a thousand pounds in hand.

It was then that it occurred to her to give a party. There were always several parties given round Ballingar at Christmas time, but of late years Bella had not been invited to any, partly because many of her neighbours had never spoken to her, partly because they did not think she would want to come, and partly because they would not have known what to do with her if she had. As a matter of fact she loved parties. She liked sitting down to supper in a noisy room, she liked dance music and gossip about which of the girls was pretty and who was in love with them, and she liked drink and having things brought to her by men in pink evening coats. And though she tried to console herself with contemptuous reflections about the ancestry of the hostesses, it annoyed her very much whenever she heard of a party being given in the neighbourhood to which she was not asked.

And so it came about that, sitting with the *Irish Times* under the picture of Abraham Lincoln and gazing across the bare trees of the park to the hills beyond, Bella took it into her head to give a party. She rose immediately and hobbled across the room to the bell-rope. Presently her butler came into the morning-room; he wore the green baize apron in which he cleaned the silver and in his hand he carried the plate brush to emphasize the irregularity of the summons.

'Was it yourself ringing?' he asked.

'It was, who else?'

'And I at the silver!'

'Riley,' said Bella with some solemnity, 'I propose to give a ball at Christmas.'

'Indeed!' said her butler. 'And for what would you want to be dancing at your age?' But as Bella adumbrated her idea, a sympathetic light began to glitter in Riley's eye.

'There's not been such a ball in the country for twenty-five years. It will cost a fortune.'

'It will cost a thousand pounds,' said Bella proudly.

The preparations were necessarily stupendous. Seven new servants were recruited in the village and set to work dusting and cleaning and polishing, clearing out furniture and pulling up carpets. Their industry served only to reveal fresh requirements; plaster mouldings, long rotten, crumbled under the feather brooms, worm-eaten mahogany floorboards came up with the tin tacks; bare brick was disclosed behind the cabinets in the great drawing-room. A second wave of the invasion brought painters, paper-hangers and plumbers, and in a moment of enthusiasm Bella had the cornice and the capitals of the pillars in the hall regilded; windows were reglazed, banisters fitted into gaping sockets, and the stair carpet shifted so that the worn strips were less noticeable.

In all these works Bella was indefatigable. She trotted from drawing-room to hall, down the long gallery, up the staircase, admonishing the hireling servants, lending a hand with the lighter objects of furniture, sliding, when the time came, up and down the mahogany floor of the drawing-room to work in the French chalk. She unloaded chests of silver in the attics, found long-forgotten services of china, went down with Riley into the cellars to count the few remaining and now flat and acid bottles of champagne. And in the evenings when the manual labourers had retired exhausted to their gross recreations, Bella sat up far into the night turning the pages of cookery books, comparing the estimates of rival caterers, inditing long and detailed letters to the agents for dance bands, and most important of all, drawing up her list of guests and addressing the high double piles of engraved cards that stood in her escritoire.

Distance counts for little in Ireland. People will readily drive three hours to pay an afternoon call, and for a dance of such importance no journey was too great. Bella had her list painfully compiled from works of reference, Riley's more up-to-date social knowledge and her own suddenly animated memory. Cheerfully, in a steady childish hand-writing, she transferred the names to the cards and addressed the envelopes. It was the work of several late sittings. Many of those whose names were transcribed were dead or bedridden; some whom she just remembered seeing as small children were reaching retiring age in remote corners of the globe; many of the houses she wrote down were blackened shells, burned during the troubles and never rebuilt; some had 'no one living in them, only farmers'. But at last, none too early, the last envelope was addressed. A final lap with the stamps and then later than usual she rose from the desk. Her limbs were stiff, her eyes dazzled, her tongue cloyed with the gum of the Free State post office; she felt a little dizzy, but she locked her desk that evening with the knowledge that the most serious part of the work of the party was over. There had been several notable and deliberate omissions from the list.

'What's all this I hear about Bella giving a party?' said Lady Gordon to Lady Mockstock. 'I haven't had a card.'

'Neither have I yet. I hope the old thing hasn't forgotten me. I certainly intend to go. I've never been inside the house. I believe she's got some lovely things.'

With true English reserve the lady whose husband had

leased Mock Hall never betrayed the knowledge that any party was in the air at all at Fleacetown.

As the last days approached Bella concentrated more upon her own appearance. She had bought few clothes of recent years, and the Dublin dressmaker with whom she used to deal had shut up shop. For a delirious instant she played with the idea of a journey to London and even Paris, and considerations of time alone obliged her to abandon it. In the end she discovered a shop to suit her, and purchased a very magnificent gown of crimson satin; to this she added long white gloves and satin shoes. There was no tiara, alas! among her jewels, but she unearthed large numbers of bright, nondescript Victorian rings, some chains and lockets, pearl brooches, turquoise earrings, and a collar of garnets. She ordered a coiffeur down from Dublin to dress her hair.

On the day of the ball she woke early, slightly feverish with nervous excitement, and wriggled in bed till she was called, restlessly rehearsing in her mind every detail of the arrangements. Before noon she had been to supervise the setting of hundreds of candles in the sconces round the ball-room and supper-room, and in the three great chandeliers of cut Waterford glass; she had seen the supper tables laid out with silver and glass and stood the massive wine coolers by the buffet; she had helped bank the staircase and hall with chrysanthemums. She had no luncheon that day, though Riley urged her with samples of the delicacies already arrived from the caterer's. She felt a little faint; lay down for a short time, but soon rallied to sew with her own hands the crested buttons on to the liveries of the hired servants.

The invitations were timed for eight o'clock. She wondered whether that were too early – she had heard tales of parties that began very late – but as the afternoon dragged on unendurably, and rich twilight enveloped the house, Bella became glad that she had set a short term on this exhausting wait.

At six she went up to dress. The hairdresser was there with a bag full of tongs and combs. He brushed and coiled her hair

84

and whiffed it up and generally manipulated it until it became orderly and formal and apparently far more copious. She put on all her jewellery and, standing before the cheval glass in her room, could not forbear a gasp of surprise. Then she limped downstairs.

The house looked magnificent in the candlelight. The band was there, the twelve hired footmen, Riley in knee breeches and black silk stockings.

It struck eight. Bella waited. Nobody came.

She sat down on a gilt chair at the head of the stairs, looked steadily before her with her blank, blue eyes. In the hall, in the cloakroom, in the supper-room, the hired footmen looked at one another with knowing winks. 'What does the old girl expect? No one'll have finished dinner before ten.'

The linkmen on the steps stamped and chafed their hands.

At half-past twelve Bella rose from her chair. Her face gave no indication of what she was thinking.

'Riley, I think I will have some supper. I am not feeling altogether well.'

She hobbled slowly to the dining-room.

'Give me a stuffed quail and a glass of wine. Tell the band to start playing.'

The *Blue Danube* waltz flooded the house. Bella smiled approval and swayed her head a little to the rhythm.

'Riley, I am really quite hungry. I've had nothing all day. Give me another quail and some more champagne.'

Alone among the candles and the hired footmen, Riley served his mistress with an immense supper. She enjoyed every mouthful.

Presently she rose. 'I am afraid there must be some mistake. No one seems to be coming to the ball. It is very disappointing after all our trouble. You may tell the band to go home.'

But just as she was leaving the dining-room there was a stir in the hall. Guests were arriving. With wild resolution Bella swung herself up the stairs. She must get to the top before the guests were announced. One hand on the banister, one on her stick, pounding heart, two steps at a time. At last she reached the landing and turned to face the company. There was a mist before her eyes and a singing in her ears. She breathed with effort, but dimly she saw four figures advancing and saw Riley meet them and heard him announce

'Lord and Lady Mockstock, Sir Samuel and Lady Gordon.'

Suddenly the daze in which she had been moving cleared. Here on the stairs were the two women she had not invited – Lady Mockstock the draper's daughter, Lady Gordon the American.

She drew herself up and fixed them with her blank, blue eyes.

'I had not expected this honour,' she said. 'Please forgive me if I am unable to entertain you.'

The Mockstocks and the Gordons stood aghast; saw the mad blue eyes of their hostess, her crimson dress; the ballroom beyond, looking immense in its emptiness; heard the dance music echoing through the empty house. The air was charged with the scent of chrysanthemums. And then the drama and unreality of the scene were dispelled. Miss Fleace suddenly sat down, and holding out her hands to her butler, said, 'I don't quite know what's happening.'

He and two of the hired footmen carried the old lady to a sofa. She spoke only once more. Her mind was still on the same subject. 'They came uninvited, those two . . . and nobody else.'

A day later she died.

Mr Banks arrived for the funeral and spent a week sorting out her effects. Among them he found in her escritoire, stamped, addressed, but unposted, the invitations to the ball.

WINNER TAKES ALL

1

WHEN Mrs Kent-Cumberland's eldest son was born (in an expensive London nursing home) there was a bonfire on Tomb Beacon; it consumed three barrels of tar, an immense catafalque of timber, and, as things turned out – for the flames spread briskly in the dry gorse and loyal tenantry were too tipsy to extinguish them – the entire vegetation of Tomb Hill.

As soon as mother and child could be moved, they travelled in state to the country, where flags were hung out in the village street and a trellis arch of evergreen boughs obscured the handsome Palladian entrance gates of their home. There were farmers' dinners both at Tomb and on the Kent-Cumberlands' Norfolk estate, and funds for a silver-plated tray were ungrudgingly subscribed.

The christening was celebrated by a garden-party. A princess stood godmother by proxy, and the boy was called Gervase Peregrine Mountjoy St Eustace – all of them names illustrious in the family's history.

Throughout the service and the subsequent presentations he maintained an attitude of phlegmatic dignity which confirmed everyone in the high estimate they had already formed of his capabilities.

After the garden-party there were fireworks and after the fireworks a very hard week for the gardeners, cleaning up the mess. The life of the Kent-Cumberlands then resumed its normal tranquillity until nearly two years later, when, much to her annoyance, Mrs Kent-Cumberland discovered that she was to have another baby.

The second child was born in August in a shoddy modern house on the East Coast which had been taken for the summer so that Gervase might have the benefit of sea air. Mrs Kent-Cumberland was attended by the local doctor, who antagonized her by his middle-class accent, and proved, when it came to the point, a great deal more deft than the London specialist.

Throughout the peevish months of waiting Mrs Kent-Cumberland had fortified herself with the hope that she would have a daughter. It would be a softening influence for Gervase, who was growing up somewhat unresponsive, to have a pretty, gentle, sympathetic sister two years younger than himself. She would come out just when he was going up to Oxford and would save him from either of the dreadful extremes of evil company which threatened that stage of development – the bookworm and the hooligan. She would bring down delightful girls for Eights Week and Commem. Mrs Kent-Cumberland had it all planned out. When she was delivered of another son she named him Thomas, and fretted through her convalescence with her mind on the coming hunting season.

2

The two brothers developed into sturdy, unremarkable little boys; there was little to choose between them except their two years' difference in age. They were both sandy-haired, courageous, and well-mannered on occasions. Neither was sensitive, artistic, highly strung, or conscious of being mis-understood. Both accepted the fact of Gervase's importance just as they accepted his superiority of knowledge and physique. Mrs Kent-Cumberland was a fair-minded woman, and in the event of the two being involved in mischief, it was Gervase, as the elder, who was the more severely punished. Tom found that his obscurity was on the whole advantageous, for it excused him from the countless minor performances of ceremony which fell on Gervase.

3

At the age of seven Tom was consumed with desire for a model motor-car, an expensive toy of a size to sit in and pedal about the garden. He prayed for it steadfastly every evening and most mornings for several weeks. Christmas was approaching.

Gervase had a smart pony and was often taken hunting. Tom was alone most of the day and the motor-car occupied a great part of his thoughts. Finally he confided his ambition to an uncle. This uncle was not addicted to expensive present giving, least of all to children (for he was a man of limited means and self-indulgent habits) but something in his nephew's intensity of feeling impressed him.

'Poor little beggar,' he reflected, 'his brother seems to get all the fun,' and when he returned to London he ordered the motor-car for Tom. It arrived some days before Christmas and was put away upstairs with other presents. On Christmas Eve Mrs Kent-Cumberland came to inspect them. 'How very kind,' she said, looking at each label in turn, 'how very kind.'

The motor-car was by far the largest exhibit. It was pillar-box red, complete with electric lights, a hooter and a spare wheel.

'Really,' she said. 'How *very* kind of Ted.'

Then she looked at the label more closely. 'But how foolish of him. He's put *Tom's* name on it.'

'There was this book for Master Gervase,' said the nurse, producing a volume labelled 'Gervase with best wishes from Uncle Ted.'

'Of course the parcels have been confused at the shop,' said Mrs Kent-Cumberland. 'This can't have been meant for Tom. Why, it must have cost six or seven pounds.'

She changed the labels and went downstairs to supervise the decoration of the Christmas tree, glad to have rectified an obvious error of justice.

Next morning the presents were revealed. 'Oh, Ger. You

are lucky,' said Tom, inspecting the motor-car. 'May I ride in it?'

'Yes, only be careful. Nanny says it was awfully expensive.'

Tom rode it twice round the room. 'May I take it in the garden sometimes?'

'Yes. You can have it when I'm hunting.'

Later in the week they wrote to thank their uncle for his presents.

Gervase wrote:

Dear Uncle Ted,

Thank you for the lovely present. It's lovely. The pony is very well. I am going to hunt again before I go back to school.

Love from Gervase.

Dear Uncle Ted [*wrote Tom*],

Thank you ever so much for the lovely present. It is just what I wanted. Again thanking you very much.

With love from Tom.

'So that's all the thanks I get. Ungrateful little beggar,' said Uncle Ted, resolving to be more economical in future.

But when Gervase went back to school he said, 'You can have the motor-car, Tom, to keep.'

'What, for *my own*?'

'Yes. It's a kid's toy, anyway.'

And by this act of generosity he increased Tom's respect and love for him a hundredfold.

4

The war came and profoundly changed the lives of the two boys. It engendered none of the neuroses threatened by pacifists. Air raids remained among Tom's happiest memories, when the school used to be awakened in the middle of the night and hustled downstairs to the basement where, wrapped in eiderdowns, they were regaled with cocoa and cake by the matron, who looked supremely ridiculous in a flannel nightgown. Once a Zeppelin was hit in sight of the school; they all crowded to the dormitory windows to see it sinking slowly in a globe of pink flame. A very young master whose health rendered him unfit for military service danced on the headmaster's tennis court crying, 'There go the baby killers.' Tom made a collection of 'War Relics', including a captured German helmet, shell-splinters, *The Times* for August 4th, 1914, buttons, cartridge cases, and cap badges, that was voted the best in the school.

The event which radically changed the relationship of the brothers was the death, early in 1915, of their father. Neither knew him well nor particularly liked him. He had represented the division in the House of Commons and spent much of his time in London while the children were at Tomb. They only saw him on three occasions after he joined the army. Gervase and Tom were called out of the classroom and told of his death by the headmaster's wife. They cried, since it was expected of them, and for some days were treated with marked deference by the masters and the rest of the school.

It was in the subsequent holidays that the importance of the change became apparent. Mrs Kent-Cumberland had suddenly become more emotional and more parsimonious. She was liable to unprecedented outbursts of tears, when she would crush Gervase to her and say, 'My poor fatherless boy.' At other times she spoke gloomily of death duties.

5

For some years in fact 'Death Duties' became the refrain of the household.

When Mrs Kent-Cumberland let the house in London and closed down a wing at Tomb, when she reduced the servants to four and the gardeners to two, when she 'let the flower gardens go', when she stopped asking her brother Ted to stay, when she emptied the stables, and became almost fanatical in her reluctance to use the car, when the bath water was cold and there were no new tennis-balls, when the chimneys were dirty and the lawns covered with sheep, when Gervase's cast-off clothes ceased to fit Tom, when she refused him the 'extra' expense at school of carpentry lessons and mid-morning milk – 'Death Duties' were responsible.

'It is all for Gervase,' Mrs Kent-Cumberland used to explain. 'When he inherits, he must take over free of debt, as his father did.'

6

Gervase went to Eton in the year of his father's death. Tom would normally have followed him two years later, but in her new mood of economy Mrs Kent-Cumberland cancelled his entry and began canvassing her friends' opinions about the less famous, cheaper public schools. 'The education is just as good,' she said, 'and far more suitable for a boy who has his own way to make in the world.'

Tom was happy enough at the school to which he was sent. It was very bleak and very new, salubrious, progressive, prosperous in the boom that secondary education enjoyed in the years immediately following the war, and, when all was said and done, 'thoroughly suitable for a boy with his own way to make in the world'. He had several friends whom he was not allowed to invite to his home during the holidays. He got his House colours for swimming and fives, played once or twice in the second eleven for cricket, and was a platoon commander in the O.T.C.; he was in the sixth form and passed the Higher Certificate in his last year, became a prefect and enjoyed the confidence of his house master, who spoke of him as 'a very decent stamp of boy'. He left school at the age of eighteen without the smallest desire to re-visit it or see any of its members again.

Gervase was then at Christ Church. Tom went up to visit him, but the magnificent Etonians who romped in and out of his brother's rooms scared and depressed him. Gervase was in the Bullingdon, spending money freely and enjoying himself. He gave a dinner-party in his rooms, but Tom sat in silence, drinking heavily to hide his embarrassment, and was later sombrely sick in a corner of Peckwater quad. He returned to Tomb next day in the lowest spirits.

'It is not as though Tom were a scholarly boy,' said Mrs Kent-Cumberland to her friends. 'I am glad he is not, of course. But if he had been, it might have been right to make the sacrifice and send him to the University. As it is, the sooner he Gets Started the better.'

7

Getting Tom started, however, proved a matter of some difficulty. During the Death Duty Period, Mrs Kent-Cumberland had cut herself off from many of her friends. Now she cast round vainly to find someone who would 'put Tom into something'. Chartered Accountancy, Chinese Customs, estate agencies, 'the City', were suggested and abandoned. 'The trouble is that he has no particular abilities,' she explained. 'He is the sort of boy who would be useful in anything – an all-round man – but, of course, he has no capital.'

August, September, October passed; Gervase was back at Oxford, in fashionable lodgings in the High Street, but Tom remained at home without employment. Day by day he and his mother sat down together to luncheon and dinner, and his constant presence was a severe strain on Mrs Kent-Cumberland's equability. She herself was always busy and, as she bustled about her duties, it shocked and distracted her to encounter the large figure of her younger son sprawling on the morning-room sofa or leaning against the stone parapet of the terrace and gazing out apathetically across the familiar landscape.

'Why can't you find something to *do*?' she would complain. 'There are *always* things to do about a house. Heaven knows I never have a moment.' And when, one afternoon, he was asked out by some neighbours and returned too late to dress for dinner, she said, 'Really, Tom, I should have thought that *you* had time for that.'

'It is a very serious thing,' she remarked on another occasion, 'for a young man of your age to get out of the habit of work. It saps his whole morale.'

Accordingly she fell back upon the ancient country house expedient of Cataloguing the Library. This consisted of an extensive and dusty collection of books amassed by succeeding generations of a family at no time notable for their patronage of literature; it had been catalogued before, in the middle of the nineteenth century, in the spidery, spinsterish hand of a relative in reduced circumstances; since then the additions and disturbances had been negligible, but Mrs Kent-Cumberland purchased a fumed oak cabinet and several boxes of cards and instructed Tom how she wanted the shelves re-numbered and the books twice entered under Subject and Author.

It was a system that should keep a boy employed for some time, and it was with vexation, therefore, that, a few days after the task was commenced, she paid a surprise visit to the scene of his labour and found Tom sitting, almost lying, in an armchair, with his feet on a rung of the library steps, reading.

'I am glad you have found something interesting,' she said in a voice that conveyed very little gladness.

'Well, to tell you the truth, I think I have,' said Tom, and showed her the book.

It was the manuscript journal kept by a Colonel Jasper Cumberland during the Peninsular War. It had no startling literary merit, nor did its criticisms of the general staff throw any new light upon the strategy of the campaign, but it was a lively, direct, day-to-day narrative, redolent of its period; there was a sprinkling of droll anecdotes, some vigorous descriptions of fox-hunting behind the lines of Torres Vedras, of the Duke of Wellington dining in Mess, of a threatened mutiny that had not yet found its way into history, of the assault on Badajoz; there were some bawdy references to Portuguese women and some pious reflections about patriotism.

'I was wondering if it might be worth publishing,' said Tom.

'I should hardly think so,' replied his mother. 'But I will certainly show it to Gervase when he comes home.'

For the moment the discovery gave a new interest to Tom's life. He read up the history of the period and of his own family. Jasper Cumberland he established as a younger son of the period, who had later emigrated to Canada. There were letters from him among the archives, including the announcement of his marriage to a Papist, which had clearly severed the link with his elder brother. In a case of uncatalogued miniatures in the long drawing-room, he found the portrait of a handsome whiskered soldier, which by a study of contemporary uniforms he was able to identify as the diarist.

Presently, in his round, immature handwriting, Tom began working up his notes into an essay. His mother watched his efforts with unqualified approval. She was glad to see him busy, and glad to see him taking an interest in his family's history. She had begun to fear that by sending him to a school without 'tradition' she might have made a socialist of the boy. When, shortly before the Christmas vacation, work was found for Tom, she took charge of his notes. 'I am sure Gervase will be extremely interested,' she said. 'He may even think it worth showing to a publisher.'

8

The work that had been found for Tom was not immediately lucrative, but, as his mother said, it was a beginning. It was to go to Wolverhampton and learn the motor business from the bottom. The first two years were to be spent at the works, from where, if he showed talent, he might graduate to the London showrooms. His wages, at first, were thirty-five shillings a week. This was augmented by the allowance of another pound. Lodgings were found for him over a fruit shop in the outskirts of the town, and Gervase gave him his old two-seater car, in which he could travel to and from his work, and for occasional week-ends home.

It was during one of these visits that Gervase told him the good news that a London publisher had read the diary and seen possibilities in it. Six months later it appeared under the title *The Journal of an English Cavalry Officer during the Peninsular War. Edited with notes and a biographical introduction by Gervase Kent-Cumberland.* The miniature portrait was prettily reproduced as a frontispiece, there was a collotype copy of a page of the original manuscript, a contemporary print of Tomb Park, and a map of the campaign. It sold nearly two thousand copies at twelve and sixpence and received two or three respectful reviews in the Saturday and Sunday papers.

The appearance of the *Journal* coincided within a few days with Gervase's twenty-first birthday. The celebrations were extravagant and prolonged, culminating in a ball at which Tom's attendance was required.

He drove over, after the works had shut down, and arrived, just in time for dinner, to find a house-party of thirty and a house entirely transformed.

His own room had been taken for a guest ('as you will only be here for one night,' his mother explained). He was sent down to the Cumberland Arms, where he dressed by candlelight in a breathless little bedroom over the bar, and arrived late and slightly dishevelled at dinner, where he sat between two lovely girls who neither knew who he was nor troubled to inquire. The dancing afterwards was in a marquee built on the terrace, which a London catering firm had converted into a fair replica of a Pont Street drawing-room. Tom danced once or twice with the daughters of neighbouring families whom he had known since childhood. They asked him about Wolverhampton and the works. He had to get up early next morning; at midnight he slipped away to his bed at the inn. The evening had bored him; because he was in love.

9

It had occurred to him to ask his mother whether he might bring his fiancée to the ball, but on reflexion, enchanted as he was, he had realized that it would not do. The girl was named Gladys Cruttwell. She was two years older than himself; she had fluffy yellow hair which she washed at home once a week and dried before the gas fire; on the day after the shampoo it was very light and silky; towards the end of the week, darker and slightly greasy. She was a virtuous, affectionate, self-reliant, even-tempered, unintelligent, high-spirited girl, but Tom could not disguise from himself the fact that she would not go down well at Tomb.

She worked for the firm on the clerical side. Tom had noticed her on his second day, as she tripped across the yard, exactly on time, bareheaded (the day after a shampoo) in a woollen coat and skirt which she had knitted herself. He had got into conversation with her in the canteen, by making way for her at the counter with a chivalry that was not much practised at the works. His possession of a car gave him a clear advantage over the other young men about the place.

They discovered that they lived within a few streets of one another, and it presently became Tom's practice to call for her in the mornings and take her home in the evenings. He would sit in the two-seater outside her gate, sound the horn, and she would come running down the path to meet him. As summer approached they went for drives in the evening among leafy Warwickshire lanes. In June they were engaged. Tom was exhilarated, sometimes almost dizzy at the experience, but he hesitated to tell his mother. 'After all,' he reflected, 'it is not as though I were Gervase,' but in his own heart he knew that there would be trouble.

Gladys came of a class accustomed to long engagements; marriage seemed a remote prospect; an engagement to her signified the formal recognition that she and Tom spent their spare time in one another's company. Her mother, with whom she lived, accepted him on these terms. In years to come, when Tom had got his place in the London showrooms, it would be time enough to think about marrying. But Tom was born to a less patient tradition. He began to speak about a wedding in the autumn.

'It would be lovely,' said Gladys in the tones she would have employed about winning the Irish sweepstake.

He had spoken very little about his family. She understood, vaguely, that they lived in a big house, but it was a part of life that never had been real to her. She knew that there were duchesses and marchionesses in something called 'Society'; they were encountered in the papers and the films. She knew there were directors with large salaries; but the fact that there were people like Gervase or Mrs Kent-Cumberland, and that they would think of themselves as radically different from herself, had not entered her experience. When, eventually, they were brought together Mrs Kent-Cumberland was extremely gracious and Gladys thought her a very nice old lady. But Tom knew that the meeting was proving disastrous.

'Of course,' said Mrs Kent-Cumberland, 'the whole thing is quite impossible. Miss Whatever-her-name-was seemed a thoroughly nice girl, but you are not in a position to think of marriage. Besides,' she added with absolute finality, 'you must not forget that if anything were to happen to Gervase you would be his heir.'

So Tom was removed from the motor business and an opening found for him on a sheep farm in South Australia.

10

It would not be fair to say that in the ensuing two years Mrs Kent-Cumberland forgot her younger son. She wrote to him every month and sent him bandana handkerchiefs for Christmas. In the first lonely days he wrote to her frequently, but when, as he grew accustomed to the new life, his letters became less frequent she did not seriously miss them. When they did arrive they were lengthy; she put them aside from her correspondence to read at leisure and, more than once, mislaid them, unopened. But whenever her acquaintances asked after Tom she loyally answered, 'Doing splendidly. And enjoying himself *very* much.'

She had many other things to occupy and, in some cases, distress her. Gervase was now in authority at Tomb, and the careful régime of his minority wholly reversed. There were six expensive hunters in the stable. The lawns were mown, bedrooms thrown open, additional bathrooms installed; there was even talk of constructing a swimming pool. There was constant Saturday to Monday entertaining. There was the sale, at a poor price, of two Romneys and a Hoppner.

Mrs Kent-Cumberland watched all this with mingled pride and anxiety. In particular she scrutinized the succession of girls who came to stay, in the irreconcilable, ever-present fears that Gervase would or would not marry. Either conclusion seemed perilous; a wife for Gervase must be well-born, well conducted, rich, of stainless reputation, and affectionately disposed to Mrs Kent-Cumberland; such a mate seemed difficult to find. The estate was clear of the mortgages necessitated by death duties, but dividends were uncertain, and though, as she frequently pointed out, she 'never interfered', simple arithmetic and her own close experience of domestic management convinced her that Gervase would not long be able to support the scale of living which he had introduced.

With so much on her mind, it was inevitable that Mrs Kent-Cumberland should think a great deal about Tomb and very little about South Australia, and should be rudely shocked to read in one of Tom's letters that he was proposing to return to England on a visit, with a fiancée and a future father-in-law; that in fact he had already started, was now on the sea and due to arrive in London in a fortnight. Had she read his earlier letters with attention she might have found hints of such an attachment, but she had not done so, and the announcement came to her as a wholly unpleasant surprise.

'Your brother is coming back.'

'Oh good! When?'

'He is bringing a farmer's daughter to whom he is engaged – and the farmer. They want to come here.'

'I say, that's rather a bore. Let's tell them we're having the boilers cleaned.'

'You don't seem to realize that this is a serious matter, Gervase.'

'Oh well, you fix things up. I dare say it would be all right if they came next month. We've got to have the Anchorages some time. We might get both over together.'

In the end it was decided that Gervase should meet the immigrants in London, vet them and report to his mother whether or no they were suitable fellow-guests for the Anchorages. A week later, on his return to Tomb, his mother greeted him anxiously.

'Well? You never wrote?'

'Wrote? Why should I? I never do. I say, I haven't forgotten a birthday or anything, have I?'

'Don't be absurd, Gervase. I mean, about your brother Tom's unfortunate entanglement. Did you see the girl?'

'Oh, *that*. Yes, I went and had dinner with them. Tom's done himself quite well. Fair, rather fat, saucer-eyes, good-tempered, I should say, by her looks.'

'Does she – does she speak with an Australian accent?'

'Didn't notice it.'

'And the father?'

'Pompous old boy.'

'Would he be all right with the Anchorages?'

'I should think he'd go down like a dinner. But they can't come. They are staying with the Chasms.'

'Indeed! What an extraordinary thing. But, of course, Archie Chasm was Governor-General once. Still, it shows they must be fairly respectable. Where are they staying?'

'Claridge's.'

'Then they must be quite rich, too. How very interesting. I will write this evening.'

11

Three weeks later they arrived. Mr MacDougal, the father, was a tall, lean man, with pince-nez and an interest in statistics. He was a territorial magnate to whom the Tomb estates appeared a cosy small-holding. He did not emphasize this in any boastful fashion, but in his statistical zeal gave Mrs Kent-Cumberland some staggering figures. 'Is Bessie your only child?' asked Mrs Kent-Cumberland.

'My only child and heir,' he replied, coming down to brass tacks at once. 'I dare say you have been wondering what sort of settlement I shall be able to make on her. Now that, I regret to say, is a question I cannot answer accurately. We have good years, Mrs Kent-Cumberland, and we have bad years. It all depends.'

'But I dare say that even in bad years the income is quite considerable?'

'In a bad year,' said Mr MacDougal, 'in a *very* bad year such as the present, the net profits, after all deductions have been made for running expenses, insurance, taxation, and deterioration, amount to something between' – Mrs Kent-Cumberland listened breathlessly – 'fifty and fifty-two thousand pounds. I know that is a very vague statement, but it is impossible to be more accurate until the last returns are in.'

Bessie was bland and creamy. She admired everything. 'It's so *antique*,' she would remark with relish, whether the object of her attention was the Norman Church of Tomb, the Victorian panelling in the billiard-room, or the central-heating system which Gervase had recently installed. Mrs Kent-Cumberland took a great liking to the girl.

'Thoroughly Teachable,' she pronounced. 'But I wonder whether she is *really* suited to Tom . . . I *wonder* . . .'

The MacDougals stayed for four days and, when they left, Mrs Kent-Cumberland pressed them to return for a longer visit. Bessie had been enchanted with everything she saw.

'I wish we could live here,' she had said to Tom on her first evening, 'in this dear, quaint old house.'

'Yes, darling, so do I. Of course it all belongs to Gervase, but I always look on it as my home.'

'Just as we Australians look on England.'

'Exactly.'

She had insisted on seeing everything; the old gabled manor, once the home of the family, relegated now to the function of dower house since the present mansion was built in the eighteenth century – the house of mean proportions and inconvenient offices where Mrs Kent-Cumberland, in her moments of depression, pictured her own declining years; the mill and the quarries; the farm, which to the MacDougals seemed minute and formal as a Noah's Ark. On these expeditions it was Gervase who acted as guide. 'He, of course, knows so much more about it than Tom,' Mrs Kent-Cumberland explained.

Tom, in fact, found himself very rarely alone with his fiancée. Once, when they were all together after dinner, the question of his marriage was mentioned. He asked Bessie whether, now that she had seen Tomb, she would sooner be married there, at the village church, than in London.

'Oh, there is no need to decide anything hastily,' Mrs Kent-Cumberland had said. 'Let Bessie look about a little first.'

*

When the MacDougals left, it was to go to Scotland to see the castle of their ancestors. Mr MacDougal had traced relationship with various branches of his family, had corresponded with them intermittently, and now wished to make their acquaintance.

Bessie wrote to them all at Tomb; she wrote daily to Tom, but in her thoughts, as she lay sleepless in the appalling bed provided for her by her distant kinsmen, she was conscious for the first time of a light feeling of disappointment and uncertainty. In Australia Tom had seemed so different from everyone else, so gentle and dignified and cultured. Here in England he seemed to recede into obscurity. Everyone in England seemed to be like Tom.

And then there was the house. It was exactly the kind of house which she had always imagined English people to live in, with the dear little park – less than a thousand acres – and the soft grass and the old stone. Tom had fitted into the house. He had fitted too well; had disappeared entirely in it and become part of the background. The central place belonged to Gervase – so like Tom but more handsome; with all Tom's charm but with more personality. Beset with these thoughts, she rolled on the hard and irregular bed until dawn began to show through the lancet window of the Victorian-baronial turret. She loved that turret for all its discomfort. It was so antique.

12

Mrs Kent-Cumberland was an active woman. It was less than ten days after the MacDougals' visit that she returned triumphantly from a day in London. After dinner, when she sat alone with Tom in the small drawing-room, she said:

'You'll be very much surprised to hear who I saw today. *Gladys.*'

'Gladys?'

'Gladys Cruttwell.'

'Good heavens. Where on earth did you meet her?'

'It was quite by chance,' said his mother vaguely. 'She is working there now.'

'How was she?'

'Very pretty. Prettier, if anything.'

There was a pause. Mrs Kent-Cumberland stitched away at a gros-point chair seat. 'You know, dear boy, that I *never interfere*, but I have often wondered whether you treated Gladys very kindly. I know I was partly to blame, myself. But you were both very young and your prospects so uncertain. I thought a year or two of separation would be a good test of whether you really loved one another.'

'Oh, I am sure she has forgotten about me long ago.'

'Indeed, she has not, Tom. I thought she seemed a very unhappy girl.'

'But how *can* you know, Mother, just seeing her casually like that?'

'We had luncheon together,' said Mrs Kent-Cumberland. 'In an A.B.C. shop.'

Another pause.

'But, look here, I've forgotten all about her. I only care about Bessie now.'

'You know, dearest boy, I never interfere. I think Bessie is a delightful girl. But are you free? Are you free in your own conscience? You know, and I do not know, on what terms you parted from Gladys.'

And there returned, after a long absence, the scene which for the first few months of his Australian venture had been constantly in Tom's memory, of a tearful parting and many intemperate promises. He said nothing. 'I did not tell Gladys of your engagement. I thought you had the right to do that – as best you can, in your own way. But I did tell her you were back in England and that you wished to see her. She is coming here tomorrow for a night or two. She looked in need of a holiday, poor child.'

When Tom went to meet Gladys at the station they stood

for some minutes on the platform not certain of the other's identity. Then their tentative signs of recognition corresponded. Gladys had been engaged twice in the past two years, and was now walking out with a motor salesman. It had been a great surprise when Mrs Kent-Cumberland sought her out and explained that Tom had returned to England. She had not forgotten him, for she was a loyal and good-hearted girl, but she was embarrassed and touched to learn that his devotion was unshaken.

They were married two weeks later and Mrs Kent-Cumberland undertook the delicate mission of 'explaining everything' to the MacDougals.

They went to Australia, where Mr MacDougal very magnanimously gave them a post managing one of his more remote estates. He was satisfied with Tom's work. Gladys has a large sunny bungalow and a landscape of grazing-land and wire fences. She does not see very much company nor does she particularly like what she does see. The neighbouring ranchers find her very English and aloof.

Bessie and Gervase were married after six weeks' engagement. They live at Tomb. Bessie has two children and Gervase has six race-horses. Mrs Kent-Cumberland lives in the house with them. She and Bessie rarely disagree, and, when they do, it is Mrs Kent-Cumberland who gets her way.

The dower house is let on a long lease to a sporting manufacturer. Gervase has taken over the Hounds and spends money profusely; everyone in the neighbourhood is content.

WORK SUSPENDED

Part One

A DEATH

1

AT the time of my father's death I was in Morocco, at a small French hotel outside the fortifications of Fez. I had been there for six weeks, doing little else but write, and my book, *Murder at Mountrichard Castle*, was within twenty thousand words of its end. In three weeks I should pack it up for the typist; perhaps sooner, for I had nearly passed that heavy middle period where less conscientious writers introduce their second corpse. I was thirty-four years of age at the time, and a serious writer. I had always been a one-corpse man. I took pains with my work and I found it excellent. Each of my seven books sold better than its predecessor. Moreover, the sale was in their first three months, at seven and sixpence. I did not have to relabel the library edition for the bookstalls. People bought my books and kept them – not in the spare bedrooms but in the library, all seven of them together on a shelf. In six weeks' time, when my manuscript had been typed, revised and delivered, I should receive a cheque for something over nine hundred pounds. Had I wished it, I could have earned considerably more. I never tried to sell my stories as serials; the delicate fibres of a story suffer when it is chopped up into weekly or monthly parts and never completely heal. Often, when I have been reading the work of a competitor, I have said, 'She was writing with an eye on the magazines. She had to close this episode prematurely; she had to introduce that extraneous bit of melodrama, so as to make each instalment a readable unit. Well,' I would reflect, 'she has a husband to support and two sons at school. She must not expect to do two jobs well, to be a good mother and a good novelist.' I chose to live modestly on the royalties of my books.

I have never found economy the least irksome; on the contrary, I take pleasure in it. My friends, I know, considered me parsimonious; it was a joke among them, which I found quite inoffensive. My ambition was to eradicate money as much as I could from my life. I acquired as few possessions as possible. I preferred to pay interest to my bank rather than be bothered by tradesmen's bills. I decided what I wanted to do and then devised ways of doing it cheaply and tidily; money wasted meant more money to be earned. I disliked profusion.

I chose my career deliberately at the age of twenty-one. I had a naturally ingenious and constructive mind and the taste of writing. I was youthfully zealous of good fame. There seemed few ways of which a writer need not be ashamed by which he could make a decent living. To produce something, saleable in large quantities to the public, which had absolutely nothing of myself in it; to sell something for which the kind of people I liked and respected would have a use; that was what I sought, and detective stories fulfilled the purpose. They were an art which admitted of classical canons of technique and taste. It was immune, too, from the obnoxious comment to which lighter work is exposed: 'How you must revel in writing your delicious books, Mr So-and-so.' My friend, Roger Simmonds, who was with me at the University and set up as a professional humorist at the same time as I wrote *Vengeance at the Vatican*, was constantly plagued by that kind of remark. Instead, women said to me, 'How difficult it must be to think of all those complicated clues, Mr Plant.' I agreed. 'It *is*, intolerably difficult.' 'And do you do your writing here in London?' 'No, I find I have to go away to work.' 'Away from telephones and parties and things?' 'Exactly.'

I had tried a dozen or more retreats in England and abroad – country inns, furnished cottages, seaside hotels out of the season – Fez was by far the best of them. It is a splendid, compact city, and in early March, with flowers springing everywhere in the surrounding hills and in the untidy patios of the Arab houses, one of the most beautiful in the world. I liked the little hotel. It was cheap and rather chilly – an indispensable austerity. The food was digestible with, again, that element of sparseness which I find agreeable. I had an intermediate place between the semi-Egyptian splendours of the tourists' palace on the hill, and the bustling commercial hotels of the new town, half an hour's walk away. The clientele was exclusively French; the wives of civil servants and elderly couples of small means wintering in the sun. In the evening Spahi officers came to the bar to play bagatelle. I used to work on the verandah of my room, overlooking a ravine where Senegalese infantrymen were constantly washing their linen. My recreations were few and simple. Once a week after dinner I took the bus to the Moulay Abdullah; once a week I dined at the Consulate. The consul allowed me to come to him for a bath. I used to walk up, under the walls, swinging my sponge-bag through the dusk. He, his wife and their governess were the only English people I met; the only people, indeed, with whom I did more than exchange bare civilities. Sometimes I visited the native cinema where old, silent films were shown in a babel of catcalls. On other evenings I took a dose of Dial and was asleep by half-past nine. In these circumstances the book progressed well. I have since, on occasions, looked back at them with envy.

As an odd survival of the age of capitulations there was at that time a British Post Office at the Consulate, used mainly, the French believed, for treasonable purposes by disaffected Arabs. When there was anything for me the postman used to come down the hill on his bicycle to my hotel. He had a badge in his cap and on his arm a brassard with the royal escutcheon; he invariably honoured me with a stiff, military salute which increased my importance in the hotel at the expense of my reputation as an innocent and unofficial man of letters. It was this postman who brought the news of my father's death in a letter from my Uncle Andrew, his brother.

My father, it appeared, had been knocked down by a motor car more than a week ago and had died without regaining consciousness. I was his only child and, with the exception of my uncle, his only near relative. 'All arrangements' had been made. The funeral was taking place that day. 'In spite of your father's opinions, in the absence of any formal instructions to the contrary [my Uncle Andrew wrote] your Aunt and I thought it best to have a religious ceremony of an unostentatious kind.'

'He might have telegraphed,' I thought; and then, later, 'Why should he have?' There was no question of my having been able to see my father before he died; participation in a 'religious ceremony of an unostentatious kind' was neither in my line nor my father's; nor – to do him justice – in my Uncle Andrew's. It would satisfy the Jellabies.

With regard to the Jellabies my father always avowed a ruthlessness which he was far from practising; he would in fact put himself to considerable inconvenience to accommodate them, but in principle he abhorred any suggestion of discretion or solicitude. It was his belief that no one but himself dealt properly with servants. Two contrasted attitudes drove him to equal fury; what he called the *'pas-devant* tomfoolery' of his childhood – the precept that scandal and the mention of exact sums of money should be hushed in their presence – and the more recent idea that their quarters should be prettily decorated and themselves given opportunity for cultural development. 'Jellaby has been with me twenty years,' he would say, 'and is fully cognisant of the facts of life. He and Mrs Jellaby know my income to the nearest shilling, and they know the full history of everyone who comes to this house. I pay them abominably and they supplement their wages by cooking the books. Servants prefer it that way. It preserves their independence and self-respect. The Jellabies eat continually, sleep with the windows shut, go to church every Sunday morning and to chapel in the evening, and entertain surreptitiously at my expense whenever I am out of the house. Jellaby's a teetotaller; Mrs Jellaby takes the port.' He rang the bell whenever he wanted anything fetched and sat as long as he wanted over his wine. 'Poor old Armstrong,' he used to say of a fellow Academician, 'lives like a Hottentot. He keeps a lot of twittering women like waitresses in a railway station buffet. After the first glass of port they open the dining-room door and stick their heads in. After the second glass they do it again. Then instead of throwing something at them, Armstrong says, "I think they want to clear," and we have to move out.'

But he had a warm affection for the Jellabies, and I believe it was largely on Mrs Jellaby's account that he allowed himself to be put up for the Academy. They, in their turn, served him faithfully. It would have been a cruel betrayal to deny them a funeral service, and I am sure my father had them in mind when he omitted any provision against it in his will. He was an exact man who would not have forgotten a point of that kind. On the other hand, he was a dogmatic atheist of the old-fashioned cast and would not have set anything down which might be construed as apostasy. He had left it to my Uncle Andrew's tact. No doubt, too, it was part of my uncle's tact to save me the embarrassment of being present.

2

I sat on my verandah for some time, smoking and considering the situation in its various aspects. There seemed no good reason for a change of plan. My Uncle Andrew would see to everything. The Jellabies would be provided for. Apart from them my father had no obligations. His affairs were always simple and in good order. The counterfoils of his cheques and his own excellent memory were his only account books; he had never owned any investments except the freehold of the house in St John's Wood, which he had bought with the small capital sum left him by his mother. He lived up to his income and saved nothing. In him the parsimony which I had inherited took the form of a Gallic repugnance to paying direct taxes or, as he preferred it, to subscribing to 'the support of the politicians'. He had, moreover, the conviction that anything he put by would be filched by the Radicals. Lloyd George's ascent to power was the last contemporary event to impress him. Since then he believed, or professed to believe, that public life had become an open conspiracy for the destruction of himself and his class. This class, of which he considered himself the sole survivor, was for him the object of romantic loyalty; he spoke of it as a Jacobite clan proscribed and dispersed after Culloden, in a way which sometimes embarrassed those who did not know him well. 'We have been uprooted and harried,' he would say. 'There are only three classes in England now – politicians, tradesmen and slaves.' Then he would particularize. 'Seventy years ago the politicians and the tradesmen were in alliance; they destroyed the gentry by destroying the value of land; some of the gentry became politicians themselves, others tradesmen; out of what was left they created the new class into which I was born, the moneyless, landless, educated gentry who managed the country for them. My grandfather was a Canon of Christ Church, my father was in the Bengal Civil Service. All the capital they left their sons was education and moral principle. Now the politicians are in alliance with the slaves to destroy the tradesmen. They don't need to bother about us. We are extinct already. I am a Dodo,' he used to say, defiantly staring at his audience. 'You, my poor son, are a petrified egg.' There is a caricature of him by Max Beerbohm, in this posture, saying these words.

My choice of profession confirmed his view. 'Marjorie Steyle's boy works below the streets in a basement, selling haberdashery at four pounds a week. Dick Anderson has married his daughter to a grocer. My son John took a second in Mods and a first in Greats. He writes penny dreadfuls for a living,' he would say.

I always sent him my books, and I think he read them. 'At least your grammar is all right,' he once said. 'Your books will translate, and that's more than can be said for most of these fellows who set up to write Literature.' He had a naturally hierarchic mind, and in his scheme of things, detective stories stood slightly above the librettos of musical comedy and well below political journalism. I once showed him a reference to *Death in the Dukeries* by the Professor of Poetry, in which it was described as 'a work of art'. 'Anyone can buy a don,' was his only comment.

But he was gratified by my prosperity. 'Family love and financial dependence don't go together,' he said. 'My father made me an allowance of thirty shillings a week for the first three years I was in London, and he never forgave it me, *never*. He hadn't cost his father a penny after he took his degree. Nor had *his* father before him. You ran into debt at the University. That was a thing I never did. It was two years before you were keeping yourself, and you went about as a dandy those two years, which I never did while I was learning to draw. But you've done very well. No nonsense about Literature. You've cut out quite a line for yourself. I saw old Etheridge at the club the other evening. He reads all your books, he told me, and likes 'em. Poor old Etheridge; he brought his boy up to be a barrister and he still has to keep him at the age of thirty-seven.'

My father seldom referred to his contemporaries without the epithet 'old' – usually as 'poor old so-and-so', unless they had prospered conspicuously when they were 'that old humbug'. On the other hand, he spoke of men a few years his juniors as 'whipper-snappers' and 'young puppies'. The truth was that he could not bear to think of anyone as being the same age as himself. It was all part of the aloofness that was his dominant concern in life. It was enough for him to learn that an opinion of his had popular support for him to question and abandon it. His atheism was his response to the simple piety and confused agnosticism of his family circle. He never came to hear much about Marxism; had he done so he would, I am sure, have discovered a number of proofs of the existence of God. In his later years I observed two reversions of opinion in reaction to contemporary fashion. In my boyhood, in the time of their Edwardian popularity, he denounced the Jews roundly on all occasions, and later attributed to them the vogue of post-impressionist painting: 'There was a poor booby called Cézanne, a kind of village idiot who was given a box of paints to keep him quiet. He very properly left his horrible canvases behind him in the hedges. The Jews discovered him and crept round behind him picking them up – just to get something for nothing. Then when he was safely dead and couldn't share in the profits they hired a lot of mercenary lunatics to write him up. They've made thousands out of it.' To the last he maintained that Dreyfus had been guilty, but when, in the early thirties, anti-Semitism showed signs of becoming a popular force, he supported the Jewish cause in many unpublished letters to *The Times*.

Similarly he was used once to profess an esteem for Roman Catholics. 'Their religious opinions are preposterous,' he said. 'But so were those of the ancient Greeks. Think of Socrates spending half his last evening babbling about the topography of the nether world. Grant them their first absurdities and you will find Roman Catholics a reasonable people – and they have civilized habits.' Later, however, when he saw signs of this view gaining acceptance, he became convinced of the existence of a Jesuit conspiracy to embroil the world in war, and wrote several letters to *The Times* on the subject; they, too, were unpublished. But in neither of these periods did his opinions greatly affect his personal relations; Jews and Catholics were among his closest friends all his life.

My father dressed as he thought a painter should, in a distinct and recognizable garb which made him a familiar and, in his later years, a venerable figure as he took his exercise in the streets round his house. There was no element of ostentation in his poncho capes, check suits, sombrero hats and stock ties. It was rather that he thought it fitting for a man to proclaim unequivocally his station in life, and despised those of his colleagues who seemed to be passing themselves off as guardsmen and stockbrokers. In general he liked his fellow Academicians, though I never heard him express anything but contempt for their work. He regarded the Academy as a club; he enjoyed the dinners and frequently attended the schools, where he was able to state his views on art in Johnsonian terms. He never doubted that the function of painting was representational. He criticized his colleagues for such faults as innocent anatomy, 'triviality' and 'insincerity'. For this he was loosely spoken of as a conservative, but that he never was where his art was concerned. He abominated the standards of his youth. He must have been an intransigently old-fashioned young man, for he was brought up in the hey-day of Whistlerian decorative painting, and his first exhibited work was of a balloon ascent in Manchester – a large canvas crowded with human drama, in the manner of Frith. His practice was chiefly in portraits – many of them posthumous – for presentation to colleges and guildhalls. He seldom succeeded with women, whom he endowed with a statuesque absurdity which was half deliberate, but given the robes of a Doctor of Music or a Knight of Malta he would do something fit to hang with the best panelling in the country; given some whiskers he was a master. 'As a young man I specialized in hair,' he would say, rather as a doctor might say he specialized in noses and throats. 'I paint it incomparably. Nowadays nobody has any to paint,' and it was this aptitude of his which led him to the long, increasingly unsaleable series of historical and scriptural groups, and the scenes of domestic melodrama by which he is known – subjects which had already become slightly ludicrous when he was in his cradle, but which he continued to produce year after year while experimental painters came and went until, right at the end of his life, he suddenly, without realizing it, found himself in the fashion. The first sign of this was in 1935, when his 'Agag before Samuel' was bought at a provincial exhibition for 750 guineas. It was a large canvas at which he had been at work intermittently since 1908. Even he spoke of it, with conscious understatement, as 'something of a white elephant'. White elephants indeed were almost the sole species of four-footed animal that was not somewhere worked into this elaborate composition. When asked why he had introduced such a variety of fauna, he replied, 'I'm sick of Samuel. I've lived with him for twenty years. Every time it comes back from an exhibition I paint out an Israelite and put in an animal. If I live long enough I'll have a Noah's ark in its background.'

The purchaser of this work was Sir Lionel Sterne.

'Honest Sir Lionel,' said my father, as he saw the great canvas packed off to Kensington Palace Gardens, 'I should dearly have liked to shake his hairy paw. I can see him well – a fine, meaty fellow with a great gold watch-chain across his belly, who's been decently employed boiling soap or smelting copper all his life, with no time to read Clive Bell. In every age it has been men like him who kept painting alive.'

I tried to explain that Lionel Sterne was the youthful and elegant millionaire who for ten years had been a leader of aesthetic fashion. 'Nonsense!' said my father. 'Fellows like that collect disjointed Negresses by Gauguin. Only Philistines like my work and, by God, I like only Philistines.'

There was also another, rather less reputable side to my father's business. He received a regular yearly retaining fee from Goodchild and Godley, the Duke Street dealers, for what was called 'restoration'. This sum was a very important part of his income; without it the comfortable little dinners, the trips abroad, the cabs to and fro, between St John's Wood and the Athenaeum, the faithful, predatory Jellabies, the orchid in his buttonhole – all the substantial comforts and refinements which endeared the world and provided him with his air of gentlemanly ease – would have been impossible to him. The truth was that, while excelling at Lely, my father could paint, very passably, in the manner of almost any of the masters of English portraiture, and the private and public collections of the New World were richly representative of his versatility. Very few of his friends knew this traffic; to those who did, he defended it with complete candour. 'Goodchild & Godley buy these pictures for what they are – my own work. They pay me no more than my dexterity merits. What they do with them afterwards is their own business. It would ill become me to go officiously about the markets identifying my own handicraft and upsetting a number of perfectly contented people. It is a great deal better for them to look at beautiful pictures and enjoy them under a misconception about the date, than to make themselves dizzy by goggling at genuine Picassos.'

It was largely on account of his work for Goodchild and Godley that his studio was strictly reserved as a workshop. It was a separate building approached through the garden, and it was excluded from general use. Once a year, when he went abroad, it was 'done out'; once a year, on the Sunday before sending-in day at the Royal Academy, it was open to his friends.

He took a peculiar relish in the gloom of these annual tea-parties, and was at the same pains to make them dismal as he was to enliven his other entertainments. There was a species of dry bright-yellow caraway cake which was known to my childhood as 'Academy cake', and appeared then and only then, from a grocer in Praed Street; there was an enormous Worcester tea service – a wedding present – which was known as 'Academy cups'; there were 'Academy sandwiches' – tiny, triangular and quite tasteless. All these things were part of my earliest memories. I do not know at what date these parties changed from a rather tedious convention to what they certainly were to my father at the end of his life, a huge, grim and solitary jest. If I was in England I was required to attend and to bring a friend or two. It was difficult, until the last two years when, as I have said, my father became the object of fashionable interest, to collect guests. 'When I was a young man,' my father said, sardonically surveying the company, 'there were twenty or more of these parties in St John's Wood alone. People of culture drove round from three in the afternoon to six, from Campden Hill to Hampstead. Today I believe our little gathering is the sole survivor of that deleterious tradition.'

On these occasions his year's work – Goodchild & Godley's items excepted – would be ranged round the studio on mahogany easels; the most important work had a wall to itself against a background of scarlet rep. I had been present at the last of the parties the year before. Lionel Sterne was there with Lady Metroland and a dozen fashionable connoisseurs. My father was at first rather suspicious of his new clients and suspected an impertinent intrusion into his own private joke, a calling of his bluff of seed-cake and cress-sandwiches; but their commissions reassured him. People did not carry a joke to such extravagant lengths. Mrs Algernon Stitch paid 500 guineas for his picture of the year – a tableau of contemporary life conceived and painted with elaborate mastery. My father attached great importance to suitable titles for his work, and after toying with 'The People's Idol', 'Feet of Clay', 'Not on the First Night', 'Their Night of Triumph', 'Success and Failure', 'Not Invited', 'Also Present', he finally called this picture rather enigmatically 'The Neglected Cue'. It represented the dressing room of a leading actress at the close of a triumphant first night. She sat at the dressing-table, her back turned on the company, and her face visible in the mirror, momentarily relaxed in fatigue. Her protector with proprietary swagger was filling the glasses for a circle of admirers. In the background the dresser was in colloquy at the half-open door with an elderly couple of provincial appearance; it is evident from their costume that they have seen the piece from the cheaper seats, and a commissionaire stands behind them uncertain whether he did right in admitting them. He did not do right; they are her old parents arriving most inopportunely. There was no questioning Mrs Stitch's rapturous enjoyment of her acquisition.

I was never to know how my father would react to his vogue. He could paint in any way he chose; perhaps he would have embarked on those vague assemblages of picnic litter which used to cover the walls of the Mansard Gallery in the early twenties; he might have retreated to the standards of the Grosvenor Gallery in the nineties. He might, perhaps, have found popularity less inacceptable than he supposed and allowed himself a luxurious and cosseted old age. He died with his 1939 picture still unfinished. I saw its early stage on my last visit to him; it was to have been called 'Again?' and represented a one-armed veteran of the First World War meditating over a German helmet. My father had given the man a grizzled beard and was revelling in it. That was the last time I saw him.

I had given up living in St John's Wood for four or five years. There was never a definite moment when I 'left home'. For all official purposes the house remained my domicile. There was a bedroom that was known as mine; I kept several trunks full of clothes there and a shelf or two of books. I never set up for myself anywhere else, but during the last five years of my father's life I do not suppose I slept ten nights under his roof. This was not due to any estrangement. I enjoyed his company, and he seemed to enjoy mine, but I was never in London for more than a week or two at a time, and I found that as an occasional visitor I strained and upset my father's household. He and they tried to do too much, and he liked to have his plans clear for some way ahead. 'My dear boy,' he would say on my first evening, 'Please do not misunderstand me. I hope you will stay as long as you possibly can, but I do wish to know whether you will still be here on Thursday the fourteenth, and if so, whether you will be in to dinner.' So I took to staying at my club or with more casual hosts, and to visiting St John's Wood as often as I could, but with formal pre-arrangements.

Nevertheless, I realized, the house had been an important part of my life. It had remained unaltered for as long as I could remember. It was a decent house, built in 1840 or thereabouts, in the contemporary Swiss mode of stucco and ornamental weather boards, one of a street of similar, detached houses when I first saw it. By the time of my father's death the transformation of the district, though not complete, was painfully evident. The skyline of the garden was broken on three sides by blocks of flats. The first of them drove my father into a frenzy of indignation. He wrote to *The Times* about it, addressed a meeting of ratepayers, and for six weeks sported a board advertising the house for sale. At the end of that time he received a liberal offer from the syndicate, who wished to extend their block over the site, and he immediately withdrew it from the market.

This was the period of his lowest professional fortunes, when his subject-pictures remained unsold, the market for dubious old masters was dropping, and public bodies were beginning to look for something 'modern' in their memorial portraits; the period, moreover, when I had finished with the University and was still dependent on my father for pocket money. It was a very unsatisfactory time in his life. I had not then learned to appreciate the massive defences of what people call the 'border line of sanity', and I was at moments genuinely afraid that my father was going out of his mind; there had always seemed an element of persecution-mania about his foibles which might, at a time of great strain, go beyond his control. He used to stand on the opposite pavement watching the new building rise, a conspicuous figure muttering objurgations. I used to imagine scenes in which a policeman would ask him to move on and be met with a wild outburst. I imagined these scenes vividly – my father in swirling cape being hustled off, waving his umbrella. Nothing of the kind occurred. My father, for all his oddity, was a man of indestructible sanity, and in his later years he found a keen pleasure in contemplating the rapid deterioration of the hated buildings. 'Very good news of Hill Crest Court,' he announced one day. 'Typhoid and rats.' And on another occasion. 'Jellaby reports the presence of prostitutes at St Eustace's. They'll have a suicide there soon, you'll see.' There was a suicide, and for two rapturous days my father watched the coming and going of police and journalists. After that fewer chintz curtains were visible in the windows, rents began to fall and the lift-man smoked on duty. My father observed and gleefully noted all these signs. Hill Crest Court changed hands; decorators', plumbers' and electricians' boards appeared all round it; a commissionaire with a new uniform stood at the doors. On the last evening I dined with my father he told me about a visit he had made there, posing as a potential tenant. 'The place is a deserted slum,' he said. 'A miserable, down-at-heel kind of secretary took me round flat after flat – all empty. There were great cracks in the concrete stuffed up with putty. The hot pipes were cold. The doors jammed. He started asking three hundred pounds a year for the best of them, and dropped to one hundred and seventy-five pounds before I saw the kitchen. Then he made it one hundred and fifty pounds. In the end he proposed what he called a "special form of tenancy for people of good social position" – offered to let me live there for a pound a week on condition I turned out if he found someone who was willing to pay the real rent. "Strictly between ourselves," he said, "I can promise you will not be disturbed." Poor beast, I nearly took his flat, he was so paintable.'

Now, I supposed, the house would be sold; another speculator would pull it to pieces; another great, uninhabitable barrack would appear, like a refugee ship in harbour; it would be filled, sold, emptied, resold, refilled, re-emptied, while the concrete got discoloured and the green wood shrank, and the rats crept up in their thousands out of the Metropolitan Railway tunnel: and the trees and gardens all round it disappeared one by one until the place became a working-class district and at last took on a gaiety and life of some sort; until it was condemned by government inspectors and its inhabitants driven further into the country and the process began all over again. I thought of all this, sadly, as I looked out at the fine masonry of Fez, cut four hundred years back by Portuguese prisoners . . . I must go back to England soon to arrange for the destruction of my father's house. Meanwhile there seemed no reason for an immediate change of plan.

3

It was the evening when I usually visited the Moulay Abdullah – the walled *quartier toléré* between the old city and the ghetto. I had gone there first with a sense of adventure; now it had become part of my routine, a regular resort, like the cinema and the Consulate, one of the recreations which gave incident to my week and helped clear my mind of the elaborate villainies of Lady Mountrichard.

I dined at seven and soon afterwards caught my bus at the new gate. Before starting I removed my watch and emptied my pockets of all except the few francs which I proposed to spend – a superstitious precaution which still survived from the first evening, when memories of Marseilles and Naples had even moved me to carry a life-preserver. The Moulay Abdullah was an orderly place, particularly in the early evening when I frequented it. I had formed an attachment for this sole place of its kind which endowed its trade with something approaching glamour. There really was a memory of 'the East', as adolescents imagine it, in that silent courtyard with its single light, the Negro sentries on either side of the lofty Moorish arch, the black lane beyond, between the walls and the water-wheel, full of the thump and stumble of French military boots and the soft pad and rustle of the natives, the second arch into the lighted bazaar, the bright open doors and the tiled patios, the little one-roomed huts where the women stood against the lamplight – shadows without race or age – the larger houses with their bars and gramophones.

I always visited the same house and the same girl – a chubby little Berber with the scarred cheeks of her people and tattooed ornaments, blue on brown, at her forehead and throat. She spoke the peculiar French which she had picked up from the soldiers, and she went by the unassuming, professional name of Fatima. Other girls of the place called themselves 'Lola' and 'Fifi'; there was even an arrogant, coal-black Sudanese named 'Whiskey-soda'. But Fatima had none of these airs; she was a cheerful, affectionate girl working hard to collect her marriage dot; she professed to like everyone in the house, even the proprietress, a forbidding Levantine from Tetuan, and the proprietress's Algerian husband, who wore a European suit, carried round the mint tea, put records on the gramophone and collected the money. (The Moors are a strict people and take no share in the profits of the Moulay Abdullah.)

To regular and serious customers it was an inexpensive place – fifteen francs to the house, ten to Fatima, five for the mint tea, a few sous to the old fellow who tidied Fatima's alcove and blew up the brazier of sweet gum. Soldiers paid less, but they had to make way for more important customers;

often they were penniless men from the Foreign Legion who dropped in merely to hear the music and left nothing behind them but cigarette ends. Now and then tourists appeared with a guide from the big hotel, and the girls were made to line up and give a performance of shuffling and hand clapping which was called a native dance. Women tourists particularly seemed to like these expeditions and paid heavily for them – a hundred francs or more. But they were unpopular with everyone, particularly with the girls, who regarded it as an unseemly proceeding. Once I came in when Fatima was taking part in one of these dances and saw her genuinely and deeply abashed.

On my visit I told Fatima that I had a wife and six children in England; this greatly enhanced my importance in her eyes and she always asked after them.

'You have had a letter from England? The little ones are well?'

'They are very well.'

'And your father and mother?'

'They, too.'

We sat in a tiled hall, two steps below street level, drinking our mint tea – or, rather, Fatima drank hers while I let mine cool in the glass. It was a noisome beverage.

'Whiskey-soda lent me some cigarettes yesterday. Will you give her them?'

I ordered a packet from the bar.

'Yesterday I had a stomach-ache and stayed in my room. That is why Whiskey-soda gave me her cigarettes.'

She asked about my business.

I had told her I exported dates.

The date market was steady, I assured her.

When I was in the Moulay Abdullah I almost believed in this aspect of myself as a philoprogenitive fruiterer; St John's Wood and Mountrichard Castle seemed equally remote. That was the charm of the quarter for me – not its simple pleasures but its privacy and anonymity, the hide-and-seek with one's own personality which redeems vice of its tedium.

That night there was a rude interruption. The gramophone

122

suddenly stopped playing; there was a scuttling among the alcoves; two seedy figures in raincoats strode across the room and began questioning the proprietress; a guard of military police stood at the street door.

Raids of this kind, to round up bad characters, are common enough in French Protectorates. It was the first time I had been caught in one. The girls were made to stand along one wall while the detectives checked their medical certificates. Then two or three soldiers stood to attention and gave a satisfactory account of themselves. Then I was asked for my *carte d'identité*. By the capitulations the French police had little authority over British subjects, and since the criminal class of Morocco mostly possessed Maltese papers, this immunity was good ground for vexation. The detectives were surly fellows, African born. Even the sacred word 'tourist' failed to soften them. Where was my guide? Tourists did not visit the Moulay Abdullah alone. Where was my passport? At my hotel. The Jamai Palace? No? Tourists did not stay at the hotel I mentioned. Was I registered at the police headquarters? Yes. Very well, I must come with them. In the morning I should have the opportunity to identify myself. A hundred francs, no doubt, would have established my respectability, but my money lay with my passport in the hotel. I did not relish a night in gaol in company with the paperless characters of the Moulay Abdullah. I told them I was a friend of the British Consul. He would vouch for me. They grumbled that they had no time for special inquiries of that kind. The Chief would see about it next morning. Then when I had despaired, they despaired too. There was clearly no money coming for them. They had been in the profession long enough to know that no lasting satisfaction results from vexing British subjects. There was a police post in the quarter and they consented to telephone from it. A few minutes later I was set at liberty with a curt reminder that it was advisable to keep my passport accessible if I wanted to wander about the town at night.

I did not return to Fatima. Instead I set off for the bus stop, but the annoyances of the night were not yet over. I was halted again at the gates and the interrogation was repeated. I explained that I had already satisfied their colleagues and had been discharged. We re-enacted the scene, with the fading hope of a tip as the recurring motive. Finally they, too, telephoned to the Consulate, and I was free to take my bus home.

They were still serving dinner at the hotel; the same game of billiards was in progress in the bar; it was less than an hour since I went out. But that hour had been decisive; I was finished with Fez; its privacy had been violated. My weekly visit to the Consulate could never be repeated on the same terms. Twice in twenty minutes the Consul had been called to the telephone to learn that I was in the hands of the police in the Moulay Abdullah; he would not, I thought, be censorious or resentful; the vexation had been mild and the situation slightly absurd – nothing more; but when we next met our relations would be changed. Till then they had been serenely remote; we had talked of the news from England and the Moorish antiquities. We had exposed the bare minimum of ourselves; now a sudden, mutually unwelcome confidence had been forced. The bitterness lay, not in the Consul's knowing the fact of my private recreations, but in his knowing that I knew he knew. It was a salient in the defensive line between us that could only be made safe by a wide rectification of frontier or by a complete evacuation. I had no friendly territory into which to withdraw. I was deployed on the dunes between the sea and the foothills. The transports riding at anchor were my sole lines of support.

In the matter of Good Conscience, I was a man of few possessions, and held them at a corresponding value. As a spinster in mean lodgings fusses over her fragments of gentility – a rosewood work-box, a Spode plate, a crested tea-kettle – which in a house of abundance would be risked in the rough and tumble of general use, I set a price on Modesty which those of ampler virtues might justly regard as fanciful.

Next day I set off for London with my book unfinished.

4

I travelled from spring into winter; sunlit spray in the Straits of Gibraltar changed to dark, heavy seas in the Bay of Biscay; fog off Finisterre, fog in the Channel, clear grey weather in the Thames estuary and a horizon of factories and naked trees. We berthed in London and I drove through cold and dirty streets to meet my Uncle Andrew.

He told me the full circumstances of my father's death; the commercial traveller, against whom a case was being brought for reckless driving, had outraged my uncle by sending a wreath of flowers to the funeral; apart from this everything had been satisfactory. My uncle passed over to me the undertaker's receipted account; he had questioned one or two of the items and obtained an inconsiderable reduction. 'I am convinced,' my uncle said, 'that there is a great deal of sharp practice among these people. They trade upon the popular conception of delicacy. In fact they are the only profession who literally rob the widow and the orphan.' I thanked my uncle for having saved me £3 18s. It was a matter of principle, he said.

As I expected, I was my father's sole heir. Besides the house and its contents I inherited £2,000 in an insurance policy which my father had taken out at the time of his marriage and, without my knowledge, kept up ever since. An injunction, in the brief will, to 'provide suitably' for the servants in my father's employment, had already been obeyed. The Jellabies had been given £250. It was clear from my father's words that he had no conception of what a suitable provision should be. Neither had I, and I was grateful to my uncle for taking responsibility in the matter. For their part the Jellabies had expected nothing. My father, as long ago as I could remember him, was accustomed to talk with relish of his approaching death. I had heard him often admonish Jellaby: 'You have joined fortune with a poor man. Make what you can while I still have my faculties. My death will be an occasion for unrelieved lamentation,' and the Jellabies, in the manner of their kind, took his words literally, kept a keen watch on all sources of perquisite, and expected nothing. Jellaby took his cheque, my uncle said, without any demonstration of gratitude or disappointment, murmuring ungraciously that it would come in quite useful. No doubt he thought no thanks were due to my uncle, for it was not his money; nor to my father, for it was no intention of his to give it. It was a last, substantial perquisite.

The Jellabies had been much in my mind, off and on, during the journey from Fez. I had fretted, in a way I have, imagining our meeting and a scene of embarrassing condolence and reminiscence, questioning the propriety of removing them immediately, if ever, from the place where they had spent so much of their lives; I even saw myself, on the Jellabies' account, assuming my father's way of life, settling in St John's Wood, entertaining small dinner parties, lunching regularly at my club and taking three weeks' holiday abroad in the early summer. As things turned out, however, I never saw the Jellabies again. They had done their packing before the funeral, and went straight to the railway station in their black clothes. Their plans had been laid years in advance. They had put away a fair sum and invested it in Portsmouth, not, as would have been conventional, in a lodging-house, but in a shop in a poor quarter of the town which enjoyed a trade in second-hand wireless apparatus. Mrs Jellaby's stepbrother had been keeping the business warm for them, and there they retired with an alacrity which was slightly shocking but highly convenient. I wrote to them some time later when I was going through my father's possessions, to ask if they would like to have some small personal memento of him; they might value one of his sketches, I suggested, for the walls of their new home. The answer took some time in coming. When it came it was on a sheet of trade-paper with a printed heading: 'T. Jellaby. Every Radio want promptly supplied for cash.' Mrs Jellaby wrote the letter. They had not much room for pictures, she said, but would greatly appreciate some blankets, as it was chilly at nights in Portsmouth; she specified a particular pair which my father had bought shortly before his death; they were lying, folded, in the hot cupboard . . .

Uncle Andrew gave me the keys of my father's house. I went straight there from lunching with him. The shutters were up and the curtains drawn; the water and electric light were already cut off; all this my uncle had accomplished in a few days. I stumbled among sheeted furniture to the windows and let in the daylight. I went from room to room in this way. The place still retained its own smell – an agreeable, rather stuffy atmosphere of cigar smoke and cantaloup; a masculine smell – women had always seemed a little out of place there, as in a London club on Coronation Day.

The house was sombre, but never positively shabby, so that, I suppose, various imperceptible renovations and replacements must have occurred from time to time. It looked what it was, the house of an unfashionable artist of the 1880s. The curtains and chair-covers were of indestructible Morris tapestry; there were Dutch tiles round the fireplaces; Levantine rugs on the floors; on the walls Arundel prints, photographs from the old masters, and majolica dishes. The furniture, now shrouded, had the inimitable air of having been in the same place for a generation; it was a harmonious, unobstructive jumble of inherited rosewood and mahogany, and of inexpensive collected pieces of carved German oak, Spanish walnut, English chests and dressers, copper ewers and brass candlesticks. Every object was familiar and yet so much a part of its surroundings that later, when they came to be moved, I found a number of things which I barely recognized. Books of an antiquated sort were all over the house in a variety of hanging, standing and revolving shelves.

I opened the french windows in my father's study and stepped down into the garden. There was little of spring to be seen here. The two plane trees were bare; under the sooty laurels last year's leaves lay rotting. It was never a garden of any character. Once, before the flats came, we used to dine there sometimes, in extreme discomfort under the catalpa tree; for years now it had been a no-man's land, isolating the studio at the farther end; on one side, behind a trellis, were

127

some neglected frames and beds where my father had once tried to raise French vegetables. The mottled concrete of the flats, with its soil-pipes and fire-escapes and its rash of iron-framed casement windows, shut out half the sky. The tenants of these flats were forbidden, in their leases, to do their laundry, but the owners had long since despaired of a genteel appearance, and you could tell which of the rooms were occupied by the stockings hanging to dry along the window-sills.

In his death my father's privacy was still respected, and no one had laid dust-sheets in the studio. 'Again?' stood as he had left it on the easel. More than half was finished. My father made copious and elaborate studies for his pictures and worked quickly when he came to their final stage, painting over a monochrome sketch, methodically, in fine detail, left to right across the canvas as though he were lifting the backing of a child's 'transfer'. 'Do your thinking *first*,' he used to tell the Academy students. 'Don't muddle it out on the canvas. Have the whole composition clear in your head before you start,' and if anyone objected that this was seldom the method of the greatest masters, he would say, 'You're here to become Royal Academicians, not great masters. If you want to write books on Art, trot round Europe studying the Rubenses. If you want to learn to paint, watch me.' The four or five square feet of finished painting were a monument of my father's art. There had been a time when I had scant respect for it. Lately I had come to see that it was more than a mere matter of dexterity and resolution. He had an historic position, for he completed a period of English painting that through other circumstances had never, until him, come to maturity. Phrases, as though for an obituary article, came to my mind: '. . . fulfilling the broken promise of the young Millais. . . Winterhalter suffused with the spirit of Dickens . . . English painting as it might have been, had there not been any Aesthetic Movement . . .' and with the phrases my esteem for my father took form and my sense of loss became tangible and permanent.

No good comes of this dependence on verbal forms. It saves

nothing in the end. Suffering is none the less acute and much more lasting when it is put into words. In the house my memories had been all of myself – of the countless home-comings and departures of thirty-three years, of adolescence like a stained tablecloth – but in the studio my thoughts were of my father and grief, nearly a week delayed, overtook and overwhelmed me. It had been delayed somewhat by the strangeness of my surroundings and the business of travel, but most by this literary habit; it had lacked words. Now the words came; I began, in my mind, to lament my father, addressing, as it were, funeral orations to my own literary memories, and sorrow, dammed and canalized, flowed fast.

For the civilized man there are none of those swift transitions of joy and pain which possess the savage; words form slowly like pus about his hurts; there are no clean wounds for him; first a numbness, then a long festering, then a scar ever ready to re-open. Not until they have assumed the livery of the defence can his emotions pass through the lines; some-times they come massed in a wooden horse, sometimes as single spies, but there is always a Fifth Column among the garrison ready to receive them. Sabotage behind the lines, a blind raised and lowered at a lighted window, a wire cut, a bolt loosened, a file disordered – that is how the civilized man is undone.

I returned to the house and darkened the rooms once more, relaid the dust-sheets I had lifted, and left everything as it had been.

5

The manuscript of *Murder at Mountrichard Castle* lay on the chest of drawers in my club bedroom, reproaching me morning, evening and night. It was promised for publication in June, and I had never before disappointed my publishers. This year, however, I should have to ask grace for a postponement. I made two attemps at it, bearing the pile of foolscap to an upper room of the club which was known as the library and used by the older members for sleeping between luncheon and tea. But I found it impossible to take up the story with any interest; so I went to my publishers and tried to explain.

'I have been writing for over eight years,' I said, 'and am nearing a climacteric.'

'I don't quite follow,' said Mr Benwell anxiously.

'I mean a turning point in my career.'

'Oh, dear, I hope you're not thinking of making a contract elsewhere?'

'No, no. I mean that I feel in danger of turning into a stock best-seller.'

'If I may say so, in very imminent danger,' said Benwell, and he made a kind of little bow from the seat of his swivel chair and smirked in the wry fashion people sometimes assume when they feel they have said something elaborately polite; a smile normally kept for his women writers; the word 'climacteric' had clearly upset him.

'I mean, I am in danger of becoming purely a technical expert. Take my father . . .' Mr Benwell gave a deferential grunt and quickly changed his expression to one of gravity suitable to the mention of someone recently dead. 'He spent his whole life perfecting his technique. It seems to me I am in danger of becoming mechanical, turning out year after year the kind of book I know I can write well. I feel I have got as good as I ever can be at this particular sort of writing. I need new worlds to conquer.' I added this last remark in compassion for Mr Benwell, whose gravity had deepened to genuine concern. I believed he would feel the easier for a little facetiousness – erroneously, for Mr Benwell had suffered similar, too serious conversations with other writers than me.

'You've not been writing *poetry* in Morocco?'

'No, no.'

'Sooner or later almost all my novelists come to me and say they have written poetry. I can't think why. It does them infinite harm. Only last week Roger Simmonds was here with a kind of play. You never saw such a thing. All the characters were parts of a motor-car – not in the least funny.'

'Oh, it won't be anything like that,' I said. 'Just some new technical experiments. I don't suppose the average reader will notice them at all.'

'I hope not,' said Mr Benwell. 'I mean, now you've found your public . . . well, look at Simmonds.'

I knew what he was thinking: 'The trouble about Plant is, he's come in for money.'

In a way he was right. The money my father had left me, and the proceeds which I expected from the sale of the house, relieved me of the need to work for two or three years; it was a matter of pure athletics to go on doing something merely because one did it well. The heap of foolscap began to disgust me. Twice I hid it under my shirts, twice the club valet unearthed it and laid it in the open. I had nowhere to keep things, except in this little hired room above the traffic.

This sense of homelessness was new to me. Before I had moved constantly from one place to another; every few weeks I would descend upon St John's Wood with a trunk, leave some books, collect others, put away summer clothes for the winter; seldom as I slept there, the house in St John's Wood had been my headquarters and my home; that earth had now been stopped, and I thought, not far away, I could hear the hounds.

My worries at this period became symbolized in a single problem; what to do with my hats. I owned what now seemed a multitude of them, of one sort and another; two of them of silk – the tall hat I took to weddings and a second I had bought some years earlier when I thought for a time that I was going to take to fox-hunting; there were a bowler, a panama, a black, a brown and a grey soft hat, a green hat from Salzburg, a sombrero, some tweed caps for use on board ship and in trains – all these had accumulated from time to time and all, with the possible exception of the sombrero, were more or less indispensable. Was I doomed for the rest of my life to travel everywhere with this preposterous collection? At the moment they were, most of them, in St

John's Wood, but, any day now, the negotiations for the sale might be finished and the furniture removed, sold or sent to store.

Somewhere to hang up my hat, that was what I needed.

I consulted Roger Simmonds, who was lunching with me. I felt as though I had known Roger all my life; actually I had first met him in our second year at Oxford; we edited an undergraduate weekly together, and had been close associates ever since. He was one of the very few people I corresponded with when I was away; we met often when I was in London. Sometimes I even stayed with him, for he and half a dozen others constituted a kind of set. We had all known each other intimately over a number of years, had from time to time passed on girls from one to the other, borrowed and lent freely. When we were together we drank more and talked more boastfully than we normally did. We had grown rather to dislike one another; certainly when any two or three of us were alone we blackguarded the rest, and if asked about them on neutral ground I denied their friendship. About Roger I used to say, 'I don't think he's interested in anything except politics now.'

This was more or less true. In the late twenties he set up as a writer and published some genuinely funny novels on the strength of which he filled a succession of jobs with newspapers and film companies, but lately he had married an unknown heiress, joined the Socialist Party, and become generally conventional.

'I never wear a hat now I am married,' said Roger virtuously. 'Lucy says they're *kulak*. Besides, I was beginning to lose my hair.'

'My dear Roger, you've been bald as a coot for ten years. But it isn't only a question of hats. There are overcoats.'

'Only in front. It's as thick as anything at the back. How many overcoats have you got?'

'Four, I think.'

'Too many.'

We discussed it at length and decided it was possible to manage with three.

'Workers pawn their overcoats in June and take them out again in October,' Roger said. He wanted to talk about his play, *Internal Combustion*. 'The usual trouble with ideological drama,' he said, 'is that they're too mechanical. I mean the characters are economic types, not individuals, and as long as they look and speak like individuals it's bad art. D'you see what I mean?'

'I do, indeed.'

'Human beings without human interest.'

'Very true. I . . .'

'Well, I've cut human beings out altogether.'

'Sounds rather like an old-fashioned ballet.'

'*Exactly*,' Roger said with great pleasure. 'It *is* an old-fashioned ballet. I knew you'd understand. Poor old Benwell couldn't. The Finsbury International Theatre are sitting on it now, and if it's orthodox – and I *think* it is – they may put it on this summer if Lucy finds the money.'

'Is she keen, too?'

'Well, not very, as a matter of fact. You see, she's having a baby, and that seems to keep her interested at the moment.'

'But to return to the question of my hats . . .'

'I tell you what. Why don't you buy a nice quiet house in the country? I shall want somewhere to stay while this baby is born.'

There was the rub. It was precisely this fear that had been working in my mind for days, the fear of making myself a sitting shot to the world. It lay at the root of the problem of privacy; the choice which torments to the verge of mania, between perpetual flight and perpetual siege; and the unresolved universal paradox of losing things in order to find them.

'Surely that is odd advice from a Socialist?'

Roger became suddenly wary; he had been caught and challenged in loose talk. 'Ideally, of course, it would be,' he said. 'But I dare say that in practice, for the first generation, we shall allow a certain amount of private property where its value is purely sentimental. Anyway, any investment you make now is bound to be temporary. That's why I feel no repugnance about living on Lucy's money . . .' Marxist ethics

133

kept him talking until we had finished luncheon. Over the coffee he referred to Ingres as a 'bourgeois' painter. When he left me I sat for some time in the leather armchair finishing my cigar. The club was emptying as the younger members went back to their work and their elders padded off to the library for the afternoon nap. I belonged to neither world. I had nothing whatever to do. At three in the afternoon my friends would all be busy and, in any case, I did not want to see them. I was ready for a new deal. I climbed to my room, began re-reading the early chapters of *Murder at Mountrichard Castle*, put it from me and faced the boredom of an afternoon in London. Then the telephone rang and the porter said, 'Mr Thurston is downstairs to see you.'

'Who?'

'Mr Thurston. He says he has an appointment.'

'I don't know anything about him. Will you ask what he wants?'

A pause: 'Mr Thurston says will you see him very particular.'

'Very well, I'll come down.'

A tall young man in a raincoat was standing in the hall. He had reddish hair and an unusually low, concave forehead. He looked as though he had come to sell some hopelessly unsuitable commodity and had already despaired of success.

'Mr Thurston?' He took my hand in a savage grip. 'You say you have an appointment with me. I am afraid I don't remember it.'

'No, well, you see, I thought we ought to have a yarn, and you know how suspicious these porter fellows are at clubs. I knew you wouldn't mind my stretching a point.' He spoke with a kind of fierce jauntiness. 'I had to give up my club. Couldn't run it.'

'Perhaps you will tell me what I can do for you.'

'I used to belong to the Wimpole. I expect you know it?'

'I'm not sure that I do.'

'No. You would have liked it. I could have taken you there and introduced you to some of the chaps.'

'That, I gather, is now impossible.'

'Yes. It's a pity. There are some good scouts there. I dare say you know the Bachelors?'

'Yes. Were you a member there, too?'

'Yes – at least, not exactly, but a great pal of mine was – Jimmie Grainger. I expect you've often run across Jimmie?'

'No, I don't think I have.'

'Funny. Jimmie knows almost everyone. You'd like him. I must bring you together.' Having failed to establish contact, Thurston seemed now to think that responsibility for the conversation devolved on me.

'Mr Thurston,' I said, 'is there anything particular you wished to say to me? Because otherwise . . .'

'I was coming to that,' said Thurston. 'Isn't there somewhere more private where we could go and talk?'

It was a reasonable suggestion. Two page boys sat on a bench beside us, the hall porter watched us curiously from behind his glass screen, two or three members passing through paused by the tape machine to take a closer look at my odd visitor. I was tolerably certain that he was not one of the enthusiasts for my work who occasionally beset me, but was either a beggar or a madman or both; at another time I should have sent him away, but that afternoon, with no prospect of other interest, I hesitated. 'Be a good scout,' he urged.

There is at my club a nondescript little room of depressing aspect where members give interviews to the press, go through figures with their accountants, and in general transact business which they think would be conspicuous in the more public rooms. I took Thurston there.

'Snug little place,' he said. 'O.K. if I smoke?'

'Perfectly.'

'Have one?'

'No, thank you.'

He lit a cigarette, drew a deep breath of smoke, gazed at the ceiling and, as though coming to the point, said, 'Quite like the old Wimpole.'

My heart sank. 'Mr Thurston,' I said, 'you have surely not troubled to come here simply to talk to me about the Wimpole Club?'

135

'No. But, you see, it's rather awkward. Don't exactly know how to begin. I thought I might lead up to it naturally. But I realize that your time's valuable, Mr Plant, so I may as well admit right out that I owe you an apology.'

'Yes?'

'Yes. I'm here under false pretences. My name isn't Thurston.'

'No?'

'No. I'd better tell you who I am, hadn't I?'

'If you wish to.'

'Well, here goes. I'm Arthur Atwater.' The name was spoken with such an air of bravado, with such confidence of its making a stir, that I felt bewildered. It meant absolutely nothing to me. Where and how should I have heard it? Was this a fellow-writer, a distant cousin, a popular athlete? Atwater? Atwater? I repeated it to myself. No association came. My visitor meanwhile seemed unconscious of how flat his revelation had fallen, and was talking away vehemently:

'Now you see why I couldn't give my name. It's awfully decent of you to take it like this. I might have known you were a good scout. I've been through hell, I can tell you, ever since it happened. I haven't slept a wink. It's been terrible. You know how it is when one's nerve's gone. I shouldn't be fit for work now even if they'd kept me on in the job. Not that I care about that. Let them keep their lousy job. I told the manager that to his face. I wasn't brought up and educated to sell stockings. I ought to have gone abroad long ago. There's no opportunity in England now, unless you've got influence or are willing to suck up to a lot of snobs. You get a fair chance out there in the colonies where one man's as good as another and no questions asked.'

I can seldom bear to let a misstatement pass uncorrected. 'Believe me, Mr Atwater,' I said, 'you have a totally mistaken view of colonial life. You will find people just as discriminating and inquisitive there as they are here.'

'Not where I'm going,' he said. 'I'm clearing right out. I'm fed up. This case hanging over me and nothing to do all day

except think about the accident. It *was* an accident, too. No
one can try and hang the blame on me and get away with it.
I was on my proper side of the road and hooted twice. It
wasn't a Belisha crossing. It was my road. The old man just
wouldn't budge. He saw me coming, looked straight at me, as
if he was daring me to drive into him. Well, I thought I'd give
him a fright. You know how it is when you're driving all day.
You get fed to the teeth with people making one get out of
their way all the time. I like to wake them up now and then
when there's no copper near, and make them jump for it. It
seems like an hour now, but it all happened in two seconds.
I kept on, waiting for him to skip, and he kept on, strolling
across the road as if he'd bought it. It wasn't till I was right on
top of him I realized he didn't intend to move. Then it was
too late to stop. I put on my brakes and tried to swerve. Even
then I might have missed him if he'd stopped, but he just
kept on walking right into me and the mudguard got him.
That's how it was. No one can blame it on me.'

It was just as my uncle Andrew had described it.

'Mr Atwater,' I said, 'do I understand that you are the man
who killed my father?'

'Don't put it that way, Mr Plant. I feel sore enough about it.
He was a great artist. I read about him in the papers. It makes
it worse, his having been a great artist. There's too little
beauty in the world as it is. I should have liked to be an artist
myself, only the family went broke. Father took me away
from school young, just when I might have got into the
eleven. Since then I've had nothing but odd jobs. I've
never had a real chance. I want to start again, somewhere
else.'

I interrupted him, frigidly I thought. 'And why, precisely,
have you come to me?'

But nothing could disabuse him of the idea that I was well
disposed. 'I knew I could rely on you,' he said. 'And I'll never
forget it, not as long as I live. I've thought everything out.
I've a pal who went out to Rhodesia; I think it was Rhodesia.
Somewhere in Africa, anyway. He'll give me a shakedown
till I get on my feet. He's a great fellow. Won't he be surprised

when I walk in on him! All I need is my passage money – third class, I don't care. I'm used to roughing it these days – and something to make a start with. I could do it on fifty pounds.'

'Mr Atwater,' I said, 'have I misunderstood you, or are you asking me to break the law by helping you to evade your trial and also give you a large sum of money?'

'You'll get it back, every penny of it.'

'And our sole connexion is the fact that, through pure insolence, you killed my father.'

'Oh, well, if you feel like that about it . . .'

'I am afraid you greatly overrate my good nature.'

'Tell you what. I'll make you a sporting offer. You give me fifty pounds now and I'll pay it back in a year plus another fifty pounds to any charity you care to name. How's that?'

'Will you please go?'

'Certainly I'll go. If that's how you take it. I'm sorry I ever came. It's typical of the world,' he said, rising huffily. 'Everyone's all over you till you get into a spot of trouble. It's "good old Arthur" while you're in funds. Then, when you need a pal it's "you overrate my good nature, Mr Atwater".'

I followed him across the room, but before we reached the door his mood had changed. 'You don't understand,' he said. 'They may send me to prison for this. That's what happens in this country to a man earning his living. If I'd been driving my own Rolls Royce they'd all be touching their caps. "Very regrettable accident," they'd be saying. "Hope your nerves have not been shocked, Mr Atwater" – but to a poor man driving a two-seater . . . Mr Plant, your father wouldn't have wanted me sent to prison.'

'He often expressed the view that all motorists of all classes should be kept permanently in prison.'

Atwater received this with disconcerting enthusiasm. 'And he was quite right,' he cried in louder tones than can ever have been used in that room except perhaps during spring cleaning. 'I'm fed to the teeth with motor-cars. I'm fed to the teeth with civilization. I want to farm. That's a man's life.'

138

'Mr Atwater, will nothing I say persuade you that your aspirations are no concern of mine?'

'There's no call to be sarcastic. If I'm not wanted, you've only to say so straight.'

'You are not wanted.'

'Thank you,' he said. 'That's all I wanted to know.'

I got him through the door, but half-way across the front hall he paused again. 'I spent my last ten bob on a wreath.'

'I'm sorry you did that. I'll refund it.'

He turned on me with a look of scorn. 'Plant,' he said, 'I didn't think it was in you to say a thing like that. Those flowers were a sacred thing. You wouldn't understand that, would you? I'd have starved to send them. I may have sunk pretty low, but I have some decency left, and that's more than some people can say even if they belong to posh clubs and look down on fellows who earn a decent living. Goodbye, Plant. We shall not meet again. D'you mind if I don't shake hands?'

That was how he left me, but it was not the last of him. That evening I was called to the telephone to speak to a Mr Long. Familiar tones, jaunty once more, greeted me. 'That you, Plant? Atwater here. Excuse the alias, won't you? I say, I hope you didn't take offence at the way I went off today. I've been thinking, and I see you were perfectly right. May I come round for another yarn?'

'No.'

'Tomorrow, then?'

'No.'

'Well, when shall I come?'

'Never.'

'No, I quite understand, old man. I'd feel the same myself. It's only this. In the circumstances I'd like to accept your very sporting offer to pay for those flowers. I'll call round for the money if you like, or will you send it?'

'I'll send it.'

'Care of the Holborn Post Office finds me. Fifteen bob they cost.'

'You said ten this afternoon.'

'Did I? I meant fifteen.'

'I will send you ten shillings. Good-bye.'

'Good scout,' said Atwater.

So I put a note in an envelope and sent it to the man who killed my father.

6

Time dragged.

The sale of the house in St John's Wood proved more irksome than I had expected. Ten years before the St John's Wood Residential Amenities Company, who built the neighbouring flats, had offered my father £6,000 for his freehold; he had preserved the letter, which was signed 'Alfred Hardcastle, Chairman'. Their successors, the Hill Crest Court Exploitation Co., now offered me £2,500; their letter was also signed Mr Hardcastle. I refused, and put the house into an agent's hands; after two months they reported one offer – of £2,500 from a Mr Hardcastle, the managing director of St John's Wood Residential Estates Ltd. 'In the circumstances,' they wrote, 'we consider this a satisfactory price.' The circumstances were that no one who liked that kind of house would tolerate its surroundings; having dominated the district, the flats could make their own price. I accepted it and went to sign the final papers at Mr Hardcastle's office, expecting an atmosphere of opulence and bluster; instead, I found a modest pair of rooms, one of the unlet flats at the top of the building. On the door were painted the names of half a dozen real estate companies, and the woodwork bore traces of other names which had stood there and been obliterated; the chairman opened the door himself and let me in. He was a large, neat, middle-aged, melancholy, likeable fellow, who before coming to business praised my father's painting with what I believe was complete sincerity.

There was no other visible staff; just Mr Hardcastle sitting among his folders and filing cabinets, telling me how he had felt when he lost his own father. Throughout all the vicissitudes of the flats this man had controlled them and lived for them; little companies had gone into liquidation; little, allied companies had been floated; the names of nephews and brothers-in-law had come and gone at the head of the notepaper; stocks had been written down and up, new shares had been issued, bonuses and dividends declared, mortgages transferred and foreclosed, little blocks of figures moved from one balance sheet to another, all in this single room. For the last ten years a few thousand pounds capital had been borrowed and lent backwards and forwards from one account to another and somehow, working sixteen hours a day, doing his own typing and accountancy, Mr Hardcastle had sustained life, kept his shoes polished and his trousers creased, had his hair cut regularly and often, bought occasional concert tickets on family anniversaries and educated, he told me, a son in the United States and a daughter in Belgium. The company to which I finally conveyed my freehold was a brand new one, registered for the occasion and soon, no doubt, doomed to lose its identity in the kaleidoscopic changes of small finance. The cheque, signed by Mr Hardcastle, was duly honoured, and when the sum, largely depleted by my solicitor, was paid into my account, I found that with the insurance money added and my overdraft taken away, I had a credit balance for the first time in my life, of rather more than £3,500. With this I set about planning a new life.

Mr Hardcastle had been willing to wait a long time to make his purchase; once it was done, however, his plans developed with surprising speed. Workmen were cutting the trees and erecting a screen of hoarding while the vans were removing the furniture to store; a week later I came to visit the house; it was a ruin; it might have been mined. Presumably there is some method in the business of demolition; none was apparent to a layman, the roof was off, the front was down, and on one side the basement lay open; on the other the walls still stood their full height, and the rooms, three-sided like stage settings, exposed their Morris papers, flapping loose in

the wind where the fireplaces and windowframes had been
torn out. The studio had disappeared, leaving a square of
rubble to mark its site; new shoots appeared here and there
in the trampled mess of the garden. A dozen or more
workmen were there, two or three of them delving away in
a leisurely fashion, the rest leaning on their tools and talking;
it seemed inconceivable that in this fashion they could have
done so much in such little time. The air was full of flying
grit. It was no place to linger. When next I passed that way,
a great concrete wing covered the site; it was cleaner than the
rest of the block and, by a miscalculation of the architects, the
windows were each a foot or two below the general line; but,
like them, were devoid of curtains.

Part Two

A BIRTH

1

MY project of settling in the country was well received by my friends.

Each saw in it a likely convenience for himself. I understood their attitude well. Country houses meant something particular and important in their lives, a system of permanent bolt-holes. They had, most of them, gradually dropped out of the round of formal entertaining; country life for them meant not a series of invitations, but of successful, predatory raids. Their lives were liable to sharp reverses; their quarters in London were camps which could be struck at an hour's notice, as soon as the telephone was cut off. Country houses were permanent; even when the owner was abroad, the house was there, with a couple of servants or, at the worst, someone at a cottage who came in to light fires and open windows, someone who, at a pinch, could be persuaded also to make the bed and wash up. They were places where wives and children could be left for long periods, where one retired to write a book, where one could be ill, where, in the course of a love affair, one could take a girl and, by being her guide and sponsor in strange surroundings, establish a degree of proprietorship impossible on the neutral ground of London. The owners of these places were, by their nature, a patient race, but repeated abuse was apt to sour them; new blood in their ranks was highly welcome. I detected this greeting in every eye.

There was also another, more amiable, reason for their interest. Nearly all of them – and, for that matter, myself as well – professed a specialized enthusiasm for domestic architecture. It was one of the peculiarities of my generation, and there is no accounting for it. In youth we had pruned our aesthetic emotions hard back so that in many cases they had reverted to briar stock; we none of us wrote or read poetry, or, if we did, it was of a kind which left unsatisfied those wistful, half-romantic, half-aesthetic, peculiarly British longings which, in the past, used to find expression in so many slim lambskin volumes. When the poetic mood was on us, we turned to buildings, and gave them the place which our fathers accorded to Nature – to almost any buildings, but particularly those in the classical tradition, and, more particularly, in its decay. It was a kind of nostalgia for the style of living which we emphatically rejected in practical affairs. The nobilities of Whig society became, for us, what the Arthurian paladins were in the time of Tennyson. There was never a time when so many landless men could talk at length about landscape gardening. Even Roger compromised with his Marxist austerities so far as to keep up his collection of the works of Batty Langley and William Halfpenny. 'The nucleus of my museum,' he explained. 'When the revolution comes, I've no ambitions to be a commissar or a secret policeman. I want to be director of the Museum of Bourgeois Art.'

He was overworking the Marxist vocabulary. That was always Roger's way, to become obsessed with a new set of words and to extend them, deliberately, beyond the limits of sense; it corresponded to some sombre, interior need of his to parody whatever, for the moment, he found venerable; when he indulged it I was reminded of the ecclesiastical jokes of those on the verge of religious melancholy. Roger had been in that phase himself when I first met him.

One evening, at his house, the talk was all about the kind of house I should buy. It was clear that my friends had very much more elaborate plans for me than I had for myself. After dinner Roger produced a copper engraving of 1767 of *A Composed Hermitage in the Chinese Taste*. It was a preposterous design. 'He actually built it,' Roger said, 'and it's still standing a mile or two out of Bath. We went to see it the other day. It only wants putting into repair. Just the house for you.'

Everyone seemed to agree.

I knew exactly what he meant. It *was* just the house one

would want someone else to have. I was graduating from the exploiting to the exploited class.

But Lucy said: 'I can't think why John should want to have a house like that.'

When she said that I had a sudden sense of keen pleasure. She and I were on the same side.

Roger and Lucy had become my main interest during the months while I was waiting to settle up in St John's Wood. They lived in Victoria Square, where they had taken a three years' lease of a furnished house. 'Bourgeois furniture,' Roger complained, rather more accurately than usual. They shut away the model ships and fire-bucket wastepaper baskets in a store cupboard and introduced a prodigious radio-gramophone; they hung their own pictures in place of the Bartolozzi prints, but the house retained its character, and Roger and Lucy, each in a different way, looked out of place there. It was here that Roger had written his ideological play.

They had been married in November. I had spent all the previous autumn abroad on a leisurely, aimless trip before settling at Fez for the winter's work. My mail at Malta, in September, told me that Roger had taken up with a rich girl and was having difficulty with her family; at Tetuan I learned that he was married. Apparently he had been in pursuit of her all the summer, unknown to us. It was not until I reached London that I heard the full story. Basil Seal told me, rather resentfully, because for many years now he had himself been in search of an heiress and had evolved theories on the subject of how and where they might be taken. 'You must go to the provinces,' he used to say. 'The competition in London is far too hot for chaps like us. Americans and Colonials want value for money. The trouble is that the very rich have a natural affinity for one another. You can see it happening all the time – stinking rich people getting fixed up. And what happens? They simply double their supertax and no one is the better off. But they respect brains in the provinces. They like a man to be ambitious there, with his way to make in the world, and there are plenty of solid, mercantile families who can settle a hundred thousand on a daughter without turning a hair, who don't care a hoot about polo, but think a Member of Parliament very fine. That's the way to get in with them. Stand for Parliament.'

In accordance with this plan Basil had stood three times – or rather had three times been adopted as candidate; on two occasions he fell out with his committee before the election. At least that was his excuse to his friends for not standing; in fact he, too, thought it a fine thing to be a Member of Parliament. He never got in, and he was still unmarried. A kind of truculent honesty which he could never dissemble for long always stood in his way. It was bitter for him to be still living at home, dependent on his mother for pocket money, liable to be impelled by her into unwelcome jobs two or three times a year while Roger had established himself almost effortlessly and was sitting back in comfort to await the World Revolution.

Not that Lucy was really rich, Basil hastened to assure me, but she had been left an orphan at an early age, and her originally modest fortune had doubled itself. 'Fifty-eight thousand in trustee stock, old boy. I wanted Lucy to take it out and let me handle it for her. I could have fixed her up very nicely. But Roger wasn't playing. He's always groaning about things being bourgeois. I can't think of anything more bourgeois than three and a half per cent.'

'Is she hideous?' I asked.

'No, that's the worst part about it. She's a grand girl. She's all right for a chap.'

'What like?'

'Remember Trixie?'

'Vaguely.'

'Well, not at all like her.'

Trixie had been Roger's last girl. Basil had passed her on to him, resumed the use of her for a week or two, then passed her back. None of us had liked Trixie. She always gave the impression that she was not being treated with the respect she was used to.

'How did he come by her?'

146

Basil told me at length, unable to hide his admiration for
Roger's duplicity in the matter. All the previous summer,
during the second Trixie period, Roger had been at work,
without a word to any of us. I remembered, now, that he had
suddenly become rather conspicuous in his clothes, affecting
dark shirts and light ties, and a generally artistic appearance
which, had he not been so bald, would have gone with long,
untidy hair. It had embarrassed Trixie, she said, when at a
bar they saw cousins of hers who were in the Air Force.
'They'll tell everyone I'm going about with a pansy.' So that
was the explanation. It was greatly to Roger's credit, we
agreed.

Improbable as it sounded, the truth was that they had met
at a ball in Pont Street, given by a relative of Roger's. He had
gone, under protest, to make up the table at dinner in answer
to an S O S half an hour before the time. Someone had fallen
out. It was five or six years since he had been in a London
ballroom and, he explained afterwards, the spectacle of his
pimply and inept juniors had inflated him with a self-esteem
which must, he said, have been infectious. He had sat next to
Lucy at dinner. She was, for our world, very young but, for
her own, of a hoary age; that is to say, she was twenty-four.
For six years she had been sent to dances by her aunt, keeping
up an unfashionable, middle stratum of life in which her
contemporaries had either married or taken to other occupa-
tions. This aunt occupied a peculiar position with regard to
Lucy; she had brought her up and now did what she described
as 'making a home' for her, which meant that she subsisted
largely upon Lucy's income. She had two other nieces
younger than Lucy, and it was greatly to their interest that
they should move to London annually for the season. The
aunt was a lady of delicate conscience where the issues of
Lucy's marriage were involved. Once or twice before she had
been apprehensive – without cause as it happened – that
Lucy was preparing to 'throw herself away'. Roger, however,
was a case that admitted of no doubt. Everything she learned
about him was reprehensible; she fought him in the full
confidence of a just cause, but she had no serviceable weapon.

147

In six years of social life Lucy had never met anyone the least like Roger.

'And he took care she shouldn't meet us,' said Basil. 'What's more, she thinks him a great writer.'

This was true. I did not believe Basil, but after I had seen her and Roger together I was forced to accept it. It was one of the most disconcerting features of the marriage for all of us. It is hard to explain exactly why I found it so shocking. Roger was a very good novelist – every bit as good in his own way as I in mine; when one came to think of it, it was impossible to name anyone else, alive, who could do what he did; there was no good reason why his books should not be compared with those of prominent writers of the past, nor why we should not speculate about their ultimate fame. But to do so struck us all as the worst of taste. Whatever, secretly, we thought about our own work, we professed, in public, to regard it as drudgery and our triumphs as successful impos- tures on the world at large. To speak otherwise would be to suggest that we were concerned with anyone else's interest but our own; it would be a denial of the *sauve qui peut* principle which we had all adopted. But Lucy, I soon realized, found this attitude unintelligible. She was a serious girl. When we talked cynically about our own work she simply thought less of it and of us; if we treated Roger in the same way, she resented it as bad manners. It was greatly to Roger's credit that he had spotted this idiosyncrasy of hers at once and played his game accordingly. Hence the undergraduate costume and the talk about the Art of the Transition. Lucy had not abandoned her young cousins without grave thought. She perfectly understood that, for them, happiness of a particular kind depended on her continued support; but she also thought it a great wrong that a man of Roger's genius should waste his talents on film scenarios and advertisements. Roger convinced her that a succession of London seasons and marriage to a well-born chartered accountant were not really the highest possible good. Moreover, she was in love with Roger.

'So the poor fellow has had to become a highbrow again,'

said Basil. 'Back exactly where he started in the New College Essay Society.'

'She doesn't sound too keen on this play of his.'

'She isn't. She's a critical girl. That's going to be Roger's headache.'

This was Basil's version of the marriage and it was substantially accurate. It omits, however, as any narrative of Basil's was bound to, the consideration that Roger was, in his way, in love with Lucy. Her fortune was a secondary attraction; he lacked the Mediterranean mentality that can regard marriage as an honourable profession, perhaps because he lacked Mediterranean respect for the permanence of the arrangement. At the time when he met Lucy he was earning an ample income without undue exertion; money alone would not have been worth the pains he had taken for her; the artistic clothes and the intellectual talk were measures of the respect in which he held Lucy. Her fifty-eight thousand in trustee stock was, no doubt, what made him push his suit to the extreme of marriage, but the prime motive and zest of the campaign was Lucy herself.

To write of someone loved, of oneself loving, above all of oneself being loved – how can these things be done with propriety? How can they be done at all? I have treated of love in my published work; I have used it – with avarice, envy, revenge – as one of the compelling motives of conduct. I have written it up as something prolonged and passionate and tragic; I have written it down as a modest but sufficient annuity with which to reward the just; I have spoken of it continually as a game of profit and loss. How does any of this avail for the simple task of describing, so that others may see her, the woman one loves? How can others see her except through one's own eyes, and how, so seeing her, can they turn the pages and close the book and live on as they have lived before, without becoming themselves the author and themselves the lover? The catalogues of excellencies of the Renaissance poets, those competitive advertisements, each man outdoing the next in metaphor, that great blurb – like a

149

publisher's list in the Sunday newspapers – the Song of Solomon, how do these accord with the voice of love – love that delights in weakness, seeks out and fills the empty places and completes itself in its work of completion; how can one transcribe those accents? Love, which has its own life, its hours of sleep and waking, its health and sickness, growth, death and immortality, its ignorance and knowledge, experiment and mastery – how can one relate this hooded stranger to the men and women with whom he keeps pace? It is a problem beyond the proper scope of letters.

I first met Lucy after I had been some weeks in London; I had seen Roger several times; he always said, 'You must come and meet Lucy,' but nothing came of these vague proposals until finally, full of curiosity, I went with Basil uninvited.

I met him in the London Library, late one afternoon.

'Are you going to the young Simmondses?' he said.

'Not so far as I know.'

'They've a party today.'

'Roger never said anything to me about it.'

'He told me to tell everyone. I'm just on my way there now. Why don't you come along?'

So we took a taxi to Victoria Square, for which I paid.

As it turned out, Roger and Lucy were not expecting anyone. He went to work now, in the afternoons, with a committee for the relief of Spanish refugees; he had only just come in and was in his bath. Lucy was listening to the six o'clock news on the wireless. She said, 'D'you mind if I keep it on for a minute? There may be something about the dock strike in Madras. Roger will be down in a minute.'

She did not say anything about a drink, so Basil said, 'May I go and look for the whisky?'

'Yes, of course. How stupid of me. I always forget. There's probably some in the dining-room.'

He went out and I stayed with Lucy in her hired drawing-room. She sat quite still listening to the announcer's voice. She was five months gone with child – 'Even Roger has to admit that it's proletarian action,' she said later – but as yet scarcely showed it in body; but she was pale, paler, I guessed, than normal, and she wore that incurious, self-regarding expression which sometimes goes with a first pregnancy. Above the sound of the wireless I heard Basil outside, calling upstairs, 'Roger. Where do you keep the corkscrew?' When they got back to the stock prices, Lucy switched off. 'Nothing from Madras,' she said. 'But perhaps you aren't interested in politics.'

'Not much,' I said.

'Very few of Roger's friends seem to be.'

'It's rather a new thing with him,' I said.

'I expect he doesn't talk about it unless he thinks people are interested.'

That was outrageous, first because it amounted to the claim to know Roger better than I did and, secondly, because I was still smarting with the ruthless boredom of my last two or three meetings with him.

'You'd be doing us all a great service if you could keep him to that,' I said.

It is a most painful experience to find, when one has been rude, that one has caused no surprise. That is how Lucy received my remark. She merely said, 'We've got to go out almost at once. We're going to the theatre in Finsbury and it starts at seven.'

'Very inconvenient.'

'It suits the workers,' she said. 'They have to get up earlier than we do, you see.'

Then Roger and Basil came in with the drinks. Roger said, 'We're just going out. They're doing the Tractor Trilogy at Finsbury. Why don't you come too? We could probably get another seat, couldn't we, Lucy?'

'I doubt it,' said Lucy. 'They're tremendously booked up.'

'I don't think I will,' I said.

'Anyway, join us afterwards at the Café Royal.'

'I might,' I said.

'What have you and Lucy been talking about?'

'We listened to the news,' said Lucy. 'Nothing from Madras.'

'They've probably got orders to shut down on it. I.D.C. have got the B.B.C. in their pocket.'

'I.D.C.?' I asked.

'Imperial Defence College. They're the new hush-hush crypto-fascist department. They're in up to the neck with I.C.I. and the oil companies.'

'I.C.I.?'

'Imperial Chemicals.'

'Roger,' said Lucy, 'we really must go if we're to get anything to eat.'

'All right,' he said. 'See you later at the Café.'

I waited for Lucy to say something encouraging. She said. 'We shall be there by eleven,' and began looking for her bag among the chintz cushions.

I said, 'I doubt if I can manage it.'

'Are we taking the car?' Roger asked.

'No, I sent it away. I've had him out all day.'

'I'll order some taxis.'

'We could drop Basil and John somewhere,' said Lucy.

'No,' I said, 'get two.'

'We're going by way of Appenrodts,' said Lucy.

'No good for me,' I said, although, in fact, they would pass the corner of St James's, where I was bound.

'I'll come and watch you eat your sandwiches,' said Basil.

That was the end of our first meeting. I came away feeling badly about it, particularly the way in which she had used my Christian name and acquiesced in my joining them later. A commonplace girl who wanted to be snubbing would have been conspicuously aloof and have said 'Mr Plant', and I should have recovered some of the lost ground. But Lucy was faultless.

I have seen so many young wives go wrong on this point. They have either tried to force an intimacy with their husband's friends, claiming, as it were, continuity and identity with the powers of the invaded territory, or they have cancelled the passports of the old régime and proclaimed that fresh application must be made to the new authorities and applicants be treated strictly on their merits. Lucy seemed serenely unaware of either danger. I had come inopportunely and been rather rude, but I was one of Roger's friends; they were like his family to her, or hers to him; we had manifest defects which it was none of her business to reform; we had the right to come to her house unexpectedly, to shout upstairs for the corkscrew, to join her table at supper. The question of intrusion did not arise. It was simply that as far as she was concerned we had no separate or individual existence. It was, as I say, a faultless and highly provocative attitude. I found that in the next few days a surprising amount of my time, which, anyway, was lying heavy on me, was occupied on considering how this attitude, with regard to myself, could be altered.

My first move was to ask her and Roger to luncheon. I was confident that none of their other friends — none of those, that is to say, from whom I wished to dissociate myself — would have done such a thing. I did it formally, some days ahead, by letter to Lucy. All this, I knew, would come as a surprise to Roger. He telephoned me to ask, 'What's all this Lucy tells me about you asking us to luncheon?'

'Can you come?'

'Yes, I suppose so. But what's it all about?'

'It's not "about" anything. I just want you to lunch with me.'

'Why?'

'It's quite usual, you know, when one's friends marry. Just politeness.'

'You haven't got some ghastly foreigners you stayed with abroad?'

'No, nothing like that.'

'Well, it all seems very odd to me. Writing a letter, I mean, and everything. . .'

I rang off.

Lucy answered with a formal acceptance. I studied her writing; she wrote like a man.

153

Dear John,

Roger and I shall be delighted to lunch with you at the Ritz on Thursday week at 1.30.

Yours sincerely,
Lucy Simmonds.

Should it not have been 'Yours ever' after the 'Dear John'? I wondered whether she had wondered what to put. Another girl might have written 'Yours' with a non-committal squiggle, but her writing did not lend itself to that kind of evasion. I had ended my note, 'Love to Roger.'

Was she not a little over-formal in repeating the place and time? Had she written straight off, without thinking, or had she sucked the top of her pen a little?

The paper was presumably the choice of their landlord, in unobtrusive good taste. I smelled it and thought I detected a whiff of soap.

At this point I lost patience with myself; it was ludicrous to sit brooding over a note of this kind. I began, instead, to wonder whom I should ask to meet her – certainly none of the gang she had learned to look on as 'Roger's friends'. On the other hand, it must be clear that the party was for her. Roger would be the first to impute that they were being made use of. In the end, after due thought and one or two failures, I secured a middle-aged, highly reputable woman-novelist and Andrew Desert and his wife – an eminently sociable couple. When Roger saw his fellow guests he was more puzzled than ever. I could see him all through luncheon trying to work it out, why I should have spent five pounds in this peculiar fashion.

I enjoyed my party. Lucy began by talking about my father's painting.

'Yes,' I said, 'it's very fashionable at the moment.'

'Oh, I don't mean that,' she said in frank surprise and went on to tell me how she had stopped before a shop window in Duke Street where a battle picture of my father's was on view; there had been two private soldiers construing it together, point by point. 'I think that's worth a dozen columns of praise in the weekly papers,' she said.

154

'Just like Kipling's *Light That Failed*,' said the woman-novelist.

'Is it? I didn't know.' She told us she had never read any Kipling.

'That shows the ten years between us,' I said, and so the conversation became a little more personal as we discussed the differences between those who were born before the First World War and those born after it; in fact, so far as it could be worked, the differences between Lucy and myself.

Roger always showed signs of persecution-mania in the Ritz. He did not like it when we knew people at other tables whom he didn't know and, when the waiter brought him the wrong dish, he began on a set-piece which I had heard him use before in this same place. 'Fashionable restaurants are the same all over the world,' he said. 'There are always exactly twenty per cent more tables than the waiters can manage. It's a very good thing for the workers' cause that no one except the rich know the deficiencies of the luxury world. Think of the idea Hollywood gives of a place like this,' he said, warming to his subject. 'A *maître d'hôtel* like an ambassador, bowing famous beauties across acres of unencumbered carpet – and look at poor Lorenzo there, sweating under his collar, jostling a way through for dowdy Middle West Americans . . .' But it was not a success. Lucy, I could see, thought it odd of him to complain when he was a guest. I pointed out that the couple Roger condemned as Middle West Americans were in fact called Lord and Lady Settringham, and Andrew led the conversation, where Roger could not follow it, to the topic of which ambassadors looked like *maîtres d'hôtel*. The woman-novelist began a eulogy of the Middle West which she knew and Roger did not. So he was left with his theme un-developed. All this was worth five pounds to me, and more.

I thought it typical of the way Lucy had been brought up that she returned my invitation in a day or two.

Roger got in first on the telephone. 'I say, are you free on Wednesday evening?'

'I'm not sure. Why?'

'I wondered if you'd dine with us.'

'Not at half-past six for the Finsbury Theatre?'

'No. I work late these days at the Relief Committee.'

'What time then?'

'Oh, any time after eight. Dress or not, just as you feel like it.'

'What will you and Lucy be doing?'

'Well, I suppose we shall dress. In case anyone wants to go on anywhere.'

'In fact, it's a dinner party?'

'Well, yes, in a kind of way.'

It was plain that poor Roger was dismayed at this social mushroom which had sprung up under his nose. As a face-saver the telephone call was misconceived, for a little note from Lucy was already in the post for me. It was not for me to mock these little notes; I had begun it. But an end had to be made to them, so I decided to answer this by telephone, choosing the early afternoon when I assumed Roger would be out. He was in, and answered me. 'I wanted to speak to Lucy.'

'Yes?'

'Just to accept her invitation to dinner.'

'But you've already accepted.'

'Yes, but I thought I'd better just tell her.'

'I told her. What d'you think?'

'Ah, good, I was afraid you might have forgotten.'

I had come badly out of that.

From first to last the whole episode of the dinner was calamitous. It was a party of ten, and one glance round the room showed me that this was an occasion of what Lucy had been brought up to call 'duty'. That is to say, we were all people whom for one reason or another she had felt obliged to ask. She was offering us all up together in a single propitiatory holocaust to the gods of the schoolroom. Even Mr Benwell was there. He did not realize that Lucy had taken the house furnished, and was congratulating her upon the decorations; 'I like a London house to look like a London house,' he was saying.

Roger was carrying things off rather splendidly with a kind

of sardonic gusto which he could often assume in times of stress. I knew him in that mood and respected it. I knew, too, that my presence added a particular zest to his performance. Throughout the evening I caught him in constant inquiry of me: was I attending to this parody of himself? I was his audience, not Lucy.

The fate in store for myself was manifest as soon as I came into the room. It was Lucy's cousin Julia, the younger of the two girls Basil had told me of, the one whose début had been so disturbed by Lucy's marriage. It would not, I felt, be a grave setback. Julia had that particular kind of succulent charm – bright, dotty, soft, eager, acquiescent, flattering, impudent – that is specially, it seems, produced for the delight of Anglo-Saxon manhood. She had no need of a London season to find a happy future. 'Julia is staying with us. She is a great fan of yours,' said Lucy in her Pont Street manner; a manner which, like Roger's but much more subtly, had an element of dumb crambo in it. What she said turned out to be true.

'My word, this *is* exciting,' said Julia, and settled down to enjoy me as though I were a box of chocolates open on her knees.

'What a lot of people Lucy's got here tonight.'

'Yes, it's her first real dinner party, and she says it will be her last. She says she doesn't like parties any more.'

'Did she ever?' I was ready to talk about Lucy at length, but this was not Julia's plan.

'Everyone does at first,' she said briefly, and then began the conversation as she had rehearsed it, I am sure, in her bath. 'I knew you the moment you came into the room. Guess how.'

'You heard my name announced.'

'Oh, no. Guess again.'

An American hero would have said, 'For Christ's sake,' but I said, 'Really, I've no idea, unless perhaps you knew everyone else already.'

'Oh, no. Shall I tell you? I saw you in the Ritz the day Lucy lunched with you.'

'Why didn't you come and talk to us?'

'Lucy wouldn't let me. She said she'd ask you to dinner instead.'

'Ah.'

'You see, for years and years the one thing in the world I've wanted most – or nearly most – was to meet you, and when Lucy calmly said she was going to lunch with you I cried with envy – literally, so I had to put a cold sponge on my eyes before going out.'

Talking to this delicious girl about Lucy, I thought, was like sitting in the dentist's chair with one's mouth full of instruments and the certainty that, all in good time, he would begin to hurt.

'Did she talk about it much before she came to lunch?'

'Oh no, she just said "I'm afraid I've got to leave you today as Roger wants me to lunch with one of his old friends." So I said, "How rotten, who?" and she said, "John Plant," just like that, and I said, "*John Plant*," and she said, "Oh, I forgot you were keen on thrillers." *Thrillers*, as though you were just anybody. And I said, "Couldn't I possibly come?" and she said, "Not possibly," and then when I was crying she said I might come with her to the lounge and sit behind a pillar and see you come in.'

'How did she describe me?'

'She just said you'd be the one who paid for the cocktails. Isn't that just like Lucy, or don't you know her well enough to tell?'

'What did she say about the lunch afterwards?'

'She said everyone talked about Kipling.'

'Was that all?'

'And she thought Roger had behaved badly because he doesn't like smart restaurants, and she said neither did she, but it had cost you a lot of money, so it was nasty to complain. Of course, I wanted to hear all about *you* and what *you* said, and she couldn't remember anything. She just said you seemed very clever.'

'Oh, she said that.'

'She says that about all Roger's friends. But, anyway,

it's my turn now. I've got you to myself for the evening.'

She had. We were sitting at dinner now. Lucy was still talking to Mr Benwell. On my other side there was some kind of relative of Roger's. She talked to me for a bit about how Roger had settled down since marriage. 'I don't take those political opinions of his seriously,' she said, 'and, anyway, it's all right to be a communist nowadays. Everyone is.'

'I'm not,' I said.

'Well, I mean all the clever young people.'

So I turned back to Julia. She was waiting for me.

'D'you know you once wrote me a letter?'

'Good gracious. Why?'

'Dear Madam, – Thank you for your letter. If you will read the passage in question more attentively you will note that the down train was four minutes late at Frasham. There was thus ample time for the disposal of the bicycle bell. Yours faithfully, John Plant,' she quoted.

'Did I write that?'

'Don't you remember?'

'Vaguely. It was about *The Frightened Footman*, wasn't it?'

'Mm. Of course I knew perfectly well about the train. I just wrote in the hope of getting an answer, and it worked. I liked you for being so severe. There was another girl at school who was literary, too, and she had a crush on Gilbert Warwick. *He* wrote *her* three pages beginning, My Dear Anthea, all about his house and the tithe barn he's turned into his work-room, and ending, Write to me again; I hope you like Sylvia as much as Heather – those were two of his heroines – and she thought it showed what a better writer he was than you, but I knew just the opposite. And later Anthea did write again, and she had another long letter just like the first all about his tithe barn, and that made her very cynical. So I wrote to you again to show how different you were.'

'Did I answer?'

'No. So then all the Literary Club took to admiring you instead of Gilbert Warwick.'

'Because I didn't answer letters?'

159

'Yes. You see, it showed you were a real artist and didn't care a bit for your public, and just lived for your work.'

'I see.'

After dinner Roger said, 'Has little Julia been boring you frightfully?'

'Yes.'

'I thought she was. She's very pretty. It's a great evening for her.'

Eventually we returned to the drawing-room and sat about. Roger did not know how to manage this stage of his party. He talked vaguely of going on somewhere to dance and of playing a new parlour game that had lately arrived from New York. No one encouraged him. I did not speak to Lucy until I came to say good-bye, which was very early, as soon as the first guest moved and everyone, on the instant, rose too. When I said good-bye to her, Julia said, 'Please, I must tell you. You're a thousand times grander than I ever imagined. It was half a game before – now it's serious.'

I could imagine the relief in the house as the last of us left, Roger and Lucy emerging into one another's arms as though from shelter after a storm . . . 'So that's over. Was it as bad as you expected?' 'Worse, worse. You were splendid.' . . . perhaps they – and Julia, too? – were cutting a caper on the drawing-room carpet in an ecstasy of liberation.

'That,' I said to myself, 'is what you have bought with your five pounds.'

That evening, next day and for several days, I disliked Lucy. I made a story for all who knew him, of Roger's dinner party, leaving the impression that this was the kind of life Lucy enjoyed and that she was driving Roger into it. But for all that I did not abate my resolve to force my friendship upon her. I sought recognition. I wanted to assert the simple fact of my separate and individual existence. I could not by any effort of will regard her as being, like Trixie, 'one of Roger's girls', and I demanded reciprocation; I would not be regarded as, like Basil, 'one of Roger's friends'; still less, like Mr Benwell, as someone who had to be asked to dinner every

now and then. I had little else to think about at the time, and
the thing became an itch with me. I felt about her, I suppose,
as old men feel who are impelled by habit to touch every
third lamp-post on their walks; occasionally something happens to distract them, they see a friend or a street accident
and they pass a lamp-post by; then all day they fret and fidget
until, after tea, they set out shamefacedly to put the matter
right. That was how I felt about Lucy; our relationship
constituted a tiny disorder in my life that had to be adjusted.

That at least is how, in those earliest days, I explained my
obsession to myself, but looking at it now, down the mirrored
corridor of cumulative emotion, I see no beginning to the
perspective. There is in the apprehension of woman's beauty
an exquisite, early intimation of loveliness when, seeing
some face, strange or familiar, one gains, suddenly, a further
glimpse and foresees, out of a thousand possible futures, how
it might be transfigured by love. With Lucy – her grace daily
more encumbered by her pregnancy; deprived of sex, as
women are, by its fulfilment – the vision was extended and
clarified until, with no perceptible transition, it became the
reality. But I cannot say when it first appeared. Perhaps, that
evening when she said, about the *Composed Hermitage in the
Chinese Taste*, 'I can't think why John should want to have a
house like that,' but it came without surprise; I had sensed it
on its way, as an animal, still in profound darkness and
surrounded by all the sounds of night, will lift its head, sniff,
and know, inwardly, that dawn is near. Meanwhile, I moved
for advantage as in a parlour game.

Julia brought me success. Our meeting, so far from disil-
lusioning her, made her cult of me keener and more direct. It
was no fault of mine, I assured Roger, when he came to
grumble about it; I had not been in the least agreeable to her;
indeed, towards the end of the evening I had been openly
savage.

'The girl's a masochist,' he said, adding with deeper gloom,
'and Lucy says she's a virgin.'

'There's plenty of time for her. The two troubles are often
cured simultaneously.'

'That's all very well, but she's staying another ten days. She never stops talking about you.'

'Does Lucy mind?'

'Of course she minds. It's driving us both nuts. Does she write you a lot of letters?'

'Yes.'

'What does she say?'

'I don't read them. I feel as though they were meant for somebody else. Besides, they're in pencil.'

'I expect she writes them in bed. No one's ever gone for me like that.'

'Nor for me,' I said. 'It's not really at all disagreeable.'

'I daresay not,' said Roger. 'I thought only actors and sex-novelists and clergymen came in for it.'

'No, no, anybody may – scientists, politicians, professional cyclists – anyone whose name gets into the papers. It's just that young girls are naturally religious.'

'Julia's eighteen.'

'She'll get over it soon. She's been stirred up by suddenly meeting me in the flesh after two or three years' distant devotion. She's a nice child.'

'That's all very well,' said Roger, returning sulkily to his original point. 'It isn't Julia I'm worried about, it's ourselves, Lucy and me – she's staying another ten days. Lucy says you've got to be nice about it, and come out this evening, the four of us. I'm sorry, but there it is.'

So for a week I went often to Victoria Square, and there was the beginning of a half-secret joke between Lucy and me in Julia's devotion. While I was there Julia sat smug and gay, she was a child of enchanting prettiness. When I was absent, Roger told me, she moped a good deal and spent much time in her bedroom writing and destroying letters to me. She talked about herself, mostly, and her sister and family. Her father was a major and they lived at Aldershot; they would have to stay there all the year round now that Lucy no longer needed their company in London. She did not like Roger. 'He's not very nice about you,' she said.

'Roger and I are like that,' I explained. 'We're always foul about each other. It's our fun. Is Lucy nice about me?'

'Lucy's an angel,' said Julia, 'that's why we hate Roger so.'

Finally there was the evening of Julia's last party. Eight of us went to dance at a restaurant. Julia was at first very gay, but her spirits dropped towards the end of the evening. I was living in Ebury Street; it was easy for me to walk home from Victoria Square, so I went back with them and had a last drink. 'Lucy's promised to leave us alone, just for a minute, to say good-bye,' Julia whispered.

When we were alone, she said, 'It's been absolutely wonderful the last two weeks. I didn't know it was possible to be so happy. I wish you'd give me something as a kind of souvenir.'

'Of course. I'll send you one of my books, shall I?'

'No,' she said, 'I'm not interested in your books any more. At least, of course, I am, terribly, but I mean it's *you* I love.'

'Nonsense,' I said.

'Will you kiss me, once, just to say good-bye.'

I kissed her paternally on the cheek.

Then she said suddenly, 'You're in love with Lucy, aren't you?'

'Good heavens, no. What on earth put that into your head?'

'I can tell. Through loving you so much, I expect. You may not know it, but you are. And it's no good. She loves that horrid Roger. Oh, dear, they're coming back. I'll come and say good-bye to you tomorrow, may I?'

'No.'

'*Please*. This hasn't been how I planned it at all.'

Then Roger and Lucy came into the room with a sly look as though they had been discussing what was going on and how long they should give us. So I shook hands with Julia and went home.

She came to my rooms at ten next morning. Mrs Legge, the landlady, showed her up. She stood in the door, swinging a small parcel. 'I've got five minutes,' she said, 'the taxi's waiting. I told Lucy I had some last-minute shopping.'

'You know you oughtn't to do this sort of thing.'

'I've been here before. When I knew you were out. I pretended I was your sister and had come to fetch something for you.'

'Mrs Legge never said anything to me about it.'

'No. I asked her not to. In fact, I gave her ten shillings. You see, she caught me at it.'

'At what?'

'Well, it sounds rather silly. I was in your bedroom, kissing things – you know, pillows, pyjamas, hair brushes. I'd just got to the washstand and was kissing your razor when I looked up and found Mrs Whatever-she's-called standing in the door.'

'Good God, I shall never be able to look her in the face again.'

'Oh, she was quite sympathetic. I suppose I must have looked funny, like a goose grazing.' She gave a little, rather hysterical giggle, and added, 'Oh, John, I do love you so.'

'Nonsense. I shall turn you out if you talk like that.'

'Well, I do. And I've got you a present.' She gave me the square parcel. 'Open it.'

'I shan't accept it,' I said, unwrapping a box of cigars.

'But you must. You see, they'd be no good to me, would they? Are they good ones?'

'Yes,' I said, looking at the box. 'Very good ones indeed.'

'The best.'

'Quite the best, but . . .'

'That's what the man in the shop said. Smoke one now.'

'Julia, dear, I couldn't. I've only just finished breakfast.'

She saw the point of that. 'When will you smoke the first one? After luncheon? I'd like to think of you smoking the first one.'

'Julia, dear, it's perfectly sweet of you, but I can't honestly . . .'

'I know what you're thinking, that I can't afford it. Well, that's all right. You see, Lucy gave me five pounds yesterday to buy a hat. I thought she would – she often does. But I had to wait and be sure. I'd got them ready, hidden yesterday evening. I meant to give you them then. But I never got a proper chance. So here they are.' And then, as I hesitated, with rising voice, 'Don't you see I'd much rather give you cigars than have a new hat? Don't you see I shall go back to Aldershot absolutely miserable, the whole time in London quite spoilt, if you won't take them?'

She had clearly been crying that morning and was near tears again.

'Of course I'll take them,' I said. 'I think it's perfectly sweet of you.'

Her face cleared in sudden, infectious joy.

'There. Now we can say good-bye.'

She stood waiting for me, not petitioning this time, but claiming her right. I put my hands on her shoulders and gave her a single, warm kiss on the lips. She shut her eyes and sighed. 'Thank you,' she said in a small voice, and hurried out to her waiting taxi, leaving the box of cigars on my table.

Sweet Julia! I thought. It was a supremely unselfish present; something quite impersonal and unsentimental – no keepsake – something which would be gone, literally in smoke, in less than six weeks; a thing she had not even the fun of choosing for herself; she had gone to the counter and left it to the shopman – 'I want a box of the best cigars you keep, please – as many as I can get for five pounds.' She just wanted something which she could be sure would give pleasure.

And chiefly because she thought I had been kind to her cousin, Lucy took me into her friendship.

Roger's engraving showed a pavilion, still rigidly orthodox in plan, but, in elevation decked with ornament conceived in a wild ignorance of oriental forms; there were balconies and balustrades of geometric patterns; the cornices swerved upwards at the corners in the lines of a pagoda; the roof was crowned with an onion cupola which might have been Russian, bells hung from the capitals of barley-sugar columns; the windows were freely derived from the Alhambra; there was a minaret. To complete the atmosphere the engraver had added a little group of Turkish military performing the bastinado upon a curiously complacent malefactor, an Arabian camel and a mandarin carrying a bird in a cage.

'My word, what a gem,' they said. 'It is really all there?'

'The minaret's down and it's all rather overgrown.'

'What a chance. John must get it.'

'It will be fun to furnish. I know just the chairs for it.'

This was the first time I had been to Victoria Square since Julia left.

And Lucy said, 'I can't think why John should want to have a house like that.'

2

Lucy was a girl of few friends; she had, in fact, at the time I was admitted to their number, only two: a man named Peter Baverstock, in the Malay States, whom I never saw, and a Miss Muriel Meikeljohn, whom I saw all too often. Peter Baverstock had wanted to marry Lucy since she was seven, and proposed to her whenever he came home on leave, every eighteen months, until she married Roger, when he sent her a very elaborate wedding present, an immense thing in carved wood, ivory and gilt which caused much speculation with regard to its purpose; later he wrote and explained. I forget the explanation. I think it was the gift which, by local usage, men of high birth gave to their granddaughters when they were delivered of male twins; it was, anyway, connected with twins and grandparents, of great rarity, and a token of high esteem in the parts it came from. Lucy wrote long letters to Baverstock every fortnight. I often watched her at work on those letters, sitting square to her table, head bowed, hand travelling evenly across the page, as, I remembered reading in some book of memoirs, Sir Walter Scott's had been seen at a lighted window, writing the Waverley novels. It was a tradition of her upbringing that letters for the East must always be written on very thin, lined paper. 'I'm just telling Peter about your house,' she would say.

'How can that possibly interest him?'

'Oh, he's interested in everything. He's so far away.'

It seemed an odd reason.

Miss Meikeljohn was a pale, possessive girl, who had been a fellow boarder with Lucy in the house of a distressed gentlewoman in Vienna where they had both been sent to learn singing. They had shared a passion for a leading tenor, and had once got into his dressing-room at the Opera House by wearing mackintoshes and pretending to be reporters sent to interview him. Lucy still kept a photograph of this tenor, in costume, on her dressing-table, but she had shed her musical aspirations with the rest of her Pont Street life. Miss Meikeljohn still sang, once a week, to a tutor. It was after these lessons that she came to luncheon with Lucy, and the afternoon was hers by prescriptive right for shopping, or for a cinema, or for what she liked best, a 'good talk'. These Tuesdays were 'Muriel's days', and no one might interfere with them.

'They are the only times she comes into London. Her parents are separated and terribly poor,' Lucy said, as though in complete explanation.

When they went to the cinema or play together they went in the cheap seats because Miss Meikeljohn insisted on paying her share. Lucy thought this evidence of Miss Meikeljohn's integrity of character; she often came back from these entertainments with a headache from having had to sit so close to the screen.

The friendship was odd in many ways, notably because Miss Meikeljohn luxuriated in heart-to-heart confidences – in what my father's generation coarsely called 'taking down her back hair', an exhibition that was abhorrent to Lucy, who in friendship had all the modesty of the naked savage.

I must accept the modesty of the naked savage on trust, on the authority of numerous travel books. The savages I have met on my travels have all been formidably overdressed. But if there existed nowhere else on the globe that lithe, chaste and unstudied nudity of which I have so often read, it was there, dazzlingly, in the mind of Lucy. There were no reservations in her friendship, and it was an experience for which I was little qualified, to be admitted, as it were, through a door in the wall to wander at will over that rich estate. The idea of an occasional opening to the public in aid of the cottage hospital, of extra gardeners working a week beforehand to tidy the walks, of an upper housemaid to act as guide, of red cord looped across the arms of the chairs, of special objects of value to be noted, of 'that door leads to the family's private apartments. They are never shown', of vigilance at the hot-house for fear of a nectarine being pocketed, of 'now you have seen *everything*: please make way for the next party', and of the open palm – of all, in fact, which constituted Miss Meikeljohn's, and most people's, habit of intimacy, was inconceivable to Lucy.

When I began to realize the spaces and treasures of which I had been made free, I was like a slum child alternately afraid to touch or impudently curious. Or, rather, I felt too old. Years earlier when Lucy was in her cradle, I had known this kind of friendship. There was a boy at my private school with whom I enjoyed a week of unrestrained confidence; one afternoon, sitting with him in a kind of nest, itself a secret, which we had devised for ourselves from a gym mat and piled benches in a corner of the place where we played on wet afternoons, I revealed my greatest secret, that my father was an artist and not, as I had given it out, an officer in the Navy; by tea-time the story was all over the school, that Plant's pater had long hair and did not wash. (Revenge came sooner than I could have hoped, for this was the summer term, 1914, and my betrayer had an aunt married to an Austrian nobleman; he had boasted at length of staying in their castle; when school reassembled in September I was at the head of the mob which hounded him in tears to the matron's room with cries of 'German spy'.) It was the first and, to my mind, most dramatic of the normal betrayals of adolescence. With the years I had grown cautious. There was little love and no trust at all between any of my friends. Moreover, we were bored; each knew the other so well that it was only by making our relationship into a kind of competitive parlour game that we kept it alive at all. We had all from time to time cut out divergent trails and camped in new ground, but we always, as it were, returned to the same base for supplies, and swapped yarns of our exploration. That was what I meant by friendship at the age of thirty-four, and Lucy, finding herself without preparation among people like myself, had been disconcerted. That was the origin of what, at first, I took for priggishness in her. Her lack of shyness cut her off from us. She could not cope with the attack and defence, deception and exposure, which was our habitual intercourse. Anything less than absolute intimacy embarrassed her, so she fell back upon her good upbringing, that armoury of schoolroom virtues and graces with which she had been equipped, and lived, as best she could, independently, rather as, it is said, Chinese gentlemen of the old school can pursue interminable, courteous, traditionally prescribed conversations with their minds abstracted in realms of distant beauty.

But it was not enough. She was lonely. In particular she was cut off by her pregnancy from Roger. For a term of months she was unsexed, the roots of her love for Roger wintering, out of sight in the ground, without leaf. So she looked for a friend and, because she thought I had been kind to Julia, and because, in a way, I had responded to her in her schoolroom mood, she chose me. I had not misinterpreted her change of manner. She had made up her mind that I was to be a friend. I began, almost at once, to spend the greater part of the day in her company, and as my pre-occupation at the time was in finding a house that quest became the structure of our friendship. Together we went over the sheaves of house agents' notices, and several times we went on long expeditions together to look at houses in the country. We talked of everything except the single topic of politics. The attraction of Socialism for Lucy was double. It was a part of the break she had made with Aldershot and Pont Street, and it relieved her of the responsibility she felt for her own private fortune. Money, her money, was of great importance to her. If she had lived among the rich it would have been different; she would then have thought it normal to be

assured, for life, of the possessions for which others toiled;
she would, indeed, have thought herself rather meagrely
provided. But she had been brought up among people poorer
than herself to regard herself as somebody quite singular.
When the age came of her going to dances, her aunt had
impressed on her the danger she ran of fortune-hunters and,
indeed, nearly all the young men with whom she consorted,
and their mothers, regarded £58,000 as a notable prize.
'Sometimes by the way that girl talks,' Basil had said, 'you'd
think she was the Woolworth heiress.' It was quite true. She
did think herself extremely rich and responsible. One of the
advantages to her of marrying Roger was the belief that her
money was being put to good use in rescuing a literary genius
from wage-slavery. She was much more afraid of misusing
her money than of losing it. Thus when she was convinced
that all private fortunes like her own were very shortly to be
abolished and all undeserved prominence levelled, she was
delighted. Moreover, her conversion had coincided with her
falling in love. She and Roger had been to meetings together,
and together read epitomes of Marxist philosophy. Her faith,
like a Christian's, was essential to her marriage, so, knowing
that I was hostile, she sequestered it from me.

It was convenient for Roger to have me in attendance. He
was not domestic by nature. He did not, as some husbands
do, resent his wife's pregnancy. It was as though he had
bought a hunter at the end of the season and turned him out;
discerning friends, he knew, would appreciate the fine lines
under the rough coat, but he would sooner have shown
something glossy in the stable. He had summer business to
do, moreover; the horse must wait till the late autumn. That,
at least, was one way in which he saw the situation, but the
analogy was incomplete. It was rather *he* that had been
acquired and put to grass, and he was conscious of that
aspect, too. Roger was hobbled and prevented from taking
the full stride required of him, by the habit, long settled, of
regarding sex relationships in terms of ownership and use.
Confronted with the new fact of pregnancy, of joint ownership, his terms failed him. As a result he was restless and no

longer master of the situation; the practical business of getting
through the day was becoming onerous, so that my adhesion
was agreeable to him. Grossly, it confirmed his opinion of
Lucy's value and at the same time took her off his hands.
Then one morning, when I made my now habitual call at
Victoria Square, Lucy, not yet up but lying in bed in a chaos
of newspapers, letters and manicure tools, greeted me by
saying, 'Roger's writing.'

Couched as she was, amid quilted bed-jacket and tumbled
sheets – one arm bare to the elbow where the wide sleeve fell
back and showed the tender places of wrist and forearm, the
other lost in the warm depths of the bed, with her pale skin
taking colour against the dead white linen, and her smile of
confident, morning welcome; as I had greeted her countless
times and always with a keener joy, until that morning I
seemed to have come to the end of an investigation and held
as a certainty what before I had roughly surmised – her
beauty rang through the room like a peal of bells; thus I have
stood, stunned, in a Somerset garden, with the close turf wet
and glittering underfoot in the dew, when, from beyond the
walls of box, the grey church tower had suddenly scattered
the heavens in tumult.

'Poor fellow,' I said. 'What about?'

'It's my fault,' she said, 'a detective story,' and she went on
to explain that since I had talked to her about my books, she
had read them – 'You were perfectly right. They *are* works of
art. I had no idea' – and talked of them to Roger until he had
suddenly said, 'Oh, God, another Julia.' Then he had told her
that for many years he had kept a plot in his mind, waiting
for a suitable time to put it into writing.

'He'll do it very well,' I said. 'Roger can write anything.'

'Yes.'

But while she was telling me this and I was answering, I
thought only of Lucy's new beauty. I knew that beauty of that
kind did not come from a suitable light or a lucky way with
the hair or a sound eight hours' sleep, but from an inner
secret; and I knew this morning that the secret was the fact of
Roger's jealousy. So another stage was reached in my falling

171

in love with Lucy, while each week she grew heavier and slower and less apt for love, so that I accepted the joy of her companionship without reasoning. Lucy and I were like characters in the stock intrigue of Renaissance comedy, where the heroine follows the hero in male attire and is wooed by him, unknowing, in the terms of rough friendship.

In these weeks Lucy and I grew adept in construing the jargon of the estate agents. I had a clear idea of what I required. In the first place, it must not cost, all told, when the decorators and plumbers had moved out and the lawyers been paid for the conveyance, more than £3,000; it must be in agricultural country, preferably within five miles of an antiquated market town, it must be at least a hundred years old, and it must be a *house*, no matter how dingy, rather than a cottage, however luxurious; there must be a cellar, two staircases, high ceilings, a marble chimneypiece in the drawing-room, room to turn a car at the front door, a coach-house and stable yard, a walled kitchen garden, a paddock and one or two substantial trees – these seemed to me the minimum requisites of the standard of gentility at which I aimed, something between the squire's and the retired admiral's. Lucy had a womanly love of sunlight and a Marxist faith in the superior beauties of concrete and steel. She had, moreover, a horror, born of long association, of the rural bourgeois with whom I was determined to enrol myself. I was able to excuse my predilection to others by describing it as Gallic; French writers, I explained, owed their great strength, as had the writers of nineteenth-century England, to their middle-class status; the best of them all owned square white houses, saved their money, dined with the mayor and had their eyes closed for them at death by faithful, repellent house-keepers; English and American writers squandered their energy in being fashionable or bohemian or, worst of all, in an unhappy alternation between the two. This theme went down well with Mr Benwell, who, in the week or two after I expounded it to him, gave deathless offence to several of his authors by exhorting them to be middle-class, too, but it left Lucy unimpressed. She thought the object of my search grotesque, but followed in a cheerful and purely sporting spirit as one may hunt a fox which one has no taste to eat.

The last occasion of her leaving London before her confinement was to look at a house with me, below the Berkshire downs. It was too far to travel comfortably in a day, and we spent the night with relatives of hers near Abingdon. We had by now grown so accustomed to one another's company that there seemed nothing odd to us in Lucy proposing me as a guest. Our host and hostess, however, thought it most irregular, and their manifest surprise was a further bond between us. Lucy was by now eight months with child, and at the back of her relatives' concern was the fear that she might be delivered prematurely in their house. They treated her with a solicitude that all too clearly was a rebuke to my own easy-going acceptance of the situation. Try how I might to realize the dangers she ran, I could never feel protective towards Lucy. She looked, we agreed, like Tweedledum armed for battle, and I saw her at this time as preternaturally solid, with an armour of new life defending her from the world. Biologically, no doubt, this was a fallacy, but it was the attitude we jointly accepted, so that we made an immediate bad impression by being struck with *fou rire* in the first five minutes of our visit, when our hostess whispered that she had fitted up a bedroom for Lucy on the ground floor so that she should not be troubled by stairs.

The house we had come to see proved, like so many others, to be quite uninhabitable. Its owner, in fact, was living in his lodge. 'Too big for me these days,' he said of the house which, when he opened it to us, gave the impression of having been designed as a small villa and wantonly extended, as though no one had remembered to tell the workmen when to stop and they had gone on adding room to room like cells in a wasp-nest. 'I never had the money to spend on it,' the owner said gloomily; 'you could make something of it with a little money.'

We went upstairs and along a lightless passage. He had

been showing people over this house since 1902, he said, and with the years he had adopted a regular patter. 'Nice little room this, very warm in the winter . . . You get a good view of the downs here, if you stand in the corner . . . It's a dry house. You can see that. I've never had any trouble with damp . . . These used to be the nurseries. They'd make a nice suite of spare bedroom, dressing-room and bath if you didn't . . .' and at that point, remembering Lucy, he stopped abruptly and in such embarrassment that he scarcely spoke until we left him.

'I'll write to you,' I said.

'Yes,' he said with great gloom, knowing what I meant. 'I sometimes think the place might do as a school. It's very healthy.'

So we drove back to Lucy's relatives. They wanted her to dine in bed or, anyway, to go to her room and lie down until dinner. Instead she came out with me into the evening sunlight, and we sat in what Lucy's relatives called their 'blue garden', reconstructing a life story of the sad little man who had shown us his house. Lucy's relatives thought us and our presence there and our whole expedition extremely odd. There was something going on, they felt, which they did not understand, and Lucy and I, infected by the atmosphere, became, as it were, confederates in this house which she had known all her life; in the garden where, as a little girl, she had once, she told me, buried a dead starling, with tears.

After this expedition Lucy remained in London, spending more and more of her time indoors. When I finally found a house to suit me, I was alone.

'You might have waited,' said Lucy. It seemed quite natural that she should reproach me. She had a share in my house. 'Damn this baby,' she added.

3

In the last week before the birth of her child Lucy began for the first time to betray impatience; she was never, at any time, at all apprehensive – merely bored and weary and vexed past bearing by the nurse who had now taken up residence in the house. Roger and Miss Meikeljohn had made up their minds that she was going to die. 'It's all this damned pre-natal care,' said Roger. 'Do you realize that maternal mortality is higher in this country than it's ever been? D'you know there are cases of women going completely bald after childbirth? And permanently insane? It's worse among the rich than the poor, too.'

Miss Meikeljohn said: 'Lucy's being so wonderful. She doesn't *realize*.'

The nurse occupied herself with extravagant shopping lists. 'Does *everyone* have to have all these things?' Lucy asked, aghast at the multitude of medical and nursery supplies which began to pour into the house. 'Everyone who can afford them,' said Sister Kemp briskly, unconscious of irony. Roger found some comfort in generalizing. 'It's anthropologically very interesting,' he said, 'all this purely ceremonial accumulation of rubbish – like turtle doves brought to the gates of a temple. Everyone according to his means sacrificing to the racial god of hygiene.'

He showed remarkable forbearance to Sister Kemp, who brought with her an atmosphere of impending doom and accepted a cocktail every evening, saying, 'I'm not really on duty *yet*,' or 'No time for this *after the day*.'

She watched confidently for The Day, her apotheosis, when Lucy would have no need for Roger or me or Miss Meikeljohn, only for herself.

'I shall call you Mrs Simmonds until The Day,' she said. 'After that you will be my Lucy.' She sat about with us in the drawing-room, and in Lucy's bedroom where we spent most of the day, now; like an alien, sitting at a café; an alien anarchist, with a bomb beside him, watching the passing life of a foreign city, waiting for his signal from the higher powers, the password which might come at once or in a very few days, whispered in his ear, perhaps, by the waiter, or scrawled on the corner of his evening newspaper – the signal that the hour of liberation had come when he would take possession of all he beheld. 'The fathers need nearly as much care as the mothers,' said Sister Kemp. 'No, not another, thank you, Mr Simmonds. I've got to keep in readiness, you know. It would never do if baby came knocking at the door and found Sister unable to lift the latch.'

'No,' said Roger. 'No, I suppose it wouldn't.'

Sister Kemp belonged to a particularly select and highly paid corps of nurses. A baby wheeled out by her, as it would be daily for the first month, would have access to certain paths in the Park where inferior nurses trespassed at the risk of cold looks. Lucy's perambulator would thus be socially established, and the regular nurse, when she took over, would find her charge already well known and respected. Sister Kemp explained this, adding as a concession to Lucy's political opinions, 'The snobbery among nurses is terrible. I've seen many a girl go home from Stanhope Gate in tears.' And then, *esprit de corps* asserting itself, 'Of course, they ought to have known. There's always Kensington Gardens for *them*.'

Once Sister Kemp had attended a house in Seamore Place, in nodding distance of Royalty, but the gardens there, though supremely grand, had been, she said, 'dull', by which we understood that even for her there were close circles. Roger was delighted with this. 'It's like something out of Thackeray,' he said and pressed for further details, but Lucy was past taking relish in social survivals; she was concerned only with the single, physical fact of her own exhaustion. 'I hate this baby already,' she said. 'I'm going to hate it all my life.'

Roger worked hard at this time, in the mornings at his detective story, in the afternoons at his committee for Spanish aid. Miss Meikeljohn and I tried to keep Lucy amused with increasingly little success. Miss Meikeljohn took her to concerts and cinemas where, now, she allowed Lucy to buy the seats, as extreme comfort was clearly necessary for her. I took her to the Zoo, every morning at twelve o'clock. There was a sooty, devilish creature in the monkey house named Humboldt's Gibbon which we would watch morosely for half an hour at a time; he seemed to exercise some kind of hypnotic fascination over Lucy; she could not be got to other cages. 'If I have a boy I'll call him Humboldt,' she said. 'D'you know that before I was born, so Aunt Maureen says, my mother used to sit in front of a Flaxman bas-relief so as to give me ideal beauty. Poor mother, she died when I was born.' Lucy could say that without embarrassment because she felt no danger in her own future. 'I don't care how disagreeable it's going to be,' she said. 'I only want it soon.'

Because of my confidence in her, and my resentment of the proprietary qualms of Roger and Miss Meikeljohn, I accepted her attitude; and was correspondingly shocked when the actual day came.

Roger telephoned to me at breakfast time. 'The baby's begun.'

'Good,' I said.

'What d'you mean, good?'

'Well, it is good, isn't it? When did it start?'

'Last night, about an hour after you left.'

'It ought to be over soon.'

'I suppose so. Shall I come round?'

He came, yawning a great deal from having been up all night. 'I was with her for an hour or two. I always imagined people stayed in bed when they were having babies. Lucy's up, going about the house. It was horrible. Now she doesn't want me.'

'What happened exactly?'

He began to tell me and then I was sorry I had asked. 'That nurse seems very good,' he said at the end. 'The doctor didn't come until half an hour ago. He went away again right away. They haven't given her any chloroform yet. They say they are keeping that until the pains get worse. I don't see how they could be. You've no conception what it was like.' He stayed with me for half an hour and read my newspapers. Then he went home. 'I'll telephone you when there's any news,' he said.

Two hours later I rang up. 'No,' he said, 'there's no news. I said I'd telephone you if there was.'

'But what's happening?'

'I don't know. Some kind of lull.'

'But she's all right, isn't she? I mean they're not anxious.'

'I don't know. The doctor's coming again. I went in to see her, but she didn't say anything. She was just crying quietly.'

'Nothing I can do, is there?'

'No, how could there be?'

'I mean about lunch or anything. You don't feel like coming out?'

'No, I ought to stay around here.'

The thought of the lull, of Lucy not speaking, but lying there in tears, waiting for her labour to start again, pierced me as no tale could have done of cumulative pain; but beyond my sense of compassion I was not scared. I had been smoking a pipe; my mouth had gone dry, and when I knocked out the smouldering tobacco the smell of it sickened me. I went out into Ebury Street as though to the deck of a ship, breathing hard against nausea, and, from habit more than sentiment, took a cab to the Zoo.

The man at the turnstile knew me as a familiar figure. 'Your lady not with you today, sir?'

'No, not today.'

'I've got five myself,' he said.

I did not understand him and repeated foolishly, 'Five?'

'Being a married man,' he added.

Humboldt's Gibbon seemed disinclined for company. He sat hunched up at the back of his cage, fixing on me a steady and rather bilious stare. He was never, at the best of times, an animal who courted popularity. In the cage on his left lived a sycophantic, shrivelled, grey monkey from India who salaamed for titbits of food; on his right were a troupe of patchy buffoons who swung and tumbled about their cage to attract attention. Not so Humboldt's Gibbon; visitors passed him by – often with almost superstitious aversion and some such comment as 'Nasty things'; he had no tricks, or, if he had, he performed them alone, for his own satisfaction, after dark, ritualistically, when, in that exotic enclave among the stucco terraces, the prisoners awake and commemorate the jungles where they had their birth, as exiled darkies, when their work is done, will tread out the music of Africa in a vacant lot behind the drug-store.

Lucy used always to bring fruit to the ape; I had nothing, but, to deceive him, I rattled the wire and held out my empty fingers as though they held a gift. He unrolled himself, revealing an extraordinary length of black limb, and came delicately towards me on toes and finger-tips; his body was slightly pigeon-chested and his fur dense and short, his head spherical, without the poodle-snout of his neighbours – merely two eyes and a line of yellow teeth set in leather, like a bare patch worn in a rug. He was less like a man than any of his kind, and he lacked their human vulgarity. When, at short range, he realized that I held nothing for him he leapt suddenly at the bars and hung there, spread out to his full span, spiderish, snarling with contempt; then dropped to the floor and, turning about, walked delicately back to the corner from which I had lured him. So I looked at him and thought of Lucy, and the minutes passed.

Presently I was aware of someone passing behind me from the salaaming monkey to the troupe of tumblers, and back again, and at either side peering not at the animals but at me. I gazed fixedly at the ape, hoping that this nuisance would pass. Finally a voice said, 'I say.'

I turned and found Arthur Atwater. He was dressed as I had seen him before, in his raincoat, though it was a fine, warm day, and his soft grey hat, worn at what should have been a raffish angle but which, in effect, looked merely lopsided. (He explained the raincoat in the course of our conversation, saying, 'You know how it is in digs. If you leave anything behind when you go out for the day, someone's sure to take a fancy to it.') 'It is Plant, isn't it?' he said.

'Yes.'

179

'Thought so. I never forget a face. They call it the royal gift, don't they?'

'Do they?'

'Yes, that and punctuality. I'm punctual, too. It's a curious thing because you see, actually, though I don't make any fuss about it in the position I'm in, I'm descended from Henry VII.' There seemed no suitable answer to this piece of information so, since I was silent, he added suddenly, 'I say, you do remember me, don't you?'

'Vividly.'

He came closer and leant beside me on the rail which separated us from the cage. It was as though we stood on board ship and were looking out to sea, only instead of the passing waters we saw the solitary, still person of Humboldt's Gibbon. 'I don't mind telling you,' said Atwater, 'I've had a pretty thin time of it since we last met.'

'I saw you were acquitted at the trial. I thought you were very fortunate.'

'Fortunate! You should have heard the things the beak said. Things he had no right to say and wouldn't have dared say to a rich man, and said in a very nasty way, too – things I shan't forget in a hurry. Mr Justice Longworth – *Justice*, that's funny. Acquitted without a stain! – innocent! Does that give me back my job?'

'But I understood from the evidence at the trial that you were under notice to go anyway.'

'Yes. And why? Because sales were dropping. Why should I sell their beastly stockings for them anyway? Money – that's all anyone cares about now. And I'm beginning to feel the same way. When do you suppose I had my last meal – my last square meal?'

'I've really no idea, I'm afraid.'

'Tuesday. I'm hungry, Plant – literally hungry.'

'You could have saved yourself the sixpence admission here, couldn't you?'

'I'm a Fellow,' said Atwater with surprising readiness.

'Oh.'

'You don't believe that, do you?'

180

'I have no reason not to.'

'I can prove it; look here – Fellow's tickets, two of them.' He produced and pressed on my attention two tickets of admission signed in a thin, feminine hand. 'My dear Atwater,' I said, 'these don't make you a Fellow; they've merely been given you by someone who is – not that it matters.'

'Not that it matters! Let me tell you this. D'you know who gave me these? – the mother of a chap I know; chap I know well. I dropped round to see him the other evening, at the address I found in the telephone book. It was his mother's house as it happened. My pal was abroad. But, anyway, I got talking to the mother and told her about how I was placed and what pals her son and I had been. She seemed a decent old bird. At the end she said, "How very sad. Do let me give you something," and began fumbling in her bag. I thought at least a quid was coming, and what did she give me? These tickets for the Zoo. I ask you!'

'Well,' I said, with a tone as encouraging as I could manage, for it did seem to me that in this instance he had been unfairly disappointed, 'the Zoo is a very pleasant place.'

At this suggestion Atwater showed a mercurial change of mood from resentment to simple enthusiasm. 'It's wonderful,' he said, 'there's nothing like it. All these animals from all over the world. Think what they've seen – forests and rivers, places probably where no white man's ever been. It makes you long to get away, doesn't it? Think of paddling your canoe upstream in undiscovered country, with strings of orchids overhead and parrots in the trees and great butterflies, and native servants, and hanging your hammock in the open at night and starting off in the morning with no one to worry you, living on fish and fruit – that's life,' said Atwater.

Once again I felt impelled to correct his misconceptions of colonial life. 'If you are still thinking of settling in Rhodesia,' I said, 'I must warn you you will find conditions very different from those you describe.'

'Rhodesia's off,' said Atwater. 'I've other plans.'

He told me of them at length, and because they distracted

181

me from thinking of Lucy, I listened gratefully. They depended, primarily, on his finding a man of his acquaintance – a good scout named Appleby – who had lately disappeared as so many of Atwater's associates seemed to have done, leaving no indication of his whereabouts. Appleby knew of a cave in Bolivia where the Jesuits, in bygone years, had stored their treasure. When they were driven out, they put a curse on the place, so that the superstitious natives left the hoard inviolate. Appleby had old parchments which made the matter clear. More than this, Appleby had an aerial photograph of the locality, and by a special process known to himself, was able to treat the plate so that auriferous ground came out dark; the hill where the Jesuits had left their treasure was almost solid black; the few white spots indicated chests of jewels and, possibly, bar platinum. 'Appleby's idea was to collect ten stout fellows who would put up a hundred quid each for our fares and digging expenses. I'd have gone like a shot. Had it all fixed up. The only snag was that just at that time I couldn't put my hands on a hundred quid.'

'Did the expedition ever start?'

'I don't think so. You see a lot of the chaps were in the same position. Besides old Appleby would never start without me. He's a good scout. If I only knew where he hung out I should be all right.'

'Where used he to hang out?'

'You could always find him at the old Wimpole. He was what our barman called one of the regulars.'

'Surely they would know his address there?' I kept talking. As long as I was learning about old Appleby I had only half my mind for Lucy.

'Well, you see, the Wimpole's rather free and easy in some ways. As long as you're a good chap you're taken as you come and no questions asked. Subs. are paid by the month; you know the kind of place. If you're shy of the ante, as we used to call it, the doorman doesn't let you in.'

'And old Appleby was shy of the ante?'

'That's it. It wasn't a thing to worry about. Most of the chaps one time or another had been shown the door. I expect it's the same at your club. No disgrace attached. But old Appleby's a bit touchy and began telling off the doorman good and proper, and then the secretary butted in and, to cut a long story short, there was something of a schmozzle.'

'Yes,' I said, 'I see.' And even as I spoke all interest in Appleby's schmozzle faded completely away and I thought of Lucy, lying at home in tears, waiting for her pain. 'For God's sake, tell me some more.' I said.

'More about Appleby?'

'More about anything. Tell me about all the chaps in the Wimpole. Tell me their names one by one and exactly what they look like. Tell me your family history. Tell me the full details of every job you have ever lost. Tell me all the funny stories you have ever heard. Tell my fortune. Don't you see, I want to be *told*?'

'I don't quite twig,' said Atwater. 'But if you are trying to hint that I'm boring you . . .'

'Atwater,' I said earnestly, 'I will pay you just to talk to me. Here is a pound, look, take it. There. Does that look as though I was bored?'

'It looks to me as though you were balmy,' said Atwater, pocketing the note. 'Much obliged all the same. It'll come in handy just at the moment, only as a loan, mind.'

'Only as a loan,' I said, and we both of us lapsed into silence, he, no doubt, thinking of my balminess, I of Lucy. The black ape walked slowly round his cage raking the sawdust and nut shells with the back of his hand, looking vainly for some neglected morsel of food. Presently there was an excited scurry in the cage next to us; two women had appeared with a bunch of bananas. 'Excuse me, please,' they said and pushed in front of us to feed Humboldt's Gibbon; then they passed on to the grey sycophant beyond, and so down all the cages until their bag was empty. 'Where shall we go now?' one of them said. 'I don't see the point of animals you aren't allowed to feed.'

Atwater overheard this remark; it worked in his mind so that by the time they had left the monkey house, he was in another mood. Atwater the dreamer, Atwater the good scout, and Atwater the underdog seemed to appear in more or less regular sequence. It was Atwater the good scout I liked best, but one clearly had to take him as he came. 'Feeding animals while men and women starve,' he said bitterly.

It was a topic; a topic dry, scentless and colourless as a pressed flower; a topic on which in the school debating society one had despaired of finding anything new to say – 'The motion before the House is that too much kindness is shown to animals, proposed by Mr John Plant, Headmaster's House' – nevertheless, it was something to talk about.

'The animals are paid for their entertainment value,' I said. 'We don't send out hampers to monkeys in their own forests' – Or did we? There was no knowing what humane ladies in England would not do – 'We bring the monkeys here to amuse us.'

'What's amusing about that black creature there?'

'Well, he's very beautiful.'

'Beautiful?' Atwater stared into the hostile little face beyond the bars. 'Can't see it myself.' Then rather truculently, 'I suppose you'd say he was more beautiful than me.'

'Well, as a matter of fact, since you raise the point . . .'

'You think that thing beautiful and feed it and shelter it, while you leave me to starve.'

This seemed unfair. I had just given Atwater a pound; moreover, it was not I who had fed the ape. I pointed this out.

'I see,' said Atwater. 'You're paying me for my entertainment value. You think I'm a kind of monkey.'

This was uncomfortably near the truth. 'You misunderstand me,' I said.

'I hope I do. A remark like that would start a rough-house at the Wimpole.'

A new and glorious idea came to me. 'Atwater,' I said, cautiously, for his oppressed mood was still on him. 'Please do not take offence at my suggestion but, supposing I were to pay – as a loan, of course – would it be possible for us, do you think, to lunch at the Wimpole?'

He took the suggestion quite well. 'I'll be frank with you,' he said. 'I haven't paid this month's sub. yet. It's seven and sixpence.'

'We'll include that in the loan.'

'Good scout. I know you'll like the place.'

The taxi driver, to whom I gave the address 'Wimpole Club', was nonplussed. 'Now you've got me,' he said. 'I thought I knew them all. It's not what used to be called the "Palm Beach"?'

'No,' said Atwater, and gave more exact directions.

We drove to a mews off Wimpole Street ('It's handy for chaps in the motor business Great Portland Street way,' said Atwater). 'By the way, I may as well explain, I'm known as Norton at the club.'

'Why?'

'Lots of the chaps there use a different name. I expect it's the same at your club.'

'I shouldn't be surprised,' I said.

I paid the taxi. Atwater kicked open a green door and led me into the hall where a porter, behind the counter, was lunching off tea and sandwiches.

'I've been out of town,' said Atwater. 'Just dropped in to pay my subscription. Anyone about?'

'Very quiet,' said the porter.

The room into which he led me was entirely empty. It was at once bar, lounge and dining-room, but mostly bar, for which a kind of film-set had been erected, built far into the room, with oak rafters, a thatched roof, a wrought-iron lantern and an inn-sign painted in mock heraldry with quartered bottles and tankards.

'Jim!' cried Atwater.

'Sir.' A head appeared above the bar. 'Well, Mr Norton, we haven't seen you for a long time. I was just having my bit of dinner.'

'May I interrupt that important function and give my friend here something in the nature of a snorter' – this was a new and greatly expanded version of Atwater the good scout. 'Two of your specials, please, Jim.' To me, 'Jim's specials are famous.' To Jim, 'This is one of my best pals, Mr Plant.' To me, 'There's not much Jim doesn't know about me.' To Jim, 'Where's the gang?'

'They don't seem to come here like they did, Mr Norton. There's not the money about.'

'You've said it.' Jim put two cocktails on the bar before us. 'I presume, Jim, that since this is Mr Plant's first time among us, in pursuance of the old Wimpole custom, these are on the house?'

Jim laughed rather anxiously. 'Mr Norton likes his joke.'

'Joke? Jim, you shame me before my friends. But never fear. I have found a rich backer; if we aren't having this with you, you must have one with us.'

The barman poured himself out something from a bottle which he kept for the purpose on a shelf below the bar, and said, 'First today,' as we toasted one another. Atwater said, 'It's one of the mysteries of the club what Jim keeps in that bottle of his.' I knew; it was what every barman kept, cold tea, but I thought it would spoil Atwater's treat if I told him.

Jim's 'special' was strong and agreeable.

'Is it all right for me to order a round?' I asked.

'It's more than all right. It's perfect.'

Jim shook up another cocktail and refilled his own glass.

'D'you remember the time I drank twelve of your specials before dinner with Mr Appleby?'

'I do, sir.'

'A tiny bit spifflicated that night, eh, Jim?'

'A tiny bit, sir.'

We had further rounds; Jim took cash for the drinks – three shillings a round. After the first round, when Atwater broke into his pound note, I paid. Every other time he said, 'Chalk it up to the national debt,' or similar reference to the fiction of our loan. Soon Jim and Atwater were deep in reminiscence of Atwater's past.

After a time I found my thoughts wandering and went to telephone to Victoria Square. Roger answered. 'It seems things are coming more or less normally,' he said.

'How is she?'

'I haven't been in. The doctor's here now, in a white coat like an umpire. He keeps saying I'm not to worry.'

'But is she in danger?'

'Of course she is, it's a dangerous business.'

'But I mean, more than most people?'

'Yes. No. I don't know. They said everything was quite normal, whatever that means.'

'I suppose it means she's not in more danger than most people.'

'I suppose so.'

'Does it bore you my ringing up to ask?'

'No, not really. Where are you?'

'At a club called the Wimpole.'

'Never heard of it.'

'No. I'll tell you about it later. Very interesting.'

'Good. Do tell me later.'

I returned to the bar. 'I thought our old comrade had passed out on us,' said Atwater. 'Been sick?'

'Good heavens, no.'

'You look a terrible colour, doesn't he, Jim? Perhaps a special is what he needs. I was sick that night old Grainger sold his Bentley, sick as a dog . . .'

When I had spent about thirty shillings Jim began to tire of his cold tea. 'Why don't you gentlemen sit down at a table and let me order you a nice grill?' he asked.

'All in good time, Jim, all in good time. Mr Plant here would like one of your specials first just to give him an appetite, and I think rather than see an old pal drink alone, I'll join him.'

Later, when we were very drunk, steaks appeared which neither of us remembered ordering. We ate them at the bar with, at Jim's advice, great quantities of Worcester sauce. Our conversation, I think, was mainly about Appleby and the need of finding him. We rang up one or two people of that name, whom we found in the telephone book, but they disclaimed all knowledge of Jesuit treasure.

It must have been four o'clock in the afternoon when we left the Wimpole. Atwater was more drunk than I. Next day

I remembered most of our conversation verbatim. In the mews I asked him: 'Where are you living?'

'Digs. Awful hole. But it's all right now I've got money – I can sleep on the Embankment. Police won't let you sleep on the Embankment unless you've got money. Vagrancy. One law for the rich, one for the poor. Iniquitous system.'

'Why don't you come and live with me. I've got a house in the country, plenty of room. Stay as long as you like. Die there.'

'Thanks, I will. Must go the Embankment first and pack.'

And we separated, for the time, he sauntering unsteadily along Wimpole Street, past the rows of brass plates, I driving in a taxi to my rooms in Ebury Street, where I undressed, folded my clothes, and went quietly to bed. I awoke, in the dark, hours later, in confusion as to where I was and how I had got there.

The telephone was ringing next door in the sitting-room. It was Roger. He said that Lucy had had a son two hours ago; he had been ringing up relatives ever since. She was perfectly well; the first thing she had asked for when she came round from the chloroform was a cigarette. 'I feel like going out and getting drunk,' said Roger. 'Don't you?'

'No,' I said. 'No, I'm afraid not,' and returned to bed.

4

When I got drunk I could sleep it off and wake in tolerable health; Roger could not; in the past we had often discussed this alcoholic insomnia of his and found no remedy for it except temperance. After telephoning to me he had gone out with Basil; he looked a wreck next morning.

'It's extraordinary,' he said. 'I've got absolutely no feeling about this baby at all. I kept telling myself all these last months that when I actually saw it, all manner of deep-rooted, atavistic emotions would come surging up. I was all set for a deep spiritual experience. They brought the thing in and showed it to me. I looked at it and waited – and nothing at all happened. It was just like the first time one takes hashish - or being "confirmed" at school.'

'I knew a man who had five children,' I said. 'He felt just as you did until the fifth. Then he was suddenly overcome with love; he bought a thermometer and kept taking its temperature when the nurse was out of the room. I daresay it's a habit, like hashish.'

'I don't feel as if I had anything to do with it. It's as though they showed me Lucy's appendix or a tooth they'd pulled out of her.'

'What's it like? I mean, it isn't a freak or anything?'

'No, I've been into that; two arms, two legs, one head, white – just a baby. Of course, you can't tell for some time if it's sane or not. I believe the first sign is that it can't take hold of things with its hands. Did you know that Lucy's grandmother was shut up?'

'I had no idea.'

'Yes. Lucy never saw her, of course. It's why she's anxious about Julia.'

'Is she anxious about Julia?'

'Who wouldn't be?'

'How soon can you tell if they're blind?'

'Not for weeks, I believe. I asked Sister Kemp. She said "The very idea" and whisked the baby off as if I wanted to injure it, poor little brute. D'you know what Lucy calls Sister Kemp now? – Kempy.'

'It's not possible.'

It was true. I went in to see her for five minutes and twice during that time she said 'Kempy.' When we were alone for a minute I asked her why. 'She asked me to,' said Lucy, 'and she's really very sweet.'

'Sweet?'

'She was absolutely sweet to me yesterday.'

I had brought some flowers, but the room was full of them. Lucy lay in bed; slack and smiling. I sat down by her and held her hand. 'Everyone's been so sweet,' she said. 'Have you seen my baby?'

'No.'

'He's in the dressing-room. Ask Kempy to show you.'

'Are you pleased with him?'

'I love him. I do really. I never thought I should. He's such a *person*.'

This was incomprehensible.

'You haven't gone bald?' I said.

'No, but my hair's terrible. What did you do yesterday?'

'I got drunk.'

'So did poor Roger. Were you with him?'

'No,' I said, 'it was really very amusing.' I began to tell her about Atwater, but she was not listening.

Then Sister Kemp came in with more flowers – from Mr Benwell.

'How sweet he is,' said Lucy.

This was past bearing – first Sister Kemp, now Mr Benwell. I felt stifled in this pastry-cook's atmosphere. 'I've come to say good-bye,' I said. 'I'm going back to the country to see about my house.'

'I'm so glad. It's lovely for you. I'm coming to see it as soon as I'm better.'

She did not want me, I thought; Humboldt's Gibbon and I had done our part. 'You'll be my first guest,' I said.

'Yes. Quite soon.'

Sister Kemp went with me to the landing. 'Now,' she said, 'come and see something very precious.'

There was a cradle in Roger's dressing-room, made of white stuff and ribbons, and a baby in it.

'Isn't he a fine big man?'

'Magnificent,' I said, 'and very sweet . . . Kempy.'

190

·POSTSCRIPT

THE date of this child's birth was 25 August, 1939, and while Lucy was still in bed the air-raid sirens sounded the first false alarm of the second World War. And so an epoch, my epoch, came to an end. Intellectually we had foreseen the event, and had calmly discussed it, but our inherited habits continued to the last moment.

Beavers bred in captivity, inhabiting a concrete pool, will, if given the timber, fatuously go through all the motions of damming an ancestral stream. So I and my friends busied ourselves with our privacies and intimacies. My father's death, the abandonment of my home, my quickening love of Lucy, my literary innovations, my house in the country – all these had seemed to presage a new life. The new life came, not by my contrivance.

Neither book – the last of my old life, the first of my new – was ever finished. As for my house, I never spent a night there. It was requisitioned, filled with pregnant women, and through five years bit by bit befouled and dismembered. My friends were dispersed. Lucy and her baby moved back to her aunt's. Roger rose from department to department in the office of Political Warfare. Basil sought and found a series of irregular adventures. For myself plain regimental soldiering proved an orderly and not disagreeable way of life.

I met Atwater several times in the course of the war – the Good-scout of the officer's club, the Under-dog in the transit-camp, the Dreamer lecturing troops about post-war conditions. He was reunited, it seemed, with all his legendary lost friends, he prospered and the Good-scout predominated. Today, I believe, he holds sway over a large area of Germany. No one of my close acquaintance was killed, but all our lives, as we had constructed them, quietly came to an end. Our story, like my novel, remained unfinished – a heap of neglected foolscap at the back of a drawer.

SCOTT-KING'S
MODERN EUROPE

MARIAE IMMACULATAE ANTONIAE
CONIUGIS PRUDENTIORIS
AUDACI CONIUGI

IN 1946 Scott-King had been classical master at Granchester for twenty-one years. He was himself a Granchesterian and had returned straight from the University after failing for a fellowship. There he had remained, growing slightly bald and slightly corpulent, known to generations of boys first as 'Scottie', then of late years, while barely middle-aged, as 'old Scottie'; a school 'institution', whose precise and slightly nasal lamentations of modern decadence were widely parodied.

Granchester is not the most illustrious of English public schools, but it is, or, as Scott-King would maintain, was, entirely respectable; it plays an annual cricket match at Lord's; it numbers a dozen or so famous men among its old boys, who, in general, declare without apology: 'I was at Granchester' – unlike the sons of lesser places who are apt to say: 'As a matter of fact I was at a place called – You see, at the time my father . . .'

When Scott-King was a boy and when he first returned as a master, the school was almost equally divided into a Classical and a Modern Side, with a group of negligible and neglected specialists called 'the Army Class'. Now the case was altered and out of 450 boys scarcely 50 read Greek. Scott-King had watched his classical colleagues fall away one by one, some to rural rectories, some to the British Council and the B.B.C., to be replaced by physicists and economists from the provincial universities, until now, instead of inhabiting solely the rare intellectual atmosphere of the Classical Sixth, he was obliged to descend for many periods a week to cram lower boys with Xenophon and Sallust. But Scott-King did not repine. On the contrary he found a peculiar relish in contemplating the victories of barbarism and positively rejoiced in his reduced station, for he was of a type, unknown in the New World, but quite common in Europe, which is fascinated by obscurity and failure.

'Dim' is the epithet for Scott-King and it was a fellow-feeling, a blood-brotherhood in dimness, which first drew him to study the works of the poet Bellorius.

No one, except perhaps Scott-King himself, could be dimmer. When, poor and in some discredit, Bellorius died in 1646 in his native town of what was then a happy kingdom of the Habsburg Empire and is now the turbulent modern state of Neutralia,* he left as his life's work a single folio volume containing a poem of some 1,500 lines of Latin hexameters. In his lifetime the only effect of the publication was to annoy the Court and cause his pension to be cancelled. After his death it was entirely forgotten until the middle of the last century, when it was reprinted in Germany in a collection of late Renaissance texts. It was in this edition that Scott-King found it during a holiday on the Rhine, and at once his heart stirred with the recognition of kinship. The subject was irredeemably tedious – a visit to an imaginary island of the New World where in primitive simplicity, untainted by tyranny or dogma, there subsisted a virtuous, chaste and reasonable community. The lines were correct and melodious, enriched by many happy figures of speech; Scott-King read them on the deck of the river steamer as vine and turret, cliff and terrace and park, swept smoothly past. How they offended – by what intended or unintended jab of satire, blunted today; by what dangerous speculation – is not now apparent. That they should have been forgotten is readily intelligible to anyone acquainted with the history of Neutralia.

Something must be known of this history if we are to follow Scott-King with understanding. Let us eschew detail and observe that for three hundred years since Bellorius's death his country has suffered every conceivable ill the body politic is heir to. Dynastic wars, foreign invasion, disputed successions, revolting colonies, endemic syphilis, impover-

* The Republic of Neutralia is imaginary and composite and represents no existing state.

ished soil, masonic intrigues, revolutions, restorations, cabals, juntas, pronunciamentos, liberations, constitutions, *coups d'état*, dictatorships, assassinations, agrarian reforms, popular elections, foreign intervention, repudiation of loans, inflations of currency, trades unions, massacres, arson, atheism, secret societies – make the list full, slip in as many personal foibles as you will, you will find all these in the last three centuries of Neutralian history. Out of it emerged the present republic of Neutralia, a typical modern state, governed by a single party, acclaiming a dominant Marshal, supporting a vast ill-paid bureaucracy whose work is tempered and humanized by corruption. This you must know; also that the Neutralians, being a clever Latin race, are little given to hero-worship and make considerable fun of their Marshal behind his back. In one thing only did he earn their full-hearted esteem. He kept out of the second World War. Neutralia sequestered herself and, from having been the cockpit of factious sympathies, became remote, unconsidered, *dim*; so that, as the face of Europe coarsened and the war, as it appeared in the common-room newspapers and the common-room wireless, cast its heroic and chivalrous disguise and became a sweaty tug-of-war between teams of indistinguishable louts, Scott-King, who had never set foot there, became Neutralian in his loyalty and as an act of homage resumed with fervour the task on which he had intermittently worked, a translation of Bellorius into Spenserian stanzas. The work was finished at the time of the Normandy landings – translation, introduction, notes. He sent it to the Oxford University Press. It came back to him. He put it away in a drawer of the pitch-pine desk in his smoky gothic study above the Granchester quadrangle. He did not repine. It was his opus, his monument to dimness.

But still the shade of Bellorius stood at his elbow demanding placation. There was unfinished business between these two. You cannot keep close company with a man, even though he be dead three centuries, without incurring obligations. Therefore at the time of the peace celebrations Scott-King distilled his learning and wrote a little essay, 4,000 words long, entitled *The Last Latinist*, to commemorate the coming tercentenary of Bellorius's death. It appeared in a learned journal. Scott-King was paid twelve guineas for this fruit of fifteen years' devoted labour; six of them he paid in income tax; with six he purchased a large gunmetal watch which worked irregularly for a month or two and then finally failed. There the matter might well have ended.

These, then, in a general, distant view, are the circumstances – Scott-King's history; Bellorius; the history of Neutralia; the year of Grace, 1946 – all quite credible, quite humdrum, which together produced the odd events of Scott-King's summer holiday. Let us now 'truck' the camera forward and see him 'close-up'. You have heard all about Scott-King, but you have not yet met him.

Meet him, then, at breakfast on a bleak morning at the beginning of the summer term. Unmarried assistant masters at Granchester enjoyed the use of a pair of collegiate rooms in the school buildings and took their meals in the common-room. Scott-King came from his classroom where he had been taking early school, with his gown flowing behind him and a sheaf of fluttering exercise papers in his numb fingers. There had been no remission of war-time privations at Granchester. The cold grate was used as ash-tray and waste-paper basket and was rarely emptied. The breakfast table was a litter of small pots, each labelled with a master's name, containing rations of sugar, margarine and a spurious marmalade. The breakfast dish was a slop of 'dried' eggs. Scott-King turned sadly from the sideboard. 'Anyone,' he said, 'is welcome to my share in this triumph of modern science.'

'Letter for you, Scottie,' said one of his colleagues. ' "The Honourable Professor Scott-King, Esquire." Congratulations.'

It was a large, stiff envelope, thus oddly addressed, emblazoned on the flap with a coat of arms. Inside was a card and a letter. The card read:

His Magnificence the Very Reverend the Rector of the University of Simona and the Committee of the Bellorius Tercentenary Celebration Association request the honour of Professor Scott-King's

198

assistance at the public acts to be held at Simona on July 28th-August 5th, 1946. R.S.V.P. His Excellency Dr Bogdan Antonic, international secretary of the Committee, Simona University, Neutralia.

The letter was signed by the Neutralian Ambassador to the Court of St James's. It announced that a number of distinguished scholars were assembling from all over the world to do honour to the illustrious Neutralian political thinker Bellorius and delicately intimated that the trip would be without expense on the part of the guests.

Scott-King's first thought on reading the communication was that he was the victim of a hoax. He looked round the table expecting to surprise a glance of complicity between his colleagues, but they appeared to be busy with their own concerns. Second thoughts convinced him that this sumptuous embossing and engraving was beyond their resources. The thing was authentic, then; but Scott-King was not pleased. He felt, rather, that a long-standing private intimacy between himself and Bellorius was being rudely disturbed. He put the envelope into his pocket, ate his bread and margarine, and presently made ready for morning chapel. He stopped at the secretary's office to purchase a packet of crested school writing paper on which to inscribe 'Mr Scott-King regrets . . .'

For the strange thing is that Scott-King was definitely blasé. Something of the kind has been hinted before, yet, seeing him cross the quadrangle to the chapel steps, middle-aged, shabby, unhonoured and unknown, his round and learned face puckered against the wind, you would have said: 'There goes a man who has missed all the compensations of life – and knows it.' But that is because you do not yet know Scott-King; no voluptuary surfeited by conquest, no colossus of the drama bruised and rent by doting adolescents, nor Alexander, nor Talleyrand, was more blasé than Scott-King. He was an adult, an intellectual, a classical scholar, almost a poet; he was travel-worn in the large periphery of his own mind, jaded with accumulated experience of his imagination. He was older, it might have been written, than the rocks on which he sat; older, anyway, than his stall in chapel; he had died many times, had Scott-King, had dived deep, had trafficked for strange webs with Eastern merchants. And all this had been but the sound of lyres and flutes to him. Thus musing, he left the chapel and went to his class-room, where for the first hours he had the lowest set.

They coughed and sneezed. One, more ingenious than the rest, attempted at length to draw him out as, it was known, he might sometimes be drawn: 'Please, sir, Mr Griggs says it's a pure waste of our time learning classics,' but Scott-King merely replied: 'It's a waste of time coming to me and *not* learning them.'

After Latin gerunds they stumbled through half a page of Thucydides. He said: 'These last episodes of the siege have been described as tolling like a great bell,' at which a chorus rose from the back bench, 'The bell? Did you say it was the bell, sir?' and books were noisily shut. 'There are another twenty minutes. I said the book tolled like a bell.'

'Please, sir, I don't quite get that, sir, how can a book be like a bell, sir?'

'If you wish to talk, Ambrose, you can start construing.'

'Please, sir, that's as far as I got, sir.'

'Has anyone done any more?' (Scott-King still attempted to import into the lower school the adult politeness of the Classical Sixth.) 'Very well, then, you can all spend the rest of the hour preparing the next twenty lines.'

Silence, of a sort, reigned. There was a low muttering from the back of the room, a perpetual shuffling and snuffling, but no one spoke directly to Scott-King. He gazed through the leaded panes to the leaden sky. He could hear through the wall behind him the strident tones of Griggs, the civics master, extolling the Tolpuddle martyrs. Scott-King put his hand in his coat pocket and felt the crisp edges of the Neutralian invitation.

He had not been abroad since 1939. He had not tasted wine for a year, and he was filled, suddenly, with deep homesickness for the South. He had not often nor for long visited those enchanted lands; a dozen times perhaps, for a few weeks – for one year in total of his forty-three years of life – but his treasure and his heart lay buried there. Hot oil and garlic and spilled wine; luminous pinnacles above a dusky wall; fireworks at night, fountains at noonday; the impudent, inoffensive hawkers of lottery tickets moving from table to table on to the crowded pavement; the shepherd's pipe on the scented hillside – all that travel agents ever sought to put in a folder, fumed in Scott-King's mind that drab morning. He had left his coin in the waters of Trevi; he had wedded the Adriatic; he was a Mediterranean man.

In the mid-morning break, on the crested school paper, he wrote his acceptance of the Neutralian invitation. That evening, and on many subsequent evenings, the talk in the common-room was about plans for the holidays. All despaired of getting abroad; all save Griggs, who was cock-a-hoop about an International Rally of Progressive Youth Leadership in Prague to which he had got himself appointed. Scott-King said nothing even when Neutralia was mentioned.

'I'd like to go somewhere I could get a decent meal,' said one of his colleagues. 'Ireland or Neutralia, or somewhere like that.'

'They'd never let you into Neutralia,' said Griggs. 'Far too much to hide. They've got teams of German physicists making atomic bombs.'

'Civil war raging.'

'Half the population in concentration camps.'

'No decent-minded man would go to Neutralia.'

'Or to Ireland for that matter,' said Griggs.

And Scott-King sat tight.

Some weeks later Scott-King sat in the aerodrome waiting-room. His overcoat lay across his knees, his hand luggage at his feet. A loud-speaker, set high out of harm's way in the dun concrete wall, discoursed dance music and official announcements. This room, like all the others to which he had been driven in the course of the morning, was sparsely furnished and indifferently clean; on its walls, sole concession to literary curiosity, hung commendations of government savings bonds and precautions against gas attack. Scott-King was hungry, weary and dispirited, for he was new to the amenities of modern travel.

He had left his hotel in London at seven o'clock that morning; it was now past noon and he was still on English soil. He had not been ignored. He had been shepherded in and out of charabancs and offices like an idiot child; he had been weighed and measured like a load of merchandise; he had been searched like a criminal; he had been cross-questioned about his past and his future, the state of his health and his finances, as though he were applying for per-manent employment of a confidential nature. Scott-King had not been nurtured in luxury and privilege, but this was not how he used to travel. And he had eaten nothing except a piece of flaccid toast and margarine in his bedroom. The ultimate asylum where he now sat proclaimed itself on the door as 'For the use of V.I.P.s only.'

'V.I.P.?' he asked their conductress.

She was a neat, impersonal young woman, part midwife, part governess, part shop-walker, in manner. 'Very Important Persons,' she replied without evident embarrassment.

'But is it all right for me to be here?'

'It is essential. You are a V.I.P.'

202

I wonder, thought Scott-King, how they treat quite ordinary, unimportant people?

There were two fellow-travellers, male and female, similarly distinguished, both bound for Bellacita, capital city of Neutralia; both, it presently transpired, guests of the Bellorius Celebration Committee.

The man was a familiar type to Scott-King; his name Whitemaid, his calling academic, a dim man like himself, much of an age with him.

'Tell me,' said Whitemaid, 'tell me frankly' – and he looked furtive as men do when they employ that ambiguous expression – 'have you ever heard of the worthy Bellorius?'

'I know his work. I have seldom heard it discussed.'

'Ah, well, of course, he's not in my subject. I'm Roman Law,' said Whitemaid, with an accession of furtiveness that took all grandiosity from the claim. 'They asked the Professor of Poetry, you know, but he couldn't get away. Then they tried the Professor of Latin. He's red. Then they asked for anyone to represent the University. No one else was enthusiastic, so I put myself forward. I find expeditions of this kind highly diverting. You are familiar with them?'

'No.'

'I went to Upsala last vacation and ate very passable caviare twice a day for a week. Neutralia is not known for delicate living, alas, but one may count on rude plenty – and, of course, wine.'

'It's all a racket, anyhow,' said the third Very Important Person.

This was a woman no longer very young. Her name, Scott-King and Whitemaid had learned through hearing it frequently called through the loudspeaker and seeing it chalked on blackboards, calling her to receive urgent messages at every stage of their journey, was Miss Bombaum. It was a name notorious to almost all the world except, as it happened, to Scott-King and Whitemaid. She was far from dim; once a roving, indeed a dashing, reporter who in the days before the war had popped up wherever there was unpleasantness – Danzig, the Alcazar, Shanghai, Wal-Wal; now a columnist whose weekly articles were syndicated in the popular press of four continents. Scott-King did not read such articles and he had wondered idly at frequent intervals during the morning what she could be. She did not look a lady; she did not even look quite respectable, but he could not reconcile her typewriter with the callings of actress or courtesan; nor for that matter the sharp little sexless face under the too feminine hat and the lavish style of hair-dressing. He came near the truth in suspecting her of being, what he had often heard of but never seen in the life, a female novelist.

'It's all a racket,' said Miss Bombaum, 'of the Neutralian Propaganda Bureau. I reckon they feel kind of left out of things now the war's over and want to make some nice new friends among the United Nations. We're only part of it. They've got a religious pilgrimage and a Congress of Physical Culture and an International Philatelists' Convention and heaven knows what else. I reckon there's a story in it – in Neutralia, I mean; not in Bellorius, of course, he's been done.'

'Done?'

'Yes, I've a copy somewhere,' she said, rummaging in her bag. 'Thought it might come in useful for the speeches.'

'You don't think,' said Scott-King, 'that we are in danger of being required to make speeches?'

'I can't think what else we've been asked for,' said Miss Bombaum. 'Can you?'

'I made three long speeches at Upsala,' said Whitemaid. 'They were ecstatically received.'

'Oh, dear, and I have left all my papers at home.'

'Borrow this any time you like,' said Miss Bombaum, producing Mr Robert Graves's *Count Belisarius*. 'It's sad though. He ends up blind.'

The music suddenly ceased and a voice said: 'Passengers for Bellacita will now proceed to Exit D. Passengers for Bellacita will now proceed to Exit D,' while, simultaneously, the conductress appeared in the doorway and said: 'Follow me, please. Have your embarkation papers, medical cards, customs clearance slips, currency control vouchers, passports, tickets, identity dockets, travel orders, emigration certificates, baggage checks and security sheets ready for inspection at the barrier, please.'

The Very Important Persons followed her out, mingled with the less important persons who had been waiting in a nearby room, stepped into a dusty gale behind the four spinning screws of the aeroplane, mounted the step-ladder and were soon strapped into their seats as though awaiting the attention of the dentist. A steward gave them brief instructions in the case of their being forced down over the sea and announced: 'We shall arrive at Bellacita at sixteen hours Neutralian time.'

'An appalling thought occurs to me,' said Whitemaid. 'Can this mean we get no luncheon?'

'They eat very late in Neutralia, I believe.'

'Yes, but four o'clock!'

'I'm sure they will have arranged something for us.'

'I pray they have.'

Something had been arranged but not a luncheon. The Very Important Persons stepped out some hours later into the brilliant sunshine of Bellacita airport and at once found their hands shaken in swift succession by a deputation of their hosts. 'I'd bid you welcome to the land of Bellorius,' said their spokesman.

His name, he told them with a neat bow, was Arturo Fe; his rank Doctor of Bellacita University; but there was nothing academic in his appearance. Rather, Scott-King thought, he might be a slightly ageing film actor. He had thin, calligraphic moustaches, a hint of side-whisker, sparse but well-ordered hair, a gold-rimmed monocle, three gold teeth, and neat, dark clothes.

'Madam,' he said, 'gentlemen, your luggage will be cared for. The motor-cars await you. Come with me. Passports? Papers? Do not give them a thought. Everything is arranged. Come.'

At this stage Scott-King became aware of a young woman standing stolidly among them. He had taken notice of her in

London where she had towered some six inches above the heads of the crowd.

'I come,' she said.

Dr Fe bowed. 'Fe,' he said.

'Sveningen,' she answered.

'You are one of us? Of the Bellorius Association?' asked Dr Fe.

'I speak not English well. I come.'

Dr Fe tried her in Neutralian, French, Italian and German. She replied in her own remote Nordic tongue. Dr Fe raised hands and eyes in a pantomime of despair.

'You speak much English. I speak little English. So we speak English, yes? I come.'

'You come?' said Dr Fe.

'I come.'

'We are honoured,' said Dr Fe.

He led them between flowering oleanders and borders of camomile, past shaded café tables at which Whitemaid longingly looked, through the airport vestibule to the glass doors beyond.

Here there was a hitch. Two sentries, shabbily uniformed but armed for action, war-worn, it seemed, but tigers for duty, barred their passage. Dr Fe tried a high hand, he tried charm, he offered them cigarettes; suddenly a new side of his character was revealed; he fell into demoniac rage, he shook his fists, he bared his chryselephantine teeth, he narrowed his eyes to mongol slits of hate; what he said was unintelligible to Scott-King, but it was plainly designed to wound. The men stood firm.

Then, as suddenly as it had arisen, the squall passed. He turned to his guests. 'Excuse one moment,' he said. 'These stupid fellows do not understand their orders. It will be arranged by the officer.' He dispatched an underling.

'We box the rude mens?' suggested Miss Sveningen, moving cat-like towards the soldiers.

'No. Forgive them I beg you. They think it their duty.'

'Such little men should be polite,' said the giantess.

The officer came; the doors flew open; the soldiers did

something with their tommy-guns which passed as a salute. Scott-King raised his hat as the little party swept out into the blaze of sunshine to the waiting cars.

'This superb young creature,' said Scott-King, 'would you say she was a slightly incongruous figure?'

'I find her eminently, transcendently congruous,' said Whitemaid. 'I exult in her.'

Dr Fe gallantly took the ladies under his own charge. Scott-King and Whitemaid rode with an underling. They bowled along through the suburbs of Bellacita; tramlines, half-finished villas, a rush of hot wind, a dazzle of white concrete. At first, when they were fresh from the upper air, the heat had been agreeable; now his skin began to prick and tickle and Scott-King realized that he was unsuitably dressed.

'Exactly ten hours and a half since I had anything to eat,' said Whitemaid.

The underling leaned towards them from the front seat and pointed out places of interest. 'Here,' he said, 'the anarchists shot General Cardenas. Here syndico-radicals shot the auxiliary bishop. Here the Agrarian League buried alive ten Teaching Brothers. Here the bimetallists committed unspeakable atrocities on the wife of Senator Mendoza.'

'Forgive me for interrupting you,' said Whitemaid, 'but could you tell us where we are going?'

'To the Ministry. They are all happy to meet you.'

'And we are happy to meet them. But just at the moment my friend and I are rather hungry.'

Yes,' said the underling with compassion. 'We have heard of it in our papers. Your rations in England, your strikes. Here things are very expensive but there is plenty for all who pay, so our people do not strike but work hard to become rich. It is better so, no?'

'Perhaps. We must have a talk about it some time. But at the moment it is not so much the general economic question as a personal immediate need? . . .'

'We arrive,' said the underling. 'Here is the Ministry.'

Like much modern Neutralian building the Ministry was unfinished, but it was conceived in severe one-party style. A portico of unembellished columns, a vast, blank doorway, a bas-relief symbolizing Revolution and Youth and Technical Progress and the National Genius. Inside, a staircase. On the staircase was a less predictable feature; ranged on either side like playing-cards, like a startling hand composed entirely of Kings and Knaves, stood ascending ranks of trumpeters aged from 60 to 16, dressed in the tabards of medieval heralds; more than this they wore blond bobbed wigs; more than this their cheeks were palpably rouged. As Scott-King and White-maid set foot on the lowest step these figures of fantasy raised their trumpets to their lips and sounded a flourish, while one who might from his extreme age have been father to them all, rattled in a feeble way on a little kettle-drum. 'Frankly,' said Whitemaid, 'I am not in good heart for this kind of thing.'

They mounted between the blaring ranks, were greeted on the piano nobile by a man in plain evening-dress, and led to the reception hall which with its pews and thrones had somewhat the air of a court of law and was in fact not infrequently used for condemning aspiring politicians to exile on one or other of the inhospitable islands that lay off the coast of the country.

Here they found an assembly. Under a canopy, on the central throne, sat the Minister of Rest and Culture, a saturnine young man who had lost most of his fingers while playing with a bomb during the last revolution. Scott-King and Whitemaid were presented to him by Dr Fe. He smiled rather horribly and extended a maimed hand. Half a dozen worthies stood round him. Dr Fe introduced them. Honorific titles, bows, smiles, shakes of the hand; then Scott-King and Whitemaid were led to their stalls amid their fellow-guests, now about twelve in number. In each place, on the red-plush seat, lay a little pile of printed matter. 'Not precisely esculent,' said Whitemaid. Trumpets and drum sounded without; another and final party arrived and was presented; then the proceedings began.

The Minister of Rest and Culture had a voice, never soft perhaps, now roughened by a career of street-corner har-angues. He spoke at length and was succeeded by the venerable Rector of Bellacita University. Meanwhile Scott-King studied the books and leaflets provided for him, lavish productions of the Ministry of Popular Enlightenment – selected speeches by the Marshal, a monograph on Neutralian pre-history, an illustrated guide to the ski-ing resorts of the country, the annual report of the Corporation of Viticulture. Nothing seemed to have bearing upon the immediate situation except one, a polyglot programme of the coming celebrations.

17.00 hrs. [he read]. 'Inauguration of the Ceremonies by the Minister of Rest and Culture. 18.00 hrs. Reception of delegates at the University of Bellacita. Official Dress. 19.30 hrs. Vin d'honneur offered to the delegates by the Municipality of Bellacita. 21.00 hrs. Banquet offered by the Committee of the Bellorius Tercentenary Committee. Music by Bellacita Philharmonic Youth Squadron. Evening dress. Delegates will spend the night at the Hôtel 22nd March.

'Look,' said Whitemaid, 'nothing to eat until nine o'clock and, mark my words, they will be late.'

'In Neutralia,' said Dr Arturo Fe, 'in Neutralia, when we are happy, we take no account of time. Today we are *very* happy.'

*

The Hôtel 22nd March was the name, derived from some forgotten event in the Marshal's rise to power, by which the chief hotel of the place was momentarily graced. It had had as many official names in its time as the square in which it stood – the Royal, the Reform, the October Revolution, the Empire, the President Coolidge, the Duchess of Windsor – according to the humours of local history, but Neutralians invariably spoke of it quite simply as the 'Ritz'. It rose amid sub-tropical vegetation, fountains and statuary, a solid structure, ornamented in the rococo style of fifty years ago. Neutralians of the upper class congregated there, sauntered about its ample corridors, sat in its comfortable foyer, used the concierge as a poste restante, borrowed small sums from its barmen, telephoned sometimes, gossiped always, now and then lightly dozed. They did not spend any money there. They could not afford to. The prices were fixed, and fixed high, by law; to them were added a series of baffling taxes – 30 per cent for service, 2 per cent for stamp duty, 30 per cent for luxury tax, 5 per cent for the winter relief fund, 12 per cent for those mutilated in the revolution, 4 per cent municipal dues, 2 per cent federal tax, 8 per cent for living accommodation in excess of minimum requirements, and others of the same kind; they mounted up, they put the bedroom floors and the brilliant dining-rooms beyond the reach of all but foreigners.

There had been few in recent years; official hospitality alone flourished at the Ritz; but still the sombre circle of Neutralian male aristocracy – for, in spite of numberless revolutions and the gross dissemination of free-thought, Neutralian ladies still modestly kept the house – foregathered there; it was their club. They wore very dark suits and very stiff collars, black ties, black buttoned boots; they smoked their cigarettes in long tortoiseshell holders; their faces were brown and wizened; they spoke of money and women, dryly and distantly, for they had never enough of either.

On this afternoon of summer when the traditional Bellacita season was in its last week and they were all preparing to remove to the seaside or to their family estates, about twenty of these descendants of the crusaders sat in the cool of the Ritz lounge. They were rewarded first by the spectacle of the foreign professors' arrival from the Ministry of Rest and Culture. Already they seemed hot and weary; they had come to fetch their academic dress for the reception at the University. The last-comers – Scott-King, Whitemaid, Miss Sveningen and Miss Bombaum – had lost their luggage. Dr Arturo Fe was like a flame at the reception desk; he pleaded, he threatened, he telephoned. Some said the luggage was impounded at the customs, others that the taxi driver had stolen it. Presently it was discovered in a service lift abandoned on the top storey.

At last Dr Fe assembled his scholars, Scott-King in his M.A.

gown and hood, Whitemaid, more flamboyantly, in the robes of his new doctorate of Upsala. Among the vestments of many seats of learning, some reminiscent of Daumier's law courts, some of Mr Will Hay of the music-hall stage, Miss Sveningen stood conspicuous in sports dress of zephyr and white shorts. Miss Bombaum refused to go. She had a story to file, she said.

The party trailed out through the swing doors into the dusty evening heat, leaving the noblemen to compare their impressions of Miss Sveningen's legs. The subject was not exhausted when they returned; indeed, had it arisen earlier in the year it would have served as staple conversation for the whole Bellacita season.

The visit to the University had been severe, an hour of speeches followed by a detailed survey of the archives. 'Miss Sveningen, gentlemen,' said Dr Fe. 'We are a little behind. The Municipality is already awaiting us. I shall telephone them that we are delayed. Do not put yourselves out.'

The party dispersed to their rooms and reassembled in due time dressed in varying degrees of elegance. Dr Fe was splendid, tight white waistcoat, onyx buttons, a gardenia, half a dozen miniature medals, a kind of sash. Scott-King and Whitemaid seemed definitely seedy beside him. But the little brown marquesses and counts had no eye for these things. They were waiting for Miss Sveningen. If her academic dress had exposed such uncovenanted mercies, such superb, such unpredictable expanses and lengths of flesh, what would she not show them when gowned for the evening?

She came.

Chocolate-coloured silk enveloped her from collar-bone to humerus and hung to within a foot of the ground; low-heeled black satin shoes covered feet which seemed now unusually large. She had bound a tartan fillet in her hair. She wore a broad patent-leather belt. She had a handkerchief artfully attached to her wrist by her watch-strap. For perhaps a minute, the inky, simian eyes regarded her aghast; then, one by one, with the languor born of centuries of hereditary disillusionment, the Knights of Malta rose from their places and sauntered with many nods to the bowing footmen towards the swing doors, towards the breathless square, towards the subdivided palaces where their wives awaited them.

'Come, lady and gentlemen,' said Dr Arturo Fe. 'The cars are here. We are eagerly expected at the Hôtel-de-Ville.'

*

No paunch, no jowl, no ponderous dignity of the counting-house or of civic office, no hint indeed of pomp or affluence, marked the Lord Mayor of Bellacita. He was young, lean and plainly ill at ease; he was much scarred by his revolutionary exploits, wore a patch on one eye and supported himself on a crutch-stick. 'His Excellency, alas, does not speak English,' said Dr Fe as he presented Scott-King and Whitemaid.

They shook hands. The Lord Mayor scowled and muttered something in Dr Fe's ear.

'His Excellency says it is a great pleasure to welcome such illustrious guests. In the phrase of our people he says his house is yours.'

The English stood aside and separated. Whitemaid had sighted a buffet at the far end of the tapestried hall. Scott-King stood diffidently alone; a footman brought him a glass of sweet effervescent wine. Dr Fe brought him someone to talk to.

'Allow me to present Engineer Garcia. He is an ardent lover of England.'

'Engineer Garcia, said the newcomer.

'Scott-King,' said Scott-King.

'I have work seven years with the firm Green, Gorridge and Wright Limited at Salford. You know them well, no doubt?'

'I am afraid not.'

'They are a very well-known firm, I think. Do you go often to Salford?'

'I'm afraid I've never been there.'

'It is a very well-known town. What, please, is your town?'

'I suppose, Granchester.'

'I am not knowing Granchester. It is a bigger town than Salford?'

'No, much smaller.'

'Ah. In Salford is much industry.'

'So I believe.'

'How do you find our Neutralian champagne?'

'Excellent.'

'It is sweet, eh? That is because of our Neutralian sun. You prefer it to the champagne of France?'

'Well, it is quite different, isn't it?'

'I see you are a connoisseur. In France is no sun. Do you know the Duke of Westminster?'

'No.'

'I saw him once at Biarritz. A fine man. A man of great propriety.'

'Indeed?'

'Indeed. London is his propriety. Have you a propriety?'

'No.'

'My mother had a propriety but it is lost.'

The clamour in the hall was tremendous. Scott-King found himself the centre of an English-speaking group. Fresh faces, new voices crowded in on him. His glass was repeatedly filled; it was over-filled and boiled and cascaded on his cuff. Dr Fe passed and re-passed. 'Ah, you have soon made friends.' He brought reinforcements; he brought more wine. 'This is a special bottle,' he whispered. 'Special for you, Professor,' and refilled Scott-King's glass with the same sugary froth as before. The din swelled. The tapestried walls, the painted ceiling, the chandeliers, the gilded architrave, danced and dazzled before his eyes.

Scott-King became conscious that Engineer Garcia was seeking to draw him into a more confidential quarter.

'How do you find our country, Professor?'

'Very pleasant, I assure you.'

'Not how you expected it, eh? Your papers do not say it is pleasant. How is it allowed to scandalize our country? Your papers tell many lies about us.'

'They tell lies about everyone, you know.'

'Please?'

'They tell lies about everyone,' shouted Scott-King.

'Yes, lies. You see for yourself it is perfectly quiet.'

'Perfectly quiet.'

'How, please?'

'Quiet,' yelled Scott-King.

'You find it too quiet? It will become more gay soon. You are a writer?'

'No, merely a poor scholar.'

'How, poor? In England you are rich, no? Here we must work very hard for we are a poor country. In Neutralia for a scholar of the first class the salary is 500 ducats a month. The rent of his apartment is perhaps 450 ducats. His taxes are 100. Oil is 30 ducats a litre. Meat is 45 ducats a kilo. So you see, we work.

'Dr Fe is a scholar. He is also a lawyer, a judge of the Lower Court. He edits the *Historical Review*. He has a high position in the Ministry of Rest and Culture, also at the Foreign Office and the Bureau of Enlightenment and Tourism. He speaks often on the radio about the international situation. He owns one-third share in the Sporting Club. In all the New Neutralia I do not think there is anyone works harder than Dr Fe, yet he is not rich as Mr Green, Mr Gorridge and Mr Wright were rich in Salford. And they scarcely worked at all. There are injustices in the world, Professor.'

'I think we must be quiet. The Lord Mayor wishes to make a speech.'

'He is a man of no cultivation. A politician. They say his mother . . .'

'Hush.'

'This speech will not be interesting, I believe.'

Something like silence fell on the central part of the hall. The Lord Mayor had his speech ready typed on a sheaf of papers. He squinnied at it with his single eye and began haltingly to read.

Scott-King slipped away. As though at a great distance he

descried Whitemaid, alone at the buffet, and unsteadily made his way towards him.

'Are you drunk?' whispered Whitemaid.

'I don't think so – just giddy. Exhaustion and the noise.'

'I am drunk.'

'Yes. I can see you are.'

'How drunk would you say I was?'

'Just drunk.'

'My dear, my dear Scott-King, there, if I may say so, you are wrong. In every degree and by every known standard I am very, very much more drunk than you give me credit for.'

'Very well. But let's not make a noise while the Mayor's speaking.'

'I do not profess to know very much Neutralian, but it strikes me that the Mayor, as you call him, is talking the most consummate rot. What is more, I doubt very much that he is a mayor. Looks to me like a gangster.'

'Merely a politician, I believe.'

'That is worse.'

'The essential, the immediate need is somewhere to sit down.'

Though they were friends only of a day, Scott-King loved this man; they had suffered, were suffering, together; they spoke, pre-eminently, the same language; they were comrades in arms. He took Whitemaid by the arm and led him out of the hall to a cool and secluded landing where stood a little settee of gilt and plush, a thing not made for sitting on. Here they sat, the two dim men, while very faintly from behind them came the sound of oratory and applause.

'They were putting it in their pockets,' said Whitemaid.

'Who? What?'

'The servants. The food. In the pockets of those long braided coats they wear. They were taking it away for their families. I got four macaroons.' And then swiftly veering he remarked: 'She looks terrible.'

'Miss Sveningen?'

'That glorious creature. It was a terrible shock to see her

215

when she came down changed for the party. It killed something here,' he said, touching his heart.

'Don't cry.'

'I can't help crying. You've seen her brown dress? And the hair ribbon? And the handkerchief?'

'Yes, yes, I saw it all. And the belt.'

'The belt,' said Whitemaid, 'was more than flesh and blood could bear. Something snapped, here,' he said, touching his forehead. 'You must remember how she looked in shorts? A Valkyrie. Something from the heroic age. Like some god-like, some unimaginably strict school prefect, *a dormitory monitor*,' he said in a kind of ecstasy. 'Think of her striding between the beds, a pigtail, bare feet, in her hand a threatening hairbrush. Oh, Scott-King, do you think she rides a bicycle?'

'I'm sure of it.'

'In shorts?'

'Certainly in shorts.'

'I can imagine a whole life lived riding tandem behind her, through endless forests of conifers, and at midday sitting down among the pine needles to eat hard-boiled eggs. Think of those strong fingers peeling an egg, Scott-King, the brown of it, the white of it, the shine. Think of her *biting* it.'

'Yes, it would be a splendid spectacle.'

'And then think of her now, in there, in that brown dress.'

'There are things not to be thought of, Whitemaid.' And Scott-King, too, shed a few tears of sympathy, of common sorrow in the ineffable, the cosmic sadness of Miss Sveningen's party frock.

'What is this?' said Dr Fe, joining them some minutes later. 'Tears? You are not enjoying it?'

'It is only,' said Scott-King,' 'Miss Sveningen's dress.'

'This is tragic, yes. But in Neutralia we take such things bravely, with a laugh. I came, not to intrude, simply to ask, Professor, you have your little speech ready for this evening? We count on you at the banquet to say a few words.'

*

For the banquet they returned to the Ritz. The foyer was empty save for Miss Bombaum, who sat smoking a cigar with a man of repellent aspect. 'I have had my dinner. I'm going out after a story,' she explained.

It was half-past ten whèn they sat down at a table spread with arabesques of flower-heads, petals, moss, trailing racemes and sprays of foliage until it resembled a parterre by Le Nôtre. Scott-King counted six wine glasses of various shapes standing before him amid the vegetation. A menu of enormous length, printed in gold, lay on his plate beside a typewritten place-card, 'Dr Scotch-Kink.' Like many explorers before him, he found that prolonged absence from food destroyed the appetite. The waiters had already devoured the *hors-d'œuvre*, but when at length the soup arrived, the first mouthful made him hiccup. This, too, he remembered, had befallen Captain Scott's doomed party in the Antarctic.

'Comment dit-on en français "hiccup"?' he asked his neighbour.

'Plait-il, mon professeur?'

Scott-King hiccuped. 'Ça,' he said.

'Ça c'est le hoquet.'

'J'en ai affreusement.'

'Évidemment, mon professeur. Il faut du cognac.'

The waiters had drunk and were drinking profusely of brandy and there was a bottle at hand. Scott-King tossed off a glassful and his affliction was doubled. He hiccuped without intermission throughout the long dinner.

This neighbour, who had so ill-advised him, was, Scott-King saw from the card, Dr Bogdan Antonic, the International Secretary of the Association, a middle-aged, gentle man whose face was lined with settled distress and weariness. They conversed, as far as the hiccups permitted, in French.

'You are not Neutralian?'

'Not yet. I hope to be. Every week I make my application to the Foreign Office and always I am told it will be next week. It is not so much for myself I am anxious – though death is a fearful thing – as for my family. I have seven children, all born in Neutralia, all without nationality. If we are sent back to my unhappy country they would hang us all without doubt.'

'Jugo-Slavia?'

'I am a Croat, born under the Habsburg Empire. That was a true League of Nations. As a young man I studied in Zagreb, Budapest, Prague, Vienna – one was free, one moved where one would; one was a citizen of Europe. Then we were liberated and put under the Serbs. Now we are liberated again and put under the Russians. And always more police, more prisons, more hanging. My poor wife is Czech. Her nervous constitution is quite deranged by our troubles. She thinks all the time she is being watched.'

Scott-King essayed one of those little, inarticulate, noncommittal grunts of sympathy which come easily to the embarrassed Englishman; to an Englishman, that is, who is not troubled by the hiccups. The sound which in the event issued from him might have been taken as derisive by a less sensitive man than Dr Antonic.

'I think so, too,' he said severely. 'There are spies everywhere. You saw that man, as we came in, sitting with the woman with the cigar. He is one of them. I have been here ten years and know them all. I was second secretary to our Legation. It was a great thing, you must believe, for a Croat to enter our diplomatic service. All the appointments went to Serbs. Now there is no Legation. My salary has not been paid since 1940. I have a few friends at the Foreign Office. They are sometimes kind and give me employment, as at the present occasion. But at any moment they may make a trade agreement with the Russians and hand us over.'

Scott-King attempted to reply.

'You must take some more brandy, Professor. It is the only thing. Often, I remember, in Ragusa I have had the hiccups from laughing . . . Never again, I suppose.'

Though the company was smaller at the banquet than at the *vin d'honneur*, the noise was more oppressive. The private dining-room of the Ritz, spacious as it was, had been built in a more trumpery style than the Hôtel-de-Ville. There the lofty roof had seemed to draw the discordant voices upwards into the cerulean perspective with which it was painted, and disperse them there amid the floating deities; the Flemish hunting scenes on the walls seemed to envelop and muffle them in their million stitches. But here the din banged back from gilding and mirrors; above the clatter and chatter of the dinner-table and the altercations of the waiters, a mixed choir of young people sang folk songs, calculated to depress the most jovial village festival. It was not thus, in his class-room at Granchester, that Scott-King had imagined himself dining.

'At my little house on the point at Lapad, we used to sit on the terrace laughing so loudly, sometimes, that the passing fishermen called up to us from their decks asking to share the joke. They sailed close in-shore and one could follow their lights far out towards the islands. When we were silent, *their* laughter came to us across the water when they were out of sight.'

The neighbour on Scott-King's left did not speak until the dessert, except to the waiters; to them he spoke loudly and often, sometimes blustering, sometimes cajoling, and by this means got two helpings of nearly every course. His napkin was tucked into his collar. He ate intently with his head bowed over his plate so that the morsels which frequently fell from his lips were not permanently lost to him. He swigged his wine with relish, sighing after each draught and tapping the glass with his knife to call the waiter's attention to the need of refilling it. Often he jammed glasses on his nose and studied the menu, not so much, it seemed, for fear of missing anything as to fix in his memory the fleeting delights of the moment. It is not entirely easy to achieve a Bohemian appearance in evening dress, but this man did so with his shock of grizzled hair, the broad ribbon on his pince-nez, and a three-days' growth of beard and whisker.

With the arrival of the dessert, he raised his countenance, fixed on Scott-King his large and rather bloodshot eyes, belched mildly and then spoke. The words were English; the accent had been formed in many cities from Memphis (Mo.) to Smyrna. 'Shakespeare, Dickens, Byron, Galsworthy,' he seemed to say.

This late birth of a troublesome gestation took Scott-King by surprise; he hiccuped non-committally.

'They are all great English writers.'

'Well, yes.'

'Your favourite, please?'

'I suppose Shakespeare.'

'He is the more dramatic, the more poetic, no?'

'Yes.'

'But Galsworthy is the more modern.'

'Very true.'

'I am modern. You are a poet?'

'Hardly that. A few translations.'

'I am an original poet. I translate my poems myself into English prose. They have been published in the United States. Do you read the *New Destiny*?'

'I am afraid not.'

'It is the magazine which publishes my translations. Last year they sent me ten dollars.'

'No one has ever paid me for my translations.'

'You should send them to the *New Destiny*. It is not possible, I think,' continued the poet, 'to render the poetry of one language into the poetry of another. Sometimes I translate English prose into Neutralian poetry. I have done a very beautiful rendering of some selected passages of your great Priestley. I hoped it would be used in the High Schools, but it is not. There is jealousy and intrigue everywhere – even at the Ministry of Education.'

At this moment a splendid figure at the centre of the table rose to make the first speech. 'Now to work,' said his neighbour, produced a note-book and pencil and began busily writing in shorthand. 'In the new Neutralia we all work.'

The speech was long and provoked much applause. In the course of it a note came to Scott-King by the hand of a waiter: 'I shall call on you to reply to his Excellency. Fe.'

Scott-King wrote in answer: 'Terribly sorry. Not tonight. Indisposed. Ask Whitemaid,' stealthily left his place and, still hiccuping, passed behind the table to the dining-room door.

Outside the foyer was almost deserted; the great glass dome which throughout the years of war had blazed aloft nightly, a candle in a naughty world, rose darkly. Two night porters shared a cigar behind one of the pillars; a huge empty carpet, strewn with empty chairs, lay before Scott-King in the subdued light to which a parsimonious management had reduced the earlier blaze. It was not much past midnight, but in the New Neutralia memories persisted of the revolutionary curfew, of police round-ups, of firing squads in the public gardens; New Neutralians liked to get home early and bolt their doors.

As Scott-King stepped into this silent space, his hiccups mysteriously ceased. He went through the swing doors and breathed the air of the piazza where under the arc-lamps workmen were washing away with hoses the dust and refuse of the day; the last of the trams, which all day long rattled round the fountains, had long since returned to its shed. He breathed deeply, testing, as it were, the limits of his miraculous recovery, and knew it to be complete. Then he turned back, took his key and, barely conscious, ascended.

*

During the first tumultuous afternoon and evening in Bellacita there had been little opportunity for more than the barest acquaintance between Scott-King and his fellow-guests of the Bellorius Association. Indeed, he had scarcely distinguished them from their hosts. They had bowed and shaken hands, they had exchanged nods among the University archives, they had apologized one to the other as they jostled and jogged elbows at the *vin d'honneur*; Scott-King had no share in whatever intimacies flourished after the banquet. He remembered an affable American and a Swiss of extreme hauteur and an oriental whom on general principles he assumed to be Chinese. Now on the morning following he came cheerfully to join them in the Ritz foyer in accordance with the printed programme. They were to leave at ten-thirty for Simona. His bags were packed; the sun, not yet oppressive, shone brilliantly through the glass dome. He was in the best of tempers.

He had awoken in this rare mood after a night of untroubled sleep. He had breakfasted on a tray of fruit, sitting on his veranda above the square, showering copious blessings on the palms and fountains and trams and patriotic statuary. He approached the group in the foyer with the intention of making himself peculiarly agreeable.

Of the festive Neutralians of the day before only Dr Fe and the Poet remained. The rest were at work elsewhere constructing the New Neutralia.

'Professor Scott-King, how are you this morning?'

There was more than politeness in Dr Fe's greeting; there was definite solicitude.

'Extremely well, thank you. Oh, of course, I had forgotten about last night's speech. I was very sorry to fail you; the truth was . . .'

'Professor Scott-King, say no more. Your friend Whitemaid, I fear, is not so well.'

'No?'

'No. He has sent word that he cannot join us.' Dr Fe raised exquisitely expressive eyebrows.

The Poet drew Scott-King momentarily aside. 'Do not be alarmed,' he said. 'Reassure your friend. Not a hint of last night's occurrences shall appear. I speak with the authority of the Ministry.'

'You know I'm completely in the dark.'

'So are the public. So they shall remain. You sometimes laugh at us in your democratic way for our little controls, but they have their uses, you see.'

'But I don't know what has happened.'

'So far as the press of Neutralia is concerned, nothing happened.'

The Poet had shaved that morning and shaved ruthlessly. The face he thrust near Scott-King's was tufted with cotton-wool. Now he withdrew it and edged away. Scott-King joined the group of delegates.

'Well,' said Miss Bombaum, 'I seem to have missed a whole packet of fun last night.'

'I seem to have missed it, too.'

'And how's the head this morning?' asked the American scholar.

'Seems like you had fun,' said Miss Bombaum.

'I went to bed early,' said Scott-King coldly. 'I was thoroughly over-tired.'

'Well, I've heard it called plenty of things in my time. I reckon that covered it, too.'

Scott-King was an adult, an intellectual, a classical scholar, almost a poet; provident Nature, who shields the slow tortoise and points the quills of the porcupine, has given to such tender spirits their appropriate armour. A shutter, an iron curtain, fell between Scott-King and those two jokers. He turned to the rest of the company and realized too late that jocularity was the least he had to fear. The Swiss had not been cordial the day before; this morning he was theatrical in his coldness; the Asiatic seemed to have spun himself a cocoon of silken aloofness. The assembled scholars did not positively cut Scott-King; in their several national fashions they signified that they were not unaware of Scott-King's presence amongst them. Further than this they did not go. They, too, had their shutters, their iron curtains. Scott-King was in disgrace. Something unmentionable had happened in which he was vicariously but inextricably implicated; a gross, black, inexpungible blot had fallen on Scott-King overnight.

He did not wish to know more. He was an adult, an intellectual; he was all that has already been predicated of him. He was no chauvinist. Throughout six embattled years he had remained resolutely impartial. But now his hackles rose; quite literally he felt the roots of his sparse hairs prick and tingle. Like the immortal private of the Buffs he stood in Elgin's place; not untaught certainly, nor rude, nor abysmally low-born, but poor and, at the moment, reckless, bewildered and alone, a heart with English instinct fraught he yet could call his own.

'I may have to keep the party waiting a few minutes,' he said. 'I must go and call on my colleague Mr Whitemaid.'

He found him in bed looking strange rather than ill; almost exalted. He was still rather drunk. The windows stood wide open on to the balcony and on the balcony, modestly robed in bath towels, sat Miss Sveningen eating beefsteak.

'They tell me downstairs that you are not coming with us to Simona?'

'No. I'm not quite up to it this morning. I have things to attend to here. It is not easy for me to explain.' He nodded towards the giant carnivore on the balcony.

'You spent an agreeable evening?'

'A total blank, Scott-King. I remember being with you at some kind of civic reception. I remember a fracas with the police, but that was much later. Hours must have intervened.'

'The police?'

'Yes. At some kind of dancing place. Irma here was splendid – like something in a film. They went down like nine-pins. But for her I suppose I should be in a cell at this moment instead of happily consuming bromoseltzer in your company.'

'You made a speech.'

'So I gather. You missed it? Then we shall never know what I said. Irma in her blunt way described it as long and impassioned, but incomprehensible.'

'Was it about Bellorius?'

'I rather suppose not. Love was uppermost in my mind, I think. To tell you the truth I have lost my interest in Bellorius. It was never strong. It wilted and died this morning when I learned that Irma was not of us. She has come for the Physical Training Congress.'

'I shall miss you.'

'Stay with us for the gymnastics.'

For a second Scott-King hesitated. The future at Simona was obscure and rather threatening.

'There are to be five hundred female athletes. Contortionists perhaps from the Indies.'

'No,' said Scott-King at length firmly. 'I must keep faith with Bellorius.'

And he returned to the delegates who now sat impatiently in a charabanc at the doors of the Ritz.

THE town of Simona stands within sight of the Mediterranean on the foothills of the great massif which fills half the map of Neutralia. Groves of walnut and cork-oak, little orchards of almond and lemon cover the surrounding country and grow to the foot of the walls which jut out among them in a series of sharp bastions, ingeniously contrived in the seventeenth century and never, in a long history of strife, put to the test of assault; for they enclose little of military significance. The medieval university, the baroque cathedral, twenty churches in whose delicate limestone belfries the storks build and multiply, a rococo square, two or three tiny shabby palaces, a market and a street of shops are all that can be found there and all that the heart of man can properly desire. The railway runs well clear of the town and betrays its presence only by rare puffs of white smoke among the tree-tops.

At the hour of the angelus Scott-King sat with Mr Bogdan Antonic at a café table on the ramparts.

'I suppose Bellorius must have looked out on almost precisely the same prospect as we see today.'

'Yes, the buildings at least do not change. There is still the illusion of peace while, as in Bellorius's time, the hills behind us are a nest of brigands.'

'He alludes to them, I remember, in the eighth canto, but surely today? . . .'

'It is still the same. Now they call them by different names – partisans, resistance groups, unreconcilables, what you will. The effect is the same. You need police escort to travel many of the roads.'

They fell silent. In the course of the circuitous journey to Simona, sympathy had sprung up between Scott-King and the International Secretary.

Bells deliciously chimed in the sunlit towers of twenty shadowy churches.

At length Scott-King said: 'You know I suspect that you and I are the only members of our party who have read Bellorius.'

'My own knowledge of him is slight. But Mr Fu has written of him very feelingly, I believe, in demotic Cantonese. Tell me, Professor, do you think the celebration is a success?'

'I'm not really a professor, you know.'

'No, but for the occasion all are professors. You are more professor than some who are here. I was obliged to cast my net rather wide to have all countries represented. Mr Jungman, for example, is simply a gynaecologist from The Hague, and Miss Bombaum is I do not know what. The Argentine and the Peruvian are mere students who happened to be in the country at this time. I tell you these things because I trust you and because I think you suspect them already. You have not perceived an element of deception?'

'Well, yes.'

'It is the wish of the Ministry. You see, I am their cultural adviser. They required a celebration this summer. I searched the records for an anniversary. I was in despair until by chance I hit on the name of Bellorius. They had not heard of him, of course, but then they would have been equally in the dark if he had been Dante or Goethe. I told them,' said Mr Antonic with a sad, sly, highly civilized little smile, 'that he was one of the greatest figures of European letters.'

'So he should be.'

'You really think so? You do not find the whole thing a masquerade? You think it is a success? I hope so, for you see my position at the Ministry is far from secure. There is jealousy everywhere. Imagine it, that anyone should be jealous of *me*. But in the New Neutralia all are so eager to work. They would snap up my little post greedily. Dr Arturo Fe would like it.'

226

'Surely not? He seems fully employed already.'

'That man collects government posts as in the old days churchmen collected benefices. He has a dozen already and he covets mine. That is why it is such a triumph to have brought him here. If the celebration is not a success, he will be implicated. Already, today, the Ministry have shown displeasure that the statue of Bellorius is not ready to be unveiled tomorrow. It is not our fault. It is the Office of Rest and Culture. It is the plot of an enemy named Engineer Garcia, who seeks to ruin Dr Fe and to succeed him in some of his posts. But Dr Fe will explain; he will improvise. He is of the country.'

*

Dr Fe improvised next day.

The party of savants were quartered in the main hotel of Simona, which that morning had the aspect of a war-time railway station owing to the arrival some time after midnight of fifty or sixty international philatelists for whom no accommodation had been arranged. They had slept in the lounge and hall; were, some of them, still sleeping when the Bellorius delegation assembled.

This was the day set down in the programme for the unveiling of the Bellorius statue. Hoarding and scaffolding in the town square marked the site of the proposed monument, but it was already well known among the delegates that the statue had not arrived. They had lived by rumour during the past three days, for nothing in their exhilarating experiences had quite corresponded with the printed plan. 'They say the bus has gone back to Bellacita for new tyres.' – 'Have you heard we are to dine with the Lord Mayor?' – 'I heard Dr Fe say we should not leave till three o'clock.' – 'I believe we ought all to be at the Chapter House.'. . . and so on. This was the atmosphere of the tour, and in it the social barriers which had threatened to divide them at Bellacita had quickly broken down. Whitemaid was forgotten, Scott-King found himself once more befriended, made part of a fellowship of bewilderment. They were two days on the road sleeping at places far from their original route; they were wined and feasted at unexpected hours, disconcertingly greeted by brass bands and deputations, disconcertingly left stranded in deserted squares; once they crossed paths and for several frantic hours exchanged luggage with a party of religious pilgrims; once they had two dinners within an hour of each other; once they had none. But here they were in the end where they should be, at Simona. The only absentee was Bellorius.

Dr Fe improvised.

'Miss Bombaum, gentlemen, a little addition to our programme. Today we go to pay homage to the National Memorial.' Obediently they trooped out to the bus. Some philatelists were sleeping there and had to be dislodged. With them were embarked a dozen vast wreaths of laurel.

'What are these?'

'Those are our homage.'

Red ribbons across the foliage bore the names of the countries thus curiously represented.

They drove out of the town into the land of cork-oak and almond. After an hour they were stopped and an escort of armoured cars formed up before and behind them.

'A little token of our esteem,' said Dr Fe.

'It is for fear of the partisans,' whispered Dr Antonic.

Dust from the military enveloped the bus and hid the landscape. After two hours they halted. Here on a bare hillock stood the National Memorial. Like all modern state-architecture it was a loveless, unadorned object saved from insignificance only by its bulk; a great truncated pyramid of stone. A squad of soldiers were at work seeking lethargically to expunge a message daubed across the inscribed face in red paint: 'Death to the Marshal.'

Dr Fe ignored their activities and led his party to the further side which was innocent of any legend, patriotic or subversive. Here under a fierce sun they left their wreaths, Scott-King stepping forward, when called, to represent Great Britain. The poet-journalist crouched and snapped with his camera. The escort cheered. The fatigue-men came round with their mops to see what was going on. Dr Fe said a few words in Neutralian. The ceremony was over. They had luncheon in a neighbouring town at what seemed to be a kind of barrack-canteen, a bare room decorated only by a large photograph of the Marshal; a substantial but far from sumptuous meal eaten at narrow tables on thick earthenware plates. Scott-King drank several glasses of the heavy, purplish wine. The bus had stood long in the sun and was scorching hot. The wine and the thick stew induced sleep, and Scott-King lolled away the hours of the return journey unconscious of the jungle-whispering which prevailed around him in that tropic air.

Whispering, however, there was, and it found full voice when at length the party returned to Simona.

Scott-King awoke to it as he entered the hotel. 'We must call a meeting,' the American professor was saying. 'We must vote a resolution.'

'We want a show-down,' said Miss Bombaum. 'Not here,' she added, taking stock of the stamp-collectors who still squatted in the public rooms. 'Upstairs.'

It would be tedious in the extreme to recount all that was said in Miss Bombaum's bedroom after the expulsion of two philatelists who had taken refuge there. It was tedious to sit there, thought Scott-King, while the fountains were splashing in the square and the breeze stirring among the orange leaves on the city walls. Speeches were made, repeated, translated and mis-translated; there were calls for order and small private explosions of ill-temper. Not all the delegates were present. The Swiss Professor and the Chinese could not be found; the Peruvian and Argentine students refused to come, but there were six savants in the little bedroom besides Miss Bombaum, all of them, except Scott-King, very indignant about something.

The cause of offence emerged through many words and the haze of tobacco smoke. In brief it was this: the Bellorius Association had been made dupes of the politicians. But for Miss Bombaum's insatiable curiosity nothing need ever have been known of it. She had nosed out the grim truth like a truffle and the fact was plain. The National Monument was nothing more or less than a fetish of civil strife. It commemorated the massacre, execution, liquidation – what you will – ten years back on that sunny spot of some fifty leaders of the now dominant Neutralian party by those then dominant. The delegates of the Bellorius Association had been tricked into leaving wreaths there and, worse than this, had been photographed in the act. Miss Bombaum's picture was at that moment, she said, being rushed out to the newspapers of the world. More than this they had lunched at the party Headquarters at the very tables where the ruffians of the party were wont to refresh themselves after their orgies of terrorization. What was more, Miss Bombaum said, she had just learned from a book in her possession that Bellorius had never had any connexion with Neutralia at all; he had been a Byzantine general.

Scott-King petulantly joined issue on this point. Strong words were used of him. 'Fascist beast.' – 'Reactionary cannibal.' – 'Bourgeois escapist.'

Scott-King withdrew from the meeting.

Dr Fe was in the passage. He took Scott-King's arm and silently led him downstairs and out into the arcaded street.

'They are not content,' said Dr Fe. 'It is a tragedy of the first magnitude.'

'You shouldn't have done it, you know,' said Scott-King.

'I should not have done it? My dear Professor, I wept when it was first suggested. I delayed our journey two days on the road precisely to avoid this. But would they listen? I said to the Minister of Popular Enlightenment: "Excellency, this is an international occasion. It is in the realm of pure scholarship. These great men have not come to Neutralia for political purposes." He replied coarsely: "They are eating and drinking at our expense. They should show their respect for the Régime. The Physical Training delegates have all saluted the Marshal in the Sports Stadium. The philatelists have been issued with the party badge and many of them wear it. The professors, too, must help the New Neutralia." What could I say? He is a person of no delicacy, of the lowest origins. It was he, I have no doubt, who induced the Ministry of Rest and Culture to delay sending the statue. Professor, you do not understand politics. I will be frank with you. It was all a plot.'

'So Miss Bombaum says.'

'A plot against me. For a long time now they have been plotting my downfall. I am not a party man. You think because I wear the badge and give the salute I am of the New Neutralia. Professor, I have six children, two of them girls of marriageable age. What can one do but seek one's fortune? And now I think I am ruined.'

'Is it as bad as that?'

'I cannot express how bad it is. Professor, you must go back to that room and persuade them to be calm. You are English. You have great influence. I have remarked during our journey together how they have all respected you.'

'They called me "a fascist beast." '

'Yes,' said Dr Fe simply, 'I heard it through the keyhole. They were very discontented.'

After Miss Bombaum's bedroom, the streets were cool and sweet; the touch of Dr Fe's fingers on Scott-King's sleeve was light as a moth. They walked on in silence. At a dewy flower-stall Dr Fe chose a buttonhole, haggled fiercely over the price, presented it with Arcadian grace to Scott-King and then resumed the sorrowful promenade.

'You will not go back?'

'It would do no good, you know.'

'An Englishman admits himself beaten,' said Dr Fe desperately.

'It amounts to that.'

'But you yourself will stay with us to the end?'

'Oh certainly.'

'Why, then, we have lost nothing of consequence. The celebrations can proceed.' He said it politely, gallantly, but he sighed as they parted.

Scott-King climbed the worn steps of the ramparts and sat alone under the orange trees watching the sun set.

*

The hotel was tranquil that evening. The philatelists had been collected and carted off; they left dumbly and glumly for an unknown destination like Displaced Persons swept up in the machinery of 'social engineering'. The six dissident delegates went with them, in default of other transport. The Swiss, the Chinese, the Peruvian and the Argentine alone remained. They dined together, silently, lacking a common tongue, but in good humour. Dr Fe, Dr Antonic and the Poet dined at another table, also silent, but sorrowful.

Next day the errant effigy arrived by lorry and the day following was fixed for the unveiling. Scott-King passed the time happily. He studied the daily papers, all of which, true to Miss Bombaum's forecast, displayed large photographs of the ceremony at the National Monument. He pieced together the sense of a leading article on the subject, he ate, he dozed, he visited the cool and glowing churches of the town, he composed the speech which, he was told, was expected of him on the morrow. Dr Fe, when they met, showed the reserve proper to a man of delicate feeling who had in emotion revealed too much of himself. It was a happy day for Scott-King.

Not so for his colleagues. Two disasters befell them severally, while he was pottering around. The Swiss Professor and the Chinese went for a little drive together in the hills. Their companionship was grounded on economy rather than mutual liking. An importunate guide; insensibility to the contemplative pleasures of Western architecture; a seemingly advantageous price; the promise of cool breezes, a wide panorama, a little restaurant; these undid them. When at evening they had not returned, their fate was certain.

'They should have consulted Dr Fe,' said Dr Antonic. 'He would have chosen a more suitable road and found them an escort.'

'What will become of them?'

'With the partisans you cannot say. Many of them are worthy, old-fashioned fellows who will treat them hospitably and wait for a ransom. But some are occupied with politics.

232

If our friends have fallen among those, I am afraid they will certainly be murdered.

'I did not like the Swiss.'

'Nor I. A Calvinist. But the Ministry will not be pleased that he is murdered.'

The fate of the South Americans was less romantic. The police took them off during luncheon.

'It seems they were not Argentine or Peruvian,' said Dr Antonic. 'Not even students.'

'What had they done?'

'I suppose they were informed against.'

'They certainly had a villainous appearance.'

'Oh yes, I suppose they were desperate fellows – spies, bimetallists, who can say? Nowadays it is not what you do that counts, but who informs against you. I think someone very high up must have informed against that pair. Otherwise Dr Fe could have had the business postponed until after our little ceremony. Or perhaps Dr Fe's influence is on the wane.'

*

So in the end, as was indeed most fitting, one voice only was raised to honour Bellorius.

The statue, when at last after many ineffective tugs at the controlling cord it was undraped and stood clear, stonily, insolently unabashed under the fierce Neutralian sun, while the populace huzzaed and, according to their custom, threw fire-crackers under the feet of the notables, as the pigeons fluttered above in high alarm and the full weight of the band followed the opening trumpets – the statue was appalling.

There are no contemporary portraits of Bellorius still extant. In their absence some sharp business had been done in the Ministry of Rest and Culture. The figure now so frankly brought to view had lain long years in a mason's yard. It had been commissioned in an age of free enterprise for the tomb of a commercial magnate whose estate, on his death, had proved to be illusory. It was not Bellorius; it was not the fraudulent merchant prince; it was not even unambiguously male; it was scarcely human; it represented perhaps one of the virtues.

Scott-King stood aghast at the outrage he had unwittingly committed on that gracious square. But he had already spoken and his speech had been a success. He had spoken in Latin; he had spoken from the heart. He had said that a torn and embittered world was that day united in dedicating itself to the majestic concept of Bellorius, in rebuilding itself first in Neutralia, then among all the yearning peoples of the West, on the foundations Bellorius had so securely laid. He had said that they were lighting a candle that day which by the Grace of God should never be put out.

And after the oration came a prodigious luncheon at the University. And after the luncheon he was invested with a Doctorate of International Law. And after the investiture he was put into a bus and driven with Dr Fe, Dr Antonic, and the Poet back to Bellacita.

By the direct road the journey took barely five hours. It was not yet midnight when they drove down the brilliant boulevard of the capital city. Little had been said on the road. When they drew up at the Ministry, Dr Fe said: 'So our little expedition is over. I can only hope, Professor, that you have enjoyed it a particle as much as we.' He held out his hand and smiled under the arc-lamps. Dr Antonic and the Poet collected their modest luggage. 'Good night,' they said. 'Good night. We shall walk from here. The taxis are so expensive – the double fare operates after nine o'clock.'

They walked. Dr Fe ascended the steps of the Ministry. 'Back to work,' he said. 'I have had an urgent summons to report to my chief. We work late in the New Neutralia.'

There was nothing furtive about his ascent but it was swift. Scott-King caught him as he was about to enter a lift.

'But, I say, where am I to go?'

'Professor, our humble town is yours. Where would you like to go?'

'Well, I suppose I must go to an hotel. We were at the Ritz before.'

'I am sure you will be comfortable there. Tell the porter to

234

get you a taxi and see he does not try to overcharge you.
Double fare but not more.'

'But I shall see you tomorrow?'

'I hope *very* often.'

Dr Fe bowed and the doors of the lift shut upon his bow
and his smile.

There was in his manner something more than the reserve
proper to a man of delicate feeling who had in emotion
revealed too much of himself.

'OFFICIALLY,' Mr Horace Smudge, 'we don't even know
you're here.'

He gazed at Scott-King through hexagonal spectacles across
the Pending Tray and twiddled a new-fangled fountain pen;
a multiplicity of pencils protruded from his breast-pocket and
his face seemed to suggest that he expected one of the
telephones on his desk to ring at any moment with a message
about something far more important than the matter under
discussion; he was for all the world, Scott-King thought, like
the clerk in the food office at Granchester.

Scott-King's life had been lived far from chanceries, but
once, very many years ago at Stockholm, he had been asked
to luncheon by mistake for someone else, at the British
Embassy. Sir Samson Courtenay had been *chargé d'affaires* at
the time and Scott-King gratefully recalled the air of non-
chalant benevolence with which he had received a callow
undergraduate where he had expected a Cabinet Minister.
Sir Samson had not gone far in his profession, but for one
man at least, for Scott-King, he remained the fixed type of
English diplomat.

Smudge was not as Sir Samson; he was the child of sterner
circumstances and a more recent theory of public service; no
uncle had put in a bland word for Smudge in high places;

honest toil, a clear head in the examination room, a genuine enthusiasm for Commercial Geography, had brought him to his present position as second secretary at Bellacita. 'You've no conception,' said Smudge, 'what a time we have with Priorities. I've had to put the Ambassadress off the plane twice, at the last moment, to make room for I.C.I. men. As it is I have four electrical engineers, two British Council lecturers and a trades unionist all wanting passages. Officially we have not heard of Bellorius. The Neutralians brought you here. It's their business to get you back.'

'I've been to them twice a day for three days. The man who organized everything, Dr Fe, seems to have left the Ministry.'

'You could always go by train, of course. It takes a little time but it would probably be quicker in the end. I presume you have all the necessary visas?'

'No. How long would they take to get?'

'Perhaps three weeks, perhaps longer. It's the Inter-Allied Zone Authority which holds things up.'

'But I can't afford to go on living here indefinitely. I was only allowed to bring seventy-five pounds, and the prices are terrible.'

'Yes, we had a case like that the other day. A man called Whitemaid. He'd run out of money and wanted to cash a cheque, but, of course, that is specifically contrary to the currency regulations. The consul took charge of him.'

'Did he get home?'

'I doubt it. They used to ship them by sea, you know, as Distressed British Subjects and hand them over to the police on arrival, but all that has been discontinued since the war. He was connected with your Bellorius celebration, I think. It has caused a good deal of work to us one way and another. But it's worse for the Swiss. They've had a professor murdered, and that always involves a special report on counsellor-level. I'm sorry I can't do more for you. I only deal with air priorities. You are the business of the consulate, really. You had better let them know in a week or two how things turn out.'

*

The heat was scarcely endurable. In the ten days Scott-King had been in the country, the summer seemed to change temper and set its face angrily against him. The grass had turned brown in the square. Men still hosed the streets, but the burning stone was dry again in an instant. The season was over; half the shops were shut and the little brown noblemen had left their chairs in the Ritz.

It was no great distance from the Embassy to the hotel, but Scott-King was stumbling with exhaustion before he reached the revolving doors. He went on foot, for he was obsessed now by parsimony; he could no longer eat with pleasure, counting the price of each mouthful, calculating the charge for service, the stamp duty, the luxury taxes; groaning in that scorching summer under the weight of the Winter Relief Fund. He should leave the Ritz without delay, he resolved, and yet he hesitated; once ensconced in some modest pension, in some remote side street where no telephone ever rang and no one in passage from the outer world ever set foot, might he not be lost irretrievably, submerged, unrecognizable in his dimness, unremembered? Would he perhaps, years hence, exhibit a little discoloured card advertising lessons in English conversation, grow shabbier and greyer and plumper with the limp accretions of despair and destitution and die there at last nameless? He was an adult, an intellectual, a classical scholar, almost a poet, but he could not face the future without terror. So he clung to the Ritz, empty as it was, contemptuously as he felt himself regarded there, as the one place in Neutralia where salvation might still be found. If he left, he knew it would be for ever. He lacked the assurance of the native nobility who could sit there day by day, as though by right. Scott-King's only right lay in his travellers' cheques. He worked out his bill from hour to hour. At the moment he had nearly forty pounds in hand. When he was down to twenty, he decided, he would move. Meanwhile he looked anxiously round the dining-room before starting the daily calculation of how cheaply he could lunch.

And that day he was rewarded. His number turned up. Sitting not two tables away, alone, was Miss Bombaum. He rose to greet her. All the hard epithets with which they had parted were forgotten.

'May I sit here?'

She looked up, first without recognition, then with pleasure. Perhaps there was something in his forlorn appearance, in the diffidence of his appeal, which cleared him in Miss Bombaum's mind. This was no fascist beast that stood before her, no reactionary cannibal.

'Surely,' she said. 'The guy who invited me hasn't shown up.'

A ghastly fear, cold in that torrid room, struck Scott-King, that he would have to pay for Miss Bombaum's luncheon. She was eating a lobster, he noted, and drinking hock.

'When you've finished,' he said. 'Afterwards, with coffee perhaps in the lounge.'

'I've a date in twenty minutes,' she said. 'Sit down.'

He sat and at once, in answer to her casual inquiry, poured out the details of his predicament. He laid particular stress on his financial problems and, as pointedly as he could, ordered the humblest dish on the menu. 'It's a fallacy not to eat in hot weather,' said Miss Bombaum. 'You need to keep your resistance up.'

When he had finished the recital she said, 'Well, I reckon it shouldn't be hard to fix you up. Go by the Underground.'

Blacker despair in Scott-King's haunted face told Miss Bombaum that she had not made herself clear.

'You've surely heard of the Underground? It's' – she quoted from one of her recent articles on the subject – 'it's an alternative map of Europe, like a tracing overlying all the established frontiers and routes of communication. It's the new world taking shape below the surface of the old. It's the new ultra-national citizenship.'

'Well, I'm blessed.'

'Look, I can't stop now. Be here this evening and I'll take you to see the key man.'

That afternoon, his last, as it turned out, in Bellacita, Scott-King received his first caller. He had gone to his room to sleep through the heat of the day, when his telephone rang and a voice announced Dr Antonic. He asked for him to be sent up.

The Croat entered and sat by his bed.

'So you have acquired the Neutralian custom of the *siesta*. I am too old. I cannot adapt myself to new customs. Everything in this country is as strange to me as when I first came here.

'I was at the Foreign Office this morning inquiring about my papers of naturalization and I heard by chance you were still here. So I came at once. I do not intrude? I thought you would have left by now. You have heard of our misfortunes? Poor Dr Fe is disgraced. All his offices taken from him. More than this, there is trouble with his accounts. He spent more, it appears, on the Bellorius celebrations than the Treasury authorized. Since he is out of office he has no access to the books and cannot adjust them. They say he will be prosecuted, perhaps sent to the islands.'

'And you, Dr Antonic?'

'I am never fortunate. I relied on Dr Fe for my naturalization. Whom shall I turn to now? My wife thought that perhaps you could do something for us in England to make us British subjects.'

'There is nothing I can do.'

'No, I suppose not. Nor in America?'

'Still less there.'

'So I told my wife. But she is a Czech, and so more hopeful. We Croats do not hope. It would be a great honour if you would come and explain these things to her. She will not believe me when I say there is no hope. I promised I would bring you.'

So Scott-King dressed and was led through the heat to a new quarter on the edge of the town, to a block of flats.

'We came here because of the elevator. My wife was weary of Neutralian stairs. But, alas! the elevator no longer works.'

They trudged to the top floor, to a single sitting-room full of children, heavy with the smell of coffee and cigarette smoke.

'I am ashamed to receive you in a house without an elevator,' said Mme Antonic in French; then turning to the children, she addressed them in another tongue. They bowed, curtsied, and left the room. Mme Antonic prepared coffee and brought a plate of biscuits from the cupboard.

'I was sure you would come,' she said. 'My husband is too timid. You will take us with you to America.'

'Dear madam, I have never been there.'

'To England, then. We must leave this country. We are not at our ease here.'

'I am finding the utmost difficulty in getting to England myself.'

'We are respectable people. My husband is a diplomat. My father had his own factory at Budweis. Do you know Mr Mackenzie?'

'No, I don't think so.'

'He was a *very* respectable Englishman. He would explain that we come of good people. He visited often to my father's factory. If you will find Mr Mackenzie he will help us.'

So the conversation wore on. 'If we could only find Mr Mackenzie,' Mme Antonic repeated, 'all our troubles would be at an end.' Presently the children returned.

'I will take them to the kitchen,' said Mme Antonic, 'and give them some jam. Then they will not be a nuisance.'

'You see,' said Dr Antonic as the door closed, 'she is always hopeful. Now I do not hope. Do you think,' he asked, 'that in Neutralia Western Culture might be born again? That this country has been preserved by Destiny from the horrors of war so that it can become a beacon of hope for the world?'

'No,' said Scott-King.

'Do you not?' asked Dr Antonic anxiously. 'Do you not? Neither do I.'

*

That evening Miss Bombaum and Scott-King took a cab to the suburbs and left it at a café where they met a man who had sat with Miss Bombaum in the Ritz on her first evening. No names were exchanged.

'Who's this guy, Martha?'

'An English friend of mine I want you to help.'

'Going far?'

'England. Can he see the chief?'

'I go ask. He's on the level?'

'Surely.'

'Well, stick around while I ask.'

He went to telephone and returned saying, 'The chief'll see him. We can drop him off there, then have our talk.'

They took another cab and drove farther from the city into a district of tanneries and slaughter-houses, recognizable by their smell in the hot darkness. Presently they stopped at a lightless villa.

'In there. Don't ring. Just push the door.'

'Hope you have a good trip,' said Miss Bombaum.

Scott-King was not a reader of popular novels and so was unfamiliar with the phrase 'It all happened so quickly that it was not until afterwards . . .' That, however, expressed his situation. The cab drove off as he was still stumbling up the garden path. He pushed the door, entered an empty and lightless hall, heard a voice from another room call 'Come in,' went in, and found himself in a shabby office confronting a Neutralian in the uniform of a major of police.

The man addressed him in English. 'You are Miss Bombaum's friend? Sit down. Do not be alarmed by my uniform. Some of our clients are *very* much alarmed. A silly boy tried to shoot me last week when he saw me like this. He suspected a trap. You want to go to England, I think. That is very difficult. Now if you had said Mexico or Brazil or Switzerland it would be easier. You have reasons which make England preferable?'

'I have reasons.'

'Curious. I spent many years there and found it a place of few attractions. The women had no modesty, the food upset my stomach. I have a little party on their way to Sicily. That would not do instead?'

'I am afraid not.'

'Well, we must see what can be done. You have a passport? This is lucky. English passports come very dear just now. I hope Miss Bombaum explained to you that mine is not a charitable organization. We exist to make profits and our expenses are high. I am constantly bothered by people who come to me supposing I work for the love of it. I do love my work, but love is not enough. The young man I spoke of just now, who tried to shoot me – he is buried just outside under the wall – he thought this was a political organization. We help people irrespective of class, race, party, creed or colour – for cash in advance. It is true, when I first took over, there were certain amateur associations that had sprung up during the World War – escaping prisoners, communist agents, Zionists, spies and so on. I soon put them out of business. That is where my position in the police is a help. Now I can say I have a virtual monopoly. Our work increases every day. It is extraordinary how many people without the requisite facilities seem anxious to cross frontiers today. I also have a valued connexion with the Neutralian government. Troublesome fellows whom they want to disappear pass through my hands in large numbers. How much have you got?'

'About forty pounds.'

'Show me.'

Scott-King handed him his book of travellers' cheques.

'But there are seventy pounds here.'

'Yes, but my hotel bill . . .'

'There will be no time for that.'

'I am sorry,' said Scott-King firmly. 'I could not possibly leave an hotel with my bill unpaid, especially in a foreign country. It may seem absurdly scrupulous to you, but it is one of the things a Granchesterian simply cannot do.'

The major was not a man to argue from first principles. He took men as they came and in his humane calling he dealt with many types.

'Well, I shan't pay it,' he said. 'Do you know anyone else in Bellacita?'

'No one.'

'Think.'

'There was a man called Smudge at our Embassy.'

'Smudge shall have your bill. These cheques want signing.'

242

Despite his high training, Scott-King signed and the cheques were put away in the bureau drawer.

'My luggage?'

'We do not handle luggage. You will start this evening. I have a small party leaving for the coast. We have our main clearing-house at Santa Maria. From there you will travel by steamer, perhaps not in the grand luxury, but what will you? No doubt as an Englishman you are a good sailor.'

He rang a bell on his desk and spoke to the answering secretary in Neutralian.

'My man here will take charge of you and fit you out. You speak Neutralian? No? Perhaps it is as well. We do not encourage talk in my business, and I must warn you, the strictest discipline has to be observed. From now on you are under orders. Those who disobey never reach their destinations. Good-bye and a good journey.'

Some few hours later a large and antiquated saloon car was bumping towards the sea. In it sat in extreme discomfort seven men habited as Ursuline nuns. Scott-King was among them.

*

The little Mediterranean seaport of Santa Maria lay very near the heart of Europe. An Athenian colony had thrived there in the days of Pericles and built a shrine to Poseidon; Carthaginian slaves had built the breakwater and deepened the basin; Romans had brought fresh water from the mountain springs; Dominican friars had raised the great church which gave the place its present name; the Habsburgs had laid out the elaborate little piazza; one of Napoleon's marshals had made it his base and left a classical garden there. The footprints of all these gentler conquerors were still plain to see, but Scott-King saw nothing as, at dawn, he bowled over the cobbles to the water-front.

The Underground dispersal centre was a warehouse; three wide floors, unpartitioned, with boarded windows, joined by an iron staircase. There was one door near which the guardian had set her large brass bedstead. At most hours of the day she reclined there under a coverlet littered with various kinds of food, weapons, tobacco and a little bolster on which she sometimes made lace of an ecclesiastical pattern. She had the face of a *tricoteuse* of the Terror. 'Welcome to Modern Europe,' she said as the seven Ursulines entered.

The place was crowded. In the six days which he spent there Scott-King identified most of the groups who messed together by languages. There were a detachment of Slovene royalists, a few Algerian nationals, the remnants of a Syrian anarchist association, ten patient Turkish prostitutes, four French Pétainist millionaires, a few Bulgarian terrorists, a half-dozen former Gestapo men, an Italian air-marshal and his suite, a Hungarian ballet, some Portuguese Trotskyites. The English-speaking group consisted chiefly of armed deserters from the American and British Armies of Liberation. They had huge sums of money distributed about the linings of their clothes, the reward of many months' traffic round the docks of the central sea.

Such activity as there was took place in the hour before dawn. Then the officer in charge, husband, it seemed, of the guardian hag, would appear with lists and a handful of passports; a roll would be called and a party dispatched. During the day the soldiers played poker – a fifty dollar ante and a hundred-dollar raise. Sometimes in the hours of darkness there were newcomers. The total number at the clearing station remained fairly constant.

At last on the sixth day there was a commotion. It began at midday with a call from the chief of police. He came with sword and epaulettes and he talked intently and crossly in Neutralian with the custodian.

One of the Americans, who had picked up more languages during his time in the Old World than most diplomats, explained: 'The guy with the fancy fixings says we got to get to hell out of here. Seems there's a new officer going to raid this joint.'

When the officer had gone, the custodian and his wife debated the question. 'The old girl says why don't he hand us over and get rewarded. The guy says Hell, the most likely reward they'd get would be hanging. Seems there's some stiffs planted round about.'

Presently a sea captain appeared and talked Greek. All the Underground travellers sat stock still listening, picking up a word here and there. 'This guy's got a ship can take us off.'

'Where?'

'Aw, some place. Seems they're kinda more interested in finance than geography.'

A bargain was struck. The captain departed, and the Underground conductor explained to each language group in turn that there had been a slight dislocation of plan. 'Don't worry,' he said. 'Just go quiet. Everything's all right. We'll look after you. You'll all get where you want to in time. Just at the moment you got to move quick and quiet, that's all.'

So, unprotesting, at nightfall, the strangely assorted party was hustled on board a schooner. Noah's animals cannot have embarked with less sense of the object of their journey. The little ship was not built for such cargo. Down they went into a dark hold; hatches were battened down; the unmistakable sound of moorings being cast off came to them in their timbered prison; an auxiliary diesel engine started up; sails were hoisted; soon they were on the high seas in very nasty weather.

*

This is the story of a summer holiday; a light tale. It treats, at the worst, with solid discomfort and intellectual doubt. It would be inappropriate to speak here of those depths of the human spirit, the agony and despair, of the next few days of Scott-King's life. To even the Comic Muse, the gadabout, the adventurous one of those heavenly sisters, to whom so little that is human comes amiss, who can mix in almost any company and find a welcome at almost every door – even to her there are forbidden places. Let us leave Scott-King then on the high seas and meet him again as, sadly changed, he comes at length into harbour. The hatches are off, the August sun seems cool and breathless, Mediterranean air fresh and spring-like as at length he climbs on deck. There are soldiers; there is barbed wire; there is a waiting lorry; there is a drive through a sandy landscape, more soldiers, more wire. All the time Scott-King is in a daze. He is first fully conscious in a tent, sitting stark naked while a man in khaki drill taps his knee with a ruler.

'I say, Doc, I know this man.' He looks up into a vaguely familiar face. 'You *are* Mr Scott-King, aren't you? What on earth are you doing with this bunch, sir?'

'Lockwood! Good gracious, you used to be in my Greek set! Where am I?'

'No. 64 Jewish Illicit Immigrants' Camp, Palestine.'

*

Granchester re-assembled in the third week of September. On the first evening of term, Scott-King sat in the masters' common-room and half heard Griggs telling of his trip abroad. 'It gives one a new angle of things, getting out of England for a bit. What did you do, Scottie?'

'Oh, nothing much. I met Lockwood. You remember him. Sad case, he was a sitter for the Balliol scholarship. Then he had to go into the army.'

'I thought he was still in it. How typical of old Scottie that all he has to tell us after eight weeks away is that he met a prize pupil! I shouldn't be surprised to hear you did some work, too, you old blackleg.'

'To tell you the truth I feel a little *désœuvré*. I must look for a new subject.'

'You've come to the end of old Bellorius at last?'

'Quite to the end.'

Later the head master sent for Scott-King.

'You know,' he said, 'we are starting this year with fifteen fewer classical specialists than we had last term?'

'I thought that would be about the number.'

'As you know, I'm an old Greats man myself. I deplore it as much as you do. But what are we to do? Parents are not interested in producing the "complete man" any more. They want to qualify their boys for jobs in the modern world. You can hardly blame them, can you?'

'Oh, yes,' said Scott-King. 'I can and do.'

'I always say you are a much more important man here than I am. One couldn't conceive of Granchester without Scott-King. But has it ever occurred to you that a time may come when there will be no more classical boys at all?'

'Oh, yes. Often.'

'What I was going to suggest was – I wonder if you will consider taking some other subject as well as the classics? History, for example, preferably economic history?'

'No, head master.'

'But, you know, there may be something of a crisis ahead.'

'Yes, head master.'

'Then what do you intend to do?'

'If you approve, head master, I will stay as I am here as long as any boy wants to read the classics. I think it would be very wicked indeed to do anything to fit a boy for the modern world.'

'It's a short-sighted view, Scott-King.'

'There, head master, with all respect, I differ from you profoundly. I think it the most long-sighted view it is possible to take.'

BASIL SEAL RIDES AGAIN

OR THE RAKE'S REGRESS

TO MRS IAN FLEMING

Dear Ann

In this senile attempt to recapture the manner of my youth I have resurrected characters from earlier stories which, if you ever read them, you will have forgotten.

Basil Seal was the hero of *Black Mischief* (1932) and *Put Out More Flags* (1942). Through my ineptitude the colour of his eyes changed during the intervening decade. At the end of the latter book he considered marriage with the newly widowed, very rich Angela Lyne who had long been his mistress. Ambrose Silk, an aesthete, also appeared in that book. Peter, Lord Pastmaster, first appeared as Peter Beste-Chetwynde in *Decline and Fall* (1928). His mother, later Lady Metroland, appeared there and in *Vile Bodies* (1930). Alastair Digby-Vane-Trumpington was Lady Metroland's lover in 1928 and Sonia's husband in 1942.

Albright is new: an attempt to extract something from the rum modern world of which you afford me occasional glimpses in your hospitable house.

I should have liked to drop the title in favour of what I have here used as subtitle, but it was suggested that this might smack of sharp practice to readers who saw the story in the *Sunday Telegraph* and *Esquire* and might be led to expect something new.

Ever your affec. coz.

Combe Florey
December 1962

E.W.

'Yes.'

'What d'you mean: "Yes"?'

'I didn't hear what you said.'

'I said he made off with all my shirts.'

'It's not that I'm the least deaf. It's simply that I can't concentrate when a lot of fellows are making a row.'

'There's a row now.'

'Some sort of speech.'

'And a lot of fellows saying: "Shush".'

'Exactly. I can't concentrate. What did you say?'

'This fellow made off with all my shirts.'

'Fellow making the speech?'

'No, no. Quite another fellow – called Albright.'

'I don't think so. I heard he was dead.'

'This one isn't. You can't say he stole them exactly. My daughter gave them to him.'

'All?'

'Practically all. I had a few in London and there were a few at the wash. Couldn't believe it when my man told me. Went through all the drawers myself. Nothing there.'

'Bloody thing to happen. *My* daughter wouldn't do a thing like that.'

Protests from neighbouring diners rose in volume.

'They can't want to hear this speech. It's the most awful rot.'

'We seem to be getting unpopular.'

'Don't know who all these fellows are. Never saw anyone before except old Ambrose. Thought I ought to turn out and support him.'

Peter Pastmaster and Basil Seal seldom attended public banquets. They sat at the end of a long table under chandeliers and pier-glasses, looking, for all the traditional brightness of the hotel, too bright and too private for their surroundings. Peter was a year or two the younger but he, like Basil, had scorned to order his life with a view of longevity or spurious youth. They were two stout, rubicund, richly dressed old buffers who might have passed as exact contemporaries.

The frowning faces that were turned towards them were of all ages from those of a moribund Celtic bard to the cross adolescent critic's for whose dinner Mr Bentley, the organizer, was paying. Mr Bentley had, as he expressed it, cast his net wide. There were politicians and publicists there, dons and cultural attachés, Fulbright scholars, representatives of the Pen Club, editors; Mr Bentley, home-sick for the *belle époque* of the American slump, when in England the worlds of art and fashion and action harmoniously mingled, had solicited the attendance of a few of the early friends of the guest of honour and Peter and Basil, meeting casually a few weeks before, had decided to go together. They were celebrating the almost coincident events of Ambrose Silk's sixtieth birthday and his investiture with the Order of Merit.

Ambrose, white-haired, pallid, emaciated, sat between Dr Parsnip, Professor of Dramatic Poetry at Minneapolis, and Dr Pimpernell, Professor of Poetic Drama at St Paul. These distinguished expatriates had flown to London for the occasion. It was not the sort of party at which decorations are worn but as Ambrose delicately inclined in deprecation of the honeyed words that dripped around him, no one could doubt his effortless distinction. It was Parsnip who was now on his feet attempting to make himself heard.

'I hear the cry of "silence",' he said with sharp spontaneity. His voice had assumed something of the accent of his place of exile but his diction was orthodox – august even; he had quite discarded the patiently acquired proletarian colloquialisms of thirty years earlier. 'It is apt, for, surely?, the object of our homage tonight is epitomized in that golden word. The voice which once clearly spoke the message of what I for one, and many of us here, will always regard as the most glorious decade of English letters, the nineteen-thirties,' (growls of dissent from the youthful critic) 'that voice tardily perhaps, but at long last so illustriously honoured by official recognition, has been silent for a quarter of a century. Silent in Ireland, silent in Tangier, in Telaviv and Ischia and

Portugal, now silent in his native London, our guest of honour has stood for us as a stern rebuke, a recall to artistic reticence and integrity. The books roll out from the presses, none by Ambrose Silk. Not for Ambrose Silk the rostrum, the television screen; for him the enigmatic and monumental silence of genius . . .'

'I've got to pee,' said Basil.

'I always want to nowadays.'

'Come on then.'

Slowly and stiffly they left the hotel dining-room.

As they stood side by side in the lavatory Basil said: 'I'm glad Ambrose has got a gong. D'you think the fellow making the speech was pulling his leg?'

'Must have been. Stands to reason.'

'You were going to tell me something about some shirts.'

'I did tell you.'

'What was the name of the chap who got them?'

'Albright.'

'Yes, I remember; a fellow called Clarence Albright. Rather an awful chap. Got himself killed in the war.'

'No one that I knew got killed in the war except Alastair Trumpington.'

'And Cedric Lyne.'

'Yes, there was Cedric.'

'And Freddy Sothill.'

'I never really considered I knew him,' said Basil.

'This Albright married someone – Molly Meadows, perhaps?'

'I married Molly Meadows.'

'So you did. I was there. Well, someone like that. One of those girls who were going round at the time – John Flintshire's sister, Sally perhaps. I expect your Albright is her son.'

'He doesn't look like anyone's son.'

'People always are,' said Basil, 'sons or daughters of people.'

This truism had a secondary, antiquated and, to Peter, an obvious meaning, which was significant of the extent by which Basil had changed from *enfant terrible* to 'old Pobble', the name by which he was known to his daughter's friends.

The change had been rapid. In 1939 Basil's mother, his sister, Barbara Sothill, and his mistress, Angela Lyne, had seen the war as the opportunity for his redemption. His embattled country, they supposed, would find honourable use for those deplorable energies which had so often brought him almost into the shadows of prison. At the worst he would fill a soldier's grave; at the best he would emerge as a second Lawrence of Arabia. His fate was otherwise.

Early in his military career, he lamed himself, blowing away the toes of one foot while demonstrating to his commando section a method of his own device for demolishing railway bridges, and was discharged from the army. From this disaster was derived at a later date the sobriquet 'Pobble'. Then, hobbling from his hospital bed to the registry office, he married the widowed Angela Lyne. Hers was one of those few, huge, astutely dispersed fortunes which neither international calamities nor local experiments with socialism could seriously diminish. Basil accepted wealth as he accepted the loss of his toes. He forgot he had ever walked without a stick and a limp, had ever been lean and active, had ever been put to desperate shifts for quite small sums. If he ever recalled that decade of adventure it was as something remote and unrelated to man's estate, like an end-of-term shortness of pocket money at school.

For the rest of the war and for the first drab years of peace he had appeared on the national register as 'farmer'; that is to say, he lived in the country in ease and plenty. Two dead men, Freddy Sothill and Cedric Lyne, had left ample cellars. Basil drained them. He had once expressed the wish to become one of the 'hard-faced men who had done well out of the war'. Basil's face, once very hard, softened and rounded. His scar became almost invisible in rosy suffusion. None of his few clothes, he found, now buttoned comfortably and when, in that time of European scarcity, he and Angela went to New York, where such things could then still be procured by the well-informed, he bought suits and shirts and shoes by the dozen and a whole treasury of watches, tie-pins, cuff-links and chains so that on his return, having scrupulously declared them and paid full duty at the customs – a thing he had never in his life done before – he remarked of his elder brother, who, after a tediously successful diplomatic career spent in gold-lace or starched linen allowed himself in retirement (and reduced circumstances), some laxity in dress: 'Poor Tony goes about looking like a scarecrow.'

Life in the country palled when food rationing ceased. Angela made over the house they had called 'Cedric's Folly' and its grottoes to her son Nigel on his twenty-first birthday, and took a large, unobtrusive house in Hill Street. She had other places to live, a panelled seventeenth-century apartment in Paris, a villa on Cap Ferrat, a beach and bungalow quite lately acquired in Bermuda, a little palace in Venice which she had once brought for Cedric Lyne but never visited in his lifetime – and among them they moved with their daughter Barbara. Basil settled into the orderly round of the rich. He became a creature of habit and of set opinions. In London finding Bratt's and Bellamy's disturbingly raffish, he joined that sombre club in Pall Mall that had been the scene of so many painful interviews with his self-appointed guardian, Sir Joseph Mannering, and there often sat in the chair which had belonged prescriptively to Sir Joseph and, as Sir Joseph had done, pronounced his verdict on the day's news to any who would listen.

Basil turned, crossed to the looking-glasses and straightened his tie. He brushed up the copious grey hair. He looked at himself with the blue eyes which had seen so much and now saw only the round, rosy face in which they were set, the fine clothes of English make which had replaced the American improvisations, the starched shirt which he was almost alone in wearing, the black pearl studs, the button-hole.

A week or two ago he had had a disconcerting experience in this very hotel. It was a place he had frequented all his life, particularly in the latter years, and he was on cordial terms with the man who took the men's hats in a den by the Piccadilly entrance. Basil was never given a numbered ticket and assumed he was known by name. Then a day came when he sat longer than usual over luncheon and found the man off duty. Lifting the counter he had penetrated to the rows of pegs and retrieved his bowler and umbrella. In the ribbon of the hat he found a label, put there for identification. It bore the single pencilled word 'Florid'. He had told his daughter, Barbara, who said: 'I wouldn't have you any different. Don't for heaven's sake go taking one of those cures. You'd go mad.'

Basil was not a vain man; neither in rags nor in riches had he cared much about the impression he made. But the epithet recurred to him now as he surveyed himself in the glass.·

'Would you say Ambrose was "florid", Peter?'

'Not a word I use.'

'It simply means flowery.'

'Well, I suppose he is.'

'Not fat and red?'

'Not Ambrose.'

'Exactly.'

'I've been called "florid".'

'You're fat and red.'

'So are you.'

'Yes, why not? Almost everyone is.'

'Except Ambrose.'

'Well, he's a pansy. I expect he takes trouble.'

'We don't.'

'Why the hell should we?'

'We don't.'

'Exactly.'

The two old friends had exhausted the subject.

Basil said: 'About those shirts. How did your girl ever meet a fellow like that?'

'At Oxford. She insisted on going up to read History. She picked up some awfully rum friends.'

'I suppose there were girls there in my time. We never met them.'

'Nor in mine.'

'Stands to reason the sort of fellow who takes up with undergraduettes has something wrong with him.'

'Albright certainly has.'

'What does he look like?'

'I've never set an eye. My daughter asked him to King's Thursday when I was abroad. She found he had no shirts and she gave him mine.'

'Was he hard up?'

'So she said.'

'Clarence Albright never had any money. Sally can't have brought him much.'

'There may be no connexion.'

'Must be. Two fellows without money both called Albright. Stands to reason they're the same fellow.'

Peter looked at his watch.

'Half past eleven. I don't feel like going back to hear those speeches. We showed up. Ambrose must have been pleased.'

'He was. But he can't expect us to listen to all that rot.'

'What did he mean about Ambrose's "silence"? Never knew a fellow who talked so much.'

'All a lot of rot. Where to now?'

'Come to think of it, my mother lives upstairs. We might see if she's at home.'

They rose to the floor where Margot Metroland had lived ever since the destruction of Pastmaster House. The door on the corridor was not locked. As they stood in the little vestibule loud, low-bred voices came to them.

'She seems to have a party.'

Peter opened the door of the sitting-room. It was in darkness save for the ghastly light of a television set. Margot crouched over it, her old taut face livid in the reflection.

'Can we come in?'

'Who are you? What d'you want? I can't see you.'

Peter turned on the light at the door.

'Don't do that. Oh, it's you Peter. And Basil.'

'We've been dining downstairs.'

'Well, I'm sorry; I'm busy, as you can see. Turn the light

out and come and sit down if you want to, but don't disturb me.'

'We'd better go.'

'Yes. Come and see me when I'm not so busy.'

Outside Peter said: 'She's always looking at that thing nowadays. It's a great pleasure to her.'

'Where to now?'

'I thought of dropping in at Bellamy's.'

'I'll go home. I left Angela on her own. Barbara's at a party of Robin Trumpington's.'

'Well, good night.'

'I say, those places where they starve you – you know what I mean – do they do any good?'

'Molly swears by one.'

'She's not fat and red.'

'No. She goes to those starving places.'

'Well, good night.'

Peter turned east, Basil north, into the mild, misty October night. The streets at this hour were empty. Basil stumped across Piccadilly and up through Mayfair, where Angela's house was almost the sole survivor of the private houses of his youth. How many doors had been closed against him then that were now open to all comers as shops and offices!

The lights were on. He left his hat and coat on a marble table and began the ascent to the drawing-room floor, pausing on the half-landing to recuperate.

'Oh, Pobble, you toeless wonder. You always turn up just when you're wanted.'

Florid he might be, but there were compensations. It was not thus that Basil had often been greeted in limber youth. Two arms embraced his neck and drew him down, an agile figure inclined over the protuberance of his starched shirt, a cheek was pressed to his and teeth tenderly nibbled the lobe of his ear.

'Babs, I thought you were at a party. Why on earth are you dressed like that?'

His daughter wore very tight very short trousers, slippers

and a thin jersey. He disengaged himself and slapped her loudly on the behind.

'Sadist. It's that sort of party. It's a "happening".'

'You speak in riddles, child.'

'It's a new sort of party the Americans have invented. Nothing is arranged beforehand. Things just happen. Tonight they cut off a girl's clothes with nail scissors and then painted her green. She had a mask on so I don't know who it was. She might just be someone hired. Then what happened was Robin ran out of drink so we've all gone scouring for it. Mummy's in bed and doesn't know where old Nudge keeps the key and we can't wake him up.'

'You and your mother have been into Nudge's bedroom?'

'Me and Charles. He's the chap I'm scouring with. He's downstairs now trying to pick the lock. I think Nudge must be sedated, he just rolled over snoring when we shook him.'

At the foot of the staircase a door led to the servants' quarters. It opened and someone very strange appeared with an armful of bottles. Basil saw below him a slender youth, perhaps a man of twenty-one, who had a mop of dishevelled black hair and a meagre black fringe of beard and whiskers; formidable, contemptuous blue eyes above grey pouches; a proud, rather childish mouth. He wore a pleated white silk shirt, open at the neck, flannel trousers, a green cummerbund and sandals. The appearance, though grotesque, was not specifically plebeian and when he spoke his tone was pure and true without a taint of accent.

'The lock was easy,' he said, 'but I can't find anything except wine. Where d'you keep the whisky?'

'Heavens, I don't know,' said Barbara.

'Good evening,' said Basil.

'Oh, good evening. Where do you keep the whisky?'

'It is a fancy dress party?' Basil asked.

'Not particularly,' said the young man.

'What have you got there?'

'Champagne of some kind. I didn't notice the label.'

'He's got the Cliquot rosé,' said Basil.

'How clever of him,' said Barbara.

'It will probably do,' said the young man. 'Though most people prefer whisky.'

Basil attempted to speak but found no words.

Barbara quoted:

' "His Aunt Jobiska made him drink
Lavender water tinged with pink,
For the world in general knows
There's nothing so good for a Pobble's toes." Come along, Charles, I think we've got all we're going to get here. I sense a grudging hospitality.'

She skipped downstairs, waved from the hall and was out of the front door, while Basil still stood dumbfounded.

At length, even more laboriously than he was wont, he continued upward. Angela was in bed reading.

'You're home early.'

'Peter was there. No one else I knew except old Ambrose. Some booby made a speech. So I came away.'

'Very wise.'

Basil stood before Angela's long looking-glass. He could see her behind him. She put on her spectacles and picked up her book.

'Angela, I don't drink much nowadays, do I?'

'Not as much as you used.'

'Or eat?'

'More.'

'But you'd say I led a temperate life?'

'Yes, on the whole.'

'It's just age,' said Basil. 'And dammit, I'm not sixty yet.'

'What's worrying you, darling?'

'It's when I meet young men. A choking feeling – as if I was going to have an apoplectic seizure. I once saw a fellow in a seizure, must have been about the age I am now – the Lieutenant-Colonel of the Bombardiers. It was a most unpleasant spectacle. I've been feeling lately something like that might strike me any day. I believe I ought to take a cure.'

'I'll come too.'

'Will you really, Angela? You are a saint.'

'Might as well be there as anywhere. They're supposed to

be good for insomnia too. The servants would like a holiday. They've been wearing awfully overworked expressions lately.'

'No sense taking Babs. We could send her to Malfrey.'

'Yes.'

'Angela, I saw the most awful looking fellow tonight with a sort of beard – here, in the house, a friend of Babs. She called him "Charles".'

'Yes, he's someone new.'

'What's his name?'

'I did hear. It sounded like a pack of fox hounds I once went out with. I know – Albrighton.'

'Albright,' cried Basil, the invisible noose tightening. 'Albright, by God.'

Angela looked at him with real concern. 'You know,' she said, 'you really do look rather rum. I think we'd better go to one of those starving places at once.'

And then what had seemed a death-rattle turned into a laugh.

'It was one of Peter's shirts,' he said, unintelligibly to Angela.

2

It may one day occur to a pioneer of therapeutics that most of those who are willing to pay fifty pounds a week to be deprived of food and wine, seek only suffering and that they could be cheaply accommodated in rat-ridden dungeons. At present the profits of the many thriving institutions which cater for the ascetic are depleted by the maintenance of neat lawns and shrubberies and, inside, of the furniture of a private house and apparatus resembling that of a hospital.

Basil and Angela could not immediately secure rooms at the sanatorium recommended by Molly Pastmaster. There was a waiting list of people suffering from every variety of infirmity. Finally they frankly outbid rival sufferers. A man whose obesity threatened the collapse of his ankles, and a woman raging with hallucinations were informed that their bookings were defective, and on a warm afternoon Basil and Angela drove down to take possession of their rooms.

There was a resident physician at this most accommodating house. He interviewed each patient on arrival and ostensibly considered individual needs.

He saw Angela first. Basil sat stolidly in an outer room, his hands on the head of his cane, gazing blankly before him. When at length he was admitted, he stated his needs. The doctor did not attempt any physical investigation. It was a plain case.

'To refrain from technical language you complain of speechlessness, a sense of heat and strangulation, dizziness and subsequent trembling?' said this man of science.

'I feel I'm going to burst,' said Basil.

'Exactly. And these symptoms only occur when you meet young men?'

'Hairy young men especially.'

'Ah.'

'*Young puppies.*'

'And with puppies too? That is very significant. How do you react to kittens?'

'I mean the young men are puppies.'

'Ah. And are you fond of puppies, Mr Seal?'

'Reasonably.'

'Ah.' The man of science studied the paper on his desk. 'Have you always been conscious of this preference for your own sex?'

'I'm not conscious of it now.'

'You are fifty-eight years and ten months. That is often a crucial age, one of change, when repressed and unsuspected inclinations emerge and take control. I should strongly recommend your putting yourself under a psychoanalyst. We do not give treatment of that kind here.'

'I just want to be cured of feeling I'm going to burst.'

'I've no doubt our régime will relieve the symptoms. You

will not find many young men here to disturb you. Our patients are mostly mature women. There is a markedly virile young physical training instructor. His hair is quite short but you had better keep away from the gym. Ah, I see from your paper that you are handicapped by war-wounds. I will take out all physical exercise from your timetable and substitute extra periods of manipulation by one of the female staff. Here is your diet sheet. You will notice that for the first forty-eight hours you are restricted to turnip juice. At the end of that period you embark on the carrots. At the end of the fortnight, if all goes well, we will have you on raw eggs and barley. Don't hesitate to come and see me again if you have any problem to discuss.'

The sleeping quarters of male and female inmates were separated by the length of the house. Basil found Angela in the drawing-room. They compared their diet sheets.

'Rum that it should be exactly the same treatment for insomnia and apoplexy.'

'That booby thought I was a pansy.'

'It takes a medical man to find out a thing like that. All these years and I never knew. They're always right, you know. So that's why you're always going to that odd club.'

'This is no time for humour. This is going to be a very grim fortnight.'

'Not for me,' said Angela. 'I came well provisioned. I'm only here to keep you company. And there's a Mrs Somebody next door to me who I used to know. She's got a private cache of all the sleeping-pills in the world. I've made great friends with her already. *I* shall be all right.'

On the third day of his ordeal, the worst according to *habitués* of the establishment, there came a telephone call from Barbara.

'Pobble, I want to go back to London. I'm bored.'

'Bored with Aunt Barbara?'

'Not with *her*, with *here*.'

'You stay where you're put, chattel.'

'No. *Please*, I want to go home.'

'Your home is where I am. You can't come here.'

'No. I want to go to London.'

'You can't. I sent the servants away for a fortnight.'

'Most of my friends live without servants.'

'You've sunk into a very low world, Babs.'

'Don't be such an ass. Sonia Trumpington hasn't any servants.'

'Well, she won't want you.'

'Pobble, you sound awfully feeble.'

'Who wouldn't who's only had one carrot in the last three days.'

'Oh, you are brave.'

'Yes.'

'How's mummy?'

'Your mother is not keeping the régime as strictly as I am.'

'I bet she isn't. Anyway, please, can I go back to London?'

'No.'

'You mean "No"?'

'Yes.'

'Fiend.'

Basil had gone hungry before. From time to time in his varied youth, in desert, tundra, glacier and jungle, in garrets and cellars, he had briefly endured extremities of privation. Now in the periods of repose and solitude, after the steam bath and the smarting deluge of the showers, after the long thumping and twisting by the huge masseuse, when the chintz curtains were drawn in his bedroom and he lay towel-wrapped and supine gazing at the pattern of the ceiling paper, familiar, forgotten pangs spoke to him of his past achievements.

He defined his condition to Angela after the first week of the régime. 'I'm not rejuvenated or invigorated. I'm etherealized.'

'You look like a ghost.'

'Exactly. I've lost sixteen pounds three ounces.'

'You're overdoing it. No one else keeps these absurd rules. We aren't expected to. It's like the *rien ne va plus* at roulette.

Mrs What's-her-name has found a black market in the gym kept by the sergeant-instructor. We ate a grouse pie this morning.'

They were in the well-kept grounds. A chime of bells announced that the brief recreation was over. Basil tottered back to his masseuse.

Later, light-headed and limp, he lay down and stared once more at the ceiling paper.

As a convicted felon might in long vigils search his history for the first trespass that had brought him to his present state, Basil examined his conscience. Fasting, he knew, was in all religious systems the introduction to self-knowledge. Where had he first played false to his destiny? After the conception of Barbara; after her birth. She, in some way, was at the root of it. Though he had not begun to dote on her until she was eight years old, he had from the first been aware of his own paternity. In 1947, when she was a year old, he and Angela had gone to New York and California. That enterprise, in those days, was nefarious. Elaborate laws restricted the use of foreign currencies and these they had defied drawing freely on undisclosed assets. But on his return he had made a full declaration to the customs. It was no immediate business of theirs to inquire into the sources of his laden trunks. In a mood of arrogance he had displayed everything and paid without demur. There lay the fount and origin of the deviation into rectitude that had disfigured him in recent years. As though waking after a night's drunkenness – an experience common enough in his youth – and confusedly articulating the disjointed memories of outrage and absurdity, he ruefully contemplated the change he had wrought in himself. His voice was not the same instrument as of old. He had first assumed it as a conscious imposture; it had become habitual to him; the antiquated, worldly-wise moralities which, using that voice, he had found himself obliged to utter, had become his settled opinions. It had begun as nursery clowning for the diversion of Barbara; a parody of Sir Joseph Mannering; darling, crusty old Pobble performing the part expected of him; and now the parody had become the *persona*.

His meditation was interrupted by the telephone. 'Will you take a call from Mrs Sothill?'

'Babs.'

'Basil. I just wondered how you were getting on.'

'They're very pleased with me.'

'Thin?'

'Skinny. And concerned with my soul.'

'Chump. Listen. I'm concerned with Barbara's soul.'

'What's she been up to?'

'I think she's in love.'

'Rot.'

'Well, she's moping.'

'I expect she misses me.'

'When she isn't moping she's telephoning or writing letters.'

'Not to me.'

'Exactly. There's someone in London.'

'Robin Trumpington?'

'She doesn't confide.'

'Can't you listen in on the telephone?'

'I've tried that, of course. It's certainly a man she's talking to. I can't really understand their language but it sounds very affectionate. You won't like it awfully if she runs off, will you?'

'She'd never think of such a thing. Don't put ideas into the child's head, for God's sake. Give her a dose of castor oil.'

'*I* don't mind, if *you* don't. I just thought I should warn.'

'Tell her I'll soon be back.'

'She knows that.'

'Well, keep her under lock and key until I get out.'

Basil reported the conversation to Angela. 'Barbara says Barbara's in love.'

'Which Barabara?'

'Mine. Ours.'

'Well, it's quite normal at her age. Who with?'

'Robin Trumpington, I suppose.'

'He'd be quite suitable.'

'For heaven's sake, Angie, she's only a child.'

'I fell in love at her age.'

'And a nice mess that turned out. It's someone after my money.'

'*My* money.'

'I've always regarded it as mine. I shan't let her have a penny. Not till I'm dead anyway.'

'You look half dead now.'

'I've never felt better. You simply haven't got used to my new appearance.'

'You're very shaky.'

' "Disembodied" is the word. Perhaps I need a drink. In fact I know I do. This whole business of Babs has come as a shock – at a most unsuitable time. I might go and see the booby doctor.'

And, later, he set off along the corridor which led to the administrative office. He set off but had hardly hobbled six short paces when his newly sharpened conscience stabbed him. Was this the etherealized, the reborn, Basil slinking off like a schoolboy to seek the permission of a booby doctor for a simple adult indulgence? He turned aside and made for the gym.

There he found two large ladies in bathing-dresses sitting astride a low horse. They swallowed hastily and brushed crumbs from their lips. A rubbery young man in vest and shorts addressed him sternly: 'One moment, sir. You can't come in here without an appointment.'

'My visit is unprofessional,' said Basil. 'I want a word with you.'

The young man looked doubtful. Basil drew his note case from his pocket and tapped it on the knob of his cane.

'Well, ladies, I think that finishes the work-out for this morning. We're getting along very nicely. We mustn't expect immediate results you know. Same routine tomorrow.' He replaced the lid on a small enamelled bin. The ladies looked hungrily at it but went in peace.

'Whisky,' said Basil.

'Whisky? Why, I couldn't give you such a thing even if I had it. It would be as much as my job's worth.'

'I should think it is precisely what your job *is* worth.'

'I don't quite follow, sir.'

'My wife had grouse pie this morning.'

He was a cheeky young man much admired in his own milieu for his bounce. He was not abashed. A horrible smirk of complicity passed over his face. 'It wasn't really grouse,' he said. 'Just a stale liver pâté the grocer had. They get so famished here they don't care what they're eating, the poor creatures.'

'Don't talk about my wife in those terms,' said Basil, adding; 'I shall know what I'm drinking, at a pound a snort.'

'I haven't any whisky, honest. There may be a drop of brandy in the first-aid cupboard.'

'Let's look at it.'

It was of a reputable brand. Basil took two snorts. He gasped. Tears came to his eyes. He felt for support on the wall-bars beside him. For a moment he feared nausea. Then a great warmth and elation were kindled inside him. This was youth indeed; childhood no less. Thus he had been exalted in his first furtive swigging in his father's pantry. He had drunk as much brandy as this twice a day, most days of his adult life, after a variety of preliminary potations and had felt merely a slight heaviness. Now in his etherealized condition he was, as it were, raised from the earth, held aloft and then lightly deposited; a mystical experience as though on Ganges bank or a spur of the Himalayas.

There was a mat near his feet, thick, padded, bed-like. Here he subsided and lay in ecstasy; quite outside his body, high and happy, his spirit soared; he shut his eyes.

'You can't stay here, sir. I've got to lock up.'

'Don't worry,' said Basil. 'I'm not here.'

The gymnast was very strong; it was a light task to hoist Basil on one of the trollies which in various sizes were part of the equipment of the sanatorium, and thus recumbent, dazed but not totally insensible, smoothly propelled up the main corridor, he was met by the presiding doctor.

'What have you there, sergeant?'

'Couldn't say at all. Never saw the gentleman before.'

'It looks like Mr Seal. Where did you find him?'

'He just walked into the gym, sir, looking rather queer and suddenly he passed out.'

'Gave you a queer look? Yes.'

'He rolls through the air with the greatest of ease, that darling young man on the flying trapeze,' Basil chanted with some faint semblance of tune in his voice.

'Been overdoing it a bit, sir, I wouldn't wonder.'

'You might be right, sergeant. You had better leave him now. The female staff can take over, Ah. Sister Gamage, Mr Seal needs help in getting to his room. I think the régime has proved too strenuous for him. You may administer an ounce of brandy. I will come and examine him later.'

But when he repaired to Basil's room he found his patient deeply sleeping.

He stood by the bed, gazing at his patient. There was an expression of peculiar innocence on the shrunken face. But the physician knew better.

'I will see him in the morning,' he said and then went to instruct his secretary to inform the previous applicants that two vacancies had unexpectedly occurred.

3

'The sack, the push, the boot. I've got to be out of the place in an hour.'

'Oh Basil, that *is* like old times, isn't it?'

'Only deep psycho-analysis can help me, he says, and in my present condition I am a danger to his institution.'

'Where shall we go? Hill Street's locked up. There won't be anyone there until Monday.'

'The odd thing is I have no hangover.'

'Still ethereal?'

'Precisely. I suppose it means an hotel.'

'You might telephone to Barbara and tell her to join us. She said she was keen to leave.'

But when Angela telephoned to her sister-in-law, she heard: 'But isn't Barbara with you in London? She told me yesterday you'd sent for her. She went up by the afternoon train.'

'D'you think she can have gone to that young man?'

'I bet she has.'

'Ought I to tell Basil?'

'Keep it quiet.'

'I consider it very selfish of her. Basil isn't at all in good shape. He'll have a fit if he finds out. He had a sort of fit yesterday.'

'Poor Basil. He may never know.'

Basil and Angela settled their enormous bill. Their car was brought round to the front. The chauffeur drove, Angela sat beside Basil who huddled beside her occasionally crooning ill-remembered snatches of 'the daring young man on the flying trapeze'. As they approached London they met all the outgoing Friday traffic. Their own way was clear. At the hotel Basil went straight to bed – 'I don't feel I shall ever want another bath as long as I live,' he said – and Angela ordered a light meal for him of oysters and stout. By dusk he had rallied enough to smoke a cigar.

Next morning he was up early and spoke of going to his club.

'That dingy one?'

'Heavens no, Bellamy's. But I don't suppose there'll be many chaps there on a Saturday morning.'

There was no one. The barman shook him up an egg with port and brandy. Then, with the intention of collecting some books, he took a taxi to Hill Street. It was not yet eleven o'clock. He let himself into what should have been the empty and silent house. Music came from the room on the ground floor where small parties congregated before luncheon and dinner. It was a dark room, hung with tapestry and furnished with Bühl. There he found his daughter, dressed in pyjamas and one of her mother's fur coats, seated on the floor with her face caressing a transistor radio. Behind her in the fire-place large lumps of coal lay on the ashes of the sticks and paper which had failed to kindle them.

'Darling Pobble, never more welcome. I didn't expect you till Monday and I should have been dead by then. I can't make out how the central heating works. I thought the whole point of it was it just turned on and didn't need a man. Can't get the fire to burn. And don't start: "Babs, what are you doing here?" I'm freezing, that's what.'

'Turn that damn thing off.'

In the silence Barbara regarded her father more intently. 'Darling, what have they been doing to you? You aren't yourself at all. You're tottering. Not my fine stout Pobble at all. Sit down at once. Poor Pobble, all shrunk like a mummy. Beasts!'

Basil sat and Barbara wriggled round until her chin rested on his knees. 'Famine baby,' she said. Star-sapphire eyes in the child-like face under black touselled hair gazed deep into star-sapphire eyes sunk in empty pouches. 'Belsen atrocity,' she added fondly. 'Wraith. Skeleton-man. Dear dug-up corpse.'

'Enough of this flattery. Explain yourself.'

'I told you I was bored. You know what Malfrey's like as well as I do. Oh the hell of the National Trust. It's not so bad in the summer with the charabancs. Now it's only French art experts – half a dozen a week, and all the rooms still full of oilcloth promenades and rope barriers and Aunt Barbara in the flat over the stables and those ridiculous Sothills in the bachelors' wing and the height of excitement a pheasant shoot with lunch in the hut and then nothing to eat except pheasant and . . . Well, I registered a formal complaint, didn't I?, but you were too busy starving to pay any attention, and if your only, adored daughter's happiness doesn't count for more than senile vanity . . .' she paused, exhausted.

'There's more to it than that.'

'There is *something* else.'

'What?'

'Now, Pobble, you have to take this calmly. For your own

good, not for mine. I'm used to violence, God knows. If you had been poor the police would have been after you for the way you've knocked me about all these years. I can take it; but you, Pobble, you are at an age when it might be dangerous. So keep quite calm and I'll tell you. I'm engaged to be married.'

It was not a shock; it was not a surprise. It was what Basil had expected. 'Rot,' he said.

'I happen to be in love. You must know what that means. You must have been in love once – with mummy or someone.'

'Rot. And dammit, Babs, don't blub. If you think you're old enough to be in love, you're old enough not to blub.'

'That's a silly thing to say. It's being in love makes me blub. You don't realize. Apart from being perfect and frightfully funny he's an artistic genius and everyone's after him and I'm jolly lucky to have got him and you'll love him too once you know him if only you won't be stuck-up and we got engaged on the telephone so I came up and he was out for all I know some one else *has* got him and I almost died of cold and now you come in looking more like a vampire than a papa and start saying "rot".'

She pressed her face on his thigh and wept.

After a time Basil said: 'What makes you think Robin paints?'

'Robin? Robin Trumpington? You don't imagine I'm engaged to *Robin*, do you? He's got a girl of his own he's mad about. You don't know much about what goes on, do you, Pobble? If it's only Robin you object to, everything's all right.'

'Well, who the hell do you think you are engaged to?'

'Charles of course.'

'Charles à Court. Never heard of him.'

'Don't pretend to be deaf. You know perfectly well who I mean. You met him here the other evening only I don't think you really took him in.'

'*Albright*,' said Basil. It was evidence of the beneficial effect of the sanatorium that he did not turn purple in the face, did not gobble. He merely asked quietly: 'Have you been to bed with this man?'

273

'Not to *bed*.'

'Have you slept with him?'

'Oh, no *sleep*.'

'You know what I mean. Have you had sexual intercourse with him?'

'Well, perhaps; not in bed; on the floor and wide awake you *might* call it intercourse, I suppose.'

'Come clean, Babs. Are you a virgin?'

'It's not a thing any girl likes having said about her, but I think I am.'

'*Think?*'

'Well, I suppose so. Yes, really. But we can soon change all that. Charles is set on marriage, bless him. He says it's easier to get married to girls if they're virgins. I can't think why. I don't mean a big wedding. Charles is very unsocial and he's an orphan, no father, no mother, and his relations don't like him, so we'll just be married quietly in a day or two and then I thought if you and mummy don't want it we might go to the house in Bermuda. We shan't be any trouble to you at all, really. If you want to go to Bermuda, we'll settle for Venice, but Charles says that's a bit square and getting cold in November, so Bermuda will really be better.'

'Has it occurred to either of you that you need my permission to marry?'

'Now don't get legal, Pobble. You know I love you far too much ever to do anything you wouldn't like.'

'You'd better get dressed and go round to your mother at Claridges.'

'Can't get dressed. No hot water.'

'Have a bath there. I had better see this young man.'

'He's coming here at twelve.'

'I'll wait for him.'

'You'll freeze.'

'Get up and get out.'

There followed one of those scuffles that persisted between father and daughter even in her eighteenth year which ended in her propulsion, yelping.

Basil sat and waited. The bell could not be heard in the

ante-room. He sat in the window and watched the doorstep, saw a taxi draw up and Barbara enter it still in pyjamas and fur coat carrying a small case. Later he saw his enemy strolling confidently from Berkeley Square. Basil opened the door.

'You did not expect to see me?'

'No, but I'm very glad to. We've a lot to discuss.'

They went together to the ante-room. The young man was less bizarre in costume than on their previous meeting but his hair was as copious and his beard proclaimed his chosen, deleterious status. They surveyed one another in silence. Then Basil said: 'Lord Pastmaster's shirts are too big for you.'

It was a weak opening.

'It's not a thing I should have brought up if you hadn't,' said Albright, 'but *all* your clothes look too big for *you*.'

Basil covered his defeat by lighting a cigar.

'Barbara tells me you've been to that sanatorium in Kent,' continued the young man easily; 'there's a new place, you know, much better, in Sussex.'

Basil was conscious of quickening recognition. Some faint, odious inkling of kinship; had he not once, in years far gone by, known someone who had spoken in this way to his elders? He drew deeply on his cigar and studied Albright. The eyes, the whole face seemed remotely familiar; the reflection of a reflection seen long ago in shaving-mirrors.

'Barbara tells me you have proposed marriage to her.'

'Well, *she* actually popped the question. I was glad to accept.'

'You are Clarence Albright's son?'

'Yes, did you know him? I barely did. I hear he was rather awful. If you want to be genealogical, I have an uncle who is a duke. But I barely know him either.'

'And you are a painter?'

'Did Barbara tell you that?'

'She said you were an artistic genius.'

'She's a loyal little thing. She must mean my music.'

'You compose?'

'I improvise sometimes. I play the guitar.'

'Professionally?'

'Sometimes – in coffee bars, you know.'

'I do not know, I'm afraid. And you make a living by it?'

'Not what *you* would call a living.'

'May I ask, then, how you propose to support my daughter?'

'Oh that doesn't come into it. It's the other way round. I'm doing what you did, marrying money. Now I know what's in your mind. "Buy him off," you think. I assure you that won't work. Barbara is infatuated with me and, if it's not egotistical to mention it, I am with her. I'm sure you won't want one of those "Gretna Green Romances" and press photographers following you about. Besides, Barbara doesn't want to be a nuisance to you. She's a loyal girl, as we've already remarked. The whole thing can be settled calmly. Think of the taxes your wife will save by a good solid marriage settlement. It will make no appreciable difference to your own allowance.'

And still Basil sat steady, unmoved by any tremor of that volcanic senility which a fortnight ago would have exploded in scalding, blinding showers. He was doing badly in this first encounter which he had too lightly provoked. He must take thought and plan. He was not at the height of his powers. He had been prostrate yesterday. Today he was finding his strength. Tomorrow experience would conquer. This was a worthy antagonist and he felt something of the exultation which a brave of the sixteenth century might have felt when in a brawl he suddenly recognized in the clash of blades a worthy swordsman.

'Barbara's mother has the best financial advice,' he said.

'By the way, where is Barbara? She arranged to meet me here.'

'She's having a bath in Claridges.'

'I ought to go over and see her. I'm taking her out to lunch. You couldn't lend me a fiver, could you?'

'Yes,' said Basil. 'Certainly.'

If Albright had known him better he would have taken alarm at this urbanity. All he thought was: 'Old crusty's a much softer job than anyone told me.' And Basil thought: 'I hope he spends it all on luncheon. That bank-note is all he will ever get. He deserved better.'

4

Sonia Trumpington had never remarried. She shared a flat with her son Robin but saw little of him. Mostly she spent her day alone with her needlework and in correspondence connected with one or two charitable organizations with which, in age, she had become involved. She was sewing when Basil sought her out after luncheon (oysters again, two dozen this time with a pint of champagne – his strength waxed hourly) and she continued to stitch at the framed grospoint while he confided his problem to her.

'Yes. I've met Charles Albright. He's rather a friend of Robin's.'

'Then perhaps you can tell me what Barbara sees in him.'

'Why, *you*, of course,' said Sonia. 'Haven't you noticed? He's the dead spit – looks, character, manner, everything.'

'Looks? Character? Manner? Sonia you're raving.'

'Oh, not as you are now, not even after your cure. Don't you remember at all what you were like at his age?'

'But he's a monster.'

'So were you, darling. Have you quite forgotten? It's all as clear as clear to me. You Seals are so incestuous. Why do you suppose you got keen on Barbara? Because she's just like Barbara Sothill. Why is Barbara keen on Charles? Because he's *you*.'

Basil considered this proposition with his newly resharpened wits.

'That beard.'

'I've seen you with a beard.'

'That was after I came back from the Arctic and I never played the guitar in my life,' he said.

'Does Charles play the guitar? First I've heard of it. He does all sorts of things – just as you did.'

'I wish you wouldn't keep bringing me into it.'

'Have you quite forgotten what you were like? Have a look at some of my old albums.'

Like most of her generation Sonia had in youth filled large

volumes with press-cuttings and photographs of herself and her friends. They lay now in a shabby heap in a corner of the room.

'That's Peter's twenty-firster at King's Thursday. First time I met you, I think. Certainly the first time I met Alastair. He was Margot's boy-friend then, remember? She was jolly glad to be rid of him . . . That's my marriage. I bet you were there.' She turned the pages from the posed groups of bride, bridegroom and bridesmaids to the snap-shots taken at the gates of St Margaret's. 'Yes, here you are.'

'No beard. Perfectly properly dressed.'

'Yes, there are more incriminating ones later. Look at that . . . and that.'

They opened successive volumes. Basil appeared often.

'I don't think any of them very good likenesses,' said Basil stiffly. 'I'd just come back from the Spanish front there – of course I look a bit untidy.'

'It's not clothes we're talking about. Look at your expression.'

'Light in my eyes,' said Basil.

'1937. That's another party at King's Thursday.'

'What a ghastly thing facetious photographs are. What on earth am I doing with that girl?'

'Throwing her in the lake. I remember the incident now. I took the photograph.'

'Who?'

'I've no idea. Perhaps it says on the back. Just "Basil and Betty". She must have been much younger than us, not our kind at all. I've got an idea she was the daughter of some duke or other. The Stayles – that's who she was.'

Basil studied the picture and shuddered. 'What can have induced me to behave like that?'

'Youthful high spirits.'

'I was thirty-four, God help me. She's very plain.'

'I'll tell you who she is – was. Charles Albright's mother. That's an odd coincidence if you like. Let's look her up and make sure.'

She found a *Peerage* and read: 'Here we are. Fifth daughter of the late duke. Elizabeth Ermyntrude Alexandra, for whom H.R.H. The Duke of Connaught stood sponsor. Born 1920. Married 1940 Clarence Albright, killed in action 1943. Leaving issue. Died 1956. I remember hearing about it – cancer, very young. That's Charles, that issue.'

Basil gazed long at the photograph. The girl was plump and, it seemed, wriggling; annoyed rather than amused by the horse-play. 'How one forgets. I suppose she was quite a friend of mine once.'

'No, no. She was just someone Margot produced for Peter.'

Basil's imagination, once so fertile of mischief, lately so dormant, began now, in his hour of need, to quicken and stir.

'That photograph has given me an idea.'

'Basil, you've got that old villainous look. What are you up to?'

'Just an idea.'

'You're not going to throw Barbara into the Serpentine.'

'Something not unlike it,' he said.

'Let us go and sit by the Serpentine,' said Basil to his daughter that afternoon.

'Won't it be rather cold?'

'It will be quiet. Wrap up well. I have to talk to you seriously.'

'Good temper?'

'Never better.'

'Why not talk here?'

'Your mother may come in. What I have to say doesn't concern her.'

'It's about me and Charles, I bet.'

'Certainly.'

'Not a scolding?'

'Far from it. Warm fatherly sympathy.'

'It's worth being frozen for that.'

They did not speak in the car. Basil sent it away, saying they would find their own way back. At that chilly tea-time, with the leaves dry and falling, there was no difficulty in finding an empty seat. The light was soft; it was one of the days when London seems like Dublin.

'Charles said he'd talked to you. He wasn't sure you loved him.'

'I love him.'

'Oh, *Pobble*.'

'He did not play the guitar but I recognized his genius.'

'Oh, Pobble, what are you up to?'

'Just what Sonia asked.' Basil leaned his chin on the knob of his cane. 'You know, Babs, that all I want is your happiness.'

'This doesn't sound at all like you. You've got some sly scheme.'

'Far from it. You must never tell him or your mother what I am about to say. Charles's parents are dead so they are not affected. I knew his mother very well; perhaps he doesn't know how well. People often wondered why she married Albright. It was a blitz marriage, you know, while he was on leave and there were air raids every night. It was when I was first out of hospital, before I married your mother.'

'Darling Pobble, it's very cold here and I don't quite see that all this past history has to do with me and Charles.'

'It began,' said Basil inexorably, 'when – what was her name? – Betty was younger than you are now. I threw her into the lake at King's Thursday.'

'What began?'

'Betty's passion for me. Funny what excites a young girl – with you a guitar, with Betty a ducking.'

'Well, I think that's rather romantic. It sort of brings you and Charles closer.'

'Very close indeed. It was more than romantic. She was too young at the beginning – just a girlish crush. I thought she would get over it. Then, when I was wounded, she took to visiting me every day in hospital and the first day I came out – you won't be able to understand the sort of exhilaration a man feels at a time like that, or the appeal lameness has for some women, or the sense of general irresponsibility we all had during the blitz – I'm not trying to excuse myself. I was not the first man. She had grown up since the splash in the lake. It only lasted a week. Strictly perhaps I should have married her, but I was less strict in those days. I married your mother instead. You can't complain about that. If I hadn't, you wouldn't exist. Betty had to look elsewhere and fortunately that ass Albright turned up in the nick. Yes, Charles is your brother, so how could I help loving him?'

Soundlessly Barbara rose from the seat and sped through the twilight, stumbled on her stiletto heels across the sand of the Row, disappeared behind the statuary through Edinburgh Gate. Basil at his own pace followed. He stopped a taxi, kept it waiting at the kerb while he searched Bellamy's vainly for a friendly face, drank another egg-nog at the bar, went on towards Claridges.

'What on earth's happened to Barbara?' Angela asked. 'She came in with a face of tragedy, didn't speak and now she's locked herself in your bedroom.'

'I think she's had a row with that fellow she was keen on. What was his name? Albright. A good thing really, a likeable fellow but not at all suitable. I daresay Babs needs a change of scene. Angie, if it suits you, I think we might all three of us go to Bermuda tomorrow.'

'Can we get tickets?'

'I have them already. I stopped at the travel office on my way from Sonia's. I don't imagine Babs will want much dinner tonight. She's best left alone at the moment. I feel I could manage a square meal. We might have it downstairs.'

CHARLES RYDER'S SCHOOLDAYS

CHAPTER ONE: RYDER BY GASLIGHT

INTRODUCTION

Last August one of my colleagues, examining the Evelyn Waugh file for 1970 in a search for evidence bearing on a contractual negotiation with his publishers Eyre Methuen, came upon a thirty-four-page typescript entitled *Charles Ryder's Schooldays*. There was nothing to show why this piece had been put in the 1970 file. It was a good carbon bearing the stamp of Alex McLachlan, literary type-copying specialist of St Leonards-on-Sea, described by Professor Robert Murray Davis in his book *Evelyn Waugh, Writer* as 'Waugh's long-suffering typist'. It was apparently intended for submission, since it bore on the title page the label of A. D. Peters, Literary Agent.

The manuscript could be read as a self-contained short story about the young Charles Ryder at public school. But the Evelyn Waugh diaries for 1945 suggest a different history. On 25 September 1945 he wrote: 'Yesterday I read my Lancing diaries through with unmixed shame.' Then on 2 October he wrote: '. . . my life seems more placid and happy than ever. I have begun a novel of school life in 1919 – as untopical a theme as could be found.' On 28 October: 'The last three weeks have been happy and uneventful: Laura cooking better, wine lasting out, weather splendid. I have written more of the school story . . .' This is the last mention of the enterprise in the diary entries, and there is no hint in the 1945 A. D. Peters file, now at the Humanities Research Center at the University of Texas, of what passed between Waugh and A. D. Peters on the subject.

I sought help from two authorities. Colonel Don Mac-Namara, late of the U.S. Marine Corps and now writing a thesis at the University of Texas on the relationship between Waugh and A. D. Peters, drew a blank in the 1945 files, but

285

was able to report that the original manuscript of the piece was conveyed to Texas with the rest of the Waugh material. I asked Donat Gallagher of the University of North Queensland, who is in London editing *The Complete Essays and Articles of Evelyn Waugh* for publication by Eyre Methuen in 1983, what he made of it. He has a photo-copy of the original manuscript and pointed out a large number of literals (which have been corrected for printing here), at variance with Waugh's correct spellings in manuscript, which suggest that Waugh may have been as long-suffering in his relationship with McLachlan as the latter was with him. Gallagher points out that in many respects *Charles Ryder's Schooldays* picks up detail and incident from the Lancing diaries. He makes two further observations. First, that the manuscript of *Brideshead Revisited* contains a considerable amount of material about Charles Ryder's early life and family background which does not appear in the published version of the novel. Second, he would expect Waugh to want to emphasize clearly something that does not come out in the published version of *Brideshead*: the contrast between the family backgrounds of Sebastian and Ryder. Perhaps this helps to explain Waugh's settling down, in an apparently happy and relaxed frame of mind, to embark on a novel on this subject.

What happened then has to be conjecture. We have no evidence that the piece was submitted to any magazine, and it would be surprising if any ensuing rejection letters had not been kept in the Waugh file. Perhaps Waugh and Peters agreed that the time wasn't ripe for submitting this fragment; perhaps Peters, after reading it, talked Waugh out of proceeding with the novel. My guess is that the typescript went into Peter's desk drawer and that when he was going through his desk in 1970 he found it and put it in the current file. Maybe publication here will flush out an editor who wrote a careful rejection letter in the autumn of 1945.

Charles Ryder's Schooldays, with an Introduction by Michael Sissons, was first published in *The Times Literary Supplement* on 5 March 1982.

1

There was a scent of dust in the air; a thin vestige surviving in the twilight from the golden clouds with which before chapel the House Room fags had filled the evening sunshine. Light was failing. Beyond the trefoils and branched mullions of the windows the towering autumnal leaf was now flat and colourless. All the eastward slope of Spierpoint Down, where the College buildings stood, lay lost in shadow; above and behind, on the high lines of Chanctonbury and Spierpoint Ring, the first day of term was gently dying.

In the House Room thirty heads were bent over their books. Few form-masters had set any preparation that day. The Classical Upper Fifth, Charles Ryder's new form, were 'revising last term's work' and Charles was writing his diary under cover of Hassall's *History*. He looked up from the page to the darkling texts which ran in Gothic script around the frieze. *'Qui diligit Deum diligit et fratrem suum.'*

'Get on with your work, Ryder,' said Apthorpe.

Apthorpe has greased into being a house-captain this term, Charles wrote. *This is his first evening school. He is being thoroughly officious and on his dignity.*

'Can we have the light on, please?'

'All right. Wykham-Blake, put it on.' A small boy rose from the under-school table. 'Wykham-Blake, I said. There's no need for everyone to move.'

A rattle of the chain, a hiss of gas, a brilliant white light over half the room. The other light hung over the new boys' table.

'Put the light on, one of you, whatever your names are.'

Six startled little boys looked at Apthorpe and at one another, all began to rise together, all sat down, all looked at Apthorpe in consternation.

'Oh, for heaven's sake.'

Apthorpe leaned over their heads and pulled the chain: there was a hiss of gas but no light. 'The bye-pass is out. Light it, you.' He threw a box of matches to one of the new boys who dropped it, picked it up, climbed on the table and looked miserably at the white glass shade, the three hissing mantles and at Apthorpe. He had never seen a lamp of this kind before; at home and at his private school there was electricity. He lit a match and poked at the lamp, at first without effect; then there was a loud explosion; he stepped back, stumbled and nearly lost his footing among the books and ink-pots, blushed hotly and regained the bench. The matches remained in his hand and he stared at them, lost in an agony of indecision. How should he dispose of them? No head was raised but everyone in the House Room exulted in the drama. From the other side of the room Apthorpe held out his hand invitingly.

'When you have quite finished with my matches perhaps you'll be so kind as to give them back.'

In despair the new boy threw them towards the house-captain; in despair he threw slightly wide. Apthorpe made no attempt to catch them, but watched them curiously as they fell to the floor. 'How very extraordinary,' he said. The new boy looked at the match-box; Apthorpe looked at the new boy. 'Would it be troubling you too much if I asked you to give me my matches?' he said.

The new boy rose to his feet, walked the few steps, picked up the match-box and gave it to the house-captain, with the ghastly semblance of a smile.

'Extraordinary crew of new men we have this term,' said Apthorpe. 'They seem to be entirely halfwitted. Has anyone been turned on to look after this man?'

'Please, I have,' said Wykham-Blake.

'A grave responsibility for one so young. Try and convey to his limited intelligence that it may prove a painful practice here to throw match-boxes about in evening school, and laugh at house officials. By the way, is that a work-book you're reading?'

'Oh, yes, Apthorpe.' Wykham-Blake raised a face of cherubic innocence and presented the back of the *Golden Treasury*.

'Who's it for?'

'Mr Graves. We're to learn any poem we like.'

'And what have you chosen?'

'Milton-on-his-blindness.'

'How, may one ask, did that take your fancy?'

'I learned it once before,' said Wykham-Blake and Apthorpe laughed indulgently.

'Young blighter,' he said.

Charles wrote: *Now he is snooping round seeing what books men are reading. It would be typical if he got someone beaten his first evening school. The day before yesterday this time I was in my dinner-jacket just setting out for dinner at the d'Italie with Aunt Philippa before going to* The Choice *at Wyndhams.* Quantum mutatus ab illo Hectore. *We live in water-tight compartments. Now I am absorbed in the trivial round of House politics. Graves has played hell with the house. Apthorpe a house-captain and O'Malley on the Settle. The only consolation was seeing the woe on Wheatley's fat face when the locker list went up. He thought he was a cert for the Settle this term. Bad luck on Tamplin though. I never expected to get on but I ought by all rights to have been above O'Malley. What a tick Graves is. It all comes of this rotten system of switching round house-tutors. We ought to have the best of Heads instead of which they try out ticks like Graves on us before giving them a house. If only we still had Frank.*

Charles's handwriting had lately begun to develop certain ornamental features – Greek Es and flourished crossings. He wrote with conscious style. Whenever Apthorpe came past he would turn a page in the history book, hesitate and then write as though making a note from the text. The hands of the clock crept on to half past seven when the porter's handbell began to sound in the cloisters on the far side of Lower Quad. This was the signal of release. Throughout the House Room heads were raised, pages blotted, books closed, fountain-pens screwed up. 'Get on with your work,' said Apthorpe; 'I haven't said anything about moving.' The porter and his bell passed up the cloisters, grew faint under the arch by the library steps, were barely audible in the Upper Quad, grew louder on the steps of Old's House and very loud in the cloister outside Head's. At last Apthorpe tossed the *Bystander* on the table and said 'All right.'

The House Room rose noisily. Charles underlined the date at the head of his page – *Wednesday Sept. 24th, 1919* – blotted it and put the note-book in his locker. Then with his hands in his pockets he followed the crowd into the dusk.

To keep his hands in his pockets thus – with his coat back and the middle button alone fastened – was now his privilege, for he was in his third year. He could also wear coloured socks and was indeed at the moment wearing a pair of heliotrope silk with white clocks, purchased the day before in Jermyn Street. There were several things, formerly forbidden, which were now his right. He could link his arm in a friend's and he did so now, strolling across to Hall arm-in-arm with Tamplin.

They paused at the top of the steps and stared out in the gloaming. To their left the great bulk of the chapel loomed immensely; below them the land fell away in terraces to the playing-fields with their dark fringe of elm; headlights moved continuously up and down the coast road; the estuary was just traceable, a lighter streak across the grey lowland, before it merged into the calm and invisible sea.

'Same old view,' said Tamplin.

'Give me the lights of London,' said Charles. 'I say, it's rotten luck for you about the Settle.'

'Oh, I never had a chance. It's rotten luck on *you*.'

'Oh, I never had a chance. But *O'Malley*.'

'It all comes of having that tick Graves instead of Frank.'

'The buxom Wheatley looked jolly bored. Anyway, I don't envy O'Malley's job as head of the dormitory.'

'That's how he got on the Settle. Tell you later.'

From the moment they reached the Hall steps they had to unlink their arms, take their hands out of their pockets and stop talking. When Grace had been said Tamplin took up the story.

'Graves had him in at the end of last term and said he was making him head of the dormitory. The head of Upper Dormitory never has been on the Settle before last term when they moved Easton up from Lower Anteroom after we ragged

Fletcher. O'Malley told Graves he couldn't take it on unless he had an official position.'

'How d'you know?'

'O'Malley told me. He thought he'd been rather fly.'

'Typical of Graves to fall for a tick like that.'

'It's all very well,' said Wheatley, plaintively, from across the table; 'I don't think they've any right to put Graves in like this. I only came to Spierpoint because my father knew Frank's brother in the Guards. I was jolly bored, I can tell you, when they moved Frank. I think he wrote to the Head about it. We pay more in Head's and get the worst of everything.'

'Tea, please.'

'Same old College tea.'

'Same old College eggs.'

'It always takes a week before one gets used to College food.'

'I never get used to it.'

'Did you go to many London restaurants in the holidays?'

'I was only in London a week. My brother took me to lunch at the Berkeley. Wish I was there now. I had two glasses of port.'

'The Berkeley's all right in the evening,' said Charles, 'if you want to dance.'

'It's jolly well all right for luncheon. You should see their hors d'oeuvres. I reckon there were twenty or thirty things to choose from. After that we had grouse and meringues with ices in them.'

'I went to dinner at the d'Italie.'

'Oh, where's that?'

'It's a little place in Soho not many people know about. My aunt speaks Italian like a native so she knows all those places. Of course, there's no marble or music. It just exists for the cooking. Literary people and artists go there. My aunt knows lots of them.'

'My brother says all the men from Sandhurst go to the Berkeley. Of course, they fairly rook you.'

'I always think the Berkeley's rather rowdy,' said Wheatley.

'We stayed at Claridges after we came back from Scotland because our flat was still being done up.'

'My brother says Claridges is a deadly hole.'

'Of course, it isn't everyone's taste. It's rather exclusive.'

'Then how did our buxom Wheatley come to be staying there, I wonder?'

'There's no need to be cheap, Tamplin.'

'I always say,' suddenly said a boy named Jorkins, 'that you get the best meal in London at the Holborn Grill.'

Charles, Tamplin and Wheatley turned with cold curiosity on the interrupter, united at last in their disdain. 'Do you, Jorkins? How very original of you.'

'Do you *always* say that, Jorkins? Don't you sometimes get tired of *always* saying the same thing?'

'There's a four-and-sixpenny table d'hôte.'

'Please, Jorkins, spare us the hideous details of your gormandizing.'

'Oh, all right. I thought you were interested, that's all.'

'Do you think,' said Tamplin, confining himself ostentatiously to Charles and Wheatley, 'that Apthorpe is keen on Wykham-Blake?'

'No, is he?'

'Well, he couldn't keep away from him in evening school.'

'I suppose the boy had to find consolation now his case Sugdon's left. He hasn't a friend among the underschools.'

'What d'you make of the man Peacock?' (Charles, Tamplin and Wheatley were all in the Classical Upper Fifth under Mr Peacock.)

'He's started decently. No work tonight.'

'Raggable?'

'I doubt it. But slack.'

'I'd sooner a master were slack than raggable. I got quite exhausted last term ragging the Tea-cake.'

'It was witty, though.'

'I hope he's not so slack that we shan't get our Certificates next summer.'

'One can always sweat the last term. At the University no

one ever does any work until just before the exams. Then they sit up all night with black coffee and strychnine.'

'It would be jolly witty if no one passed his Certificate.'

'I wonder what they'd do.'

'Give Peacock the push, I should think.'

Presently Grace was said and the school streamed out into the cloisters. It was now dark. The cloisters were lit at intervals by gas-lamps. As one walked, one's shadow lengthened and grew fainter before one until, approaching the next source of light, it disappeared, fell behind, followed one's heels, shortened, deepened, disappeared and started again at one's toes. The quarter of an hour between Hall and Second Evening was mainly spent in walking the cloisters in pairs or in threes; to walk four abreast was the privilege of school prefects. On the steps of Hall, Charles was approached by O'Malley. He was an ungainly boy, an upstart who had come to Spierpoint late, in a bye-term. He was in Army Class B and his sole distinction was staying power in cross-country running.

'Coming to the Graves?'

'No.'

'D'you mind if I hitch on to you for a minute?'

'Not particularly.'

They joined the conventional, perambulating couples, their shadows, lengthened before them, apart. Charles did not take O'Malley's arm. O'Malley might not take Charles's. The Settle was purely a House Dignity. In the cloisters Charles was senior by right of his two years at Spierpoint.

'I'm awfully sorry about the Settle,' said O'Malley.

'I should have thought you'd be pleased.'

'I'm not, honestly. It's the last thing I wanted. Graves sent me a postcard a week ago. It spoiled the end of the holidays. I'll tell you what happened. Graves had me in on the last day last term. You know the way he has. He said, "I've some unpleasant news for you, O'Malley. I'm putting you head of the Upper Dormitory." I said, "It ought to be someone on the Settle. No one else could keep order." I thought he'd keep Easton up there. He said, "These things are a matter of personality, not of official position." I said, 'It's been proved you have to have an official. You know how bolshie we were with Fletcher." He said, "Fletcher wasn't the man for the job. He wasn't my appointment." '

'Typical of his lip. Fletcher was Frank's appointment.'

'I wish we had Frank still.'

'So does everyone. Anyway, why are you telling me all this?'

'I didn't want you to think I'd been greasing. I heard Tamplin say I had.'

'Well, you are on the Settle and you are head of the dormitory, so what's the trouble?'

'Will you back me up, Ryder?'

'Have you ever known me back anyone up, as you call it?'

'No,' said O'Malley miserably, 'that's just it.'

'Well, why d'you suppose I should start with you?'

'I just thought you might.'

'Well, think again.'

They had walked three sides of the square and were now at the door of Head's House. Mr Graves was standing outside his own room talking to Mr Peacock.

'Charles,' he said, 'come here a minute. Have you met this young man yet, Peacock? He's one of yours.'

'Yes, I think so,' said Mr Peacock doubtfully.

'He's one of my problem children. Come in here, Charles. I want to have a chat to you.'

Mr Graves took him by the elbow and led him into his room.

There were no fires yet and the two armchairs stood before an empty grate; everything was unnaturally bare and neat after the holiday cleaning.

'Sit you down.'

Mr Graves filled his pipe and gave Charles a long, soft and quizzical stare. He was a man still under thirty, dressed in Lovat tweed with an Old Rugbeian tie. He had been at Spierpoint during Charles's first term and they had met once on the miniature range; in that bleak, untouchable epoch Charles had been warmed by his affability. Then Mr Graves was called up for the army and now had returned, the term before, as House Tutor of Head's. Charles had grown confident in the meantime and felt no need of affable masters; only for Frank whom Mr Graves had supplanted. The ghost of Frank filled the room. Mr Graves had hung some Medici prints in the place of Frank's football groups. The set of *Georgian Poetry* in the bookcase was his, not Frank's. His college arms embellished the tobacco jar on the chimney-piece.

'Well, Charles Ryder,' said Mr Graves at length, 'are you feeling sore with me?'

'Sir?'

Mr Graves became suddenly snappish. 'If you choose to sit there like a stone image, I can't help you.'

Still Charles said nothing.

'I have a friend,' said Mr Graves, 'who goes in for illumination. I thought you might like me to show him the work you sent in to the Art Competition last term.'

'I'm afraid I left it at home, sir.'

'Did you do any during the holidays?'

'One or two things, sir.'

'You never try painting from nature?'

'Never, sir.'

'It seems rather a crabbed, shut-in sort of pursuit for a boy of your age. Still, that's your own business.'

'Yes, sir.'

'Difficult chap to talk to, aren't you, Charles?'

'Not with everyone. Not with Frank,' Charles wished to say; 'I could talk to Frank by the hour.' Instead he said, 'I suppose I am, sir.'

'Well, I want to talk to you. I dare say you feel you have been a little ill-used this term. Of course, all your year are in rather a difficult position. Normally there would have been seven or eight people leaving at the end of last term but with the war coming to an end they are staying on an extra year, trying for University scholarships and so on. Only Sugdon left, so instead of a general move there was only one vacancy at the top. That meant only one vacancy on the Settle. I dare say you think you ought to have had it.'

'No, sir. There were two people ahead of me.'

'But not O'Malley. I wonder if I can make you understand why I put him over you. You were the obvious man in many ways. The thing is, some people *need* authority, others don't. You've got plenty of personality. O'Malley isn't at all sure of himself. He might easily develop into rather a second-rater. You're in no danger of that. What's more, there's the dormitory to consider. I think I can trust you to work loyally under O'Malley. I'm not so sure I could trust him to work under you. See? It's always been a difficult dormitory. I don't want a repetition of what happened with Fletcher. Do you understand?'

'I understand what you mean, sir.'

'Grim young devil, aren't you?'

'Sir?'

'Oh, all right, go away. I shan't waste any more time with you.'

'Thank you, sir.'

Charles rose to go.

'I'm getting a small hand printing-press this term,' said Mr Graves. 'I thought it might interest you.'

It did interest Charles intensely. It was one of the large features of his day-dreams; in chapel, in school, in bed, in all the rare periods of abstraction, when others thought of racing motor-cars and hunters and speed-boats, Charles thought long and often of a private press. But he would not betray to Mr Graves the intense surge of images that rose in his mind.

'I think the invention of movable type was a disaster, sir. It destroyed calligraphy.'

'You're a prig, Charles,' said Mr Graves. 'I'm sick of you. Go away. Tell Wheatley I want him. And try not to dislike me so much. It wastes both our time.'

Second Evening had begun when Charles returned to the House Room; he reported to the house-captain in charge, despatched Wheatley to Mr Graves and settled down over his Hassall to half an hour's day-dream, imagining the tall folios, the wide margins, the deckle-edged mould-made paper, the engraved initials, the rubrics and colophons of his private press. In Third Evening one could 'read'; Charles read Hugh Walpole's *Fortitude*.

Wheatley did not return until the bell was ringing for the end of evening school.

Tamplin greeted him with 'Bad luck, Wheatley. How many did you get? Was it tight?'; Charles with 'Well, you've had a long hot-air with Graves. What on earth did he talk about?'

'It was all rather confidential,' said Wheatley solemnly.

'Oh, sorry.'

'No, I'll tell *you* some time if you promise to keep it to yourself.' Together they ascended the turret stair to their dormitory. 'I say, have you noticed something? Apthorpe is in the Upper Anteroom this term. Have you ever known the junior house-captain anywhere except in the Lower Anteroom? I wonder how he worked it.'

'Why should he want to?'

'Because, my innocent, Wykham-Blake has been moved into the Upper Anteroom.'

'Tactful of Graves.'

'You know, I sometimes think perhaps we've rather misjudged Graves.'

'You didn't think so in Hall.'

'No, but I've been thinking since.'

'You mean he's been greasing up to you.'

'Well, all I can say is, when he wants to be decent, he *is* decent. I find we know quite a lot of the same people in the holidays. He once stayed on the moor next to ours.'

'I don't see anything particularly decent in that.'

'Well, it makes a sort of link. He explained why he put O'Malley on the Settle. He's a student of character, you know.'

'Who? O'Malley?'

'No, Graves. He said that's the only reason he is a schoolmaster.'

'I expect he's a schoolmaster because it's so jolly slack.'

'Not at all. As a matter of fact, he was going into the Diplomatic, just as I am.'

'I don't expect he could pass the exam. It's frightfully stiff. Graves only takes the Middle Fourth.'

'The exam is only to keep out undesirable types.'

'Then it would floor Graves.'

'He says schoolmastering is the most *human* calling in the world. Spierpoint is not an arena for competition. We have to stop the weakest going to the wall.'

'Did Graves say that?'

'Yes.'

'I must remember that if there's any unpleasantness with Peacock. What else did he say?'

'Oh, we talked about people, you know, and their characters. Would you say O'Malley had poise?'

'Good God, no.'

'That's just what Graves thinks. He says some people have it naturally and they can look after themselves. Others, like O'Malley, need bringing on. He thinks authority will give O'Malley poise.'

'Well, it doesn't seem to have worked yet,' said Charles, as O'Malley loped past their beds to his corner.

'Welcome to the head of the dormitory,' said Tamplin. 'Are we all late? Are you going to report us?'

O'Malley looked at his watch. 'As a matter of fact, you have exactly seven minutes.'

'Not by my watch.'

'We go my mine.'

'Really,' said Tamplin. 'Has your watch been put on the Settle, too? It looks a cheap kind of instrument to me.'

'When I am speaking officially I don't want any impertinence, Tamplin.'

'His watch *has* been put on the Settle. It's the first time I ever heard one could be impertinent to a watch.'

They undressed and washed their teeth. O'Malley looked repeatedly at his watch and at last said, 'Say your dibs.'

Everyone knelt at his bedside and buried his face in the bedclothes. After a minute, in quick succession, they rose and got into bed; all save Tamplin who remained kneeling. O'Malley stood in the middle of the dormitory, irresolute, his hand on the chain of the gas lamp. Three minutes passed; it was the convention that no one spoke while anyone was still saying his prayers; several boys began to giggle. 'Hurry up,' said O'Malley.

Tamplin raised a face of pained rebuke. '*Please*, O'Malley. I'm saying my dibs.'

'Well, you're late.'

Tamplin remained with his face buried in the blanket. O'Malley pulled the chain and extinguished the light, all save the pale glow of the bye-pass under the white enamel shade. It was the custom, when doing this, to say 'Goodnight'; but Tamplin was still ostensibly in prayer; in this black predicament O'Malley stalked to his bed in silence.

'Aren't you going to say "Goodnight" to us?' asked Charles.

'Goodnight.'

A dozen voices irregularly took up the cry. 'Goodnight, O'Malley . . . I hope the official watch doesn't stop in the night . . . happy dreams, O'Malley.'

'Really, you know,' said Wheatley, 'there's a man still saying his prayers.'

'Stop talking.'

'*Please*,' said Tamplin, on his knees. He remained there for half a minute more, then rose and got into bed.

'You understand, Tamplin? You're late.'

'Oh, but I don't think I can be, even by your watch. I was perfectly ready when you said "Say your dibs." '

'If you want to take as long as that you must start sooner.'

'But I couldn't with all that noise going on, could I, O'Malley? All that wrangling about watches?'

'We'll talk about it in the morning.'

'Goodnight, O'Malley.'

At this moment the door opened and the house-captain in charge of the dormitory came in. 'What the devil's all this talking about?' he asked.

Now, O'Malley had not the smallest intention of giving Tamplin a 'late'. It was a delicate legal point, of the kind that was debated endlessly at Spierpoint, whether in the circumstances he could properly do so. It had been in O'Malley's mind to appeal to Tamplin's better nature in the morning, to say that he could take a joke as well as the next man, that his official position was repugnant to him, that the last thing he wished to do was start the term by using his new authority on his former associates; he would say all this and ask Tamplin to 'back him up'. But now, suddenly challenged out of the darkness, he lost his head and said, 'I was giving Tamplin a "late", Anderson.'

'Well, remind me in the morning and for Christ's sake don't make such a racket over it.'

'Please, Anderson, I don't think I was late,' said Tamplin; 'it's just that I took longer than the others over my prayers. I was perfectly ready when we were told to say them.'

'But he was still out of bed when I put the light out,' said O'Malley.

'Well, it's usual to wait until everyone's ready, isn't it?'

'Yes, Anderson. I did wait about five minutes.'

'I see. Anyhow, lates count from the time you start saying your dibs. You know that. Better wash the whole thing out.'

'Thank you, Anderson,' said Tamplin.

The house-captain lit the candle which stood in a biscuit-box shade on the press by his bed. He undressed slowly, washed and, without saying prayers, got into bed. Then he lay there reading. The tin hid the light from the dormitory and cast a small yellow patch over his book and pillow; that and the faint circle of the gas-lamp were the only lights; gradually in the darkness the lancet windows became dimly visible. Charles lay on his back thinking; O'Malley had made a fiasco of his first evening; first and last he could not have done things worse; it seemed a rough and tortuous road on which Mr Graves had set his feet, to self-confidence and poise.

Then, as he grew sleepier, Charles's thoughts, like a roulette ball when the wheel runs slow, sought their lodging and came at last firmly to rest on that day, never far distant, at the end of his second term; the raw and gusty day of the junior steeplechase when, shivering and half-changed, queasy with apprehension of the trial ahead, he had been summoned by

Frank, had shuffled into his clothes, run headlong down the turret stairs and with a new and deeper alarm knocked at the door.

'Charles, I have just had a telegram from your father which you must read. I'll leave you alone with it.'

He shed no tear, then or later; he did not remember what was said when two minutes later Frank returned; there was a numb, anaesthetized patch at the heart of his sorrow; he remembered, rather, the order of the day. Instead of running he had gone down in his overcoat with Frank to watch the finish of the race; word had gone round the house and no questions were asked; he had tea with the matron, spent the evening in her room and slept that night in a room in the Headmaster's private house; next morning his Aunt Philippa came and took him home. He remembered all that went on outside himself, the sight and sound and smell of the place, so that, on his return to them, they all spoke of his loss, of the sharp severance of all the bonds of childhood, and it seemed to him that it was not in the uplands of Bosnia but here at Spierpoint, on the turret stairs, in the unlighted box-room passage, in the windy cloisters, that his mother had fallen, killed not by a German shell but by the shrill voice sounding across the changing-room, 'Ryder here? Ryder? Frank wants him at the double.'

2

Thursday, September 25th, 1919. Peacock began well by not turning up for early school so at five past we walked out and went back to our House Rooms and I read Fortitude *by Walpole; it is strong meat but rather unnecessary in places. After breakfast O'Malley came greasing up to Tamplin and apologized. Everyone is against him. I maintain he was in the right until he reported him late to Anderson. No possible defence for that – sheer windiness. Peacock deigned to turn up for Double Greek. We mocked him somewhat. He is trying to make us use the new pronunciation; when he said oŭ there was a wail of 'ooh' and Tamplin pronounced subjunctive soobyoongteeway – very witty. Peacock got bored and said he'd report him to Graves but relented. Library was open 5–6 tonight. I went meaning to put in some time on Walter Crane's* Bases of Design *but Mercer came up with that weird man in Brent's called Curtis-Dunne. I envy them having Frank as house-master. He is talking of starting a literary and artistic society for men not in the sixth. Curtis-Dunne wants to start a political group. Pretty good lift considering this is his second term although he is sixteen and has been at Dartmouth. Mercer gave me a poem to read – very sloppy. Before this there was a House Game. Everyone puffing and blowing after the holidays. Anderson said I shall probably be centre-half in the Under Sixteens – the sweatiest place in the field. I must get into training quickly.*

Friday 26th. Corps day but quite slack. Reorganization. I am in A Company at last. A tick in Boucher's called Spratt is platoon commander. We ragged him a bit. Wheatley is a section commander! Peacock sent Bankes out of the room in Greek Testament for saying 'Who will rid me of this turbulent priest' when put on to translate. Jolly witty. He began to argue. Peacock said, 'Must I throw you out by force?' Bankes began to go but muttered 'Muscular Christianity'. Peacock: 'What did you say?'; 'Nothing, sir'; 'Get out before I kick you.' Things got a bit duller after that. Uncle George gave Bankes three.

Saturday 27th. Things very dull in school. Luckily Peacock forgot to set any preparation. Pop. Sci. in last period. Tamplin and Mercer got some of the weights that are so precious they are kept in a glass case and picked up with tweezers, made them red hot on a bunsen burner and dropped them in cold water. A witty thing to do. House Game – Under Sixteen team against a mixed side. They have put Wykham-Blake centre-half and me in goal; a godless place. Library again. Curtis-Dunne buttonholed me again. He drawled 'My father is in parliament but he is a very unenlightened conservative. I of course am a socialist. That's the reason I chucked the Navy.' I said, 'Or did they chuck you?' 'The pangs of parting were endured by both sides with mutual stoicism.' He spoke of Frank as 'essentially a well-

*intentioned fellow.' Sunday tomorrow thank God. I may be able to
get on with illuminating 'The Bells of Heaven'.*

3

Normally on Sundays there was a choice of service. Matins
at a quarter to eight or Communion at quarter past. On the
first Sunday of term there was Choral Communion for all at
eight o'clock.

The chapel was huge, bare, and still unfinished, one of the
great monuments of the Oxford Movement and the Gothic
revival. Like an iceberg it revealed only a small part of its
bulk above the surface of the terraced down; below lay a crypt
and below that foundations of great depth. The Founder had
chosen the site and stubbornly refused to change it so that
the original estimates had been exceeded before the upper
chapel was begun. Visiting preachers frequently drew a
lesson from the disappointments, uncertainties and final
achievement of the Founder's 'vision'. Now the whole nave
rose triumphantly over the surrounding landscape, immense,
clustered shafts supporting the groined roof; at the west it
ended abruptly in concrete and timber and corrugated iron,
while behind, in a waste land near the kitchens, where the
Corps band practised their bugles in the early morning, lay a
nettle-and-bramble-grown ruin, the base of a tower, twice as
high as the chapel, which one day was to rise so that on
stormy nights, the Founder had decreed, prayers might
be sung at its summit for sailors in peril on the
sea.

From outside the windows had a deep, submarine tinge,
but from inside they were clear white, and the morning sun
streamed in over the altar and the assembled school. The
prefect in Charles's row was Symonds, editor of the Magazine,
president of the Debating Society, the leading intellectual.
Symonds was in Head's; he pursued a course of lonely study,

seldom taking Evening School, never playing any game except, late in the evenings of the summer term, an occasional single of lawn tennis, appearing rarely even in the Sixth Form, but working in private under Mr A. A. Carmichael for the Balliol scholarship. Symonds kept a leather-bound copy of the *Greek Anthology* in his place in chapel and read it throughout the services with a finely negligent air.

The masters sat in stalls orientated between the columns, the clergy in surplices, laymen in gowns. Some of the masters who taught the Modern Side wore hoods of the newer universities; Major Stebbing, the adjutant of the OTC, had no gown at all; Mr A. A. Carmichael – awfully known at Spierpoint as 'A.A.' – the splendid dandy and wit, fine flower of the Oxford Union and the New College Essay Society, the reviewer of works of classical scholarship for the *New Statesman*, to whom Charles had never yet spoken; whom Charles had never yet heard speak directly, but only at third hand as his *mots*, in their idiosyncratic modulations, passed from mouth to mouth from the Sixth in sanctuary to the catechumens in the porch; whom Charles worshipped from afar – Mr Carmichael, from a variety of academic costume, was this morning robed as a baccalaureate of Salamanca. He looked, as he stooped over his desk, like the prosecuting counsel in a cartoon by Daumier.

Nearly opposite him across the chapel stood Frank Bates; an unbridged gulf of boys separated these rival and contrasted deities, that one the ineffable dweller on cloud-capped Olympus, this the homely clay image, the intimate of hearth and household, the patron of threshing-floor and olive-press. Frank wore only an ermine hood, a BA's gown, and loose, unremarkable clothes, subfusc today, with the Corinthian tie which alternated with the Carthusian, week in, week out. He was a clean, curly, spare fellow; a little wan for he was in constant pain from an injury on the football field which had left him lame and kept him at Spierpoint throughout the war. This pain of his redeemed him from heartiness. In chapel his innocent, blue eyes assumed a puzzled, rather glum expression like those of an old-fashioned child in a room full of grown-ups. Frank was a bishop's son.

Behind the masters, out of sight in the side aisles, was a dowdy huddle of matrons and wives.

The service began with a procession of the choir: 'Hail Festal Day', with Wykham-Blake as the treble cantor. At the rear of the procession came Mr Peacock, the Chaplain and the Headmaster. A week ago Charles had gone to church in London with Aunt Philippa. He did not as a rule go to church in the holidays, but being in London for the last week Aunt Philippa had said, 'There's nothing much we can do today. Let's see what entertainment the Church can offer. I'm told there is a very remarkable freak named Father Wimperis.' So, together, they had gone on the top of a bus to a northern suburb where Mr Wimperis was at the time drawing great congregations. His preaching was not theatrical by Neapolitan standards, Aunt Philippa said afterwards; 'However, I enjoyed him hugely. He is irresistibly common.' For twenty minutes Mr Wimperis alternately fluted and boomed from the pulpit, wrestled with the reading-stand and summoned the country to industrial peace. At the end he performed a little ceremony of his own invention, advancing to the church steps in cope and biretta with what proved to be a large silver salt cellar in his hands. 'My people,' he said simply, scattering salt before him, 'you are the salt of the earth.'

'I believe he has something new like that every week,' said Aunt Philippa. 'It must be lovely to live in his neighbourhood.'

Charles's was not a God-fearing home. Until August 1914 his father had been accustomed to read family prayers every morning; on the outbreak of war he abruptly stopped the practice, explaining, when asked, that there was now nothing left to pray for. When Charles's mother was killed there was a memorial service for her at Boughton, his home village, but Charles's father did not go with him and Aunt Philippa. 'It was all her confounded patriotism,' he said, not to Charles but to Aunt Philippa, who did not repeat the remark until many years later. 'She had no business to go off to Serbia like that. Do you think it my duty to marry again?'

'No,' said Aunt Philippa.

'Nothing would induce me to – least of all my duty.'

The service followed its course. As often happened, two small boys fainted and were carried out by house-captains; a third left bleeding at the nose. Mr Peacock sang the Gospel over-loudly. It was his first public appearance. Symonds looked up from his Greek, frowned and continued reading. Presently it was time for Communion; most of the boys who had been confirmed went up to the chancel rails, Charles with them. Symonds sat back, twisted his long legs into the aisle to allow his row to pass, and remained in his place. Charles took Communion and returned to his row. He had been confirmed the term before, incuriously, without expectation or disappointment. When, later in life, he read accounts of the emotional disturbances caused in other boys by the ceremony he found them unintelligible; to Charles it was one of the rites of adolescence, like being made, when a new boy, to stand on the table and sing. The Chaplain had 'prepared' him and had confined his conferences to theology. There had been no probing of his sexual life; he had no sexual life to probe. Instead they had talked of prayer and the sacraments.

Spierpoint was a product of the Oxford Movement, founded with definite religious aims; in eighty years it had grown more and more to resemble the older Public Schools, but there was still a strong ecclesiastical flavour in the place. Some boys were genuinely devout and their peculiarity was respected; in general profanity was rare and ill-looked-on. Most of the Sixth professed themselves agnostic or atheist.

The school had been chosen for Charles because, at the age of eleven, he had had a 'religious phase' and told his father that he wished to become a priest.

'Good heavens,' his father said; 'or do you mean a parson?'

'A priest of the Anglican Church,' said Charles precisely.

'That's better. I thought you meant a Roman Catholic. Well, a parson's is not at all a bad life for a man with a little money of his own. They can't remove you except for flagrant immorality. Your uncle has been trying to get rid of his fellow at Boughton for ten years – a most offensive fellow but perfectly chaste. He won't budge. It's a great thing in life to have a place you can't be removed from – too few of them.'

But the 'phase' had passed and lingered now only in Charles's love of Gothic architecture and breviaries.

After Communion Charles sat back in his chair thinking about the secular, indeed slightly anti-clerical, lyric which, already inscribed, he was about to illuminate, while the masters and, after them, the women from the side aisles, went up to the rails.

The food on Sundays was always appreciably worse than on other days; breakfast invariably consisted of boiled eggs, overboiled and luke-warm.

Wheatley said, 'How many ties do you suppose A.A.'s got?'

'I began counting last term,' said Tamplin, 'and got to thirty.'

'Including bows?'

'Yes.'

'Of course, he's jolly rich.'

'Why doesn't he keep a car, then?' asked Jorkins.

The hour after breakfast was normally devoted to letter-writing, but today a railway strike had been called and there were no posts. Moreover, since it was the start of term, there was no Sunday Lesson. The whole morning was therefore free and Charles had extracted permission to spend it in the drawing school. He collected his materials and was soon happily at work.

The poem – Ralph Hodgson's "Twould ring the bells of Heaven The wildest peal for years, If Parson lost his senses And people came to theirs . . .' – was one of Frank's favourites. In the happy days when he had been House Tutor of Head's, Frank had read poetry aloud on Sunday evenings to any in Head's who cared to come, which was mostly the lower half of the House. He read 'There swimmeth One Who swam e'er rivers were begun, And under that Almighty Fin The littlest fish may enter in' and 'Abou Ben Adhem, may his tribe increase' and 'Under the wide and starry sky' and 'What have I done for you, England, my England . . .?' and many others of the same comfortable kind; but always before the end of the evening someone would say 'Please, sir, can we have "The Bells of Heaven"?' Now he read only to his own house but the poems, Frank's pleasant voices, his nightingales, were awake still, warm and bright with remembered fire-light.

Charles did not question whether the poem was not perfectly suited to the compressed thirteenth-century script in which he had written it. His method of writing was first to draw the letters faintly, free-hand in pencil; then with a ruler and ruling-pen to ink in the uprights firmly in Indian ink until the page consisted of lines of short and long black perpendiculars; then with a mapping-pen he joined them with hair strokes and completed their lozenge-shaped ter-minals. It was a method he had evolved for himself by trial and error. The initial letters of each line were left blank and these, during the last week of the holidays, he had filled with vermilion, carefully drawn, 'Old English' capitals. The *T* alone remained to do and for this he had selected a model from Shaw's *Alphabets*, now open before him on the table. It was a florid fifteenth-century letter which needed considerable ingenuity of adaption, for he had decided to attach it to the decorative tail of the *J*. He worked happily, entirely absorbed, drawing in pencil, then tensely, with breath held, inking the outline with a mapping-pen; then, when it was dry – how often, in his impatience, he had ruined his work by attempt-ing this too soon – rubbing away the pencil lines. Finally he got out his water colours and his red sable brushes. At heart he knew he was going too fast – a monk would take a week over a single letter – but he worked with intensity and in less than two hours the initial with its pendant, convoluted border was finished. Then, as he put away his brushes, the exhil-aration left him. It was no good; it was botched; the ink outline varied in thickness, the curves seemed to feel their way cautiously where they should have been bold; in places the colour over-ran the line and everywhere in contrast to the opaque lithographic ink it was watery and transparent. It was no good.

Despondently Charles shut his drawing book and put his things together. Outside the Drawing School, steps led down to the Upper Quad past the door of Brent's House – Frank's. Here he met Mercer.

'Hello, been painting?'

'Yes, if you can call it that.'

'Let me see.'

'No.'

'Please.'

'It's absolutely beastly. I hate it, I tell you. I'd have torn it up if I wasn't going to keep it as a humiliation to look at in case I ever begin to feel I know anything about art.'

'You're always dissatisfied, Ryder. It's the mark of a true artist, I suppose.'

'If I was an artist I shouldn't do things I'd be dissatisfied with. Here, look at it, if you must.'

Mercer gazed at the open page. 'What don't you like about it?'

'The whole thing's nauseating.'

'I suppose it *is* a bit ornate.'

'There, my dear Mercer, with your usual unerring discernment you have hit upon the one quality that is at all tolerable.'

'Oh, sorry. Anyway, I think the whole thing absolutely first-class.'

'Do you, Mercer. I'm greatly encouraged.'

'You know you're a frightfully difficult man. I don't know why I like you.'

'I know why I like you. Because you are so extremely easy.'

'Coming to the library?'

'I suppose so.'

When the library was open a prefect sat there entering in a ledger the books which boys took out. Charles as usual made his way to the case where the Art books were kept but before he had time to settle down, as he liked to do, he was accosted by Curtis-Dunne, the old new boy of last term in Brent's. 'Don't you think it scandalous,' he said, 'that on one of the few days of the week when we have the chance to use the library, we should have to kick our heels waiting until some semi-literate prefect chooses to turn up and take us in? I've taken the matter up with the good Frank.'

'Oh, and what did he say to that?'

'We're trying to work out a scheme by which library privileges can be extended to those who seriously want them, people like you and me and I suppose the good Mercer.'

'I forget for the moment what form you are in.'

'Modern Upper. Please don't think from that I am a scientist. It's simply that in the Navy we had to drop Classics. My interests are entirely literary and political. And of course hedonistic.'

'Oh.'

'Hedonistic above all. By the way I've been looking through the political and economic section. It's very quaintly chosen, with glaring lacunae. I've just filled three pages in the Suggestions Book. I thought perhaps you'd care to append your signature.'

'No, thanks. It's not usual for people without library privileges to write in the Suggestions Book. Besides, I've no interest in economics.'

'I've also written a suggestion about extending the library privileges. Frank needs something to work on, that he can put before the committee.'

He brought the book to the Art bay; Charles read 'That since seniority is no indication of literary taste the system of library privileges be revised to provide facilities for those genuinely desirous of using them to advantage.'

'Neatly put, I think,' said Curtis-Dunne.

'You'll be thought frightfully above yourself, writing this.'

'It is already generally recognized that I *am* above myself, but I want other signatures.'

Charles hesitated. To gain time he said, 'I say, what on earth have you got on your feet? Aren't those house shoes?'

Curtis-Dunne pointed a toe shod in shabby, soft black leather; a laced shoe without a toe-cap, in surface like the cover of a well-worn Bible. 'Ah, you have observed my labour-saving device. I wear them night and morning. They are a constant perplexity to those in authority. When questioned, as happened two or three times a week during my first term, I say they are a naval pattern which my father, on account of extreme poverty, has asked me to wear out. That embarrasses them. But I am sure you do not share these middle-class prejudices. Dear boy, your name, please, to this subversive manifesto.'

Still Charles hesitated. The suggestion outraged Spierpoint taste in all particulars. Whatever intrigues, blandishments and self-advertisements were employed by the ambitious at Spierpoint were always elaborately disguised. Self-effacement and depreciation were the rule. To put oneself explicitly forward for preferment was literally not done. Moreover, the lead came from a boy who was not only in another house and immeasurably Charles's inferior, but also a notorious eccentric. A term back Charles would have rejected the proposal with horror, but today and all this term he was aware of a new voice in his inner counsels, a detached, critical Hyde who intruded his presence more and more often on the conventional, intolerant, subhuman, wholly respectable Dr Jekyll; a voice, as it were, from a more civilized age, as from the chimney corner in mid-Victorian times there used to break sometimes the sardonic laughter of grandmama, relic of Regency, a clear, outrageous, entirely self-assured disturber among the high and muddled thoughts of her whiskered descendants.

'Frank's all for the suggestion, you know,' said Curtis-Dunne. 'He says the initiative must come from us. He can't go pushing reforms which he'll be told nobody really wants. He wants a concrete proposal to put before the library committee.'

That silenced Jekyll. Charles signed.

'Now,' said Curtis-Dunne, 'there should be little difficulty with the lad Mercer. He said he'd sign if you would.'

By lunch-time there were twenty-three signatories, including the prefect-in-charge.

'We have this day lit a candle,' said Curtis-Dunne.

There was some comment around Charles in Hall about his conduct in the library.

'I know he's awful,' said Charles, 'but he happens to amuse me.'

'They all think he's balmy in Brent's.'

'Frank doesn't. And anyway I call that a recommendation. As a matter of fact, he's one of the most intelligent men I ever met. If he'd come at the proper time he'd probably be senior to all of us.'

Support came unexpectedly from Wheatley. 'I happen to know the Head took him in as a special favour to his father. He's Sir Samson Curtis-Dunne's son, the Member for this division. They've got a big place near Steyning. I wouldn't at all mind having a day's shooting there next Veniam day.'

On Sunday afternoons, for two hours, the House Room was out of bounds to all except the Settle; in their black coats and with straw hats under their arms the school scattered over the countryside in groups, pairs and occasional disconsolate single figures, for 'walks'. All human habitations were barred; the choice lay between the open down behind Spierpoint Ring and the single country road to the isolated Norman church of St Botolph. Tamplin and Charles usually walked together.

'How I hate Sunday afternoons,' said Charles.

'We might get some blackberries.'

But at the door of the house they were stopped by Mr Graves.

'Hullo, you two,' he said, 'would you like to make yourselves useful? My press has arrived. I thought you might help put it together.' He led them into his room, where half-opened crates filled most of the floor. 'It was all in one piece when I bought it. All I've got to go on is this.' He showed them a wood-cut in an old book. 'They didn't change much from Caxton's day until the steam presses came in. This one is about a hundred years old.'

'Damned sweat,' muttered Tamplin.

'And here, young Ryder, is the "movable type" you deplore so much.'

'What sort of type is it, sir?'

'We'll have to find out. I bought the whole thing in one lot from a village stationer.'

They took out letters at random, set them, and took an impression by pressing them, inked, on a sheet of writing paper. Mr Graves had an album of typefaces.

'They all look the same to me,' said Tamplin.

In spite of his prejudice, Charles was interested. 'I've got it, I think, sir; Baskerville.'

'No. Look at the serifs. How about Caslon Old Style?'

At last it was identified. Then Charles found a box full of ornamental initials, menu headings of decanters and dessert, foxes' heads and running hounds for sporting announcements, ecclesiastical devices and monograms, crowns, Odd Fellows' arms, the wood-cut of a prize bull, decorative bands, the splendid jumble of a century of English job-printing.

'I say, sir, what fun. You could do all sorts of things with these.'

'We will, Charles.'

Tamplin looked at the amateurs with disgust. 'I say, sir, I've just remembered something I must do. Do you mind awfully if I don't stay?'

'Run along, old Tamplin.' When he had gone, Mr Graves said, 'I'm sorry Tamplin doesn't like me.'

'Why can't he not let things pass?' thought Charles. 'Why does he always have to comment on everything?'

'You don't like me either, Charles. But you like the press.'

'Yes,' said Charles, 'I like the press.'

The type was tied up in little bags. They poured it out, each bagful into the tray provided for it in the worn oak tray.

'Now for the press. This looks like the base.'

It took them two hours to rebuild. When at last it was assembled, it looked small, far too small for the number and size of the cases in which it had travelled. The main cast-iron supports terminated in brass Corinthian capitals and the summit was embellished with a brass urn bearing the engraved date 1824. The common labour, the problems and discoveries of erection, had drawn the two together; now they surveyed its completion in common pride. Tamplin was forgotten.

'It's a lovely thing, sir. Could you print a book on it?'

'It would take time. Thank you very much for your help. And now,' Mr Graves looked at his watch, 'as, through some grave miscarriage of justice, you are not on the Settle, I expect you have no engagement for tea. See what you can find in the locker.'

The mention of the Settle disturbed their intimacy. Mr Graves repeated the mistake a few minutes later when they had boiled the kettle and were making toast on the gas-ring. 'So at this moment Desmond O'Malley is sitting down to his first Settle tea. I hope he's enjoying it. I don't think somehow he is enjoying this term very much so far.' Charles said nothing. 'Do you know, he came to me two days ago and asked to resign from it? He said that if I didn't let him he would do something that would make me degrade him. He's an odd boy, Desmond. It was an odd request.'

'I don't suppose he'd want me to know about it.'

'Of course he wouldn't. Do you know why I'm telling you? Do you?'

'No, sir.'

'I think you could make all the difference to him, whether his life is tolerable or not. I gather all you little beasts in the Upper Dormitory have been giving him hell.'

'If we have, it's because he asked for it.'

'I dare say, but don't you think it rather sad that in life there are so many different things different people are asking for, and the only people who get what they ask for are the Desmond O'Malleys?'

At that moment, beyond the box-room, the Settle tea had reached its second stage; surfeited with crumpets, five or six each, they were starting on the éclairs and cream-slices. There was still a warm, soggy pile of crumpets left uneaten and according to custom O'Malley, as junior man, was deputed to hand them round the House Room.

Wheatley was supercilious. 'What is that, O'Malley? Crumpets? How very kind of you, but I am afraid I never eat them. My digestion, you know.'

Tamplin was comic. 'My figure, you know,' he said.

Jorkins was rude. 'No, thanks. They look stale.'

There was loud laughter among the third-year men and some of their more precocious juniors. In strict order of seniority, O'Malley travelled from boy to boy, rebuffed, crimson. All the Upper Dormitory refused. Only the fags watched, first in wonder that anyone should refuse crumpets on a cold afternoon, later with brightening expectancy as the full plate came nearer to them.

'I say, thanks awfully, O'Malley.' They soon went at the under-school table and O'Malley returned to his chair before the empty grate, where he sat until chapel silently eating confectionery.

'You see,' said Mr Graves, 'the beastlier you are to O'Malley, the beastlier he'll become. People are like that.'

4

Sunday, Sept. 28th. Choral. Two or three faints otherwise uneventful. Tried to do the initial and border for 'The Bells of Heaven' but made a mess of it. Afterwards talked to Curtis-Dunne in the library. He intrigues me. With Frank's approval we are agitating for library privileges. I don't suppose anything will come of it except that everyone will say we are above ourselves. After luncheon Tamplin and I were going for a walk when Graves called us in and made us help put up his printing press. Tamplin escaped. Graves tried to get things out of me about ragging Dirty Desmond but without success. In the evening we had another rag. Tamplin, Wheatley, Jorkins and I hurried up to the dormitory as soon as the bell went and said our prayers before Dirty D. arrived. Then when he said, 'Say your dibs' we just sat on our beds. He looked frightfully bored and said 'Must I repeat my instructions?' As the other men were praying we said nothing. Then he said, 'I give you one more chance to say your dibs. If you don't I'll report you.' We said nothing so off Dirty D. went in his dressing-gown to Anderson who was with the other house-captains at hot-air with Graves. Up came Anderson. 'What's all this about your prayers?' 'We've said them already.' 'Why?' 'Because Tamplin got a late for taking too long so we thought we'd better start early.' 'I see. Well we'll talk about it tomorrow.' So far nothing has been said. Everyone thinks we shall get beaten but I don't see how we can be. We are entirely in our rights. Geoghegan has just been round to all four of us to say we are to stay behind after first evening so I suppose we are going to be beaten.

After First Evening, when the House Room was clear of all save the four and the bell for Hall had died away and ceased, Geoghegan, the head of the house, came in carrying two canes, accompanied by Anderson.

'I am going to beat you for disobeying an order from the head of your dormitory. Have you anything to say?'

'Yes,' said Wheatley. 'We had already said our prayers.'

'It is a matter of indifference to me how often you pray. You have spent most of the day on your knees in chapel, praying all the time, I hope. All I am concerned about is that you obey the orders of the head of the dormitory. Anyone else anything to say? Then get the room ready.'

They pushed back the new men's table and laid a bench on its side across the front of the fireplace. The routine was familiar. They were beaten in the House Room twice a term, on the average.

'Who's senior? You, I think, Wheatley.'

Wheatley bent over the bench.

'Knees straight.' Geoghegan took his hips and arranged him to his liking, slightly oblique to the line of advance. From the corner he had three steps to the point of delivery. He skipped forward, struck and slowly turned back to the corner. They were given three strokes each; none of them moved. As they walked across the Hall, Charles felt the slight nausea turn to exhilaration.

'Was he tight?'

'Yes, he was rather. And damned accurate too.'

After Hall, in the cloisters, O'Malley approached Charles.

'I say, Ryder, I'm frightfully sorry about tonight.'

'Oh, push off.'

'I had to do my duty, you know.'

'Well, go and do it, but don't come and bother me.'

'I'll do anything you like to make up. Anything outside the House, that is. I'll tell you what – I'll kick anyone else in another house, anyone you care to choose. Spratt, if you like.'

'The best thing you can do is to kick yourself, Dirty Desmond, right round the cloisters.'

MORE ABOUT PENGUINS
AND PELICANS

For further information about books available from Penguins please write to Dept EP, Penguin Books Ltd, Harmondsworth, Middlesex UB7 0DA.

In the U.S.A.: For a complete list of books available from Penguins in the United States write to Dept CS, Penguin Books, 625 Madison Avenue, New York, New York 10022.

In Canada: For a complete list of books available from Penguins in Canada write to Penguin Books Canada Ltd, 2801 John Street, Markham, Ontario L3R 1B4.

In Australia: For a complete list of books available from Penguins in Australia write to the Marketing Department, Penguin Books Australia Ltd, P.O. Box 257, Ringwood, Victoria 3134.

In New Zealand: For a complete list of books available from Penguins in New Zealand write to the Marketing Department, Penguin Books (N.Z.) Ltd, P.O. Box 4019, Auckland 10.